WHAT LIES BEHIND

WHAT LIES BEHIND

J.T. ELLISON

MIRA®

MIRA

ISBN-13: 978-0-7783-1650-3

What Lies Behind

Copyright © 2015 by J.T. Ellison

For questions and comments about the quality of this book, please contact us at CustomerService@Harlequin.com.

www.MIRABooks.com

Printed in U.S.A.

First printing: June 2015
10 9 8 7 6 5 4 3 2 1

Recycling programs
for this product may
not exist in your area.

PROLOGUE

HE WATCHED. BECAUSE THAT'S WHAT HE DID. IT'S WHAT HE DID BEST.

He used to watch in person, but the gods had conspired against him, and now it was safer for him to watch remotely. Not as satisfying, but it got the job done.

When on the hunt, he lived behind the bank of computers—eating, drinking, barely leaving to shower and sleep. He watched, and bided his time. Patient. Ever patient. Said the spider to the fly.

They were so stupid, really, to think what they said and did online was remotely secure. A private direct message sent from a burner account, a text gone astray, a mistaken link. A few clicks in any direction, a little bit of malware, and he had them. Every private thought, every post, everything they shared. They were only talking to their friends, after all. They thought they were safe.

They didn't realize he was one of the nameless, faceless, *you've got the nicest smile, glad you had a fun weekend* bots out there, tracking everything they did. Gorging himself on their secrets.

The internet made stalking so much easier. He didn't even have to leave his house until he was ready. Until the urge was so bright, so intense, he couldn't stand it anymore. And under the circumstances, the ever-watchful eyes, this was a very good thing.

In the beginning, he'd relied on his own skills—his careful, meticulous planning, watching from afar with binoculars and camera lenses. Developing the film himself so no one would see an overabundance of photos of a single woman in various stages of her life and undress and grief and happiness and think there was something wrong.

Now, a few clicks, and there she would be, in all her glory. Notes to lovers, to BFFs, hearts poured out onto a keyboard. Uploads and downloads and the occasional chic self-porn. A life that was supposed to be private was his to intercept and enjoy at his leisure. And enjoy he did.

There was only one problem. He'd recognized the growing sense of dissatisfaction a few years earlier. Convenience had usurped chance. His special muscles atrophied. The watching took on a mechanical air. Distant, so distant.

The thrill of the hunt was gone. There was no danger anymore. Physical contact was only made when he came to finish the job.

He missed the chase. Ducking behind buildings, wearing disguises, renting cars. The breathless moments—had he been seen?

Smelling the perfumes left on a vanity, the shampoo in the shower, the soap in the dish. Slipping between the smooth sheets. Riffling through drawers, lace and silk gliding against the pads of his fingers. Drinking from the orange juice, touching the lettuce and eggs, leaving bits of himself behind in the sink.

They told him the new world wouldn't be as fun. That he'd have to be careful. But damn it all, he wanted more.

He wanted them all.

But he couldn't have them all. Not now. Not with so many people looking.

So he searched. He befriended and dazzled, was a shoulder to cry on.

And he found the perfect one. Another perfect one.

He took a sip from his cooling coffee, adjusted the chair, the screens. Today he would watch her, and tonight, tonight she would be his at last.

The hours passed slowly, so very slowly. The camera caught fragments of her as she moved through her apartment—it was Sunday, a day of rest. She always stayed home on Sundays. Slept in. Had a leisurely breakfast. Read magazines, painted her nails, watched a movie. Mundane things. She was a creature of habit.

Too easy. She's begging for it. She hasn't taken a precaution in years. This won't satisfy you a bit, and you know it.

He ignored the voice, as he had been since he'd picked her. The voice, whatever part of his conscience that still lived, was more of an annoyance than anything else. Sometimes it begged, cajoled. Sometimes it drove, commanded. He'd listened to it well for all his life, but lately, the voice had become less brave. Less artistic. Less everything.

Patterns create boredom. Boredom creates mistakes.

What would you have me do? Walk away?

An annoyed sigh. *Yes.*

No. Patterns are what makes the world go around. Without them, the world would descend into chaos. We would descend into chaos. I am doing my part to keep the world revolving. So shut. Up. Already.

He edged closer to the screen. Sweat trickled down his back, gathering in the groove above his pants. He shifted, pressed back against the chair. He was still in good shape, considering all the sitting he did now. He worked at it, using his own body weight to keep strong and lithe. Muscles tight, waist thin. Hair—short and chemically blond; jaw—square; teeth—perfectly straight; eyes—the lightest blue. All functioning normally, better than most men his age. The strange gift of symmetry imbued by his DNA that made him beautiful. He crossed between the races; he was a sight to behold.

That's why his friends called him Beauty.

His beauty was his camouflage. Nothing beautiful could hurt you. Nothing beautiful could betray and deceive or harm. Nothing beautiful could slice and grind and strangle.

Beauty was a deadly weapon. The one no one ever saw coming.

He grinned to himself as he watched her settle in for a Sunday afternoon nap.

Her last nap.

It was time.

And when it was over, he would turn his attentions to a more interesting prey. A challenge. Since he hadn't had one in so long.

The one who was looking for him. He would take his time. Be cautious and careful. But she would be his. If it was the last thing he did, she would be his.

TUESDAY: MORNING

What lies behind us and what lies before us are
tiny matters compared to what lies within us.

—Emerson

CHAPTER 1

Georgetown
Washington, D.C.
Tuesday morning

LAUGHTER.

They'd drunk too much, gotten too loud, too boisterous.
Mr. Smith's kicked them out a few minutes past midnight, and
they stumbled into the Georgetown night, dragged themselves
up Wisconsin and loped across M Street, tripping and clutching each other to stay upright, cackling hysterically, their heels
an incoherent tattoo on the sidewalks. People watched them,
their antics greeted with amusement or derision, depending on
the mood of the observers.

"I can't go on, I can't. Stop, Emma, please, stop."

Emma, ponytailed, blonde and lanky, fiddled with her tights
with one hand, tugged on Cameron's arm. "I gotta pee. We can't
stop now, Cam, it's just a few more blocks."

"My feet hurt. And my head." Cameron slipped, landed hard
against the plate-glass window of Starbucks. "Bump!" That set
them off again, the giggles turning into guffaws.

Emma yanked on the door to the darkened store. "Nuts. They're closed."

"Why are they closed?" Cameron whined.

"'Cause it's midnight. The witching hour. And you're not a witch, you're just a bitch. Tommy's place is just ahead. Can you make it there?"

Cameron squeezed her eyes closed, chanting the rhyme under her breath. "Not a witch, just a bitch, not a witch, just a bitch."

"You really are screwed up, aren't you? Come on." Emma dragged her to her feet, off down the darkened street.

Georgetown never truly sleeps. Even when the bars close, there are still people about—joggers, the ubiquitous construction workers, musicians and homeless, dog walkers and students, lovers and mistresses. A stew of incessant liveliness, perfect for the college-aged and the cuckolded. The romantics and the hardened.

They made it a block before Cameron stopped dead. She grabbed Emma's arm, nails digging into the soft flesh.

"Did you hear that?"

Emma strained, but one block up from M Street and two blocks over, all she heard was the tittering of the night birds and the whooshing of tires on pavement, maybe some faint, masked music. "Hear what?"

Cameron shook her head. "I thought I heard something. Someone shouted. I'm drunk. Where are we?"

Emma glanced at the sign on the corner. The numbers and letters weaved together. She shut one eye and the familiar *N* floated into range.

"We're on N Street. One more block up. Come on already."

They started off again. "How are you going to get in? I thought you two broke up. Didn't he take back his key?"

"We're not broken up. Just on a break. There's a difference. He's so busy now, with school and working. He just took on another new project. He needed some space. I understand."

"Oh. I see. You understand why you're not important to him anymore. Big of you."

"Bitch." But there was no heat behind the word.

She heard footsteps. Straightened in time to see a jogger cross the street in front of them, legs pounding out a steady rhythm. Chick could move. Emma wasn't a runner. She played tennis, quite well, but the idea of running for the sake of running was boring to her. At least on the courts there was a tangible goal.

She realized she was alone, looked over her shoulder. Cameron had stopped again, was leaning woozily on a trash can.

"Come *on*," Emma said, her tongue getting stuck on the words. She bit back a giggle and held out her hand. "We're almost there."

"Gotta rest."

"Fooocuuuus, Cameron. Don't make me leave you behind in the dark, all alone. Whooooo. Big nasty dark gonna eat you alive."

Cameron flipped Emma the bird and stumbled back to her feet. "Lesgo."

A car turned the corner, engine purring as it disappeared behind them. Now they were truly alone.

One block, turn right. Twenty steps more, then the basement apartment railing appeared on her left. Emma fished the key out of her bra. She'd known they were going to be drunk tonight. Thought a little booty call would be appropriate, even though she and Tommy had, in essence, broken up. Not because he didn't dig her; he did, she knew it. It was just school was tough on him.

She knew Tommy would be home studying, late into the night, working on some random epithelial cell or DNA splicing theory, as he always seemed to be. Medical school was hard. Hell, undergrad was hard. Harder than she'd expected. Life was hard, too, especially for a pretty young thing with just enough smarts to make it into Georgetown, but maybe not quite enough to stay there. Her parents would freak if she failed out.

Tomorrow, I'll stop drinking and partying and really study.
Tomorrow.

But for tonight, everyone needed to blow off some steam, get a little nookie. Sex was good for the brain. Raised the levels of oxytocin, serotonin, melatonin, all those tonins Tommy liked to talk about.

Emma shook her hair free of its ponytail so it would fall in a sultry mass about her shoulders, sloppily freshened her lip gloss, licked her lips and shot Cameron a look. Cam seemed like she was about to pass out. Her eyes were half-shut, the smile on her face dreamy and stupid.

Emma slipped as she went down the five stairs to Tommy's front door. She grabbed the railing with both arms, clung on, the metal biting cruelly into her rib cage. She managed not to drop the key, but one sky-high platform peep-toe clattered toward the door, hitting it with a thump.

"Whoops," she said, laughing. Cameron hooted like it was the best trick she'd ever seen.

Emma put a finger to her lips. "Shhh. God, you're gonna wake the whole street." She righted herself with dignity, squared her shoulders and put the key in the lock.

"Aren't you going to knock?" Cameron asked.

"Why?" Emma replied, jiggling the key, then turning the knob. The door swung open into darkness.

"Darn it. He's asleep," Emma said, looking back over her shoulder. "Better be quiet, Cam. Can you be quiet?"

"Go in, for Chrissakes. I need a drink."

Emma took off her other heel and stepped inside, the straps looped on her index finger. It was dark, so dark she couldn't see anything. She ran her hand along the wall by the door, found the light switch. The lamp in the foyer cast its yellow glow into the hallway. Tommy's bike was leaning against the wall. Careful not to knock it over, she pulled Cameron inside and shut the door. Made her way down the hall into the living room.

Turned on the light. Saw red, and it took a moment for reality to penetrate her margarita-fogged brain.

Red.

Not red.

Blood.

Blood, *everywhere*. The sofa, the floor, the wall by the two-seater bar.

Emma stood frozen, unable to move. Cameron was busy getting sick behind her, gagging and choking. Only then did the smell of the blood hit her, meaty and raw, like steaks left too long in the refrigerator, their surface shiny and green.

Want to run, want to hide, want to go away.

Something kept her rooted to the spot. "Tommy?" she called.

There was no answer.

"Stay here," she told Cameron, an unnecessary direction. Cam was on her hands and knees, moaning, trying and failing to scrabble backward away from the living room and the vomit. She bumped up against the hallway wall and ducked her head into her hands, eyes squeezed tightly shut. She wasn't going to be of any help.

Careful to avoid stepping in the blood, Emma moved along the edges of the living room. Tommy's bedroom was down the hall. It was dark. There were no sounds but Cameron's low keening, which sent shivers down Emma's spine.

"Please," she said, uncertain to whom the plea was directed. Please don't let this be Tommy's blood. Please don't let him be hurt. Please don't let him be dead. *Please please please please please.*

His door was shut. She steeled herself, took two deep breaths. The smell was worse here, tighter, fresher. Almost alive in its awfulness.

She opened the door, flipped on the light.

Screams.
Over and over and over again.
Screams.

CHAPTER
2

Georgetown

SIRENS RENT THE NIGHT AIR.

The wailing jolted Dr. Samantha Owens from sleep. She listened for a moment, heard them growing louder. They were close. Too close. Several of them, caterwauling through the night as they came near. Instead of peaking and fading, blue lights suddenly flashed on the opposite wall of her bedroom, rotating frantically. The sirens ended with a squawk, but the lights continued their alternating strobes. Based on the angle of the flashes, they'd stopped on O Street.

Her home in Georgetown was generally quiet and calm in the darkness. A few drunk kids every once in a while, hollering as they wound their way back to campus, but rarely something like this.

Clearly, something terrible had happened.

Sam was used to sirens. Living in the city meant they were a regular, nightly, daily occurrence. Sirens used to be the precursor to her part in the festivities, so she always registered their noise. Sirens used to mean her phone was going to ring, and she'd have to drop everything and rush to a crime scene. But that was another life, in another city. One she tried very hard to put behind her.

Her phone wasn't going to ring, but habits die hard. She glanced at the clock—one in the morning.

She got up, pulled a brush through her shoulder-length brown hair, slipped a warm cashmere sweater over her thin T-shirt, pulled on black leggings and a pair of leather ankle boots. Grabbed a pashmina and tossed it around her shoulders.

Autumn was in full swing, and the late-September temperatures had dropped precipitously over the past week, making D.C. shiver. The bedroom, too, was cold, empty of Xander and his internal furnace. He was on assignment, a close-protection detail with one of his old Army buddies, Chalk. Trevor Reeves Worthington III on his driver's license, but Chalk forever to his Army mates, named for his propensity to write everything down.

It had only been three weeks since Xander and Chalk had hung out their shingle, made the business official, and they'd already been in high demand. She was glad to see Xander re-engage with the world, though she had to admit, it was a bit of a shame. She liked the idea of him up in the woods with Thor at his side, doing his best Thoreau, leading the occasional fishing party, hiking solitary through the woods. The new gig was intense, all-hours, and took him away too much for her liking. Plus, his main job was to throw himself in front of a bullet should the need arise, and she wasn't at all comfortable with the thought.

She started down the stairs, whistled for Thor. The German shepherd was waiting for her already, ears pricked. She knelt beside him, buried her face in his fur. He was warm, like his daddy, had been curled in a ball in his sheepskin bed, dreaming doggy dreams. He nuzzled her and licked her on the nose gently, then went to stand by the door, alert and ready.

"Let's go out the back, baby."

He hurried to her side, and she fastened his lead. She opened the back door, was rewarded with a gust of chilly air, and the voices that carried from the other side of her privacy fence.

You have stooped to a new level, Owens, trying to eavesdrop on a crime scene.

But she went to the far fence, skirting the eternity pool, Thor stuck to her leg like glue. Put her head against the wood. If she turned slightly sideways, she could see through the double slats.

It was so familiar, the shouts and calls. The first responders were there, the police, too. An ambulance was parked on the corner. As she watched, EMTs scrambled toward it with a stretcher. One was kneeling on the gurney itself, straddling a body of indeterminate sex, performing CPR with single-minded intensity.

The open doors of the ambulance blocked the rest. Moments later, they slammed shut and it left in a hurry, sirens wailing. The fire trucks followed, calm now, big beasts rumbling into the night.

The police stayed.

Definitely not a good sign.

She wondered if her friend Darren Fletcher, the newly minted homicide lieutenant, would show. She didn't know why she assumed it was a homicide, or an attempted homicide, given that someone had been brought out at a rush. It could be anything. More than likely, at this time of night, it was a simple domestic dispute. Someone was punched, had a bloody nose, a black eye, then things got out of control. She ran through the neighbors she knew on O Street, people she'd waved to when walking Thor, imagining them in various states of fury and undress.

Maybe a heart attack. Or a stroke. Embolism, aneurysm, overdose.

God, you are cheery, aren't you?

She heard one of the cops say, "Hernandez, while you're at it, go ahead and call the OCME. We'll need them."

And she knew. Something inside her gave a little buzz. Death comes in all forms, from all directions. Expected or by surprise, it was the greatest common denominator, the great equalizer. She felt an affinity with the grimness, couldn't help that. But she had a choice, now. A choice to walk away from the carnage, from the horror. To face death on her own terms, especially since she'd agreed to work with the FBI on their more esoteric cases. A deal made all the more tantalizing because they wouldn't be dragging her out of bed in the middle of the night to parade, yawning, to a crime scene, where she'd face death in all its incarnations, as she had for so many years as a medical examiner.

She had a more immediate choice, as well. She could open the gate, walk around the block, stand with the crowd of neighbors who'd come to watch the show. Or she could go back inside and return to bed. She'd be able to get several more hours of sleep if she went inside now.

You're not the M.E. anymore, Sam. She stepped away from the fence.

Thor took advantage of the nocturnal walk to do his business, then she followed him into the silent house, feeling strangely hollow. As she closed the door behind her and watched Thor scoot back to bed, something made her pull out her cell phone and send Fletcher a text.

What's up on O Street?

She knew it wasn't too late for him; he was a night owl, especially now that he was seeing FBI Agent Jordan Blake. He'd be up, one way or another. She sent another, this time to Xander.

Miss you.

She poured herself a finger of Ardbeg, thought about it,

brought the bottle with her to the couch. Sat down. Took off her boots.

Waited.

Didn't know exactly what she was waiting for.

She spared a glance at the file folders on the coffee table in front of her. She'd left them scattered carelessly in frustration before climbing the stairs to bed. Crime scene and autopsy photos spilled out of the manila folders, coupled with her notes and Baldwin's notes and toxicology reports, all jumbled together on the smoky glass. She'd pulled all the autopsy reports from the files and stacked them neatly on the side table; they were her reading material and were proving to be an even bigger frustration than the case itself. This massive, sprawling, unnamed and unacknowledged case.

There were so many pathologists, coroners, methods, regulations, jurisdictions. No one did a postmortem exactly the same, much less were handling several of the individual cases as if there was a criminal component. She'd begun to feel she was interpreting without a Rosetta stone.

When John Baldwin had talked her into coming on board the FBI as a consultant to the behavioral analysis unit, BAU II, to work with his infamous group of profilers, he'd promised she could pick her cases. True to his word, he'd brought her to Quantico, gotten her set up with passes and emails and paperwork galore, then set her loose in the BAU file room. They had so much work, and so few people to handle it, any help was welcome.

And whether she was trying to prove her worth to her new team, or to herself, she'd chosen the big daddy of them all. A stack of files that were getting dusty, because no one could manage to link them, even though there was a single similarity between each victim—every woman was from the same hometown. New Orleans.

She'd seen the box, labeled Cold Case. Read the previous

profiler's report. There was nothing tying them together. The women had died by various means. Stabbings and stranglings and gunshots, one a cardiac arrest from a drug overdose, even a bridge jumper. Nothing highly unusual, nothing esoteric, nothing sexually motivated or even creepy. On the surface at least.

Baldwin had a feeling about the cases, had spent years compiling the ones he thought fit a pattern, and she'd learned to trust his gut when it came to crime. Despite the sometimes innocuous causes of death, the link to New Orleans shouted "connection" to him. But he couldn't definitively tie all the cases together, nor could anyone on his staff.

Sam had looked through the files in the storage room, shaking her head. The murders did seem unrelated—they were spread all over the country, with different MOs, different murder weapons, different victimologies of all ages and races and socioeconomic levels. And yet, like Baldwin, she sensed the tenuous thread holding them. All of these women had been murdered by the same person. She could just feel it. There was something here. This was a series. Eight of them at last count, over more than twenty years.

Baldwin had just added what he thought might be number nine to the stack, a young woman named Olivia Rives, who'd been found shot to death in Minneapolis last month.

Nine dead. Multiple jurisdictions. No apparent links outside of a hometown and a profiler's hunch.

A nightmare.

She shot the Ardbeg, poured another and gathered up the thick stack of papers on the side table. No sense going back to bed just this moment. She'd read a while more, keep filling her brain with the disparate notes of nine different autopsy reports by nine different doctors and coroners.

Maybe this time, something would be different.

CHAPTER 3

McLean, Virginia

ROBIN SOULEYRET'S PHONE RANG AT 3:23 A.M. EYES SNAPPING OPEN, SHE saw the number on the caller ID. Surprised, she palmed the receiver. "You know better than to call in the middle of the night unless someone is dead. So who died?"

There was silence.

"Amanda? What is it? Are you okay?"

Nothing. Then a click.

That was odd. Robin sat up in the bed, realized she was still naked, glanced at the empty spot beside her. Felt the pillow. It was cold. He'd left. She tamped down the feeling that churned in the pit of her stomach. Annoyance? Relief? Sorrow? She didn't know, but this was their deal. No strings, and definitely no feelings. They were just filling a need for each other.

With a sigh, she reached down and grabbed the shirt she'd been wearing off the floor, pulled it on and dialed Amanda's phone back.

It went straight to voice mail. Her sister's lilting voice filled her ears. "This is Mandy. You know what to do."

Robin tried to keep the irritation from her tone. Well, most of it, anyway.

"You woke me up, little sister. Care to call me back, tell me what's up?"

Lying back against the pillows, she stared at the ceiling. Wished Riley hadn't been in such a hurry to split. She wouldn't have minded making him breakfast. Just this once.

The room was dark around her, empty, but not lonely, never lonely. She'd chosen this life, known what it would be—all work, and no play. No real lasting relationships, with friends or lovers, no kids, no normality. Just a constant string of challenges, issues to be overcome. She'd realized long ago she was just an ant among other ants in a very strange hill, crawling across the world, bumping into a crumb here and there. Some were even big enough to take back to their queen.

Which made her think about Amanda again. She tried the phone once more, to no avail.

A vague uneasiness flooded her system. Maybe Amanda had dialed her number accidentally. Butt-dialed her. Or decided what she wanted to say wasn't important enough to wake Robin in the middle of the night.

"Fat chance of that, you little bonehead. Where are you?"

She'd never get back to sleep at this rate. She got up, made a pot of strong Turkish coffee, measured in some sugar so it would be *orta şekerli*, just sweet enough to add to the flavor, bring out the chocolate notes without overwhelming the richness. She inhaled the fumes as it began to boil, craving the dark, deep taste.

Her Turkish friends would be aghast at her drinking coffee in the middle of the night, but as she liked to point out to them, she was an American, not Turkish, and by God she'd drink it whenever she wanted—in the morning, before her dinner, in the middle of the night. So there.

Cup in hand, she made her way through the cottage to the back porch. The sky was as dark as the coffee, beginning its los-

ing battle with the sun, which was still three hours off. She re-
dialed Amanda's phone.

Nothing.

Took a sip of the coffee, listened to the night things chirping
and crawling in the bushes, imagined the birds and mice having an intimate, elegant cocktail party under the bough of the
fir tree. Breaking bread with the enemy. Her specialty.

When she'd finished the coffee, she knew it was time to make
the call. She hated to do it, but she had no choice. Mandy was
her little sister, headstrong and brave, but prone to getting herself into situations that involved delicate extrications. The girl
seemed to live for close calls, and she managed well, considering. She'd only asked for help once, a month ago. Robin had
been forced to turn her down, unable to break away from her
own messed-up world to help. They hadn't spoken since, and
Robin was missing her impetuous sister.

She dialed the number.

Listened to the greeting.

Punched in an extension.

Waited a moment, then hung up.

A heartbeat later, the phone rang.

She answered, surprised to hear Riley's voice on the other
end. "Robin?"

"What are you doing on the desk? I figured you'd be at home,
sound asleep." Or in my bed, sound asleep. Or wide-awake, an
even better scenario.

The unspoken words shimmered around her, golden threads
of need and desire. She needed to get a handle on these nascent
emotions, and quickly. Riley wasn't thinking about champagne
and roses and candlelight every time he bedded her, she knew
that. Of course, Riley didn't see the glorious colors dancing
around his words, either.

"I got called in. There's been an incident in Georgetown."

The golden threads dissipated with a pop and something like

fear skittered up her back. She didn't recognize the sensation right away. She hadn't been afraid in a very long time.

"Anything I can do?" she said, careful to stay neutral.

Riley's voice cracked a bit. "I'm comin' over. You sit tight."

Riley was from Texas, and no matter what, when he was upset, or tired, or drunk, little bits of an accent floated through his teeth, tripping off his tongue in blues and reds, like the flag.

The quivery, uncontrolled feeling coursed through her again. It *was* fear, she thought—deep, abiding, acrid and horrible. It filled her nostrils and played along the edges of her skin. "Riley. Tell me right now. What's happened?"

His great gusting sigh scared her even more. Riley was a rock. Nothing rattled him.

She already knew what he was going to say, felt herself sliding out of the chair, to the cold concrete patio, as if being closer to the earth would help cushion the blow.

"It's Amanda, Robin. She's been killed."

The stark word danced around her, sharp needles poking and prodding.

Killed. Killed. Killed.

You knew you should have helped her. Why didn't you swallow your pride and call?

She's dead, and it's your fault. Your fault. Your fault.

"That's not possible," she whispered.

But it was true. She could feel the emptiness in the world. The spot that housed her sister, always tangible and reachable, was gone.

She dropped the phone, didn't hear Riley say, "I'll be there in five minutes. You stay put."

Amanda.

Mandy.

Gone.

Black. Black and gray, swirling, choking, drawing her down,

the words covering her like a scratchy blanket, drawing tighter, suffocating.

It is your fault, Robin.

CHAPTER 4

Georgetown

DARREN FLETCHER PULLED UP TO THE CRIME SCENE WITH THE REMNANTS OF
a hurried to-go cup of coffee in his hand. He parked, drained
the cup, grimacing—the coffee had gone cold, and bitter with
it—and waited for the caffeine to hit his system so he wouldn't
yawn in front of his team. It didn't work; he felt a jaw-cracking
one coming on. Ducked his head down, let it overtake him.
He'd been asleep when the call came.

The yawn made him feel better. More alert. He dropped the
coffee cup into the drink holder and got out of the car.

Every crime scene was the same. There were the usual crowds
of neighbors clustered together along the sidewalk. Yellow crime
scene tape was wound around the stop sign at the corner of O
and Wisconsin, effectively blocking traffic from driving down
the street. He expected the same was true at the other end of
the block. Nodded to himself. They were handling things well.

A patrol officer held the clipboard, standing relaxed against
a tree. He straightened when he saw Fletcher.

"Evening, sir. Got us a mess."

"So I hear. Who's on it?"

"Detective Hart's talking to the witnesses right now." He gestured down the sidewalk, where Fletcher's old partner and now lead detective stood by a pair of girls, both tearstained and rumpled. "Dude's girlfriend found them. They're pretty shook up."

"I bet. Thanks, Hernandez."

Fletcher signed in, went down the stairs. He could smell the blood before he saw it. When he stepped through the hall into the main room, with all the crime scene lights burning brightly, the blood seemed chaotic in its motion, streams and spatters of red going everywhere.

He sighed. A long night ahead for his team.

They all knew Fletcher liked to look at things by himself. Two crime scene techs saw him come in and melted away, allowing their boss a clean scene to walk through.

One said in passing, "Watch the blood in the hall. It's pretty thick as you go into the bedroom."

Fletcher nodded his thanks and walked through by himself once, placing things. The tech was right. The blood *was* thick and smeary, almost as if the body had been dragged into the bedroom from the living room.

As he entered the master, he saw a woman's body leaning against the bed, arms by her sides, a crumpled marionette. Her skin was blue; milky, slitted eyes stared at nothing. Skids of blood stained the carpet, the bed, the walls. Life's blood, clearly. A six-inch blade lay quietly on the comforter, next to a small, dirty-white plastic tent with a green light inside to designate a significant piece of evidence, and the number seven written on it.

Crime scene markers.

There was another green-lit one on the dresser, perched next to a piece of paper.

He'd been told this was a murder-suicide. Here was the murder.

The suicide was not present for his own party. He'd been

transported to George Washington University Hospital, in extreme distress.

The crime scene was messy, unwieldy, complicated. Not the worst he'd ever seen, but bad enough. It would take a week to sort through all the blood. And with two victims, it would cost him a mint. He couldn't help but see the dollar signs—he had a budget now, new responsibilities. He needed to keep control of things. And DNA testing was expensive. A necessary evil, of course, but pricey all the same.

The note was on the dresser, a page ripped from a notebook, written in a slanting hand, the letters blocked, like an architect's script, but leaning heavily to the right, as if the building plans attached to it were sliding down a hill.

You made me do this.

He left it there, made his way out of the apartment, up the stairs, breathing deeply of the city air, happy to let its gassy stink clear his sinuses of the reek of death. Spared a quick glance at the tall back windows of the house one street over. Samantha Owens lived there, and he was surprised she wasn't over here already, marching around, giving orders. Of course, she wasn't a part of his world, not really, just an interesting bystander who brought him the strangest cases.

He liked the idea of her working for the FBI. She needed the challenge.

The lights in her bedroom were dark. He shook off thoughts of his friend. He needed to attend to his witnesses before they were useless.

Emma and Cameron were their names. Both undergrad students at Georgetown. Both highly intoxicated still, though scared into some semblance of sobriety. Underage, too, of course, which meant trouble for whoever was serving them tonight, but he didn't spare more than a moment's thought to that issue. Not his problem.

The taller of the two was standing by the squad car, her arms wrapped around her body as if she could hold herself together. He imagined she'd never seen anything like this. It would scar her for life. And the other one—prettier, softer, but…less, somehow, than her friend—was well on her way to being medicated by the EMTs. The horror of violent death took people differently. Some freaked out, some got quiet. Some enjoyed the ruckus, found ways to make it all about them. Others shook, and were never right again.

Hart nodded to him as he approached. He looked as tired as Fletcher felt.

"Hey, boss. This is Emma Johnson. She found the victims. Cameron Saint, her friend. They came to visit Mr. Cattafi this evening and found them." He gestured back toward the house.

The girl Hart had identified as Emma kept glancing at the house. Her voice was soft, hurting. "Is Tommy going to make it?"

Fletcher could smell the liquor on her breath. She'd been crying; her eyes were red and puffy. "I don't know, ma'am. Can you run me through your night? Tell me what happened?"

"I just wanted to stop by and see him," she said.

"They'd broken up," Cameron added. Emma came to life, anger on her face as she gave her friend a nasty look.

Her friend shrugged. "What? You did. He was there with another woman, anyway. And he tried to kill her. You dodged a bullet, you ask me."

Emma sighed in disgust, turned to Fletcher with old eyes. "We're on a break. I still have my key. He's been really busy lately. School's been really hard on him."

"Where does Mr. Cattafi go to school?"

"He's an M.D./Ph.D. candidate at Georgetown. He's going to cure cancer. Already has."

"Mmm-hmm. And you broke up when?"

"Two weeks ago."

"Did you know he was seeing someone new?"

The words were small. "No. No, I didn't."

"Where were you tonight?"

"Just…all over the place. Barhopping."

"And people can confirm this?"

"Oh. My. Gawd. You think I had something to do with this? Are you mental?"

"Careful, Miss Johnson," Hart said.

"My father will be very interested to hear your accusations. Do you have any idea who I am?"

Fletcher stopped himself from laughing. "No, Miss Johnson. I have no idea who you are, nor do I care. Now you can settle down, or we can have this chat in my office. Do you want that?"

"Calm down, Emma. He's not kidding," Cameron said.

Emma huffed a bit, then raised her chin. "No. I don't care to continue this line of questioning without a lawyer present."

Hart glanced at Fletcher, who nodded. Hart whipped out his cuffs, turned Emma Johnson around and calmly placed them on her wrists, all the while ignoring her squeaks of shock at his rough treatment. "When my father hears this, he's going to get you fired!"

Cameron groaned and leaned back against the police cruiser. She met Fletcher's eyes as if to say, *Hey, I can't do anything with her when she's fired up like this.*

"Miss Saint? Would you like to continue this conversation, or would you, too, like a lawyer present?"

"Yes, sir, I would. I mean, no, sir, I'm all good." Flustered, she continued. "Emma didn't do this, sir. She's been with me all night."

"Shut *up*, Cameron. We need to get my dad's lawyers here."

Cameron drew herself up and gave her friend a baleful glare. "*You* shut up, Emma. You're making a fool out of yourself." And to Fletcher, "We have fake IDs—we were in Mr. Smith's most of the night. You can check. They booted us and we walked up here. *She* wanted a booty call. She's just drunk. She gets stupid when she drinks. Let her go, please. We stumbled into this, and we don't know anything."

Her words rang true, and Fletcher nodded. "Did you see anyone in the neighborhood as you were walking here? Anything that stood out? Cars that seemed suspicious, people who were out of place?"

Cameron looked at the ground, then back to him. "Sir, I apologize, but I had a lot to drink tonight. I wasn't noticing much of anything besides where to put my foot next to make it up the hill, and then tossing my cookies when I saw all that blood. Besides, it's Georgetown. There's always a bunch of people around. I didn't notice anyone who looked wrong, but I wasn't paying a lot of attention, either."

Emma had had a change of heart. "There was a jogger. That's the only person I saw. But it was a woman. She was coming down the hill."

"Young, old? Hair color?"

"She had a baseball cap on, and those reflective sneakers. That's all I remember."

Fletcher believed her. "All right. Unhook her, Hart."

Emma looked like she was about to say something, but Cameron shook her head and she stopped. Hart released the cuffs, and Emma rubbed her wrists and muttered, "Thanks."

Cameron grabbed her friend's hand. "Can we go now?"

Fletcher did his best disappointed-dad routine. "You two behaved incredibly irresponsibly tonight. You could have been killed. I hope you realize that. Now, give me the fake IDs."

"Yes, sir," they chimed in unison.

They dug in their bags and came up with the bits of plastic. He pocketed them. "Detective Hart will make sure you get home all right. I'll most likely want to talk to you again, when you've had a chance to sober up, and clean up. Give him all your information. And, girls? I hear about you doing anything out of step again, I won't be Mr. Nice Guy. You hear me?"

They nodded, and Fletcher jerked his head toward the car. "Get them home," he said to Hart, then walked back to his own car.

What a mess. What a huge mess.

His phone was sitting on the console. There was a text from Sam—sure enough, she had noticed the hubbub. He was tempted to go knock on her door, let her make him a decent cup of coffee. Her boyfriend, Xander, was addicted. They always had some sort of delicious brew on hand. But the text was over an hour old. She may have gone to bed when she didn't hear back from him.

He sent her a quick note back, then got started with the paperwork.

There'd be no sleep for him tonight.

CHAPTER 5

BIRDS. ALL SHE COULD HEAR WAS BIRDS.

Chirping, singing, flitting against the glass feeder. Sweet little songbirds going mad outside the window.

Sam cracked open her right eye, then the left, pulled herself upright with a little groan. Touched her forehead, saw the remnants of the Scotch in the glass on the coffee table. Papers fell to the floor in a cascade, a gentle susurration off her chest.

She'd fallen asleep on the couch, waiting for something... She couldn't remember.

Thor saw her stirring. His head shot up, and she could swear the dog smiled.

"Yeah, yeah, I'll get your breakfast in a minute."

He *woofed* softly, set his muzzle on his paws.

She picked up the papers, stacked them carefully. Remembered to put Sausalito on top. She wanted to revisit that scene. A houseboat in the northern part of the city, abandoned and neglected. It stood out among the brighter, shinier, newly constructed and renovated, not only because of its dilapidation, but because its owner visited only once a year, in the summer, and when a body had been found in the salon, the owner hadn't come to see to things.

Something there.

The sirens. O Street. She remembered now. Flipped on the television, knowing well enough that if it were as bad as she suspected, the local news would be all over it.

They were talking about the weather. Sunny and chilly all week, some rain here and there, then a series of perfect D.C. fall days ahead.

She grabbed her phone. Fletcher had texted her back, some- time around three in the morning. She hadn't heard the ding.

Bad one. Double stabbing. One deceased, one in ICU. Si- rens wake you up?

Then a second text, ten minutes later.

Apparently not.

She smiled, his sarcasm evident, started to write him back, then jumped as the phone began chirping in her hand. Xander. She answered with a smile. She really did miss him.

"Hi, babe."

"You were up late." His voice was deep, still rough with sleep, and she felt like he'd wrapped her in his arms from afar.

"Something happened on O Street, late. Double stabbing. Cops everywhere. I couldn't get back to sleep."

"Are you okay? Was it someone we know?"

"I don't think so. I'm fine, just tired."

"I'm sorry I didn't call you back. I was on all night." He yawned. "Vigilance never sleeps."

"You haven't gotten any sleep? You need rest, Xander."

"I know. I'll grab a few winks in a minute. I wanted to talk to you first."

A shimmer of absurd pleasure shot through her. Even ex- hausted, he wanted her.

"Is the job going well? Nothing dangerous happening?"

"It is. All's well. We'll be wrapped shortly, and I can come home as soon as we put these guys on a plane back to London. I have good news, though. We already have a gig for next week."

She couldn't help the frown, pushed it away. This was a good thing. She didn't have the right to hold him back just because she enjoyed having him around at all hours.

"Good. I'm glad." She couldn't help herself. "Hopefully the job is local?"

He started to laugh. "Why, Dr. Owens. Do you miss me?"

"Oh, hush. Thor is going nuts without you here."

"Uh-huh. I hear you. Give him a scratch for me. Clients' flight leaves at 0930, then I'm headed your way. I'll be in by let me see, 1300 hours. Maybe we can walk down to Clyde's. I'm dying for a decent burger. These guys ate sushi all week."

"That sounds great. Can't wait. Fly safe."

"Have a nice day off. Love you." And he was gone before she had a chance to say it back.

"I love you, too," she whispered, and set the phone on the table. She fingered the simple diamond band he'd given her a few weeks earlier, opening the door to a more permanent future together.

She wasn't in a rush. They were together in all the ways that mattered. There was no real reason to make it legal. She wasn't going anywhere, and neither was he.

She hopped up from the couch, washed her hands thoroughly, ignoring the little voice counting *one Mississippi, two Mississippi* in the back of her head, then called Fletcher.

He answered on the first ring, quite jovial considering the time. "Heya, sleeping beauty. What happened, the battery die on your phone again?"

"Again? It was just the one time. I fell asleep, waiting for *you* to get back to me. What in the world happened last night?"

"Stabbing. Probably domestic. One dead, one gravely injured.

Couple of students found them. I'm waiting for a briefing on it in ten minutes. Want to meet me after for breakfast?"

"Yeah, I can do that. I don't have classes today." But he'd know that. Fletcher always seemed to have radar for her schedule. "Besides, I'm banging my head against the wall on a case. I could use the fresh air, maybe a fresh perspective."

"Meet me at Le Pain, then, in thirty minutes."

The short walk to Le Pain Quotidien was refreshing, just as she'd hoped. She was glad Fletcher had invited her to join him—with all the new work she was doing, the craziness of the past few months, she hadn't made many friends in D.C. yet. It was nice to get asked out on a breakfast date.

She got a table by the windows, and true to his word, twenty minutes later, Fletcher walked through the doors. Dressed in his usual gray suit and white shirt, unshaven and dark hair mussed, he looked more like he'd rolled out of bed instead of walking out of his office. He was frowning, scanning the restaurant in true cop form, before he joined her. She'd given him the chair that faced the door.

He gave her a quick hug and sat down, signaling to the waiter for a cup of coffee.

"To what do I owe the honor of your presence this morning?" she asked.

"I have a meeting down the street at ten. I'm telling you, being the LT isn't all it's cracked up to be. I spend more time in meetings than at crime scenes. It's becoming oppressive."

"I know exactly what you mean. I'm amazed anything gets done in the world, considering how many meetings we have. I had a faculty meeting last week that's sole purpose was to schedule another faculty meeting."

The waiter came, and they ordered—croissants for her, a ham and Gruyère tartine for him—and when he moved away,

Fletcher leaned forward and spoke quietly. "You wanna go to a crime scene with me?"

Sam had just picked up her coffee cup. It stopped midair. She clapped her right hand to her heart. "Oh, Fletcher. You say the sweetest things."

"Stow it, Owens. Is that a yes?"

"Of course it is. Right now?"

"We'll eat first. Then we'll go. Unless you've gotten squeamish in your old age and can't handle a nasty scene on a full stomach."

She rolled her eyes. "*I* can handle anything."

"Good."

"Out of curiosity, what is it exactly you'd like me to see?"

"All sorts of things. Tell me, have you ever heard of a kid at Georgetown Med named Thomas Cattafi?"

"Is that who was attacked? No, I haven't heard the name. He's not in any of my classes."

"He's a fourth year."

"That explains it."

"It's his apartment where the attack took place. It's probably in my head, but something about it all doesn't feel right. I spoke at length to his ex-girlfriend in the wee hours of the morning, and again just a bit ago. She and her BFF got hammered and dropped by for a booty call—she still had a key. Walked in, saw blood everywhere, called 9-1-1. BFF confirms every inch of the story."

"You think she did it, and the BFF is lying to cover for her?"

"I rousted the bartender at Mr. Smith's. He corroborates their story. He'd been serving them since seven or so. The two were cut off around midnight, sent drunk as skunks out into the dark. They're lucky they didn't get hurt. No, I think she's telling the truth. Though she was a pain in my ass last night." He mimicked the girl's high-pitched voice, and stamped his foot under the table. "'Don't you know who I am?'"

"Who was she?"

"Ah, hell, her dad's some big-shot here in town. Works for the attorney general. He was mighty pissed when he heard his precious underage princess was not only caught drunk at her ex's house but had just been let out of cuffs after mouthing off to me. Can you still ground a kid when they're nineteen?"

Sam laughed a bit. "Yeah, if they rely on your money to live." She could just imagine it. Then, seeing Fletcher was still distracted, she asked, "So what's not right about it? The crime scene, I mean, not the overindulged debutantes."

He fiddled with his coffee cup. "Weren't you an overindulged debutante?"

"And now you know why I recognized her for what she was."

They laughed, then he grew serious. "You ever get that sixth sense that what you're seeing isn't the real story?"

"Sure. All the time. It's part of what I do—did—trying to see past the obvious to find out the truth."

"So the ex—her name's Emma, by the way—said Tommy was having some trouble at school. I asked her, was he overloaded, too much work, that kind of stuff? And she says no, it was something else. Something serious. He wouldn't talk about it, broke up with her, pushed her out of his life."

"Sounds like a typical fourth year to me. Too much work, not enough time for actual living."

He shook his head briefly. "You're probably right. But then he and his new lover end up with knife wounds. She's dead, he still might die. There's a case to be made for murder-suicide, but…it doesn't feel as random as it might otherwise, I guess. Tell me, what do you know about curing cancer?"

CHAPTER
6

ROBIN WAS STILL. SHE HADN'T MOVED SINCE THE WEE HOURS, SINCE THE PHONE call and coffee and news and seething spiral of black oppressive knowledge had shut her down.

Riley sat next to her, not touching, whistling something under his breath. Rachmaninoff, she thought, or wait, no, it was one of the songs from the movie soundtrack of *Braveheart*.

Maybe she'd been asleep, drifted off, maybe she'd been sunk into meditation. She realized she was hearing him, the soft sibilance of his lips, so close, but never farther away, and shook herself slightly. The sun had come up. The sky to her west was hazy, the color of weak tea. The rustlings of the night creatures was long past. It would rain today.

Real. It was real. Amanda was dead.

A searing pain filled her chest. Red, she was red, everywhere. It rushed over her body, biting, stinging. She reached out to touch it, surprised when her finger touched skin, and the red absorbed into her, disappeared.

Not now, Robbie. You can't go down that hole again.

Riley had told her everything when he arrived, about the

boy who'd killed her sister, that she'd been taken to the D.C. morgue, that there would be an autopsy. That the boy who killed her had tried to kill himself, too, but was still alive.

Her legs were asleep. She'd stacked them beneath her before she'd gone into her empty place, the place she went to cope with anything overwhelming or hurtful, or when the synesthesia got to be too much. The empty place had gotten her through Afghani jails and snakebites and gunshots and torture. Had gotten her through her father's death. It was a wellspring of nothingness, a virtual blank spot in her psyche filled with nothing but soft, calming white noise. She entered it when the pain was too great, and emerged when her subconscious recognized she could deal with things again.

It was a valuable tool. One she hadn't thought she'd need ever again.

Swallowing, she realized the cup of coffee was still in her hand. The dregs were cold but she was parched. She let the chewy thickness linger in her mouth, realized she would never again drink the brew without thinking of her sister, a gash in her neck, dead in Georgetown.

Red, red, red.

Stop.

She shut her eyes briefly, and the moment passed. It had taken her years to learn how to control her curse, her gift, her otherness. Now it came to her gently, when she allowed it, pastels and soft things, but fear or horror killed her ability to control it. And she needed to be in control right now.

Amanda was supposed to die very, very old, or in the field somewhere, a hero's death, not at the wrong end of a knife less than five miles from her sister's loving arms.

Why hadn't she said she was coming to the States? Why hadn't she called? Robin would have protected her, done anything for her. Even if there was animosity between them, they were all that was left.

Amanda had called. A month prior. *And you were too far up your own miserable ass to help. This is your fault.*

There would be no tears, but her throat thickened, and she swallowed hard, again and again, until she realized the bile was rising; there was nothing she could do to stop it.

She jumped up and vomited over the railing.

Riley jumped up, too, one hand on her back, the other entangled in her long blond hair, pulling it back. He made shushing noises as if she were a child who'd had a bad dream. And she let him comfort her, using the only language either of them knew anymore—the dirty grayness of grief that helped with the shock of losing someone you love too soon.

When her stomach had finally settled, she sat back on the chair and met his eyes. They were pretty eyes. An odd shade of blue, dark and deep as the ocean, they were his best feature. The rest had been handsome, once, before. Before a knife to the forehead and ten years on the ground in too many countries to count wore even that out of him, and left him weary, battle torn and hungry for things she could barely give him. He was like a piece of granite, carved from the earth, silent and deadly.

"You're back," he said. It wasn't a question, but the interrogatory was evident. She'd scared him, collapsing in on herself like that, only to emerge choking and flailing over the rail.

"Yes. Do they know why?" she asked, surprised at how rusty she sounded, like a pipe left years in the rain.

He shook his head. "It's too early. If the boy wakes up, the police will certainly question him. But he's barely hanging on."

"She called me. At 3:23 this morning. She didn't say a word."

Riley frowned. "Not possible. She was already gone."

Robin picked up her cell phone. Showed him the incoming call.

"Someone has her phone," he said.

She shook her head. "No. It was probably one of the cops, checking her contacts for someone to notify."

"And when they found your name, and you answered, they decided not to tell you?"

"Maybe I'm not listed as her next of kin."

He touched her arm. "Robin. You are. You know you are."

"It was a murder-suicide, you said."

"There was a note. You're sure you've never heard of Thomas Cattafi?"

She shook her head. "I haven't. And a note, that's not enough to go on. It doesn't mean there wasn't someone else with them. Someone that killed her, and tried to kill him."

"What was she working on again?"

At that, Robin sucked in her breath and looked away. "You know I don't know. We hadn't been in touch for a while. She called me a month back, said she'd gotten into some trouble, wanted me to come bail her out. I was up to my ass in alligators with the failed meet in Kirkuk. There was no stopping to help her. So I said no. Told her she needed to learn how to deal with these things herself. That's the last time we talked." Hazy green clouds surrounded her head. The letters *N* and *O* rotated slowly, turning white in the mist.

"Jesus. I'm sorry."

She sniffed once, hard, then snapped to, waving her hands to dissipate the cloud. It went away dutifully, and when she opened her eyes again, she saw nothing but the backyard she loved, with the feeders and flowers grown out of control, the water, roaring past. Her very own jungle. Control.

"Riley, we need to investigate. Get Alicia to run the call logs into my phone. I don't care what sort of excuse she needs to make, who she needs to promise what, just find out where my sister's phone was when she...when it was used to call me."

"I don't think that's a good idea. We'll need clearance—"

"Riley Dixon, when is the last time you asked for clearance to run a phone call?"

His jaw flexed, the muscle in his cheek jumping. She'd hit a nerve. Good. But she softened her voice the tiniest bit.

"I don't know what Amanda was up to. But I will find out what happened to her. Are you going to help me or not?"

"I'll help you, Robbie. But I can't promise you're going to like where this leads. What if she's involved in something bad? What if you find out there's some sort of attack coming, and she's a part of it?"

She nodded, and stood, arms tight around her waist.

"Riley, she's not. She'd never be involved in anything to hurt us."

"Have you seen today's bulletin? On the threat to the nation's natural aquifers? What if someone hit our water supply here in D.C.? Just strolled right up to the plant on Roosevelt and popped something in the water."

"Wouldn't happen, Riley. There are fail-safes to make sure nothing biological can get through."

"You don't know that. Read the bulletin. It's scary stuff. There are too many threats to count. Amanda could have stumbled across the wrong person and they tried to recruit her into doing their dirty work."

"Then I absolutely need to find out what she was involved in."

He ran a hand through his brown hair, the bicep flexing. Hard. He'd always been so hard, all sinew and bone and flesh, muscles tightly coiled, a big cat, ready to pounce or leap away at a moment's notice.

"I'm going to have to call in a favor or two."

"Thank you, Riley."

He gave her a brief hug, cold lips pressed to her forehead, and left, stalking out through the living room, his heels banging on the hardwood. That man could walk silently across a field of broken glass; she knew he meant it to make a point. He was doing this against his will.

Well, so was she.

Riley would work things from his end, seeking out who had called using Mandy's phone. There was one phone call she needed to make. If there was anyone who might know what Mandy was involved in, Atlantic would be the one.

She put in word that she needed to talk to him, then sat back and waited.

And waited. And waited.

CHAPTER 7

CANCER? SAM FELT THE QUICK FLASH OF ALARM, TRIED TO KEEP HERSELF IN check. "Are you okay? Are you sick?"

Fletcher shook his head. "Oh, no, this isn't about me. Emma said Cattafi was involved in cancer research. He's doing some sort of specialized microbiology internship that has been making waves. Cellular differentiation or something like that. Stem cells, cancer vaccines, all sort of really cutting-edge stuff."

"What's a fourth year doing in research? That's usually post-doctoral work."

"Kid's a prodigy, from what I've heard. Juggling internships. Someone said he was in the M.D./Ph.D. program. So he's at GW in a coma. There was a woman with him—her name was Amanda Souleyret. She didn't make it."

He was messing with his spoon, putting it in his cup, taking it out. The fidgeting was uncharacteristic. Clearly, something had him rattled.

"And?"

"And..." The spoon went back in the coffee cup with a clatter. "On the surface, it looks like a domestic. He stabbed her, stabbed himself. He had the knife in his hand. The spatter patterns are consistent with an attack. It's cut-and-dried. Only thing that saved his life is his ex-girlfriend getting drunk and deciding she wanted a reconciliatory booty call and stumbling right into the scene. If she hadn't shown up when she did... It was a near thing. EMTs managed to get a heartbeat. He's not doing well. His family is flying in. Probably brain-dead—they may be looking at organ donation."

Sam had a vivid flash from the night before, the EMT working frantically, giving CPR. "That's terrible. But...?"

He looked at her finally, really looked, met her eyes and smiled. "You know me too well, don't you?"

The food came, and they waited for the waiter to clear off before they continued the conversation. Sam ripped off a chunk of croissant, lavishly buttered it. "I know when you're building up to something. So spit it out."

"The ID on the woman had a red flag. This is between us, right?"

She crossed her heart, waved the flaky pastry at him. "You, me and my croissant."

"She's blacked out in the system."

"What does that mean?"

"It means I can't do my job, because someone doesn't want me to know who she really is, and what she really does."

"Oh. That is rather odd. What do you think, she's some sort of agent? A spy? We are in D.C., after all."

He looked serious all of a sudden, put a hand on the back of his neck and squeezed. "That would be my guess. I don't know what agency she's from, whose side she's on. What I do know is ten minutes after I got to work this morning, I was told that there'd been a meeting scheduled at State, and my presence was requested. Either I'm about to be relieved of this case, or they're going to send me on a wild-goose chase."

"Fun times, my friend. You always catch the coolest cases."

"Which is why I was thinking, maybe if you have a look-see, I'll have a better sense of what's happening. I don't know what a spy would be doing having a fight with a kid in med school. It's probably just domestic, like I said, but..."

"No worries, Fletch. I'm happy to help, as always."

Her cell phone rang. She apologized, pulled it out of her pocket. Glanced at the screen, saw the call was coming from Quantico. John Baldwin. In a way, he was her new boss.

"Fletch, forgive me, I have to answer this."

He held up a hand. "No worries. Go ahead."

She stood and walked outside, determined not to disturb everyone around her with the call.

"Baldwin?"

His deep voice sounded stressed. "Sam, good morning. I hope you're doing well."

"I am. Out of the house and everything, having breakfast with Fletcher. What's up?"

"Ah, that's good. I'm glad you're already with him. Has he told you about the murder near your house last night?"

She grew wary. "He has. Plus I saw parts of it—the sirens woke me. Why?"

"The female victim, Amanda Souleyret? She was one of ours."

"She was FBI?"

"Yes. A longtime undercover agent, working...well, what she specialized in is most likely irrelevant, considering. I was told this looks like a domestic situation."

"That's what Fletcher said."

"Such a shame. No one even knew Amanda was in the US much less that she was dating someone here. I don't know how she found the time. She works primarily overseas, as an investigator for a French company called Helix International. Have you ever heard of it?"

Now Sam really was on alert. "As it happens, I have. They're in the same business as Xander, albeit on a much larger scale.

They do everything from close protection to industrial investigations."

"That's right. Amanda is—she was—a very talented agent, capable of handling most anything thrown her way. She's been on an undercover op that's stretched for over a year. Anyway, there's a briefing scheduled at ten at the State Department. Fletcher's already on the guest list. They wanted me there, but I'm flying out to Denver in an hour. Just between you and me, we might have another Hometown murder."

"You're kidding. That's two this month alone. He's accelerating."

"Yes, he is. I have to get out to Denver and see what's happening. Can you go to State in my stead? See what they have to say, take notes. Call me after, fill me in?"

"Of course," she said coolly, but her mind was going a thousand miles an hour. Why her? Why not pull someone from the Hoover Building to go, someone on Baldwin's direct staff? What did she have to offer this investigation? Especially if it had been bumped to this level, which felt awfully strange for a domestic case. Why would the State Department want to stick their oar into a lovers' spat gone horribly wrong?

She kept her mouth shut, though. When she'd agreed to come on board Baldwin's team, he'd been very clear that sometimes she'd be getting her hands dirty in all facets of his investigative life. It's why he wanted her in particular, someone he could trust, someone who understood the way things worked, but was an outsider.

"Great," Baldwin said. "I've already called in your DOB and social, just be sure you have your driver's license on you. They're on alert today, as you can imagine. I'll call you when I land in Denver and you can brief me."

"Sounds good. Talk to you then."

She hung up, hugged her arms around her body. A kid on a skateboard zoomed past her, calling out to a friend behind him, the small transparent wheels clattering on the sidewalk, the answering shouts. Cars whizzed by, people walked the streets with smiles on their faces.

Carefree. Careless. Too young to realize how precarious life truly is, too involved in their own moment to imagine what could happen.

She went back inside. Fletcher had finished his sandwich, and her croissant, too.

"Sorry, I was starving," he said. "I already ordered you a new one."

"We better get it to go."

A shadow crossed his face. "Gotta go to work?"

"Actually, *we* have to go to work. I just got called in on your murder. You better take me to that crime scene pronto."

CHAPTER 8

Teterboro Airport
New Jersey

XANDER WHITFIELD SLOUCHED IN THE CHAIR AT THE GATE, SHADES FIRMLY IN place. While he looked like a sleeping tourist trying to catch an uncomfortable nap before his flight, he was on high alert.

He watched his partner, Chalk, move through the room near the principal, waiting for the nod telling him it was time to move. They had a loose box around their principal—a wealthy British industrialist named James Denon, who didn't want it known he had a protection detail on him while he visited his interests in the States—and his people. Their job had been to blend into the crowd everywhere the team went.

So far, they'd done well. Not great—they'd had one small mishap when Chalk turned the wrong way for a moment and the principal had gotten too far ahead of them—but good. Xander wasn't entirely thrilled with this lurking-from-afar crap, but sometimes the principal got to make the call. Once the doors to the plane closed, he and Chalk would be done and on their way, thousands of dollars richer and with a glowing recommendation to boot. Just what they needed to get their new company off the ground.

This part of the operation was the trickiest. Whipping out their weapons at an airport was a surefire way to get noticed. If a bogey were to make a move now, they would have to counter it with subtle, quick and meaningful brute force.

Xander was fine with that. It had been ages since he'd been in an honest-to-God fight. He wouldn't mind sinking his fists into a bad guy's face.

It wouldn't happen today. The job had been simple, straightforward. James Denon was well-liked by his people, his company and his country. There had been no signs of trouble all week. The people who hated him were half a world away, and the trip had been on close hold, so they had no idea he was in the States.

They'd timed their arrival well. The wait was short; after only fifteen minutes, their principal's flight was ready. This was the beauty of Teterboro, New Jersey's private airport. The crowds were smaller, the people waiting for private flights and charters. The usual program—parking, security, long wait times at the gates—wasn't at all the same.

Good for the principal, but more difficult for Xander to fit in. They'd been lucky today; there was a group of private high schoolers being ferried to Canada, and they were creating quite a bit of distraction. Enough for Xander to find a spot along the periphery and look like one of their chaperones, exhausted already by their energy.

Behind the mirrored lenses, he watched the small crowd. Their principal began making his way toward the doors. Xander gave Chalk the nod, stood, stretched. Moved toward the double glass doors to the tarmac, gave things a look-see. All clear. He spoke quietly into his hand mike. "We're a go. Plane's here."

Chalk, standing four feet away, touched the principal on the shoulder, gestured unobtrusively toward the door. Xander kept watch while the principal and his people dutifully paraded out the door, across the tarmac and into the plane.

Five minutes later, it was done. The flight attendant had closed the door, and the plane pulled away, engines purring.

"A final all clear," Xander said, and felt the tension of the past few days leak away.

Chalk strolled toward the exit, and Xander followed, cautious to watch their backs. No reason to get made just because the operation was over.

They met up in the parking lot. They had rented two cars. They'd take them back to JFK, drop them and the job would officially be over.

"That went well," Chalk said.

"It did. And now he'll tell all his friends. Let's get to JFK. I want to go home."

Chalk's phone rang. He answered with his usual, "Hoo-rah." A moment later his face turned white.

Xander instinctively put his hand on his weapon at his belt, a sweet little SIG Sauer he preferred for close-up work.

"What is it? What happened?"

Chalk didn't answer, just made a helicopter with his finger and about-faced smartly, back toward the private terminal. Xander stepped next to him. A moment later, Chalk hung up.

"That was Denon. They're turning the plane around, some sort of mechanical problem. Looks like you and I aren't done just yet."

They were at the entrance now, and there was a lot of activity inside. Xander saw four airport employees running toward the back doors. The private schoolers were gathered together at the southern end of the room, pushing toward the windows, staring, one of their chaperones waving her hands to get them to stay put.

Xander ignored everyone around him but Chalk, tuned them out, lasered his focus. "What's the issue, did he say?"

"No. He's justifiably concerned."

"Think it's directed at him?"

"I don't know, but we better be ready for anything when that plane lands."

"If it is, they knew we were on him. They waited until we left to make a move."

"That's pretty fucking sophisticated. I haven't seen a tail, or anything to indicate we were being observed."

Xander nodded. "Me, either. Could his itinerary have leaked? He's a good target, we both know that. The threat assessment showed plenty of people who want him dead."

"If so, someone inside his senior staff or the folks he met with did it. No one else knows he's here."

They jogged through the doors, went straight to the back and out onto the tarmac. With the hullabaloo, no one thought to stop them. So much for being inconspicuous, though.

"Sam is going to skin me alive if I don't get home tonight."

Chalk shot him a grin. "Cheer up, lover boy. If our principal goes splat, you can get right on the next plane south."

"If our principal goes splat, we're done for. You take the terminal, I'll meet the plane. Cover my six."

He would be totally exposed, but there was no help for it. Chalk disappeared into the shadows behind him, and Xander stood with the other employees, his arms crossed, staring toward the empty tarmac. He listened hard to the charter employees. Apparently, the engine lights had flashed red, and the pilot wasn't about to try a transatlantic flight with possible trouble. It could be a simple mechanical issue.

Xander had a feeling that wasn't the case. Just a small frisson of *something*, up the back of his neck. He scanned the area. Murmured, "All clear," into his mike.

A few moments later, the Gulfstream came into view.

Xander stepped to the side, out of earshot, and phoned James

Denon, who answered sounding rather panicky. "What's happening? They won't tell us what's happening."

"We're here, sir, we're waiting on you. There's nothing apparent on the ground. Are you all right?"

"I am. What in bloody hell is going on?"

"They're saying it was an engine problem. Chances are, that's all this is. You just sit tight once they land. If they force you to disembark, make sure you come out last. I'll be waiting for you at the foot of the stairs. We can follow the same protocol as before, staying out of sight, but right now, I think we should stick close."

"I agree. Something feels off."

"Roger that, sir. You hang tight inside as long as they'll let you."

Xander hung up and casually turned, scoping the building behind him. He still had his shades on, eyes roving right, then left. He couldn't see Chalk, which was good. His adrenaline was surging, running hard through his body, so hard his hands were fighting the urge to shake. *Breathe, Xander. Breathe.*

The Gulfstream touched down, a small puff of white smoke rising from its tires. It headed toward the terminal, then suddenly altered course and began taxiing toward the southern hangar instead of the terminal. A radio crackled on the hip of the employee standing nearest him.

"This is Gulfstream 890. Got another warning light, we're leaking oil. Gonna head directly into the hangar. We'll disembark the passengers before we go in. Better find another plane, looks like we're going to be out of commission for a while."

There were sharp curses from the assembled crowd, but Xander ignored them.

The hangar.

A hundred yards away.

Xander had eyes on it, but he wasn't close enough to scope it properly. He scanned the building rapidly, looking for anything out of place. There was something, near the roof, twenty degrees to the right. A shadow. As he watched, the shadow pulled back slightly, and there was a flash. A mirrored flash.

His adrenaline shot into overdrive, and he clicked on his comms unit.

"Chalk, buddy, we got a shooter on top of the hangar."

"Roger. Can you take him?"

"I need to get closer, and higher. If I start heading his way, he'll know I saw him. You're gonna have to end around, let me get into position."

"There's a metal ladder behind me, runs up the side of the terminal building. The two buildings are about the same height. Should be the right angle."

"This might draw some attention to our client."

"Better attention than dead. I'll cover Denon, you take the shooter. Out."

Xander heard the whine of the engines. He was out of time. He broke with the employees and quick-walked to the edge of the terminal. Went up the ladder, wishing like hell he had his M4. He'd have a better chance of taking the guy out that way.

His mind was preternaturally calm, clear, crisply assessing everything. Wind speed, atmosphere, angle. The lack of a load in the SIG, the best place to take the shot. Up on the roof now, and of course there was very little to hide behind.

He'd lost eyes on his target, but he scooted to the north edge of the roof, and found him again. The assassin was low now, crouched against the concrete buttress. Relaxed, but ready, a M2010 ESR trained on the crowd below. Xander recognized a professional at work, and his heart sank.

Xander clicked his mike. "I'm in position. Son of a bitch has an M2010."

Chalk whistled. "Can you take him out?"

Xander took off his sunglasses. Laid on his stomach, inched to the edge. The terminal's high roof was a boon; he had a down angle on the shooter.

"Xander? Talk to me, buddy. What's happening up there?"

"Shh. I'm concentrating."

Chalk's voice raised slightly. "Concentrate faster, the plane door's opening."

God, he would kill for a set of binoculars, or even a range finder. He made the distance between the two buildings, from the end of his muzzle to the shooter's head, at just under a hundred yards.

Doable.

Xander shut his eyes, then opened and refocused. Modulated his breathing. Rolled onto his knees. Braced, got his grip perfect. Ignored Chalk in his ear saying, "Tick tock, buddy, time's running out. They're making them all disembark. I've counted three, that's the staff. Denon's going to be out next."

He watched the shooter on the roof swivel his rifle down, finger in the trigger. It was time.

Xander braced his arms. Felt a wind gust, made a small adjustment. Swallowed, and squeezed.

The gun moved smoothly in his hands, and the shooter on the opposite roof collapsed, his rifle catapulting over the concrete buttress to the tarmac below.

"Threat eliminated."

CHAPTER 9

Georgetown
O Street
Tommy Cattafi's apartment

SAM ADMIRED THE BUILDING THAT HOUSED CATTAFI'S APARTMENT. HIS PLACE
was in the basement of a beautiful three-story redbrick town house. An overgrown Norway maple was planted in front of the house, its broad leaves just beginning to show a tinge of yellow. In a few weeks, Georgetown would be a riot of colors, putting on a show, but for now, it was still green, only a bit less vibrant and deflated than even a week before.

Crime scene tape fluttered in the breeze. A patrol officer sat in his vehicle, unseeing, staring into his lap. The scene hadn't been fully released yet. It would be another day or two at least before that happened and the cleanup could begin. The reparation of lives torn asunder by those left behind. As if by cleaning away the blood and gore, a life could be set to rights again.

Sam thought about the kid in the hospital, and his family flying to see him, to make life and death decisions on his behalf, and a familiar sense of hopelessness filled her. Senseless violence always did.

The cop still hadn't noticed them standing five feet from his vehicle. Fletcher arched an eyebrow at her and put a finger to his lips. He squared his shoulders, put on his best glower and marched up to the patrol car.

When the young patrol saw Fletcher, he jumped out of the car, fumbling his phone into his pocket, and practically saluted. Sam bit back a laugh—Fletcher's new position was a source of great pride for him, and if terrorizing the junior officers made him happy, so be it.

The young officer stammered a greeting. "Lieutenant, I didn't know you were coming by."

"Officer Beggs. Are we finding the crime scene less than scintillating this morning?"

"No, sir. Not at all, sir."

"Hmm. This is Dr. Samantha Owens. We'll only be a minute. You have the sign-in sheet?"

"Yes, sir." Beggs reached into the patrol car and came out with the clipboard. Fletcher signed himself and Sam into the crime scene. "I'm sorry, sir. I should have been ready for your arrival."

"Yes, you should have. What if Chief Armstrong had walked up to you playing with your dick in the front seat of your car?"

The patrol's face turned beet red. "Sir, I was texting my girl-friend that I wouldn't be home for a while. I wasn't—"

Fletcher started to laugh. "Relax, kid. I'm playing with you. You're fine. Go back to whatever it was you were doing." And to Sam, "Come on."

She gave the kid her best apologetic *yes, he's an idiot* smile and followed Fletcher to the steps that led down to Cattafi's apartment.

Sam shook her head. "Why must you torture the youngsters?"

"Oh, that was nothing. You should have seen the hazing we got when I was coming up. These kids are so protected, the worst we can do is hassle 'em a little. We can't get mean with them."

"Still, Fletch. You're a leader now."

"Yeah, that's me. The leader. Leaderman!" He put his hands on his hips and braced his legs apart, turned his head to the side in his best superhero pose. "I should have a giant *L* on my shirt."

"And a cape. Don't forget the cape."

"Lieutenant Leaderman. I like it."

"I don't know, Leaderman. You'd probably have to wear lederhosen or something, just to go with the theme."

"Screw that, Owens. I'm wearing tights and a cape, or I'm not gonna play."

"You are five. You know that, don't you?"

He smirked at her. "You have no idea."

The banter felt good, right. But it was time to be serious now. Sam snapped on nitrile gloves and followed Fletcher down the stairs.

Fletcher turned off the goofball, turned on the cop. "You know some of the story, but I'd like you to give me your impressions based on what you see. Be prepared, it's a bloody mess."

He swung open the door, and they went inside.

The hallway was dimly lit. The windows were low and the space didn't have much light. But it was surprisingly spacious, with dark hardwood floors and white walls. They walked past a kitchenette with brown granite countertops and stainless appliances into a decent-size great room with a large flat-screen TV and a relatively new black leather couch.

"Someone spruced up this place," Sam said.

"Apparently, Cattafi. He likes to renovate in his spare time. Landlord was all for it—it will only improve the rental value for a new renter."

"Spare time? When I was in med school, spare time meant shoving in two slices of pizza while mentally rehearsing the vascular system and getting horizontal as quickly as possible for as long as I could."

"Horizontal, eh?" he said with a leer.

"Sleeping," she replied forcefully, but couldn't help blushing. There'd been quite a bit of horizontal rumba while she was in med school, too, with her love, Eddie Donovan, away from home. He was gone now, but it wasn't lost on her that Eddie was the reason she was standing here, in a blood-spattered apartment in Georgetown, her own house and new life, a new love, only a block away.

Eddie had been an officer in Xander's Ranger unit in the Army. Their shared loved for the man was an unbreakable bond between them.

"Earth to Owens."

She came back to the apartment. "Sorry, Fletch. Daydreaming."

"If you're ready, then..." He gestured toward the small hallway, and she stepped through into the living room.

Fletcher wasn't kidding. The place was a bloody mess. Dark stains were everywhere. The bar to the kitchen, the floor into the hall, the walls.

"Someone went pretty nuts in here."

Sam shook her head. "It's arterial spray. The velocity can be shocking. I assume this is Souleyret's blood, since she's the one who's dead. She's clearly missing quite a lot of it."

"That's what it looks like. Keep going."

Sam stepped carefully, avoiding the bloody trail of shuffling footprints that smeared down the hallway. She hugged the wall, edged into the bedroom. Things were worse in here, the meaty scent of the blood intensified in the smaller space. She could see where Souleyret had bled out; she'd crawled across the small bedroom floor until she bumped up against the base of the bed. The rug was stained crimson, with a small, nearly bloodless impression in the middle. Sam could see the girl, curled up against the bed, arms around legs as she died. The bedclothes themselves were rumpled and stained with blood. The wall behind the bed was decorated with cast-off spatter in a morbid Jackson Pollock–esque pattern.

"Where was Cattafi found?" she asked.

"There. Other side of the bed. Like he fell off."

She moved carefully to the other side of the room. There was a lot of blood on the floor here, too, similarly spaced, with a bloodless impression. "He was half on, half off?" she asked.

"Yes. Three great big wounds to his torso, the knife in his hand."

"Photos?"

"Plenty of them. But first, tell me, what do you see?"

She shut her eyes briefly and let the scene coalesce before her. Heard the screams of Souleyret, tried to envision the step-by-step that led to the great gouts of blood spread throughout the apartment. A bottle fly bumbled drunkenly past her ear. She opened her eyes, swatted at it. Amazing how the food chain supplemented itself. Less than twelve hours in and new lives were already springing up.

"Conventional wisdom says Cattafi stabbed her in the living room. She managed to get away and dragged herself into the bedroom. He followed her, administered one last cut, then stabbed himself in the chest three times. He did leave a note."

Sam was already shaking her head. "No. That's not it. Look."

She pointed to the floor, showed Fletcher a scrape in the trail of blood. A fuzzy footprint, barely discernible, with the heel and toe in the wrong spot to support his theory. "He was backing in here. Blocking whoever had attacked them from getting to Souleyret again. He was protecting her. When the blood's run, you'll find his is in the living room, too. There was definitely a third party involved."

Fletcher was looking at her like she'd just conjured water out of thin air. He knelt down, looked closer at the footprint. Walked it off mentally, stood with a grunt.

"You're right. Damn it. How did you do that? You saw the whole scene."

"I…" She stopped. He was right. What the hell had just happened? Was she suddenly psychic? Able to discern from the scene what had happened just by its proximity?

A feeling of dread ran through her. No. She wasn't. And she wasn't reimagining the crime scene, either. She'd seen it before. Or one that looked damn close to it.

CHAPTER 10

SAM WALKED THROUGH THE CRIME SCENE ONCE MORE, TRACING THE BACK-ward steps of Thomas Cattafi. Everything was muddled; the blood had dried in streaky brown swooshes, but now that she knew what she was looking for, she could clearly see his steps. It went that way sometimes; when the blood was fresh, it was hard to see exactly what had happened. That's why it took so long to release crime scenes—good homicide detectives would come back two or three times to see how the scene changed as it aged.

She thought about the files on her coffee table. The Hometown Killer stabbed several of his victims. Could he have struck again, so soon, this time in Georgetown? And was this the reason Baldwin wanted her on the case? He sensed yet another connection?

No. She was reading into the crime scene, projecting all the horrors from the files she'd been reading the night before. It was all in her imagination.

She dragged her attention back to Fletcher, who was visibly upset. "This is staged to look like a murder-suicide. The note, the blood being dispersed, everything. But it's a setup. How did we miss this?"

"Sometimes a zebra is a zebra," Sam said. "And sometimes a zebra is an elephant in disguise."

He cocked his head. "Huh?"

"Occam's razor. Your team went to the most logical conclusion because that's what the scene was meant to present. What exactly do we know about Amanda Souleyret?"

Fletcher caught the tone in her voice. "Not much. We just took her body out of here an hour ago. Why?" he asked slowly.

"Do you know where she's from?"

Fletcher's dark eyes were troubled. "We don't know much at all. Just the basics. It's early days in the investigation. I figured her family can fill us in."

"I'd like to be there. To talk to them, I mean."

"Sam, what aren't you telling me?"

Sam ignored him. She bent, looked closer at the small breakfast bar. "Here," she said quietly. "It started here."

Fletcher nodded, ran a hand across his chin. He hadn't shaved and the hairs rasped against his palm. "That's what my blood spatter analyst said, too. First strike left that lovely castoff." He pointed at the ceiling. Spots of blackened blood speckled the white. "I'd say whoever killed her was in a rare temper."

Sam could envision the knife, gliding silver through the air, an overhand arc. Landing with a *thunk* into the woman's neck, the arterial spray shooting. Souleyret's screams, if she had screamed, would have been cut off as quickly as they started. And then he'd stabbed her again and again, driving her back into the bedroom, where Cattafi had tried to defend her, had put himself in the killer's path.

She admired him for it. It would most likely cost him his life, but at least he'd die a hero. A waste, either way.

"Tell me what you know, Sam."

"I don't know anything, Fletch. For a moment, the scene seemed familiar. Just to satisfy my curiosity, when we finish up here, let's stop back at my place. I'll take a look at my files, see what's niggling at me about this."

He took her word for it. She tucked the odd feeling of familiarity away. She'd look at it later. There were other questions that needed to be answered. Most importantly, what was an undercover FBI agent doing in the apartment of a Georgetown University medical student?

She took a deep breath, trying to clear her head. Smelled something off, something close. Deeper than the tang of blood and the effluvia of dead bodies. Sweet, almost flowerlike, but not. She couldn't place it, had never come across the scent before. It wasn't pleasant, and it wasn't a natural part of the crime scene, she was sure. It smelled a bit like overripe honeysuckle, but sharper, with some mint, perhaps, both scents overlaid with a sickly rot that made her gorge rise.

Where was it coming from? She saw nothing unusual, or out of place, except for the copious streaks of blood.

"Fletch, come here. Do you smell anything?"

Fletcher breathed in deep. "Blood and gore and carpet cleaner. Maybe some old pot smoke. Bacon grease."

"Nothing flowerlike? Like old flowers left to mold in a vase of water?"

"Like the way patchouli smells? I've never liked it, but I can't say—"

"No, that's not it."

Fletcher came closer, sniffing. "Ugh. Yeah, I smell it now. What the hell? It wasn't here earlier."

Sam edged to the breakfast bar, wrinkled her nose as the smell grew stronger. She looked closer at the bar. Runnels of blood had come off the counter, streamed down the paneling. There was a break in the blood, almost as if a ruler had been placed in the down flow and the blood had run over it in a perfect line.

"Do you have a Maglite?" she asked.

"Sure," Fletcher replied, handing her the flashlight he'd stuffed in his jacket pocket.

She shone the light on the edges of the counter, then down into the paneling. In one small area, about twelve inches across, the blood dribbled into nowhere, just plain disappeared. There was an edge here, a break in the wood. It was almost indistinguishable from the other panels—it looked like a normal seam where the pieces met. She reached out and pressed the edge, and a panel popped open. The scent gusted forth, and she stepped back, gagging.

"Christ, what is that?"

Sam pulled the waist of her T-shirt up to cover her nose. She flashed the light into the small space. Saw a silver handle. Using her gloved hand, she pulled it open.

And immediately began backing away again.

Son of a bitch.

"Fletcher, alert HAZMAT. Now."

His head jerked toward her. "What is it? What's in there?"

"It's a wine refrigerator, but the power's been cut."

"Let me see."

"Don't—"

He stepped around her. "What is this stuff? Some sort of science experiment?"

Sam grabbed his arm and pulled him backward, toward the front door. "Without examining it closely, I can't say for sure. There's a bottle labeled *Vibrio cholerae*."

At his blank look, she explained. "Cholera, Fletch. And there's more than one vial in there. Cattafi has an unsecured refrigerator full of transmissible, possibly deadly bacteria and viruses. Ones that shouldn't be anywhere but in a secure lab."

"What do you mean, deadly bacteria and viruses? What the hell?"

She glanced back at the refrigerator. "It looks like Thomas Cattafi was being a bad, bad boy."

CHAPTER 11

McLean, Virginia

RILEY CALLED ROBIN JUST PAST TEN. SHE WAS STILL AT THE HOUSE. SHE'D called in sick, which raised a few eyebrows, but to hell with them. She hadn't had a sick day since she'd woken up in Ramstein, Germany, three years earlier, pumped full of shrapnel from the remnants of a roadside IED. A blindingly red day, it was all she could remember, a fog of puce, sucking at her, draining her dry. Later, when she was healed, she remembered the screams, and was happy the fog had taken away the memories.

She rubbed her left side, where the scars were the worst. She couldn't be upset about them. She was the only one who'd survived intact. Another five feet and that wouldn't have been the case. She'd be missing legs and arms, like the rest of the team, not just her spleen and a kidney. Aside from the lingering headaches and occasional blackouts and swirls of colors when people talked or were emotional, she was just fine. Mostly fine.

She answered the phone with trepidation, wondered where her nerve had gone.

"What's happening?"

"A lot. The police just called HAZMAT to Cattafi's apartment."

"HAZMAT? What in the hell?"

"I don't know. Was Amanda still on that vaccine scam?"

"I think so. She was working it hard a few months ago, I know. But, Riley, seriously, we hadn't talked in a few weeks. I don't know if it has anything to do with her. Might be the boyfriend's troubles."

"Speaking of, Alicia traced the call made to your cell phone this morning. It pinged off the tower closest to Amanda's town house on Capitol Hill."

Robin pulled a cup down from the cabinet, the delicate china from her parents' wedding set, went about making a cup of tea. "As far as I know, she has that place rented out to a couple of congressional aides. She wouldn't go there if she came to town. She'd just grab a hotel room, or stay with me." Or go stay with a boyfriend Robin knew nothing about. "Someone should do a welfare check, just in case."

"I'll send Lola."

Lola Jergens was Riley's particular pet. Petite, wheat blonde, small enough to fit in his pocket, attractive in a bland, generic, easy-to-forget-her-face way, he'd been grooming her to handle the more discreet needs of their workload around town. He took her on assignment sometimes, too. Robin had to admit, Lola was a good choice. They could count on her to be subtle. Then she thought about it, and changed her mind.

"No. I'll go. I have a key. It will save us some time. Where is the phone now?"

"After the call, it drops off the grid."

"Destroyed?"

"Most likely. Listen, Robbie, you have to operate under the assumption that whoever has, or had, that phone knows where you are. Knows who you are."

She patted the Glock under her arm, though he couldn't see

the action. "Worry not. I'm ready for anything. Just so you know, I put a call in to Atlantic. We'll see if he knows anything about this."

"Good, that's good. Do I want to know what HAZMAT is going to find?"

"I haven't the foggiest. But I'm going to go take a look in her files, see what I can dig up."

"Has Metro been in touch yet?"

"I would assume they're having a hard time finding me. I'll go to them once we know what's really happening."

A surge of red filled the air. *Mop up your mess, little sister.* Followed by a swirl of canary yellow. *How dare you die on me!*

"Be careful, Robbie. Stay in touch."

"Always."

Robin logged in to her secure home system and immediately went to her email account. Checked to see if there was anything from Amanda officially, saw nothing. She logged out, crossed platforms, went to Gmail and tried Amanda's account. Prayed she hadn't changed the password—not that it would matter; Robin could get in, it would simply take more time—but she was lucky. The password was the same, and moments later, her sister's private correspondence was open.

She ignored the inbox, went directly to the drafts folder. It was a common trick—give two people access to a single account, and communicate through the drafts without ever sending the email, thus ensuring absolute privacy.

There was a single draft email in the file, dated three hours earlier. Addressed to Amanda, no subject. Five innocuous words.

Did you get it in?

There was nothing else in the folder.

Robin quickly scanned the remaining emails, saw nothing outside the norm.

Did she get *what* in? And to where?

She itched to get her hands on Amanda's laptop and her phone. There wasn't much Robin could do accessing remotely on her own computer, but with Mandy's, if she'd not erased the history each night as she should, Robin might be able to re-create the drafts folder, see what other messages might be in there. Better yet, her phone might have a cached version of the drafts inbox, which would hold the earlier messages.

What could she have been trying to bring in? The vaccines, yes, Robin knew about that project. Was there something in them? Something deadly, or earth-shattering?

Something worth dying for?

Drumming her fingers on the table, little puffs of slate rising from the taps, she decided.

She'd go to Mandy's house, look around a bit, then it was time to see what Metro had discovered.

CHAPTER 12

Teterboro Airport
New Jersey

BELOW XANDER, AS THE TARMAC EXPLODED INTO ACTION—A CACOPHONY OF shouts and screams and the background roar of a plane's engines reversing as it landed—Xander slid down to the roof, rolled to his back and stared at the sky. He hadn't thought this through, had only reacted. From the moment the SIG was in his hand, his forefinger caressing the trigger, the end was clear. He'd gone into a trance of perfect focus and eliminated the threat. What he was trained to do.

Clouds scudded past, lacing the blue sky with billows of white. Calming, comforting. Skies were all different. Some forbidding, some beautiful. He'd lain on roofs and grounds across the world, waiting, planning, watching—frightened and cold and overwhelmed at times—and the sky had always been with him.

He thought back to the moment Chalk approached him about starting the firm, realized that he'd never fully conceptualized what might happen. He'd known intellectually he might be forced to kill again, but he was supposed to be in *protection* now, damn it all. Saving lives, not taking them.

For a life he'd just taken, no question about it. He rolled over onto his stomach again, looked over the edge to the target. The man he'd shot was slumped over the parapet, arms dangling. A rusty smear was giving in to gravity, spreading slowly down the concrete.

He came back to himself, realized Chalk was going mad in his ear.

"Mutant, talk to me. What's wrong? I can't hear you, repeat, I can't hear you!"

"Chalk," he said quietly, and his friend calmed immediately.

"You okay, buddy? That was one hell of a shot. You want to come on down?"

Come down, face the world, the scrutiny. He didn't know what upset him more, that he'd so calmly negated the threat, or that he'd never questioned the only course of action was to take the threat down. Could he have done something different? He'd reacted, unthinking, and the fallout was going to be insane.

Face it, Whitfield. You're a stone-cold killer. Always have been, always will.

Killing is my business, and business has been good.

"Coming."

He shoved down the dark thoughts, forced himself to his feet. Climbed down the ladder to the scene below.

Their principal was out of sight, but the Teterboro Airport security was not. Chalk had clearly been trying to explain what was happening, but the Teterboro cops were more inclined to arrest the two men with concealed weapons, especially the one who'd done the shooting, and ask questions later.

Xander handed over his SIG, suffered being slammed against a yellow cinder-block wall, legs and arms spread-eagled and roughly frisked. He let them put cuffs on him without a fight.

Chalk wasn't being nearly as calm. He'd managed to get James Denon isolated before they started the Gestapo act with Xander, and was dancing around the cops trying to explain their role in the situation. Denon was finally tapped to confirm who they were, and with his testimony, the cops relaxed a bit. They took off Chalk's cuffs, but kept Xander chained, seated at a chipped table that looked like it had been recycled from a prison.

Xander heard sirens coming closer. They'd called the New Jersey state police, probably the FBI, too. An ambulance, though it wouldn't be necessary. A meat wagon was more appropriate. News trucks would follow. Xander knew they needed to get Denon out of there immediately.

After a few more minutes of chaos, their bona fides were established, and Xander was uncuffed for the time being. He stood, rubbing his chafed wrists. The last time he'd been in cuffs was during counterinsurgency training. They made him feel caged, something he fought against. Once, the comforts of the military, its regimented days, worked for him. Now, he simply wanted to be free.

Threats were still lingering in the air, the Teterboro cops glaring and bristling. When the state police arrived, they would make the call. Xander had a feeling he knew how this was going to go down—the cuffs would go back on, he'd be transported, arraigned, bail set. He would have to call Sam to come get him; Chalk didn't have the means to spring him, not yet.

Not how he wanted things to go today.

Finally, Xander and Chalk were escorted to Denon's isolated room; the door closed quickly behind them. Denon shot a hard glance at the handle as the lock *thunked* home, but shrugged and took a deep breath. He was a handsome man, foppish blond hair, fit and trim, very British schoolboy grows up and does well for himself. He was charming and smart and, despite the attempt on his life, was pale but composed. Xander thought he was handling the attempted assassination with a great deal of calm.

Denon pointed to the ceiling, then deliberately turned his back to the camera. They joined him in the middle of the room, a scrum against the digital intrusion. "Who was the shooter?" he asked quietly.

Xander shook his head. "We don't know yet. There will be an investigation, obviously, which is out of our hands now. We'll try to keep it quiet, but there's no telling how the airport police will work with the New Jersey cops. This could be all over the news in twenty minutes."

"It's already leaking out." Denon showed them a tweet from a local account, someone who'd been at Teterboro and took pictures of the dead man dangling off the roof. "It's only a matter of time before they connect this with me."

Xander straightened, put his arms behind his back, parade rest. "I apologize, sir. I know you wanted to keep your visit and our involvement quiet. This isn't what we had in mind. I am fully prepared to take responsibility for the situation and keep your name out of it, if at all possible."

Denon gave him an incredulous look. "You just saved my life, and you're apologizing and offering to take the fall? Bloody hell, man, you're my hero. If you hadn't acted so quickly, I'd be on that tarmac with a bullet in me." He clapped Xander on the shoulder. "Thank you. Both of you. You acted in my best interest, and I refuse to let them prosecute you, in my name, or in yours. We'll get this situation straightened, you have my word."

Xander nodded. "Thank you, sir. Mr. Worthington will get you back on track here shortly. I'm sure the police will need a statement from you, so I'm assuming it will be at least an hour before you'll be able to leave."

Denon's schoolboy face split into a winning grin, and Xander felt a measure of relief when he said, "To be honest, Mr. Whitfield, I think I'd rather stick by your side for the time being. I don't want to see you get railroaded for doing your job. And I want to know who the hell just tried to kill me."

CHAPTER 13

Georgetown
O Street
Thomas Cattafi's apartment

IT DIDN'T TAKE LONG FOR THE BIG GUNS TO ARRIVE, WEARING THEIR SPACE-
age polymer suits, hooked into oxygen. Sam and Fletcher were
taken through a portable decontamination unit, had blood samples drawn and were told to stay put. Phones, her purse, shoes,
everything, was taken away.

Sam had an awful sense of déjà vu; she'd been through something similar a few months back, when a crazed man had used a
homegrown biological weapon to gas the Foggy Bottom Metro
station and she'd been sitting at ground zero at the George Washington University Hospital waiting to be cleared to go home.

She pushed the thought away. No sense revisiting the past
until she knew what she was dealing with. Or whom.

Thomas Cattafi. She didn't know the name—no reason she
should, really, if he was a fourth-year M.D./Ph.D. student. Two
years of med school, four years of specialized research, then back
to the med school side to finish the clinical rotations. A hellish
tract, one few students wanted, and fewer survived. Sam was

only working with the first-year forensic pathology students, the dewy-eyed youngsters who thought everything about med school was cool. Soon enough, they'd become hardened and cynical, like everyone else.

What in the hell was a student doing with a refrigerator full of pathogens? Even if he was an M.D./Ph.D. candidate, there was no reason to have the items at his home. They belonged in a lab. Cattafi was involved in something bad, that was for sure. Something this woman, Amanda Souleyret, had brought to his door?

And what about the scene felt so familiar?

Since she had a few moments of leisure, she thought back to the Hometown Killer files, the autopsy photos, ran everything through her head. Two of the women in the series had been stabbed—Terri Snow from Topeka and Jan Tovey from San Francisco. Blood everywhere, the women's bodies found in the bedroom. The Snow crime scene was the one that struck her as familiar.

You're reaching, Samantha.

She wanted to call Baldwin, demand a briefing, but he was on a plane. There was nothing he could do for her right now. She'd shot him an email before they took her phone, told him to get back to her the moment he landed. She had a problem, and he needed to be secure before he reached out. The last thing she needed was someone capturing the message and leaking this to the press. Hopefully they'd be cleared before he started burning up the wires.

She watched the HAZMAT team move about, smelled the intense scent of rain coming. Worried, but just a little, about whether she'd been exposed to something horrible. The refrigerator had been empty of wine and unplugged, so the pathogens weren't at the right temperature, nor were they specially packaged. It was almost as if Cattafi had been working on something, been interrupted and hurriedly shut the pathogens away in the refrigerator. Forgotten to plug it in.

Or someone had purposely unplugged it.

When and for how long it had been turned off was anyone's guess—it had its own power source, so they'd have to track all that down, too.

She hadn't touched anything, and all the discs and vials she'd seen looked like they'd been properly handled and were sealed, except for the one that was cracked, leaking and smelling awful. But one never knew. A list of hemorrhagic diseases ran through her mind, countdowns, worried doctors, isolation chambers, right into visions of blood gushing from various orifices, leaking from fissures cracking open in her porcelain skin, until she shook her head to physically stop the thoughts.

There was nothing to be done right now. Everyone who'd come in contact with Cattafi for the past few weeks would have to be examined, all the crime scene investigators tested. This was a mess of epic proportion.

The autopsy of Amanda Souleyret was postponed, her body in isolation, until they knew more about what was happening. There was no sense infecting the morgue if it could be avoided.

She soothed herself with a single thought—if Cattafi had been symptomatic, they'd have already heard from the hospital. Went back to worrying about a more immediate problem.

The pack of vials and discs had seemed undisturbed, but she'd noticed there was a single spot in the tray of vials that was empty. She hoped like hell there wasn't something missing, something the killer had taken.

And with that thought, the scene began to make more sense.

She was wrong. There was nothing familiar here. Cattafi had been targeted because someone knew about his little lab.

She watched the HAZMAT team work, moving slowly, like they were underwater. Felt a bit like she was underwater herself, isolated and alone, though Fletcher was with her.

"You okay?" she asked him.

"Mmm-hmm. Annoyed more than anything."

"This is turning into something more than it first seemed."

He gave her a sharp glance. "With you, it always does." But there was humor in his voice. "Entertain me. I'm bored."

"You're joking, right? What do you want me to do, tell you a bedtime story?"

"While that has its own compelling set of responses, I was thinking more along the lines of what sort of work Amanda Souleyret might be doing that's drawn the attention of the FBI."

"Oh, it's speculation you want. I'm good at that." She settled herself more comfortably on the table they'd been given to sit on. "All right. You'll find out soon enough. Souleyret is undercover FBI."

"Really?"

"Yeah. She was working for a company called Helix."

"Explain."

"Helix is a huge European firm with offices in several countries that run all kinds of private investigations, from industrial espionage to pharmaceutical investigations. They also work on pharmaceutical espionage. Trademark infringements, ripping off formularies, passing off generics as the real thing. There's a more…physical component to what they do, as well. An entire division of close protection, K and R—kidnap and ransom—the whole gamut. It's like what Xander and his buddy are doing, only on a much bigger scale."

"Like the Pinkertons?"

She smiled, imagining Xander and Chalk in suits and fedoras. "Something like that. Perhaps a little less gunplay, a little more computer-driven research. But yes. They're essentially detectives, and protectors of the realm."

"And whichever realm pays the best gets their undying loyalty?"

"For the term of the contract."

"So what's an FBI asset doing there?"

"It's a great place for her, really. They have unlimited funds and unlimited access all across Europe. Until we know exactly what project she was working on, we won't know how they benefited her, but until she got herself dead, she had it good. Xander and Chalk, they're just starting out. Competing with a behemoth company like Helix is hard."

"And yet they're going to try."

"Some people want more discreet protection. That's going to be their niche."

"You're good with that? Him being all heroic and stuff?"

She hesitated before answering, and he nodded, touched her knee. "Don't worry. You don't need to tell me. I can see you're worried about it, though."

"Close protection is dangerous, especially if they start working overseas. I don't necessarily want to see him go back into Iraq or Afghanistan. Everything that happened with Eddie Donovan, the fratricide, it messed him up. That's all."

"Then we should make sure to find him work here. I'll put the word out, if you like."

She gave him that heartbreaking smile of hers. "Thank you, Fletcher. I appreciate that."

Jesus, no matter how much in love, in lust or whatever he was with another woman, the sight of Samantha Owens at full wattage still made his gonads clench. He decided he liked the reaction. To hell with it not being proper for friends to get those feelings.

He cleared his throat. "All right. Another question. Did Souleyret bring the pathogens into the country with her? And if so, how the hell would she transport them? If she worked in France, she had to go through customs somewhere when she got over here. How in the world could they miss this?"

"Maybe a private flight to a private airport? The last time I traveled overseas, security sent the bags through the scanner as usual, with no special scrutiny on my personal stuff, even though I had a bottle of vitamins in there. It wouldn't be hard to package these as some sort of medicine and slip them through. You can take anything on a flight if you have a prescription for it, or it looks like it belongs. We're sort of on an honor system."

"Her bags would still have to be checked at the private airports, but you have a point. The question is, where did she come in, and when?"

She grinned at him again, teeth flashing white. "I guess that's what you're going to have to figure out, aren't you? Sounds like you've got your work cut out for you."

"And you're not going to help at all, are you?"

"Hey, I'm not Nancy Drew. I'm the mind of reason here. I do the science. The mystery is yours to sort out."

"And sort it I will. Look who's here at last." He waved to Lonnie Hart, who pulled his black Caprice to the curb and waved back. Fletcher was glad to see him. Hart had been his partner for years. They'd been detectives together for almost eight, partners for six. Hart had a keen mind, a laconic attitude and an ongoing love affair with his weight bench. When Fletcher moved up the ladder, he'd brought Hart along with him. Hart's promotion was Fletcher's only stipulation to accepting the lieutenant position.

Hart gave them an ironic salute and went to find the head of the HAZMAT team, a buxom woman named Sophie Lewis. They talked together for a moment, then he gave Fletcher a thumbs-up.

Sam knocked into his shoulder. "That looks like good news."

And it was.

CHAPTER
14

DISASTER AVERTED, PROBABLY, AT LEAST FOR THE TIME BEING. FIELD TESTS
were negative for live, dangerous pathogens, but they were asked
to stay in isolation for the time being. People would stop by
every once in a while to update them. Feeding time at the zoo.
Fletcher was going mad just sitting here, watching. He wanted
to help. Even with a tentative all clear, he needed to do something to take his mind off the idea of tiny invisible razorlike
creatures multiplying in his bloodstream, inching him toward
a slow and certain death.

The list of pathogens grew as the morning wore on, bacteria
and viruses and diseases that were deadly and transmissible, all
mixed together unsecured in the Georgetown apartment. There
were names Fletcher was familiar with, or at least could puzzle out: *Clostridium botulinum, Salmonella enteritidis, diarrheagenic
Escherichia coli,* SARS coronavirus, HIV. And a few he couldn't,
specifically something Sam said was a generic hemorrhagic fla-
vivirus—as if there was anything generic about hemorrhagic
viruses—plus a mosquito-borne alphavirus called chikungunya,
and something in a nasty pink solution with a handwritten label:
Gransef. No one had heard of that one before.

Fletcher was livid. How his crime scene techs had missed the refrigerator of doom, as he'd mentally dubbed it, was lost on him. It had taken Sam all of ten minutes to find it. There was going to be a shitstorm back at headquarters. In the meantime, he needed to find out what the hell Thomas Cattafi was doing with all these pathogens in his hidden refrigerator, and why he and Amanda Souleyret had been attacked.

And what vial, if any, was missing from the lot. The vials were in a plastic carrier, and one slot was open. When Sam had pointed it out, his stomach dropped to his knees. That lone emptiness freaked him out more than anything.

The meeting at State had been pushed back to noon. Sam had the day off but asked a crime scene tech to relay a message to her TA, Stephanie, to handle anything that might come up during the afternoon. Though unable to return to work, her insatiable curiosity was keeping her mood buoyed. He could see she was starting to chafe at being left out, like him, as the HAZMAT team began retrieving the pathogens from Cattafi's apartment, but she watched the proceedings with bright eyes.

She'd never last at Georgetown. He'd been surprised when she accepted the position in the first place, surprised she'd agreed to upend her life and move to D.C. If there was ever a woman who should have a badge, a lifeline into investigations, it was her. Her passion for the job was clear, and while he had no doubt she was passionate about teaching, too, he couldn't imagine it could be nearly as fun as what they'd stumbled into this morning.

At least Baldwin had talked her into consulting for the FBI. She had a gift, and Fletcher was happy someone was going to be able to use it.

Towering clouds were gathering briskly over the Potomac. With heart-stopping suddenness, the sun disappeared. He could hear gentle rumbles of thunder in the distance. Watching the curtain rise on the show, he understood how the ancients looked at storms as a form of the gods arguing. He could do with a little divine interference himself.

He needed to get cleared so he could go over to George Washington University Hospital and see how Thomas Cattafi was faring. The folks at GW had been warned to treat him as a HAZMAT, though by now, with all the people who'd come into contact with him, if he'd fucked up and mishandled any of the pathogens in his apartment, they were all screwed. The same went for Souleyret's body—the morgue had been cautioned to treat her autopsy with the utmost of care.

Always something, Fletcher thought.

A tech came with their phones, handed them off. They were still wrapped in plastic. "They're ringing off the hook. Deal with it."

Sam immediately grabbed hers and started listening to messages. Fletcher did the same—a call from Armstrong, chewing his ass out for getting exposed to this shit and tying up the investigation, and by the way, *I hope you're okay*; Hart, on his way over; Jordan, his *I think I can safely call her my girlfriend*, wanting to know if he was free for lunch on Friday, when she arrived back in town; and oddly, his ex-wife, Felicia, who rarely reached out, asking if he could take Tad this weekend.

Nothing that helped the case.

When he finished, he saw Sam was on the phone, eyes averted. She glanced his way, then hung up. He leaned over to her. "Who are you talking to? No, let me guess. Xander."

She gave him a crooked grin. "If you must know, that was Amado. He was going to post the woman in an hour. I asked if I could stop by and watch. He agreed to wait until we finish the meeting at the State Department first. It will take them a while to set up the precautions, anyway. They've done some preliminary blood work to see if anything stands out. So far, she's showing clean."

Fletcher sighed in relief. "Good. Hopefully she hadn't gotten into anything. I'll go with you. I want both our eyes on this."

"It's going to be an interesting one, that's for sure. None of the vials were disturbed, but the refrigerator had been turned off. The C-bot—sorry, botulism—had begun breaking down. It wasn't perfectly sealed, and that's what the terrible smell was. The proteins began to decompose, just like flesh."

"I'll take your word for it. Is botulism a hazard?"

She shook her head. "It is a disease, not an airborne patho-gen, which is the only reason we're being isolated here instead of locked down in a containment unit. No, I don't think there's any real danger from any of these, so long as they're treated properly. But it's quite convenient that he had the wine fridge built into the bar. If you didn't know it was there, you'd never find it."

"But maybe the killer did find it. There might be a vial miss-ing. Hell, we're going in circles. We need to find out what Sou-leyret was doing with Cattafi in the first place."

"Yes, we do. I have word in to Baldwin. As soon as he lands in Denver, he'll call. He told me he didn't think her current as-signment had anything to do with her death, but that was when we thought this was a domestic. Now that we're dealing with a potential double murder, we have to approach it in a whole new light. Face it, Fletch. You're stuck with me."

He grinned at her. "What a perfectly horrible thought."

Hart came by a few minutes later. Arms bulging, neck now sweating. He had a hand on the Glock at his waist, an impen-etrable look spread across his face.

Fletcher put up his hands.

"Don't shoot, Occifer. I ain't drunk."

"You're demented, that's what you are," Hart replied. "And cleared. All the field tests are negative. You're fine, you're out of isolation. All the brain rot is from natural causes." He turned to Sam with a smile. "Good to see you, Doc. This loon roped you into another case?"

"Hey, I'm your commander—you can't call me a loon."

Hart rolled his eyes. "Doc, I ever tell you about the time me and Fletch were down in Loudon County on a domestic? Turns out this guy'd been doing it with his goat, and the wife caught him going at it in the barn, lost it, grabbed the closest weapon and pumped him full of bird shot. Dude dies with his, ahem, boots on, so to speak. Now, Fletch here, he's trying to figure out how we save this poor goat, so he—"

Sam was already giggling, and Fletcher reached out like he was going to smack Hart's arm, but thought better of touching him. "Don't you dare say another word, or I'll bump you back to uniform. Tell me what's happening at the hospital. How's Cattafi?"

Hart flashed him a grin, then got serious. "Dude lost a lot of blood. He's not giving too many signs of waking up anytime soon. His family's on a flight in from Michigan. They'll be in—" he checked his watch "—by one or two. There are big storms in Chicago and their plane was delayed. Your dead chick has a sister. We're trying to locate her to do notification now. There's not a lot of info floating around about either one of them, and the vic lived overseas. We're trying to track it all down. I figure you're gonna want to talk to the families when we round them up, at the very least."

"Kind of you to save them for me."

"Yeah, yeah. The sacrifices I make."

"Cattafi's parents wrecked?"

"They're as distraught as you can imagine. Claim the kid's some sort of supergenius. Gonna cure cancer, all that."

"I keep hearing that. Anything on the traffic cams? I noticed one on the corner."

"We're looking at everything between ten and two. And we're going to recanvass the area. There's a camera mounted a few doors down, but the folks weren't home when we knocked."

"Good. Anything we can get will help. Sam, you know his professors at Georgetown, right? Can you get us in to talk to them?"

She nodded. "Of course. I'll go set something up right now."

She walked a little ways down the leafy green street, punching numbers in her cell phone.

Hart gave him the fish eye. "What are you doing, dragging her in here? She's a civilian, Fletcher, albeit a talented one. You can't keep involving her in our cases. It's not seemly."

"Now, now, don't get your panties in a wad. She's a legitimate part of the investigation. Apparently, our female vic was undercover FBI. Sam's taking John Baldwin's place for the time being while he deals with another case."

"Whose idea was that?"

Fletcher smiled. "Lonnie, worry not, okay? I wouldn't do anything to compromise this investigation. She's got a knack for this—took her all of ten minutes to dig out the hidden refrigerator. Speaking of which, I trust you've told Robertson I'm gunning for him?" Mel Robertson was the head of the crime scene unit—it was his boys and girls who'd screwed the pooch.

"Robertson is quaking in his size-fourteen boots." A few spatters of rain started, and Hart popped a baseball cap onto his bald pate.

Fletcher put the file he was holding over his own head as a shield. "I'm not kidding. If Robertson ain't gonna take this seriously, I'll let Armstrong go after him. What sort of bullshit is this, that we can't trust our own crime scene techs to do their jobs?"

"You sound like a bureaucrat." But Hart was smiling. He liked the idea of Robertson getting chewed out.

"I *am* a bureaucrat. Now."

Sam was walking back toward them, a worried look on her face. When she reached them, Fletcher shared his file folder with her.

"What's the matter?"

She bit her lip. "Thomas Cattafi isn't a student at Georgetown anymore. He was kicked out two weeks ago. The dean says he can't discuss it over the phone. We'll have to go see him to find out more."

CHAPTER 15

Teterboro Airport
New Jersey

XANDER WAS ONCE AGAIN STANDING WITH HIS HANDS BEHIND HIS BACK, shifting his weight from foot to foot to alleviate the boredom. As predicted, when the New Jersey cops had rolled in, he'd been recuffed and brought to another interrogation room inside the Teterboro Airport, then left to cool his heels while the powers that be decided what to do with him. The room was a dingy white, a twin to the one he'd been in with Chalk and Denon, nothing more than a table, four chairs and a camera bolted high in the northeast corner. No windows, nothing to allow him to entertain himself.

Left to his own devices, he'd begun brooding about the shooting again. He'd done the right thing, he knew it, but the image of the shooter crumpling over the parapet replayed in his mind. He hadn't killed anyone since he'd separated from the Army, taken his honorable discharge and walked away into the woods. For the first several weeks, he'd even done catch and release on the damn trout he landed, simply because he couldn't stand the thought of harming anything else.

That ended. Of course it did. His sense returned. But he'd not taken a human life since that last firefight in Jalālābād, and he'd hoped he never would have to again.

If he was going to have a career in close protection, clearly he was going to have to realign his priorities.

The door opened, and a plainclothes officer he hadn't seen before walked in. He uncuffed Xander, handed him a bottle of water, shook his hand.

"Arlen Grant. New Jersey State Police. Seems you've had yourself an interesting day." Grant was tall and lanky, a solid jaw, just this side of forty, hair about to thin but not there yet, with a sleek gray suit and a chunky stainless-steel watch, a Fitbit trainer on the opposite wrist. He had the hungry look of a man who'd lost weight recently, and would do most anything to sink his teeth into a thick steak and fries instead of salad and veggies.

"You could say that."

"Why don't you tell me the story, top to bottom, then we'll talk about your next steps."

Xander assessed Grant openly. He seemed friendly enough. Almost too friendly. All of Xander's warning bells went off.

"Am I under arrest?"

"No, no, nothing like that. I want to hear the story in your own words, man-to-man. That's all."

Xander wasn't stupid. He saw where this was headed, heard something in Grant's voice that made him go on alert. He didn't trust the man.

He hated to do it, because in his capacity as a security agent he'd done his job—protected his principal—but he had to protect himself, too. The facts were indisputable. He'd killed a man, on American soil, in front of a dozen witnesses, with only James Denon and Chalk's word for it that it wasn't a well-planned hit. There was no choice, not anymore, not the way Grant was looking at him, like a bird who's spied a juicy worm across a dew-wet lawn.

"I'll need a lawyer present, and then I'm happy to tell you the whole story."

Grant's expression didn't change, though he waited for a heartbeat, staring straight into Xander's eyes. He didn't say another word, just stood and walked out of the room.

Fuck.

Grant had been expecting the demand. They knew if Xander had half a brain he would lawyer up. Grant had come in as a test.

Ante up.

Xander thought furiously—who was he going to call? He hadn't exactly kept in close touch with many people since he'd left the Army, just a few Ranger buddies, and they weren't lawyers. Were they going to keep him here, or take him somewhere else? He'd need to let Sam know.

At the thought of her, he felt his resolve start to crumble. *Way to go, man. You're about to get yourself arrested for murder. Now there's a phone call to sow marital bliss.*

She'd leap into action, he was sure of it. She'd know a good lawyer; she knew everyone, it seemed. And better calling Sam than calling his parents out in Colorado. This wasn't cow tipping, which was the charge the last time he'd been arrested. Their kindly town sheriff had cuffed him, marched him up the mountain to his parents' farm and let them mete out the justice, so it wouldn't go on his record.

Good old Sheriff Houghton. Dead now, but well remembered in Xander's hometown of Dillon as a great, fair, equitable lawman. Thanks to him, Xander shoveled goat shit for a month.

The door opened, and Grant came back in, a curious look on his face.

"I'm getting my phone call, right?" Xander said.

"Don't worry about it. There's a dude on his way here right now, criminal defense hotshot out of New York. Sean Lawhon. Heard of him?"

Xander shook his head.

"Best shark that money can buy. You have a fan in Mr. Denon. He engaged the lawyer's services on your behalf before you and I ever talked. So. We'll just sit here and stare at each other until he arrives. Between you and me, I want to stay away from the cameras."

Great, the media was here. Xander nodded once, curtly. He still needed to call Sam, more so now, before she saw it on TV.

"Am I allowed to make a call?"

"Are you going to talk about the case?"

"Just want to give someone a heads-up. I'd hate for her to get the wrong idea."

"Why don't we wait for Mr. Lawhon, then you can do whatever you want. I wouldn't want to trample your rights or anything." He pulled out his cell phone and began playing a rousing game of solitaire. Judging from the slowness of the clicks, he was losing.

Xander gritted his teeth at Grant's sarcasm. He'd dealt with men like him plenty of times—either he'd chill when he saw Xander had only been doing his job, and get all sorts of friendly, or he'd go for the jugular. There weren't going to be any in-betweens. And they would never be friends; a connection would not be made.

Which was fine. He didn't need more friends.

Xander drank his water, and when he set the empty bottle down, there was a knock at the door. Grant gave his screen one last, doleful glance, then opened the door.

The lawyer was a kid. Xander was only thirty-six, but Lawhon looked at least a decade younger—tan and blond and thick through the shoulders. He looked like he'd be good for a pickup game at the gym. He did not look like a threat.

Which was probably why he was successful. Subterfuge and camouflage.

"Mr. Whitfield? I'm Sean Lawhon. Fine mess you've gotten yourself into." He smiled, showing slightly crooked teeth. His parents hadn't sprung for braces; Lawhon was a self-made man. "We'll get this all straightened out in a jiff. No reason to think we won't be out of here quickly. Is there, Detective Grant?"

Grant watched the show, a pointed look on his otherwise homely face. "He killed a man, Mr. Lawhon. Let's not lose sight of the facts."

Lawhon flipped like a switch, the friendliness gone. He looked at Grant like he was an alien. His voice was no longer pleasant, it was grim and angry. "We're not dealing with a security guard shooting an intruder in a building. This is a trained, and licensed, I might add, professional who stopped an assassination attempt. To even hold him is unconscionable. You should be ashamed of yourself, Detective Grant. This man was doing his duty to his client."

Grant yawned, showing a gold molar.

"Take it up with the judge, Lawhon. Grand jury is already seated for another case. I'm sure we could push this onto the docket by morning."

Xander watched the exchange with interest. Grant's attitude was pissing the kid off. The anger was genuine now, not fabricated for Xander's benefit.

"Give me a break. There's not going to be a grand jury. They'd laugh you out of the room, much less even consider indicting. We all know you're just being difficult because you can."

Grant's face tightened at that remark. Lawhon continued his assault. "Why are you still here? Planning to listen in while I talk to my client?"

"Naw," Grant said. "Just wondering what it is about you city boys and your fancy suits. Enjoy." He shut the door behind him, and Lawhon took a quick breath, straightened his lapels, turned to Xander and smiled.

"That guy is a raging dickhead. We've never gotten along." The pal tone was back.

"I see that. What did he do?"

"Divorced my sister last year, without a lot of warning. Crushed her. Though he's always been an ass, that's nothing new. We're all just one big happy family." Lawhon set up on the table, briefcase open, phone out, yellow notepad, Montblanc fountain pen. He saw Xander eyeing the pen. "Gift from my parents when I graduated law school. It was my grandfather's."

"Was he a lawyer, too?"

"A writer actually. Parents wanted me to go the same route— the pen is mightier than the sword, all that. Lost their minds when I decided to go to law school. They're just a couple of hippies, have a commune up in Albany. They didn't want me working for The Man."

Xander felt his spirits lift. "As are mine. In Colorado. My folks were rabid when I told them I was going to enlist."

"I know. I read your file on the way over. You've got a fascinating background." A glint in the blue eyes. "May I call you Moonbeam?"

"If you want to get your teeth knocked down your throat, sure thing."

Lawhon smiled again, lips closed this time. "Alexander, then."

"Xander's fine. What's their plan? Are they going to charge me?"

Lawhon became all business. "They're considering it. You stalling Grant made them nervous. There's a bevy of cops out there. Half of them want to shake your hand, half want to see you strung up."

"Grant made me uncomfortable. I had a sergeant way back who used to buddy up to us grunts, then use what we told him to make our lives hell. I got the sense Grant would do the same."

"You're a shrewd judge of character. Despite my own personal drama, Grant does have a reputation. He isn't one to be messed with. He's a true believer. There's no gray in his world. You'd already be in a cell if you'd talked to him. Now, tell me about the shooting. Whatever possessed you to pull the trigger?"

"Dude was about to take out my principal. I didn't have a choice."

Saying it aloud made him feel better. He'd done right. He'd done his job.

"The principal being James Denon, head of Denon Industries, one of the world leaders in oil and gas, mining and the like."

"Correct. He had business in the city, hired our firm to do his protection. He wanted to be subtle—he didn't want anyone to know he'd been to the States."

"So he chose a small, untried firm out of Washington, D.C.?"

"Small, yes. Untried? Hardly. We've got more experience in these matters than most."

"New, then. A new firm."

"All right. Yes. New."

"Any idea why he chose you?"

"We were recommended to Mr. Denon by a friend."

Lawhon tipped his head. "What friend?"

"My partner booked the job. You'll have to ask him for a name."

"I'll do that. The man you shot hasn't been identified. He had a sniper rifle and enough ammunition to kill every person on that tarmac. Why were you so sure he was going after Denon?"

Xander shifted in his seat. It was a good question, and he needed to be sure of his answer. "Logic. It was a setup. Had to be. Whoever took out the contract on Denon knew we were his people on the ground, and knew our procedures. Once Denon was on the plane and in the air, he ceased to be our responsibility. We were leaving when we got the call the plane was coming back. It was a well-orchestrated plan to get us out of the way."

Lawhon sat back in the chair. "Pretty elaborate."

"Yes. Whoever wants him dead hired someone who knows close-protection protocols." And was using a United States Army–issue enhanced sniper rifle, one Xander himself had used many a time. He didn't mention that tidbit.

"How did you know for sure the guy was after Denon?"

"Once the plane taxied back and the passengers disembarked, he had multiple opportunities to shoot whomever he wanted. The tarmac was full of people. He was waiting. We'd told Denon to make sure he was last off the plane. I did not engage until it was clear the principal was in mortal danger."

At that, Xander leaned forward, caution forgotten.

"I didn't shoot until I saw his finger go for the trigger, Mr. Lawhon. I wouldn't kill a man in cold blood for the fun of it. That's not how I roll."

Lawhon watched him for a moment. "No," he said softly. "I don't believe you would. So here's the deal. We're going in with a justifiable homicide claim. You were protecting your boss, whose life was in danger, who hired you to look after him. I think that will fly, no problem. If not, we'll take it up with the judge. He'll see reason."

"Jesus, this isn't going to go further than this, is it?"

"You mean to arraignment and a trial? I hope not. It's going to be up to Grant how far he wants it pursued."

"Then let's get him in here and I'll give a statement. I'm ready to talk, to explain my side of things. I can't sit here anymore, pretending all is well with the world."

"First, we need to talk about a media strategy."

"What?"

"Regardless of how this goes down, Xander, you're going to be the lead at the top of the hour on every news channel in the country. Your name and image will be put out there. Like the cops sitting outside this door, half the people will want to congratulate you, half will want you prosecuted. Unfortunately, it's the latter half who are the most vocal. So we need to be prepared. I want you safe, out of harm's way and out of a jail cell."

"Okay. If you say so."

"Good." Lawhon smiled again. "Now, tell me everything."

CHAPTER 16

THE MOMENT THEY WERE GIVEN THE GO-AHEAD, FLETCHER AND SAM GOT INTO his car and made the short drive to the Georgetown University campus. The dean of the medical school, Dr. Nate Simpson, and Sam's immediate boss, Dr. Hilary Stag, were waiting for them in the dean's office.

Hilary looked genuinely upset; the smile lines around her usually merry eyes were set and grim. The dean looked no better—a happy, rotund man with a white goatee and wire-rim glasses, Sam had always thought he looked a bit like Santa Claus, minus the red suit, but this morning he was frowning and dour.

What, exactly, had Tommy Cattafi done?

After the introductions were made, Dean Simpson settled down to business. "No sense beating around the bush. If Cattafi survives, and I do hope he does, despite all of this, you can ask him yourself what he was up to."

Hilary crossed her long legs. She was wearing sheer hose that made a *shurring* noise each time she moved. "He was found in the gross anatomy lab, Samantha. In a state of undress. One of the corpses had been…interfered with."

The expression on Fletcher's face was priceless. Sam wasn't quite as fazed; it happened, more than people realized. Whether a natural proclivity toward necrophilia, or an attachment formed during the semester, Cattafi wouldn't be the first student caught diddling a corpse, nor would he be the last.

"Why wasn't I told about this?" Sam asked. She was teaching a new class of forensic gross anatomy to the first years. It was part of the new pathology program.

"It wasn't in your lab, to start with—it was Dr. Wilhelm's. And we chose to handle it internally because we had no real evidence that the boy had been doing anything of a...sexual nature."

"Then why was he undressed?" Fletcher asked.

"We asked Mr. Cattafi the same thing. His shirt was unbuttoned—we asked why. He refused to answer."

Sam sat forward in her chair. "If it wasn't sexual, Hilary, what exactly was he caught doing? You need to tell us everything."

The dean glanced at Hilary, then nodded.

"Please understand, we must ask that you keep this confidential. If word got out, it could severely damage the reputation of the school."

Fletcher started to say something, but Sam put a hand on his arm. "No problem. We'll keep this just between us, unless it becomes absolutely necessary to the investigation. Deal?"

"He was taking tissue samples from the reproductive organs, the brain, the heart, the liver. We saw this on film, of course, after he was caught. When the janitor walked in on him, Mr. Cattafi's bags were packed, his shirt was open and he had a needle in Mr. Anderson's vas deferens."

Sam saw Fletcher glance at his crotch and bit back a smile.

"How new to the program is Mr. Anderson?"

"I believe he arrived only a few days before the incident."

Fletcher looked blank. Sam said, "We use fresh cadavers. There is a regular supply."

"I see," Fletcher said, grimacing.

"Was Cattafi going after sperm, do you think?" Sam asked.

"I don't know," the dean said. "Why would he be?"

"I'm wondering, Dean, if Cattafi was as advanced as everyone says. Perhaps he was simply experimenting."

"Or he's some sort of freak, and we didn't weed him out early enough."

Hilary put a hand on the dean's arm. "I hadn't thought of it before, this situation has been so alarming and unsettling. But I think Samantha might be on to something. I knew Thomas. He didn't strike me as the aberrant type. He was very interested in stem cells and regeneration. He'd done work in the field, even landed a plum internship last summer at Stanford in their Regenerative Medicine program. He's interned for several prestigious firms."

The dean was anything but mollified, but he backed down. "Be that as it may, as I said before, Mr. Cattafi refused to speak to us about the matter. We told him if he didn't defend himself, he'd be expelled, and he simply shook his head and shrugged. I found it highly perplexing. Mr. Cattafi was one of our finest students. He had another two years of research ahead before he came back for his clinical work, yes, but I have no doubt he would have graduated at the top of his class when all was said and done. He already had offers from research teams, from residency programs—the Pasteur Institute wanted him. He was something special, and everyone who came in contact with him knew it."

"I've been hearing this all morning. What exactly was so special about him?" Sam asked.

The dean scratched his chin. "He is…a genius. Ahead of his time. Conceptually, experimentally. As Dr. Stag said, he had a fascination with regeneration—of cells and tissue, but eventually, whole body. He was applying his talents to a cancer vaccine, and from what I know, was damn close to having a breakthrough. He believed he would eventually conquer death itself, and I have to tell you, Dr. Owens, I believed him. If anyone could, it was Thomas Cattafi. The boy's as talented as any I've seen in my tenure at this school."

"Yet you kicked him out."

The dean's face whitened, his hand gripped the arm of his chair. "I had no choice. He refused to defend his actions, to explain his rather unorthodox situation. And now he's been stabbed, and might not live. Trust me, Dr. Owens, I've been rethinking my decision since the day it happened."

Fletcher closed his notebook, crossed his legs, spoke conversationally. "Between us chickens, do you have any idea what Cattafi would be doing with cholera and *E. coli* and a few other unsavories in a refrigerator at his house?"

They both looked startled, and Sam knew that was news. It started her thinking, though. From all she'd heard, it sounded as if Cattafi was stealing tissue samples, bone marrow and semen and the like, not trying to get his jollies with the corpse. If he believed in regeneration, maybe, just maybe, he'd hit on something that he thought could be used to *prevent* the illnesses he had in his refrigerator. Or something in his cancer work was applicable to the pathogens he had.

Dr. Frankenstein.

You're making leaps again, Owens. Keep that to yourself. You're not in a bloody science-fiction film.

"Did Thomas have any benefactors here in town? People who were helping him, off campus?" she asked.

Hilary nodded. "He'd recently accepted a fellowship with David Bromley, at GW's med school. They were in Africa until just before the semester started. You know we've been working hard to cross-pollinate the two universities for a massive International Medicine program. Bromley took one look at Cattafi and began his seduction. From all accounts, they were inseparable."

"What's Bromley's specialty?" Sam asked.

"Virology," Hilary answered. "He's one of the preeminent virologists in the world."

Sam's mind started spinning. Maybe she wasn't as far off as she'd first thought.

Fletcher glanced at his watch. "I hate to do this, but we have another meeting. Thank you so much for your time. I will do my best to respect your wishes about keeping this incident private, but please understand, if it becomes necessary, I will have to include it in the files."

The dean stood and extended his hand. "We understand, Lieutenant. Thank you for coming."

Hilary rose, as well. "Samantha, Stephanie and I would be happy to cover your classes for the next couple of days, if you need to see to this."

Sam was tempted to protest, but knew it would be for the best. Between this and Baldwin's new cases, she might just be out of pocket for a little while.

"Thank you, Hilary. That would be a great help."

The rain had pushed through by the time they finished. The skies were lightening in the west. A fresh breeze swept Sam's hair off her shoulders. Virology, an undercover FBI agent, a student playing with fire. Fletcher's instinct had been right on the money—there was something more here than met the eye.

As they walked back to the car, Sam said, "I'm beginning to see a story emerge that makes sense, at least on Cattafi's side."

"Yes. Genius doctor does freaky stuff to bodies, news at eleven. So now we just need to figure out what he was doing with Amanda Souleyret and a fridge full of pathogens. You said you needed to stop by your place, look at your files. Let's head to your house next, then."

She shook her head. "No, that's all right. It was my imagination. Guess I won't make much of a profiler, after all. Cattafi was the target, I'm sure. With all the stuff in his fridge, his connections to Bromley, his bizarre actions—someone wanted something he had. Either Souleyret was in the wrong place at the wrong time..."

"Or she brought him the pathogens and was going to take whatever he stole from the bodies in the lab."

"Or that. We do need to find out where his lab was, visit this Bromley fellow at GW. And Souleyret...I don't know, Fletch. Let's get to the briefing, see if we can't flesh her out a bit. Victimology always helps. We just need more information."

A lot more.

"Your wish is my command."

She smiled. "Careful. I might start wishing all sorts of unsavory things, and then you'll be in trouble. Tell me, the girls who found him. What's their story? Do you think they're telling the truth? What were they really doing there in the middle of the night?"

"The kid claimed it was a booty call," Fletcher said.

"And you believe her?"

"I do. She was drunk enough last night that her belligerence rang true."

"So he's a popular guy with the ladies."

"No kidding."

"Is Lonnie the lead on this?"

"Hart? Hell, yes. He'll keep me informed as things change. You know how this goes—he's in the information-gathering stage. We'll have a better idea of who this cat was, and what the woman was doing there, and why Cattafi had a fed die in his apartment when we get out of this meeting with State, I'm sure."

Sam stared out the window, unseeing. Nothing made sense right now. She forced away the small thrill of excitement that went through her, recognizing an adrenaline burst at the idea of a case.

You're hopeless, Owens. You're turning into a regular Miss Marple.

She realized suddenly that she was incandescently happy at the thought.

CHAPTER 17

McLean, Virginia

ROBIN DRESSED CAREFULLY, VERY PROPER D.C. IN A BLACK SKIRT, WHITE SILK top, cropped black jacket, pumps. She twisted her blond hair into a knot at the base of her neck, put a Glock .27 in a shoulder harness, nestled under her arm. Felt like she was dressing for a funeral, which, in a way, she was.

The drive into the city would only take fifteen minutes; she was just over the Potomac on Chain Bridge Road. The Gold Coast, they called it, for good reason. The real estate along the Potomac had always been pricey; in the past fifteen years, it had ballooned comically. A buyer would be hard-pressed to find anything without six zeroes on the end of the list price on her street.

She, lucky girl, had not the money for the area, but rented a cottage on the grounds of a larger home. Something simple, easily managed. She wasn't one for big responsibilities. Though she always felt an odd qualm as she drove off the grounds, as if she was driving past a country club she wasn't allowed to join. Her landlords were friends, a French couple she'd met in Algiers who'd been stationed in D.C. during the nineties. When he retired, they kept the house, all eight bedrooms and twelve bathrooms of decorated-to-the-hilt glory. As was common with their kind of people, wanderlust kept them on the road continuously, and the D.C. house remained largely unoccupied, which Robin thought was a shame. It should be filled with kids screaming and their friends hanging out and secrets, a miasma of colors forming a life, a home.

François and Jacqueline had invited her in with open arms, and she appreciated knowing she could have a safe, secure place in their forested backyard, her own aerie overlooking the churning brown waters of the Potomac.

Being back in D.C. was in and of itself a good thing, though she missed her old life, missed waking to strange, spicy smells, the sharp metal of guns and shimmers of cobalt and roan in the air. She liked not knowing what the sunrise would throw her way. Liked being off balance. That's where she operated best, on the screaming, bleeding edge.

She'd lost a step after the bombing.

She hadn't wanted to admit it. But when she'd recovered and the wounds knitted, she'd gone out on her first mission, something easy—a quick assassination, intelligence already gathered, a target needing to get dead right away. It was designed to get her back in the saddle, and instead she'd frozen halfway through when an unexpected surface-to-air missile roared overhead, left herself exposed, lying stock-still in the sand like a wounded deer—*Red! Red! Red!*—unable to pull the trigger. Through the scope, she watched her target get into his truck and drive away, whistling. The moment was lost, the mission parameters unmet, the intelligence, hours and hours of work, squandered.

She'd requested leave. It had been granted. And she red-assed it back to D.C. to her little cottage on the river and didn't come out for months.

Until Riley Dixon had come banging on her door, sick of hearing her excuses, and started the colors again.

She smiled a little thinking of the row they'd had that night, which had ended horizontally. Then she remembered Mandy, stopped smiling. Got behind the wheel of her black Lexus— a hybrid, not out of any love for the environment, but so she could drive the D.C. area HOV lanes unencumbered by extra passengers—and set off into the city.

Logic dictated she go to the cops immediately, identify herself as the victim's grieving sister. Find out the details, the smallness of her sister's last moments, her last breaths. Start putting answers to why into the ether.

She'd go to Amanda's place first, then go see the cops.

Because she was a coward now.

Capitol Hill was already teeming with life, gazellelike interns in stilettos running the last two blocks from the Metro to their offices under the appreciative glances of the black-clad police, armed with M4s, standing sentry on every corner; men in blue suits and bow ties and horn-rimmed Wayfarers walking with purpose; taxis speeding by; tourists and locals all mixing it up on the sidewalks. She cast a longing glance at the Hawk and Dove bar as she drove by, ever a favorite of her people.

A few more turns and she was away from the commotion and into the more residential area off Constitution Avenue.

Amanda's town house was a three-story shotgun on Lexington Place, with a small plot in front that served as a landscaped garden. The house boasted a tiny porch, and a one-car garage in the back. Robin took a lap around the block to see if anything felt off, then went down the alley and parked in the driveway. The place was quiet; the young men who rented from Mandy were surely already off to work. She didn't see anything unusual, other than an overlay of dew on the small back deck, like the neighbor's sprinklers had run. It was threatening rain but it hadn't started yet.

Which was odd. It was late September. What little grass the

neighbors had wouldn't be around much longer. Why waste money trying to keep it alive for another few weeks?

She stepped closer to the fence to glance over, was met with the sudden barking of a dog, deep and throaty. Ah. That's why. Someplace for Rover to squat.

Reading something into the dewdrops, Robbie. That's why you're out of the field.

She edged up onto the back deck and inserted her key in the lock. Waited a moment, then slipped inside and closed the door behind her.

It was too quiet.

It didn't smell right.

No coffee dregs. No breakfast dishes in the sink. The air was stale and old, and very, very cold.

Cautious now, she pulled her Glock, kicked off her heels. Moved quietly through the bottom floor. There was a catchall desk in the corner of the living room. Someone had stirred through the household detritus—mail and flyers and grocery lists and magazines were scattered across the desk and onto the floor.

Looking for something. All the hair on her neck stood on end.

Up the stairs, creeping, quiet as a mouse, her breath the only sound.

The two men were together, face-to-face, on the floor of the master bedroom. One was bound, hands tied roughly behind his back. The other was loose, long limbs splayed out, as if he'd reached for his friend in the last moments.

There was no blood, but each had a small froth of foam around their mouths. They'd been fed poison of some kind.

She didn't need to check their pulses—they were clearly cyanotic and clearly dead—but she did, anyway, out of habit more than anything else.

Dead. Sprinkled with gray.

She stood, went to the front window, looked out onto the street. Dialed Riley.

"Problem. Z squared, Amanda's place." It was their own code, a personal shorthand her team developed to bypass any eaves-droppers on the lines who might be familiar with standard mili-tary speak. She heard the sharp intake of breath.

"Let me scramble this." A moment later. "All right. We're safe. I'll send help."

Help was a cleaning crew.

"I think that's premature. This has nothing to do with us. Let's allow it to play out."

"You sure?"

She nodded, looking at the young men. Too young. In the wrong place at the wrong time. They'd been treated roughly. There was bruising around their throats and…what was that, wedged under the unbound boy?

She stepped quickly, lightly, used the Glock to slide the piece of paper out. Handwritten, spiky script, practically scribbled. Hurriedly written. Wrong, all wrong.

I'm sorry, I had no choice. It's better this way.

Another note. She'd been right, damn it. Cattafi probably hadn't killed her sister. And whoever had was looking for some-thing, and tying up the loose ends as they went.

"Are you there?"

"Yes. There's a note. Same basic scenario as Mandy."

"Murder-suicide?" Silence. White space. Then he asked qui-etly, "What are the odds?"

"That's what I'm wondering. Perhaps the police were hasty in their assessment of the scene in Georgetown. These two have been dead at least a day."

And the blood began running hard, pumping slick and wet through her veins, adrenaline pushing with it. If Mandy hadn't been killed by Cattafi, who had killed her?

And why?

The email came back to her.

Did you get it in?

The email was the key. Whoever sent it was behind this, she was sure of it.

And Amanda had *it*, whatever that may be.

Or did.

CHAPTER 18

FLETCHER WAS BEHIND THE WHEEL, THE WIPERS SQUEAKING AWAY THE DOWN-pour, and Sam was thinking about the news they'd received. A bigger picture was beginning to form.

"I think we're onto something with all this regeneration talk. Cattafi might have been harvesting cells to use in his experiments. That explains him removing ejaculate and blood from the cadavers. Not terribly ethical, but not unheard of. Especially if he was trying to prove a theory—regenerating a cadaver's cells makes for a convincing presentation."

"What?" Fletcher asked, cutting off a bike messenger without braking.

"Whoa. You nearly hit that kid."

"Yeah, well, he shouldn't have been driving through a red light. Would serve him right."

"You haven't heard a thing I just said. What put you in such a foul mood all of a sudden?"

"I don't know. Maybe it's the idea of messing with the dead. I don't get it."

He glanced over at Sam. She raised an eyebrow.

"You do know who you're talking to, right? What I do?"

Fletcher went quiet. The rain pattered harder. His wipers were due for a change; the one on her side left a wide streak in the middle, making her center line of vision blurry. The tension built in the car.

"What is it, Fletch? Spit it out."

"I mean, what you do, it's for the greater good. No one likes an autopsy."

"I beg to differ, but I hear what you're saying. Go on."

"I don't know, the idea of a room full of cadavers, kids cutting them up to learn how they work, and Cattafi, partially undressed near one, messing with the body...ugh."

"There are some people who find the dead highly erotic."

"Okay, stop trying to gross me out."

She laughed. "And some find great peace with the dead. Me, for instance."

"Peace? Really?"

She nodded. "They don't exactly talk back, you know. Not out loud, anyway."

"Hmm. I've never asked you why, Sam. Why did you choose pathology over being a regular doctor? You'd have made a great surgeon." He touched the scar on his neck. She'd given it to him, a month earlier, in the woods near Great Falls, when he'd been shot by a suspect, and nearly bled out. "If you hadn't been there..."

"But I was."

"Exactly my point. You could be saving lives, not dissecting them."

She looked out the window. They were passing through the area of town aptly named Foggy Bottom, one of the oldest in the city. She saw a red door—the home of one of her favorite old haunts, the Red Lion, and the entrance across the way to the Metro. People streamed past in droves, umbrellas up, a dance of the sugarplum fairies in reds and greens and blues and blacks. "My mother said the same thing to me when I was sixteen and told her I wanted to be a pathologist."

"You knew that early?"

"I'd always known I wanted to go to med school, and I didn't have any problems with dissection. I was in advanced biology, we did a tour of the morgue, witnessed an autopsy. It was fascinating."

"But you were only sixteen. Surely you had other interests. Boys, shoes…"

She glanced at him. "Do I strike you as the shoes type?"

He pointed at her feet. "How much did those cost?"

She raised her leg, looked at the supple calfskin Frye boot. Not obscenely expensive, but pricey enough. "Touché."

He laughed. "So what is it, really?"

She gathered her thoughts, tried to find the right words. It was an odd compulsion, and she appreciated why people had a hard time understanding. "You've been in enough autopsies. Have you ever noticed, Fletch, that we're all the same inside? For the most part, identical little machines that whir day in and day out until something, or someone, bids them to stop?"

"I've never really thought about it."

"Now's your chance. We *are* all alike inside. Everything is meant to work together. The placement, the mechanism, the engine, is sheer and utter perfection. So, if we're all alike inside, then there's something that makes us individuals. More than our body type, or our face, because once even that's stripped away, it's clear the skin is just a machine casing.

"Whether it's an id, or a soul or a spirit, there's an ineffable *something* inside that makes us unique, makes each person who they are. How do we make decisions? Why do some of us go bad, become criminals, murderers? Why are some of us shy, and some outgoing? Loving, hateful? Philanthropists, misers. Why are some brilliant, some average, some subpar?" She flipped her

hair off her shoulders. "Maybe I'm looking for the last bits of…
it, whatever *it* is, that makes us who we are. Maybe it's that I'm
curious about what makes the machine stop. Either way, everyone deserves an answer to why their lives ended. It's my job to
find those answers."

Fletcher was engrossed now, all earlier discomfort gone. The
philosophy behind life always interested him. "Do you think
Nocek feels like that? That it's more than a job? Is that why you
like him so much?"

"Yes, I do. Not all of us see it this way, mind you. But some
of us, I think, are searching for something more. Some answer
that there *is* more."

She realized she'd never said that aloud. But it was true.

"Think about this. You can't destroy matter. We're finding
that cells live on in the body even after death. Stem cells, for
example, can be harvested and used up to seventeen days postmortem. We can take sperm from the dead and use it to make
babies. Perhaps more lingers on that we're not aware of yet."

"The regeneration talk got you thinking?"

She nodded, played with the ring on her finger. "Scientists
have always been fascinated by death, dying and regeneration.
It's not too much of a leap, especially if you think about Cattafi
taking tissue samples and the like. By all accounts he's a brilliant
young scientist. It stands to reason he might be experimenting."

Fletcher shuddered, his hands gripping the wheel tightly. Sam
noticed his knuckles were red and slightly bruised, like he'd
punched something.

"Sorry. I know that's a freaky thought."

"You could say that. Where's his lab, then? I didn't see anything in his apartment that seemed capable of experimentation."

"I didn't, either. Add that to the list of things we need to
track down. Maybe his ex-girlfriend or his family will know. Or
maybe he did all his work with Bromley, the virologist at GW.
And what was his connection to this undercover FBI agent? I

don't want to make any leaps until we get a better idea of what he was up to."

"Speaking of leaps, you're working a case with Baldwin. May I ask?"

"Sure. It's a bunch of murders no one has ever been able to connect into a real series, save one commonality. All the women are from New Orleans. They've been killed in various ways, all over the country, for years. They have wildly different victimologies, multiple MOs. Baldwin thinks they're linked, though there is nothing forensically tying them together. I've been going over the files, and while I can't see the connection yet, it feels all wrong. Baldwin and I both think this is a serial. And there's been two new murders in the past month that fit the pattern. The evidence from those scenes might help us pull things together."

"Gut instinct?"

"Yes. Sometimes it's the very best way to solve a case."

And they arrived at the State Department.

When Fletcher handed over their IDs, they were quickly waved through and given directions on where to park. They were expected.

Sam was starting to understand how the intricacies of the D.C. government systems worked—if you were on the list, you were golden. And if not? Good luck.

They were met in the lobby by a young woman in a black pantsuit, with hip black glasses and white-blond hair slicked back in a ponytail. She was thin and tall and lovely, her accent vaguely Southern in the genteel way of broadcast journalists and character actresses.

"Lieutenant Fletcher, Dr. Owens. I'm Ashleigh Cavort, head of Public Affairs. If you'll follow me?"

"Georgia?" Sam asked.

Cavort smiled. "You're good. Dahlonega. Born and raised. You?"

"Nashville. I've been to Dahlonega. It's a sweet little town."

"*Little* being the operative word," Cavort said, ending the conversation. They followed her, winding through the halls, into an elevator, decanting out on the third floor directly into a conference room. Three people were inside, waiting for them.

Cavort got them seated, handed out confidentiality agreements with a knowing shrug—the price of doing business in D.C. was a permanent gag order on everything you learned— brought them coffee while they signed, then took a seat herself and introduced the other three people.

"Shannon Finders, Counterterrorism, Brian de Lete, Narcotics and Law Enforcement, and Jason Kruger, Africa desk. We're just waiting for Undersecretary Girabaldi, and we'll get you briefed and out of here."

Girabaldi. Sam knew Regina Girabaldi's name. She was head of Arms Control and International Security for State. Her confirmation hearings had been legendary—between being a hardline Republican hawk nominated by a Democrat administration and her former life as a CIA field agent, her nomination had drawn fire from across the board, including a poorly organized march on the Capitol and multitudes of death threats. Sam didn't get it—the woman was brilliant, and completely dedicated to the country. But Sam stayed the hell out of politics if she could help it. That was a world she didn't want to understand.

Moments later, the doors opened and a sharp-dressed grayhaired woman stepped through. She wore a Chanel jacket and straight black skirt, expensive but sensible sling-back pumps. Her sheer black hose had a seam directly up the back, enhancing her rather curvy calves, a spot of sexiness in an otherwise conservative display. She wasn't tall, but carried herself like an Amazon. Sam couldn't help herself; she sat up straighter when Girabaldi's appraising eyes fell on her.

Girabaldi nodded to the people from State, nodded to Sam and Fletcher, sat and glanced quickly around the room.

"Where do we stand?"

Brian de Lete, who, despite his elegant name, sounded like he'd rolled off the bus from South Boston with a wicked hangover, spoke up. "As you know, Amanda Souleyret was stabbed to death last night in the home of a young med student named Thomas Cattafi. The cops are calling it a domestic incident. There was a note that read, 'You made me do this.' She—"

Girabaldi eyes were black and piercing. She fixed her gaze on de Lete. "What the hell was she doing in the States? She was supposed to be in Paris."

Jason Kruger stepped in. He seemed to be a grave man, with dark skin and soulful eyes, and an accent Sam had a hard time placing. He moved between American and British and South African, depending on the words he used.

"We think she flew in last night and went straight to Cattafi. As far as we know, she hadn't been made. She just picked the wrong boyfriend. He killed her, nearly killed himself. It's a shame, but it's not related to…" He dropped off, and Sam and Fletcher shared a glance. Fletcher started to interject, but Girabaldi looked at him, held up a hand.

"A moment, please, Lieutenant. Mr. Kruger, do we have records of her being with this young man?" Then, almost to herself, "A lovers' spat. What a stupid way for her extraordinary life to end."

"No, ma'am, not entirely." Kruger tapped a finger on the pad of paper in front of him. "Cattafi isn't dead, not yet, anyway. We may have a chance to interview him. Find out what she told him that made him go crazy and kill her."

Sam watched the undersecretary purse her lips and stare out the window. What in the hell was going on here?

Fletcher must have read her mind. He leaned forward. "I'm sorry to interrupt, but you're misinformed. This was not a murder-suicide. Cattafi did not kill Souleyret. The evidence is quite compelling—they were attacked by a third party. We think the note was a part of the staging of the scene."

This was news, and Girabaldi ran a hand through her sleek gray bob, clearly distressed. Sam thought she wouldn't make a very good poker player, which was surprising, given her position. She hadn't known many politicians who weren't experts at being able to hide their emotions. Either she had a glass face, or Amanda Souleyret was closer to the undersecretary than they knew.

"You're saying it wrong," she snapped. "It's Souleyret, like Chevrolet. And this is distressing news, very distressing indeed. Why wasn't I informed immediately?"

Heads dropped around the table; her team didn't like being chastened.

Fletcher shot Sam a glance. "That information has not been released yet."

There were murmurs around the table, echoes of relief, Sam thought, that their asses were being covered.

"Why don't you tell us everything, Lieutenant, then we can finish our briefing," Cavort said.

"First, can you back up a minute? Dr. Owens and I haven't been fully briefed. We know quite a bit about Thomas Cattafi, but we don't know anything about Amanda Souleyret. Who is this woman? I assume she works for you. And do you know why someone might want to kill her?"

Girabaldi's shoulders tensed, but her voice was surprisingly gentle. "Lieutenant Fletcher, Amanda Souleyret was one of the finest operatives I've ever had the honor to work with. She was fearless, capable and, as of yesterday, in France, on assignment, investigating an international pharmaceutical anomaly. Or so we thought. She's been out of touch for some time, which told us she was very close to achieving her goal, and it wasn't safe to check in."

"I'll bite. What's a pharmaceutical anomaly?" Fletcher asked.

"She had infiltrated an international company based in France that we believe is manufacturing and selling counterfeit medicines. She's been—had been—deep undercover for the past year, and for her to break cover, pull out and fly to the States, without warning us she was coming, means something major happened."

"What's the State Department doing investigating a pharmaceutical firm?" Fletcher asked.

Girabaldi merely shook her head. "That's classified."

"All right," Fletcher said, annoyance creeping into his voice. "Did she fit in? Was she fluent in the language, the culture? What I'm really asking is, could she have been found out? And someone from France followed her to D.C. and killed her?"

"Anything is possible. Yes, she was fluent, and yes, she was able to fit into the fabric of her environment well. It was part of her training. Now, would you please brief us on the specifics of the crime scene? What makes you so sure Cattafi was not the perpetrator?"

Fletcher ran them through the scene. Girabaldi listened without flinching, then interrupted yet again. "Other than the blood, what was collected from the scene? Amanda should have been carrying a laptop, or tablet, at the very least. A satellite phone. We'll need her phone, her personal effects, everything, brought to State immediately for our own internal examination. I would request that you refrain from having your people go through any of these items. Because the work she was doing is classified, they don't have the appropriate clearances."

Fletcher's brows drew together. "I saw the evidence log early this morning, and I don't recall anything of the sort at the scene. No laptops at all, actually. I'll have to recheck the evidence list, but I don't believe there were any electronic devices identified as Ms. Souleyret's. There was a desktop computer and cell phone that belonged to Mr. Cattafi, but they have yet to be fully examined. As you know, our investigation is just beginning."

He shifted in his seat. "And Madam Undersecretary, as I mentioned earlier, we're pretty well convinced a third party killed Ms. Souleyret and did their best to take out Mr. Cattafi, too. The more information you can give us about her, the quicker we'll be able to find her killer."

Girabaldi ran a hand through the sleek gray bob again. Sam realized it was a nervous gesture. Nervous, or maybe even scared. The woman looked at her team, and her lips drew back into what could be categorized as a smile if the circumstances were different. Sam was reminded of a fox she'd once seen on her back deck in Nashville. Brazen little thing had stood its ground when she came out to shoo it away; she'd worried it might be rabid. It had the same look on its face as Girabaldi did now.

"We'll get you all the information you need, Lieutenant," Girabaldi said. "But for the time being, we need you to classify this as a domestic dispute and close the case."

CHAPTER 19

FLETCHER SHOOK HIS HEAD. "WAIT A MINUTE, HERE. THIS ISN'T A DOMESTIC dispute gone wrong. It's a murder, and from the precarious state of Thomas Cattafi, about to be a double. I won't be able to classify it otherwise."

Girabaldi shrugged, and the insouciance of the gesture made Sam go on alert. The woman definitely knew more about this than she was letting on.

"I'm sure you'll figure something out. I know how resourceful you are, Lieutenant."

Ashleigh Cavort spoke up, that pale ponytail swinging around her neck like a noose. "Lieutenant Fletcher, there's more. In addition to closing the case, we think it would be best for you to put out word that Thomas Cattafi has died. You'll be given a specific backgrounder on Amanda Souleyret, and we need you to use the information therein for all official statements and correspondence. We can't jeopardize her operation, even if she is dead."

Sam bit her lip. Fletcher was too well-versed in the D.C. machine to respond appropriately: *you're out of your ever-loving mind if you think that's going to happen.* Instead, he took a deep breath and nodded slowly. "Are you claiming jurisdiction?"

Girabaldi shook her head. "No. Officially, we aren't involved at all, nor, as I understand, is the FBI, outside of Dr. Owens consulting. This meeting never happened, you were never here. Best-case scenario for us—you close the case for the record, but off the record, run a very quiet investigation and help us figure out what's happened. Because of the classified nature of Amanda's work, we can't have anyone knowing about this. Too many lives are at stake. Simply put out word this was a murder-suicide that's ended tragically, and we can help you manage the rest from behind the scenes."

Fletcher's eyebrows rocketed skyward. "Do you realize the level of coordination it would take to make all that happen in silence? Hospital workers, nurses, half the police force..." He broke off, shaking his head. "And you want me to keep it to myself and handle it all alone? Is there anything else we can do for you, Madam Undersecretary? Change the color of the sky, perhaps?"

Girabaldi gave him a half smile. "There's no need for sarcasm, Lieutenant. This is a matter of national security, and every piece of the investigation is need to know. We need you to cooperate and help us out. I would consider this a personal favor. When the time is right, if the time ever becomes right, you can quietly move the case to your homicide files. I know how the D.C. police do so love their close rates."

Fletcher leaned forward, put his hands flat on the table. Sam wondered if he was going to get up and walk out, but he simply said, "I don't think you understand. I don't have the power to do this. There are too many people involved already. Cops, EMTs, hospital employees, reporters. Witnesses. Homeland Security has a finger in the pie, too, now that we've had to call in HAZMAT, there's—"

Girabaldi's eyes nearly popped from her skull. "You did *what*?"

Fletcher had the good grace not to look affronted. "Ma'am,

some of us follow protocol. If you wanted a cover-up, you needed to get up earlier."

She narrowed her eyes, but sat back and crossed her arms. "What happened? Why was HAZMAT involved?"

"Cattafi had a refrigerator full of illegal pathogens. We didn't have a choice. We had to protect the scene and the neighborhood."

"And you didn't mention this before?"

"You interrupted me before I had a chance to get to it. What the hell was your chick doing with Cattafi? Do you even know?"

Girabaldi's eyes sought the heavens. "God save me from these people," she muttered, then looked at Sam and Fletcher. "Sorry, I didn't mean you. No, I don't know what Amanda was doing with Thomas Cattafi."

"Until we establish their ties, we're going to have a hard time figuring out this case."

Girabaldi looked at her team. "Can we have the room, please?"

The four staffers stood and exited without a word. When the door was shut, Girabaldi turned exhausted eyes to Fletcher.

"Lieutenant, I know our requests are atypical. And I do understand it would take a herculean effort on your behalf to completely shut the door on this investigation. But, please, I need you to keep this as close held as possible. I do *not* want to be out making the rounds of the Sunday talk shows trying to explain this situation. Do I make myself clear?"

Sam didn't think *that* was the most politic way to get Fletch to cooperate. He didn't respond well to demands. She wasn't surprised to see a matching look of exasperation on his face.

"So you don't know what she was doing with Cattafi, but I take it you know what the pathogens were doing at the kid's apartment?"

"Amanda was probably bringing material in to test. Cattafi wasn't on our—anyone's—radar. He'd be a safe place to store them if she couldn't get them to us. And don't worry about it.

Those aren't pathogens. Those are test vaccines. There's no real danger from them."

Fletcher was getting fed up with all the double-talk and subterfuge. Sam could see the impatience in his balled-up fists. "Test on what? Or on whom?" he said slowly.

Girabaldi cleared her throat. "I could lose my job for telling you this."

"Without all the information, we're going to have a hard time bringing Amanda's killer to justice. Besides, we signed the nondisclosures. We aren't stupid. You can trust me, ma'am. Trust us. I think you're going to have to."

She nodded, leaned closer across the table. "Last year, some bad vaccines were shipped into Africa. We don't know who was behind the shipment. Amanda has been trying to find out where they're coming from. All the manufactured vaccines have markers in them, almost like DNA. And the vaccines themselves are DNA-based and administered with a gene gun, so the sequence of the DNA might act as a fingerprint to trace back to the source. Amanda has been smuggling batches of vaccines under development out of every company who might have a part in this. Not only the vaccines themselves, but the vials that contain them, the material used in the suspension liquids for the vaccines, the gene guns, everything that goes into making and distributing the vaccines. Are you following?"

"Yes. Different companies create different components and you have to test them all to see where the bad ones are coming from."

She gave him an appreciative look. "Exactly. It's been grueling for her. And for us. Clearly she was able to get out another batch, and it must have been a sudden opportunity if she didn't have time to signal. Though why she didn't make us aware, I guess we won't ever know. We could have protected her."

"What do you mean, bad vaccines?" Sam asked.

"Bad as in worthless. Selling them on the black market, saying they were a cure-all for every household African disease you can think of. There are no cures for many of the hemorrhagic diseases in Africa. It's snake oil."

Sam wondered if that was the whole truth. She thought about Tommy Cattafi and his interest in regeneration. "Madam Undersecretary, are you sure there isn't something else going on with the vaccines?"

She looked surprised by the question. "Like what?"

"This seems like a lot of trouble to go to for inactive, unworkable medicines. If they cause no harm, this is unethical, but it isn't criminal. And you're concerned enough to put an operative in play to infiltrate—what, ten companies, twelve?"

"Eight so far," Girabaldi replied.

"Infiltrate eight separate companies, risking life and limb, for snake oil? What's really wrong with the vaccines?"

CHAPTER 20

GIRABALDI SAT BACK IN HER SEAT. "JOHN BALDWIN TOLD ME YOU WERE SMART."

"I appreciate the compliment. Now, would you mind telling us what's really going on here?"

"Be careful what you wish for, Dr. Owens." She straightened her jacket, smoothed her hair. "You're aware that transportation, financial and bioterror are the biggest threats we face today. We work tirelessly to thwart attacks on our country, and on our people abroad, through highly sophisticated monitoring of possible hotbeds of terror."

"Spying, you mean," Fletcher said.

Girabaldi gave him a cold look, then continued. "Do you recall a biological event in 2006 in Israel, where several Israelis died after receiving a flu vaccination?"

Sam nodded. "Of course. It was big news at the time. A potential bioterrorism scare."

"That's right. As it turned out, Israel was a fluke. It wasn't an actual attack, as far as we could tell. All of the vaccines were given by a single nurse who was ill, and she passed along her infection to the people she inoculated. Four of them did not survive. Sad, but not an attack.

"However, ever since this event, we've been closely monitoring anything that could be related to vaccines and bioterrorism. Amanda was our lead on discovering and disturbing these threats. Since we recognize the dangers we face from a sophisticated bioterrorism attack, we gave her every resource we have to do her job."

Sam was starting to get uncomfortable. Bioterrorism scared the living hell out of her—she knew just how easy it would be to enact, given the appropriate circumstances. She told Girabaldi that.

"Scares the hell out of me, too, Dr. Owens. As it did Amanda. Last year, she discovered an association between measles vaccinations and an outbreak of a virulent viral hemorrhagic fever in Africa. It was similar in nature to Lassa and Ebola, but new. Something no one had seen before. And dreadful. The mortality rate was nearly one hundred percent. The virologists who are familiar with it have been operating under the assumption it may have come from the bat population, which is logical. As the forests get smaller, the hunters must go farther afield to find food, and they come into contact with new, infected animals. *Voilà*, new viruses are discovered, much to the people's detriment."

"But the vaccinations were responsible?" Sam asked.

"We believe that to be the case. Every person who died of this new virus was inoculated for measles at a specific Médecins Sans Frontières station out in the bush, all during a single week's time frame. The outbreak could have turned into an epidemic, but the bodies of all the victims were gathered up and burned in a mass cremation. The ashes were buried, the vaccinations halted and the outbreak stopped. The batch of tainted vaccines was destroyed, as well. Vaccinations resumed a week later, no one else sickened and the outbreak was written off as a fluke." She shook her head. "Another fluke."

Sam was horrified. "Didn't anyone in Africa put the two things together? The medication and the delayed mortality response? They track these incidents closely."

"Yes, they do," Girabaldi said. "But sometimes the powers that be don't release all they know. Amanda found the records, which showed that the remaining tainted vaccines were taken off-site by a man with a British accent, as he was described, who promised to see them destroyed. The man has disappeared, and there is no trace of the vaccines he took with him.

"Amanda was convinced they'd just witnessed a dry run, a test of something much more sinister than a batch of tainted vaccines. And she felt strongly this man was planning to use the information gained to increase their effectiveness and utilize them for an attack."

"Had Amanda found the proof of all of this?" Fletcher asked.

Girabaldi shook her head. "Honestly, I don't know exactly what she found. She'd been cabling me information as the search went on, but as far as I know, she hadn't made any real discoveries. Trust me, she would have told me immediately if she'd found him. All we know about this man is what Amanda had been able to track down, which has been very little. She had a vague physical description, which varies from person to person, and she hadn't seen him herself." She paused, then shook her head. "Though I must assume she stumbled across something quite terrible if she was murdered, as you say."

"Could we be looking at a case of genocide? Or are we just dealing with some very, very bad people?" Sam asked.

"I am afraid we're dealing with the latter. You'd be amazed what people will do for money, Dr. Owens. There are two components to this case. One, who is behind it? And two, where did the tainted vaccines come from? The second we find out, we will blow the whistle and prosecute to the fullest extent of the law. Amanda was getting close."

"Why haven't you gone public with this?" Sam asked. "And why wouldn't you just stop all the vaccinations in Africa immediately? It seems the only safe thing to do."

"And create a panic? Do you know how many deaths are prevented each year with these vaccinations? Besides, the people Amanda has been chasing are cockroaches. If we let them know we're onto them, they'll simply scurry back into the woodwork. And we will lose all hope of finding the tainted vaccines and stopping this attack."

Sam glanced at Fletcher. "Unfortunately, Madam Undersecretary, I think these people, or this man, knew quite well Amanda was onto him. And that's why she's lying in the morgue right now."

Girabaldi was already pale. At this, her cheeks flushed, and Sam could have sworn tears pricked at the corners of the woman's eyes.

"Unfortunately, Dr. Owens, I believe you're absolutely right."

Sam tapped her pen on the notepad in front of her, thinking. "If she was so close... We have the 'vaccines' from Cattafi's apartment. Maybe it's actually the tainted medications disguised. Perhaps Amanda managed to find some and get it into the country, and whoever killed her didn't discover them at Cattafi's apartment."

"Which means they'll be looking elsewhere for them," Fletcher said.

Girabaldi seemed pleased with their quick grasp of the situation. "If that's the case, we need to have everything you discovered delivered to our scientists as quickly as possible. The problem is, one is lying in a hospital, nearly dead, from what you tell me."

"Thomas Cattafi?"

"Yes. Do you think he will survive?"

Fletcher didn't answer, clearly surprised by this reversal. "So you *do* know what she was doing with him."

"Yes."

"You lied to us?"

"I didn't want to reveal the truth in front of my staff. This case is sensitive, and on a need-to-know basis. We're trying to protect our people, Lieutenant. Surely you understand that."

"Fine. You want to tell me why Thomas Cattafi was working on this, instead of a professional? He's just a kid. Still in school."

Girabaldi looked momentarily surprised, then shook her head. "Thomas is a brilliant young man. He and Amanda have known each other for several years. He's more capable than anyone else in our government. And more discreet, as well." She leaned forward. "Will he survive?"

"I don't know," Fletcher said. "That's the truth."

"I'm still confused as to why you haven't simply brought in your very best people and shut this operation down," Sam said.

Girabaldi sat back, flipped a hand through her hair. Sam got the sense she was deciding how much to say, and exactly how to say it. "Trust me, if I thought we could, I would have. We don't need a sledgehammer here. We need a scalpel. The fewer people involved at this point, the better."

"But they could be gearing up to murder more innocent people." Sam realized she sounded utterly incredulous, and with good cause. "We're the United States. We can stop them from—"

"Yes," Girabaldi interrupted calmly. "And we're going to. But without knowing who is behind this, identifying all the players, following the money trails back to the individuals at the corporations... Dr. Owens, surely you understand how undercover work goes. The whole point is for it to be undercover. If we were to just announce this to the world, as I mentioned before, they'd pack up shop and disappear, starting over somewhere else. We must stay the course. We're so close now."

Fletcher sighed. "Who else is working on this with Cattafi?"

"His mentor, David Bromley. Bromley is one of the preeminent virologists in the country. His specialty is hemorrhagic fevers. He's in Africa right now, trying to find more evidence of this cover-up. So now you understand why we can't lose Thomas."

"Why smuggle in the vaccines? If that's what they are, I mean."

"Well, goodness, it's not like Mr. Cattafi can walk into the CDC and ask for samples of these diseases and viruses to work on in private. They're closely controlled, closely monitored. Anything Amanda could get out was done in great secrecy. She put herself at great risk. But without Tommy, and without Amanda's notes, there's nothing more for us to go on. We won't be able to stop the attack she was so sure was coming."

Fletcher pushed a pad of paper toward the undersecretary. "I assume you have a list of suspects. If she's been digging around this case for a year, surely you have names of the people who'd want to stop her, people who might kill to protect their secrets? Write them down. I'll go talk to them all and get to the bottom of this."

"Amanda had the names, not I. We were trying to keep the information safe, and that sometimes means not sharing." Girabaldi sighed. "We need to protect Mr. Cattafi. And the best way to do that is to put out word he's died, and hopefully whoever was after her will leave him be. And you have to find Amanda's computer. Her killer must have taken it, and we truly can't afford for word of this investigation to get out."

Fletcher sighed and scratched his forehead like he was getting a headache. "At the very least, I'll have to bring my boss into the loop. There is no way I can do this without his express approval. Especially now. The media saw the HAZMAT team, they're already talking."

"Certainly, tell your immediate superior," Girabaldi said. "But you're going to have to work with me on this. Find out who killed Amanda, and do it quietly. Right now, we can't trust anyone. I didn't even want to bring you into the case, but a friend told me you could be relied upon to cooperate. No offense meant."

"None taken. What friend?"

She didn't answer.

Fletcher sighed heavily. "Madam Undersecretary, I'm sorry, but there's no way this is going to happen the way you want. We aren't the State Department. I'm D.C. homicide. We are accountable for *all* of our actions."

Her eyes narrowed, but she didn't take the bait. "Oh, Lieutenant, I think you'll find a way. Amanda's work will be for naught if word gets out what she was doing. Someone wanted her stopped. And if the killer finds out Cattafi is still alive, he'll assume the boy knows everything, and come after him again and again until they have a dead body to parade through the streets. And don't think they won't."

"This is D.C., ma'am, not Mogadishu."

Girabaldi smiled her vulpine grin, and Sam felt a chill go down her spine. "You don't get it, do you, Lieutenant? I've been very forthcoming with you. I'm no longer asking."

"Be that as it may, telling me to shelve an investigation into a possible double murder is out of bounds. I won't be able to make it happen."

Sam recognized Fletcher was at the boiling point. He wouldn't be diplomatic anymore. Now was the time to step in.

"Madam Undersecretary, what do you expect the FBI's role to be in this investigation? I know Ms. Souleyret was our operative, though she reported to you. I need to know what you want us to do here. I can't imagine the director is going to stand back and allow a cover-up to happen."

Girabaldi took a breath, swiveled her gaze, touched her hand to her brow. Her entire demeanor changed. She became downright maternal.

"John Baldwin is a particular friend of mine, and he knows Amanda. I asked him to be here today because Amanda was technically an FBI employee. As such, Dr. Baldwin's vision and discretion is necessary. He understands the intricacies of what's happening. He spoke very highly of you, said you and Lieutenant Fletcher both possess a keen sense of…imagination when it comes to law enforcement."

In other words, Souleyret liked to break the rules, and they were going to uncover all sorts of irregularities that would require a lot of looking the other way.

"I see."

"Do you?" Girabaldi's mouth thinned, the gentle manner disappeared. "We need to find out who killed her, and where her notes are. This is a matter of grave importance. Time is running out."

Sam wasn't about to let the older woman back her down. "So you keep saying. I don't know how you expect us to do our jobs with only half the information. We don't even know where she was in the past few weeks. I assume—"

Girabaldi checked her watch, a heavy gold Rolex, and stood up. "We can't afford to assume anything, Dr. Owens. Thank you for your help. I must leave you now. I'm sorry for the circumstances that have brought us together, but I look forward to your report. I'll make sure my people get you what you need."

They'd been dismissed.

Girabaldi stood and nodded, then left the room. De Lete and Kruger had been waiting outside the door; they went with her like puppies following their mama.

Shannon Finders, the counterterrorism lead, came back into the room, as did the PR contact, Ashleigh Cavort. Wanting to make sure anything said or done was politically correct, for sure.

"Do you need a break?" Finders asked, all smiles. Her voice was deep and soft, gentle even, completely at odds with her intense, important title. Sam guessed she shouldn't make assumptions. Just because the woman sounded like a kindergarten teacher didn't mean she wasn't tough as nails. Indeed, the

juxtaposition probably worked well for her. Kill 'em with kind-
ness and rip their heads off when they were least expecting it.

Sam shook her head. "No. Let's keep moving forward. Undersecretary Girabaldi said you'd have information for us?"

"I need to be in another meeting." Finders handed them both
business cards. "You can call me directly if you find anything
of note. I'll pass it on to the undersecretary." She glanced at her
watch. "We all want the same thing, Dr. Owens. I'll do all I
can to help. Please excuse me."

Cavort followed the counterterrorism chief out of the conference room, stopping for a moment by the door to say, "Just
hang out. I'll be back in a moment."

Great, Sam thought. *Now we have even more questions than answers.*

Fletcher stared after them. "What the hell are they up to?"

"I don't know," Sam said.

"Well, I'll tell you something, Doc. I do believe we're being
played."

"Are you going to play along?"

Fletcher shoved his hands in his pockets, shoulders hunched.
"I don't know that I have a choice at this point. If there's even
a hint of the possibility of a terrorist attack, and we didn't do
everything we could to stop it? No. They're up to something."

Sam tapped her fingers on the table. "I think you're absolutely
right. They're being way too up-front. There's something else
going on here, something they aren't telling us."

Fletcher grinned. "I knew I liked you, Owens. Always willing to see the dark side of things. I agree, they are setting us
up. But for what?"

Sam got up and poured a second cup of coffee. "And why?
Why us?"

"Because we don't matter. We're expendable. If this operation has been ongoing for over a year? If as much is at stake as
they claim? They need someone to throw to the wolves when

and if it all goes south. That's the only reason I can fathom that we're here, being given the white-glove treatment."

She knew he was right. It would be easy to put blame on Fletcher's head in the media if things went south. Hers, too. She was a nobody in this world, easily scapegoated if necessary. She wondered, though, what exactly Girabaldi had planned if John Baldwin had been in the room. Because if there was ever someone who couldn't be compromised and shot down, it was him.

"These aren't dumb people. Why in the world do you think they assume we'll cooperate?" she asked.

"Because they can make my life very difficult if I don't."

"Then how are we going to pull this off? Can you run a dual investigation—closing the case on one hand but still investigating?"

"I can, yes. Do I want to? Hell, no. I just got this job, and I like it. I don't want to get run out on a rail because I'm bending the rules to accommodate State."

"Will you tell Hart what you're up to?"

His face stilled. "They asked me not to tell anyone but Armstrong, and I aim to please."

She saw the message in his eyes: *we'd best not talk here. We don't know who's listening.*

She nodded once, brief and curt, to let him know she got it.

Outside the glass walls of the conference room, Sam saw heads begin to turn. Television was a fundamental part of every government office, where 24/7 news channels ran continuously. As she watched, several people in the offices across the hall started getting to their feet and staring at the television screens.

Fletcher caught the movement, as well. "Uh-oh. Something's up."

"Shall we go see? Are we even allowed? I don't want to get shouted at for leaving the conference room without an escort."

"I don't know why not. What's the worst that can happen?

They ask us to cover up the fact that we left the conference room without authorization?"

She laughed, and they made their way to the nearest television. A huge red banner scrolled along the bottom of the television: Assassination Attempt Thwarted at Teterboro Airport.

Sam felt her heart race. She hurried back into the conference room and grabbed her cell, speed-dialed Xander as she returned to the television. His phone rang unchecked.

Fletcher shot her a glance. "What is it?"

She stared at the TV. "That."

Xander was crossing the screen, looking exceptionally grim, arms behind his back, being walked toward a building.

"What the hell?" Fletcher asked, then turned to a worker bee standing near him. "What's happening?"

"The dude in cuffs shot a man at Teterboro."

"He's a professional. He didn't just shoot a man for the fun of it," Sam snapped, voice hard, and the worker bee paled and nodded.

She tried Xander's phone again. Nothing. It had been turned off. Not even the voice mail came on.

Oh, God, Xander. What have you gotten yourself into?

CHAPTER 21

Teterboro Airport
New Jersey

XANDER FINISHED HIS STORY AND SAT BACK, TAKING A LONG DRINK OF WATER.
Lawhon had taken copious notes; he now read through these,
marking bits here and there. After a few minutes, he looked up,
eyes bright with excitement.

"Great. This is all great. We'll be able to craft a media story
no one will question. The court of public opinion will be on
your side by nightfall, I promise you that."

"A media story? No. No way. I'm still not comfortable taking this to the media."

"Xander, trust me. You aren't going to have a choice. They
were swarming the place when I drove up. Footage has leaked
on Twitter. You're already in this, my friend. And the court of
public opinion can make or break you."

The door opened, and Arlen Grant stuck his head in. He
looked queasy, like the news he was about to impart had left a
bad taste in his mouth. At Lawhon's gesture, he came in and set
Xander's cell phone and gun on the table gently.

"You're free to go, Mr. Whitfield."

Lawhon hopped to his feet. "You aren't pressing charges?"

Grant shook his head. "They've identified the shooter. He's wanted in a dozen countries. Congratulations, Mr. Whitfield. Seems like you managed to kill a professional assassin who has a serious body count and is on every watch list out there."

Xander didn't know whether to be relieved or more worried. If the would-be assassin wasn't a crazy, and he'd killed a pro, there would be more coming. He thought about the sniper rifle the man was carrying, which was standard issue for the US Army.

"What's the man's name? Who is he working for?"

"No idea," Grant replied. "And who knows what his real name is. He was traveling under a Spanish passport with the name Hector Senza on it. Real picture, but that's not his real name, or I'll eat my hat. We've contacted the Spanish consulate. So far, they're disavowing the man."

Xander stood. "And you're just letting me go. I can leave, head home, and all is forgotten?"

"Less paperwork that way. Mr. Denon wants a word first. Then yes, you're free to go. I'm sure the feds will have some questions for you, but I'm done with you. Good luck out there. Try not to kill anyone else."

And he turned and walked off.

Xander glanced at Sean Lawhon, who looked disappointed, to say the least.

"Good for you, bad for me," he said with a shrug. "It would have been a great case. I'm not kidding about the media, though. We should make a plan, decide who you'll talk to, who you'll do interviews with."

"That would be no one. There's no way. I can't go out there and drum up publicity, not with what I do. And I certainly don't want to put a bigger target on myself than is already there."

"Target?"

"If Grant is right, and this Senza character is an established pro, I killed someone's pet. I doubt that will go over well. These are the type of people who hold a grudge, and won't stop until they get their revenge. Chances are, whoever took the contract out on Mr. Denon will try again. And then they'll come for me, too."

"You don't think you're exaggerating a bit?"

Xander shook his head. "No, I don't. I've lived in this world for a very long time. I've carried a gun by my side day and night for the past eighteen years. I know how they think, and I know how serious they are. Denon has enemies. And now, so do I."

Lawhon paled a bit. "You keep my card in case anything else goes down. You may still need some media training. You're going to be approached by all the networks. I'd be happy—"

"Sean, no offense, but I won't be giving any interviews. All I want is to get back to D.C. I can handle the media from there."

Lawhon shook Xander's hand. "Luck to you, then. If you need a proxy, you give me a call. It was good to meet you, Xander Moon." He grinned, lifted his bag and grandfather's pen and left, as well.

Xander took a deep breath, picked up his phone. It had been turned off. God knew what they'd done to it. He didn't want to be paranoid, but it was possible there was tracking software newly installed, allowing the New Jersey Staties to watch his every move. For the moment, he didn't care. The call would be expected; if he didn't make it, they'd know he was onto them. He dialed Sam, and she answered on the first ring.

"Xander. Thank God. Are you okay? You're all over television."

Great. So it had already begun.

"Hi, babe. I'm all right. It's all a big misunderstanding. They've just released me. I'm going to get back down to D.C. before anyone changes their mind."

"What happened?"

"Not on the phone, okay? It hasn't been with me the whole time."

"Ah."

He heard her intake of breath, sent up a prayer of thanks that he'd found himself an extremely intelligent woman who understood his world so completely.

"Give me two hours," he said. "Meet me at the house?"

"I'll do my best. Baldwin called me in on a case. I can't talk about *it*, either," she said wryly.

"All right. Keep in touch, should anything change. I love you. See you soon."

He hung up, feeling much calmer. Her voice did that to him. Level-headed, strong, smart. God, he wished she'd agree to marry him already. He made up his mind to pursue this line of thought the moment he was home and she was home and this whole mess was over. Took his cell phone apart, removed the battery and sim card. He tossed the battery in the trash can, pocketed the remaining pieces and stepped out into the corridor.

Grant was standing anxiously by the door, a grimace on his lean face. Xander realized this was the man's standard look, like the world was coming to an end.

"Mr. Denon's waiting."

I bet he is, Xander thought. "Thank you. Is he...?"

"There's a plane on the tarmac."

"Ah. I see. Well." He strode past Grant without further comment. There was a small Gulfstream outside the glass doors, stairs lowered. Chalk was at the base of them. His face lit up when he saw Xander. Slapped him on the back and said, low, "Get the fuck on the plane already, before they change their minds."

Xander climbed the stairs two at a time, Chalk on his heels. He pulled up the stairs and the door closed with a *thunk*.

James Denon was inside the plane, sitting midcabin. His three-person team, looking startled, were scattered through the back of the plane. They eyed Xander with everything from fear to awe.

He nodded at them, then took a seat. Chalk sat opposite him, and they were wheels up in another two minutes. Xander began breathing again, not realizing he'd been holding his breath.

What a morning.

Denon pulled a decanter out of the wall, and three glasses. Poured, handed them out. It was a fine single-malt; Xander recognized it as one of Sam's favorites—Lagavulin.

Xander tipped his glass toward the two men and threw the whiskey against the back of his throat. Set the glass down. "Thanks. Now. Someone want to tell me who the hell Hector Senza is, and where we're going?"

Denon smiled. "Relax. I'm flying you back to D.C. I've arranged for another plane to take us back tomorrow. In light of what happened, Mr. Worthington felt it best I alter my plans. It will give my people in the UK time to make contingency arrangements."

"It might give the people who are trying to kill you time to set up another attack, too," Chalk said. "But it's worth the risk, I think."

"Perhaps." He toyed idly with a napkin. Denon was distinctly less cheerful now than he was this morning. It was all sinking in. Almost dying did that to a man. "But now that we know someone wants me dead, I can approach my security a little differently."

He waved his hand at the small contingent with him. Xander ran their names through his head. Louis Bebbington, chief financial officer of Denon Industries; George Everson, the IT guru; and Maureen Heedles, Denon's head of research. Bebbington was a numbers geek through and through, down to the thin tie and too-tight pants, a particularly British style choice. He and Heedles were middle-aged; Everson was younger, African-American, *a dapper lad*, as Denon had called him when they first met. Heedles was the more interesting of the three to look at—she had smartly styled ash-brown hair, which framed her face well, and one brown eye and one blue, a remarkably distinct heterochromia. All three were quiet and subdued, talking softly among themselves while their boss sat with his new bodyguards. The idea that he might have been killed, and that someone had orchestrated it, had clearly frightened them all.

Xander wondered what process Denon used to decide who would be by his side when he traveled, and made a note to look into the backgrounds of the three people sitting behind him. They were all trusted members of the company. Denon prized privacy above all things, strictly controlling his interviews and appearances, and Xander knew you had to be the best at what you did to score a spot on his team. Denon expected, and received, the top efforts from everyone around him, at all times. And he had to be on his guard against anyone who might slack off, or betray him, or leak information or mess up in the slightest.

It was an exhausting way to live, a life Xander couldn't imagine wanting.

He didn't see any reason to beat around the bush. "We did a full threat assessment before you came and saw nothing that seemed out of place. You certainly have upset some people in your time, but I didn't see anything active. Do you have any idea who might have a contract out on you, Mr. Denon? And who would know your movements, and that we were involved in your protection?"

Chalk shook his head slightly, and Xander tried to rein in his temper. He was boiling mad, he realized suddenly—furious and upset and trying like hell to remember his training and shove the anger down into his boot heel, because he couldn't let anything ruffle him, not now. He knew it was the aftermath of the morning's escapades, and frustration at nearly being beaten. It would pass soon enough. Adrenaline did wonky things to your system after a shooting. He knew that from too many rooftops, too many triggers pulled. He took a breath.

"I'm sorry, sir. We'd prepared for every contingency for your protection, went through every checklist, and there was nothing on the street about a contract. The state cop, Grant, told me the man was traveling on a Spanish passport. You piss off someone in Spain?"

Denon nodded. "Probably. I piss people off everywhere, Mr. Whitfield. It's part of my job. I don't know who was behind this. But I trust I can keep you and Mr. Worthington—"

"Sir, please. Trey, or Chalk. Mr. Worthington is my father."

"Trey, then. I'd like to keep you two on. Hopefully you can find out who has it in for me."

Xander narrowed his eyes at the man. "Not that we don't appreciate the vote of confidence, but wouldn't your own security services be better equipped for this kind of investigation, sir?"

Denon shook his head and smiled sadly. He leaned in so he wouldn't be overheard. "Unfortunately, gentlemen, I'm afraid my instincts tell me this is something best kept out of house. And since you've proven your loyalty to me in such a spectacular fashion… Well."

Xander met Chalk's eyes. He was right—Denon suspected the attack had come from within.

"All right, sir. We can do that. We'll get on it right away."

"Thank you," he said softly.

Xander grabbed a cocktail napkin and wrote a note to Denon.

Is there someone on the plane you suspect?

He passed it over, and Denon's eyebrows hiked up to his hairline. But he pulled a fountain pen from his shirt pocket, wrote on the napkin and pushed it back.

No. Never. These three are the ones I'd trust with my life.

Xander showed Chalk the napkin. He nodded, pulled out his laptop, began to type. Xander knew he was backgrounding the people on the plane. Sometimes the people closest to you were the ones you should trust the least.

Xander folded the napkin and put it in his pocket. Denon was eyeing him, whether impressed by his astuteness or something else, he didn't know.

Keep your enemies close. Denon was either crazy or brave, he wasn't sure which.

He cast a glance toward the back of the plane. Louis Bebbington, George Everson and Maureen Heedles. Trusted associates. Scared to death. How many people did Denon employ? And did any of them hold a grudge? This wasn't going to be an easy case, he knew it.

"I need to chill for a minute. Don't mind me." Xander tossed back some more Scotch, then settled back into the leather, and shut his eyes for a minute, resetting.

He wasn't kidding Sean Lawhon. There were going to be repercussions. To the shooting, to protecting Denon. He needed to make a few plans of his own—how to protect himself and Sam, and the fragile world they lived in.

He'd killed a killer. Word would get out.

CHAPTER 22

State Department
Washington, D.C.

ASHLEIGH CAVORT RETURNED TO THE CONFERENCE ROOM WITH A SLIM MANILA folder. "Here's the file on Agent Souleyret. I'm happy to escort you out now." At the front doors, she nodded earnestly, ponytail swinging. "Do keep in touch," she said with a bright, happy smile. Like they were going on a vacation, or moving to another city.

The rain had pushed through, and Sam breathed the sweet, clean air of a just-washed city, relieved to leave the State Department. She didn't like the idea of participating in a cover-up, there could be a possible terrorist attack in the works, she was worried as hell about Xander. And Fletcher was too quiet, planning and plotting something. All the pressure was getting to her.

The file on Amanda Souleyret was exceptionally thin. Sam paged through it, distressed to see how little information was given. Fletcher pointed the car toward Fourteenth Street. He wanted to go straight to the morgue and get the autopsy out of the way before they started talking to people.

Sam agreed. Better to have all the tangible facts in place, and then they could make the rest come together. She was still quite sure Girabaldi had been lying to them, trying to throw them off the scent of something much, much bigger. Why else would State have stuck their long noses into the case? Why not let the homicide team run down the killer?

And why ask them to start a cover-up?

She had a terrible feeling they weren't going to want the answer to whom the State Department thought was behind the killing. Something was wrong with Girabaldi's requests. She just didn't know what.

She slapped the file closed. "Souleyret's file is embarrassingly incomplete. Everything about her life before she joined the FBI is redacted, and the current information is barely enough to do a background on her. Her permanent address is up on Capitol Hill, but she rents out her house. She has one sister, Robin, but there is no information about her. Her father is dead, her mother gone since the girls were young. The only useful thing in here—she was decorated, two years ago, with the FBI Shield of Bravery."

"For what?"

"Wouldn't you like to know? There are no details about what she did to deserve it, or even what case she'd been involved in."

When Ashleigh Cavort had handed Sam the file, she'd done so with a shrug of knowledge—there was nothing here that was going to help. She told Fletcher as much.

"This is a waste of our time. All we have here is basically her height, weight and social. There's nothing we can use, outside of tracking down why she was awarded the medal. Why'd they even bother?"

"Sam, I rarely question the intentions of our government. God knows why they do anything. The woman was an FBI agent. I'm sure there are files on her that you can access."

"Well, if I can't, Baldwin certainly can." She glanced at her watch, the silver-and-gold Tag Heuer her parents had given her when she graduated from high school. "I wonder what's taking him so long to call me back? He should be on the ground by now."

"Couldn't you call down to the Hoover Building and ask?"

She glanced at her watch again. "Let me just try him one more time."

But Baldwin's phone went directly to voice mail. She left a message, asked him to call as soon as he could and rang off. His plane must have been delayed.

A moment later, a text message came in. It was from Baldwin.

Tied up for the foreseeable future on this case, but I think I know what you're looking for. Contact Charlaine Shultz in my office, tell her what you need.

Amazing how he could anticipate. It had always unnerved her, his ability to sense what people needed. It was what made him a great investigator, being able to see past the obvious. But it could be off-putting at times.

She dialed the main number at Quantico and asked the operator to put her through to Dr. Charlaine Shultz in the BAU II.

A few moments later, Charlaine's soft Southern voice came on the line.

"Charlaine, it's Samantha Owens. How are you?"

"Sam! It's good to hear from you. Everything okay up there in D.C.?"

"Not perfect, but okay. Did Baldwin tell you I'd be calling?"

"He just texted me. You need info on our girl?"

Sam noticed everyone was being careful not to openly use Souleyret's name. "I do. I have the basics, but it's telling me nothing. Can you help?"

"I'll pull together everything you might need and get a courier on his way to you immediately. Where should I send him?"

"The OCME in D.C. if you could. I'll be there for the next couple of hours. We're about to—"

"I know." There was a soft sigh. "Poor thing. Always liked her. I hope you find what you're looking for."

D.C.'s Office of the Chief Medical Examiner was now housed in a beautiful new state-of-the-art building off E Street, just down the street from NASA. It was a huge improvement from their old, unpleasant quarters. Sam hadn't particularly liked going to the old shop—it was dank and dismal, nothing like the setup she'd had in Nashville at Forensic Medical. But the new building, which fit in nicely with the other office buildings in the area, was well equipped and staffed by excellent people, including her friend Amado Nocek.

Amado had offered her a position at the OCME, but she'd declined. The oppressiveness of the place would have driven her mad. Now that they had new digs, she wouldn't be as unhappy, but she was enjoying teaching, more than she imagined she would. She was blessed with Hilary, who recognized early on having an active investigator on staff would enhance the credibility of the new forensic pathology program. She had more freedom than she'd had in years, and she had to admit she liked it. The rigidity of being the head medical examiner for the state of Tennessee—the grind, the politics, the constant influx of the dead, day in and day out—had become oppressive, even before the floods. She knew she was on the right path now.

The thought of the raging waters brought her family to mind, as it always did. *I miss you all so much.*

Simon's face began to sneak into the edges of her mind, the twins, too, with their silly grins, but she firmly pushed them all away, counting as she breathed. *One Mississippi.* Not now. *Two Mississippi.* There was so much to do, so many people to talk to. *Three Mississippi.* Decisions to be made. She couldn't be waylaid by panic, by grief. *Four Mississippi.* There would be time to indulge in memories later. Right now, there were people counting on her.

Her heart rate dropped, and her hands unclenched. *Okay. You're okay.*

Close. Too close. Fletcher was well aware of her little problem, but he was on the phone, chewing someone out, and hadn't seemed to notice her momentary loss of control. Good.

Now she just had to figure out what the hell she was doing.

Sam was used to being a part of an investigation, not driving one. She had a sudden vision of her best friend, Taylor Jackson, the homicide lieutenant in Nashville, and straightened her shoulders. Taylor would know exactly what steps to take to find out what Girabaldi was up to. Sam decided to call her when they got out of the autopsy, even if only to hear her voice.

Taylor was also engaged to John Baldwin, and he bounced a lot of information off her pretty head. Perhaps there'd be movement on both the cases she was suddenly working on.

Lost in her own thoughts, she hadn't realized Fletcher had parked the car on the street in front of the OCME until she heard him say, "I'm here, I gotta go. Thanks for letting me know. But it still doesn't let Robertson off the hook. Tell him to prepare for my wrath, because he's going to hear all about it. Okay. Bye."

"What was that about?"

"What Girabaldi's toady said was true. None of the pathogens were active. They were vaccines. Or attempts at vaccines. So we weren't in any danger."

She smiled. "Feel better?"

"Hell, yes. The idea of that stuff crawling around my body... yeah, I'm very happy. And this will help us shut down the investigation quicker. If Souleyret and Cattafi had live pathogens sitting around, we'd be dealing with a whole different level of investigation. As it is, I think I can craft something that will shut down the media ballyhoo, and we'll go forward with the claims of a domestic dispute. It's just a matter of keeping Cattafi's dirty laundry out of the mix. Our PR folks are putting

together a statement right now saying he succumbed to his injuries. This was a domestic dispute that ended in a murder-
suicide. End of case."

"So you're going to go forward with a cover-up?"

His hands tightened on the steering wheel. "For now."

"Fletcher, why?"

"To buy us some time. Girabaldi's right. If the killer knows
Cattafi's alive, he might come back for him. I want to at least
get his story out of this. How he was connected to Souleyret."

"What about the families? How do you propose to contain
them?"

"His parents are still stuck on the tarmac at O'Hare, so we
can afford to put them off for a bit. Let's get moving, shall we?
Maybe we can have a resolution before they land and we try to
convince them to pretend their son is dead."

Sam didn't think the plan was a good one, but what the hell
did she know? She trusted Fletcher. If he thought they could
pull this off, then she'd do her best to help.

And buying time was a good thing. She wanted to see what
exactly had happened to Amanda Souleyret before she formed
any real opinions.

CHAPTER 23

OCME

AMADO NOCEK WAS WAITING FOR THEM INSIDE THE LOBBY OF THE OCME, A serene look on his otherwise homely face. Tall, much too thin and oddly angular, his whole countenance insectlike, he'd put up with ridiculous nicknames like Lurch and Fly Man since childhood. But where some saw a six-foot-six praying mantis, Sam saw a dear friend. Amado was one of her favorites. Cultured and intelligent, brought up in Europe, he was an excellent dining partner, and an even better pathologist.

He shook Fletcher's hand, gave Sam a brief hug. "Lieutenant. Samantha. It is good to see you both. You are prepared for the autopsy of Ms. Souleyret?"

Her name had such a lilt in his Neapolitan accent. It made her sad.

"We are. You've heard there were no pathogens, correct? That the vials were vaccines?"

The buglike head tipped to one side. "I am hearing many things in reference to this case. I suspect none are entirely false, and none are entirely true. Am I close?"

Sam nodded. "We're a bit confused, too, Amado."

"I am receiving a great deal of external direction, as well. The autopsy report, for example. We are to transmit it directly to you, Lieutenant, and not put it in the official system." Nocek's feathery eyebrows were hiked nearly to his receding hairline. "Do you know where that request came from?"

Fletcher rolled his eyes. "I'm afraid I do, and I'm not at liberty to say. Just roll with it, Dr. Nocek. It will be easier on you that way."

"I see. Then let us do the autopsy, and see what the body tells us."

At the sinks, they washed up, got gloved and masked, and five minutes later, they were in a separate autopsy suite made for private autopsies—posts that were especially sensitive, bodies in advance stages of decomposition or ones that had been exposed to chemical or biological hazards. Sam had been in here once before, during the biological attack scare a few months earlier, posting the body of a congressman exposed to an airborne toxin.

Amanda Souleyret's body was laid out on the stainless-steel slab. Amado's tech had already done the prep work. The flat-screen monitor showed the full-body radiographs; the body was naked and had been washed.

Sam was surprised by the pristine condition of the body. Amanda Souleyret's torso was scratched and there was antemortem bruising, but she observed no apparent stab wounds, which didn't jibe with the crime scene.

Amado caught her look of confusion. "The wounds are in her back."

"Ah." Sam walked to the other side of the body and saw a small puncture in Souleyret's neck, clearly the source of much of the blood at Cattafi's apartment.

"She was wearing a long-sleeve T-shirt and jeans when they brought her in. They were extensively bloodstained."

Casual clothes. Good for travel. She made a mental note:

Check the file Charlaine's sending—how did Souleyret get back into the country?

"Shoes?"

"Boots. Military-style. In the bag, just there."

Sam saw the bulging white trash bag on the table near the wall, nodded.

"So she wasn't undressed, hadn't taken off her shoes and gotten comfortable?"

"That is correct."

"Can we turn her, please?" Sam asked.

Nocek nodded, went to the woman's head. Sam stationed herself at her waist, and they turned her over slowly.

Here the damage was dreadful. The wounds were stark against the fair flesh of her back, red gashes that gaped wide like heavy-lidded eyes. Sam quickly counted them, six in all—one cut in the right side of her neck, two extremely deep ones below each scapula, the other three varying from deep to superficial.

Fletcher was standing a few feet away. "So she was running away when she was stabbed?"

Sam nodded. "The neck wound came first. That slowed her down long enough for her attacker to hit her in the lungs, one on each side. The rest were reaches. Amado?"

"Yes, I believe you are correct. There are very few defensive wounds. There was nothing under her nails—no breaks, matter, anything. It fits with the theory of her running away." He *tsked*, as if in sympathy with the girl's plight. "There is something else I believe you should see. On external examination, we discovered a tampon in place. Subsequently, we removed the tampon. This is not an unusual occurrence, save for this. There was no indication our guest was menstruating. The tampon was clean of any biological material I would normally associate with its usage."

Now that *was* interesting. "Has it been disposed of?"

Amado shook his head, pointed toward a small tray on the counter. "I saved it. Its placement and status felt...off."

They moved Souleyret's body back into position, then Sam went over to the tampon. It wasn't pristine, but there was no blood. She glanced at Fletcher, who was eyeing her with the kind of horror most men do when faced with anything oriented to a woman's monthly cycle, and bit back a laugh.

"It won't bite, Fletch. I promise. I just want to test it. It could be laced with drugs. I've seen it before."

She took a scalpel and teased the edge of the cotton apart, clipping a bit to put into a tube for testing. She set the tampon back onto the tray, then something caught her eye. A dark edge inside the tampon itself.

"What is that?" Fletcher asked.

Sam used her small forceps, got a grip on the thing. It came out easily. She turned it over, looked at Fletcher with a grin.

"A micro SD chip. Now that's a handy place to carry something you need to sneak into the country."

"What do you think is on it?"

"I have no idea." She turned to Nocek. "Do you have a secure server, one that doesn't hook into the OCME network? This could be classified information. I don't want to get you in trouble."

"No, we do not, not in the way you need. Just as we can access anything from any computer in the building to put up on the screen here, technically speaking, it could go the other way, should someone want to snoop. Normally, this is a wonderful way for all of our doctors and technicians and administration to access files. For instance, should I have a death I believe is linked to another, I can call up the previous files and do a comparison on the spot, without leaving the autopsy suite or waiting for files to be delivered.

"In this case, if this is sensitive information, I believe you would be safer trying to open the contents away from any sort of wireless network. We are trustworthy, but I do not want you to get into any trouble down the road."

"Thank you for your candor, Amado," she said, and he inclined his head slightly in acknowledgment. Such a graceful man, she thought, both in action and speech.

Sam put the SD card in an evidence bag and handed it to Fletcher, who looked at it like it might explode. "Chain of custody," she said with a smile.

His hand convulsed on the bag, and he placed it carefully on the table beside him.

"Let's get going," he said. "Get her posted. I'm eager to see what's on this SD card."

"Me, too," Sam said. "Amado? Shall we?"

He nodded, pulling up his mask. "Let us go inside our guest, and see what else may be happening."

And without further ado, his scalpel flashed in the overhead lights, and the Y-incision was made.

CHAPTER 24

SAM AND AMADO WENT THROUGH THE REST OF THE AUTOPSY WITH RELATIVE ease, while Fletcher called one of his computer geeks to bring a secure laptop so he could take a look at the micro SD card.

Amado did the oral recitation of Souleyret's wounds so his report would be easier to compile when he was finished. Sam, used to both dictation and writing specifics on a whiteboard, took a few notes of her own. They sawed and weighed and dissected companionably, as if they'd been working together for years.

The initial Y-incision had shown little subcutaneous fat, and coupled with the girl's oversized calf muscles and lithe build, Sam took her for a runner. Her heart was beautiful. There was nothing remarkable about the woman's head, nose or throat, though Sam could tell she had been delicately pretty while she still breathed, fit and healthy. Amado was correct—she had not been menstruating.

It was her lungs that told the tale. Souleyret had died of hemothoraxes of both her right lung, the result of a four-inch-deep stab wound, and another on the left, three inches deep, between her ribs in the eighth intercostal space, puncturing the lung and causing the hemothorax. There was quite a bit of blood in her lungs; despite the gash in her neck and all the arterial spray, she hadn't bled out. Which meant a good deal of the blood at the crime scene must have come from Thomas Cattafi, something the crime scene techs would realize once they began processing the evidence.

Three of the six stab wounds were superficial, though two inches deep. It was impossible to tell which of the two deeper wounds was the culprit, but Sam was comfortable with Amado's conclusion that the hemothoraxes had killed her. The perpetrator was right-handed; the wounds were horizontally oriented and were deeper on the right posterior than the left.

The rest of Souleyret's autopsy was nominal. She'd never carried a child to term, something Sam noted with as little internal imagination as possible. Her liver and kidneys were clean, her brain matter coiled tightly. She hadn't eaten in the few hours before she died.

Unless there was something significant in her blood, which had already been sent to the OCME's in-house lab with specialized instructions to test for all sorts of unusual diseases more common to the African continent than the normal tox screens would cover, she had certainly died as a result of the stabbing.

Stabbed in the back. Sam wondered again if there was some significance to the crime scene, or if it was just her imagination on overdrive. Something just felt so strange about all of this. And it wasn't only seeing what made Amanda Souleyret tick, as it were.

And the tampon…now that was one for her annals. She'd pulled all sorts of things from orifices over the years, most of them drug related, some the result of pleasure gone wrong, but she'd never had information smuggled in a tampon before.

Fletcher, who had promptly set the bag with the SD card down once Sam had handed it to him, had finally been coaxed closer to the "thing," as he called it, lying quiet in its bag on the small metal tray, which he eyed from time to time with great distaste. "I suppose this is one advantage to being a woman. Smuggling is easier."

"This is true. Something this small, she could have swallowed it, but stowing it in a tampon is a much less messy proposition."

"Ugh."

"Quite."

"What's on it?" he wondered aloud for the twentieth time.

Amado had called a tech to close the incisions, and joined them, staring at the innocuous bit of fiber. "When I was younger, I once knew a man in Naples who was a smuggler. Diamonds, mostly, and other jewels. His partner took them from the hotel rooms of the rich who stayed in the city. He always struck rooms that faced the Bay of Naples. He would place the jewelry in trash bags, and throw them off the balconies toward the cliffs. Then his people would walk the cliffs, ostensibly cleaning up the trash, and take the jewels at their leisure."

Sam was amused by the story. "I can't imagine you being friends with a lawbreaker, Amado."

"Not friends, Samantha. Never that."

"So how did they smuggle out the jewels? I assume they needed to get them out of the country? If they had them in hand, couldn't they just cash them in?"

"Your assumption is correct. They wished to move the jewels out of the country, exchange them for money. At the time, there was an alert at the borders for this man. If he tried to fly, or to drive across the border, he would be caught. So he used a woman in a similar way. A bag of jewels, liberated from their settings, followed by a tampon. The border patrols were thorough searchers, but when they spied the string, they backed away."

He grinned once, haughtily, and not necessarily amused. "Old mythologies die hard, do they not? And so the jewels were taken across the border, sold for exorbitant prices and the man was not caught for many years. They called him l'Ombre—the Shadow. He was one of the most successful cat burglars in history. He died recently, a very rich old man. I believe someone was writing a book about his escapades."

Sam was charmed. "He sounds like an absolute scoundrel, Amado. How in the world did you know him?"

His face was eloquently blank. "The woman who crossed the borders for him was my mother."

CHAPTER 25

NOCEK'S SOBERING REVELATION ENDED THE AFTERNOON'S EXERCISE. THEY cleaned up and, casting a last glance at Souleyret's now-stitched and empty body, Sam said a quick prayer for the woman's soul, and they left the autopsy suite.

Amado escorted them to the lobby. "I will send an official report to your email address this evening, Lieutenant Fletcher. It was pleasant seeing you once again. Samantha, we are still engaged for the symphony next week? I look forward to our evening with Rachmaninoff."

"As do I, Amado. I'll see you next Friday. Thank you for your help today."

At that moment, Fletcher's tech hurried through the doors, bringing the secure laptop, and was closely followed by the courier from Quantico sent by Charlaine Shultz. Fletcher went to deal with his guy, and Sam greeted the courier. He was a kid, a newly minted agent who'd probably just graduated. He had a fresh haircut, a red tie and was out of breath, like he'd run from Quantico.

"Dr. Owens? I'm Agent Marcos Daniels. I have the package Dr. Shultz prepared for you."

Sam held out a hand. "Thanks for bringing it. Glad you didn't get a ticket on the way. You must have just broken the land speed record from Quantico."

He shook his head. "I'm afraid I have to bring it back when you're done reading. I'm your shadow until you do."

"All right," Sam said. "Once Lieutenant Fletcher is finished, I believe we're heading to the homicide offices. I'll ride with you and start looking over the file. We might be a minute, though. Catch your breath."

"Yes, ma'am." He nodded sharply, subsided into a chair and took three deep breaths. Sam loved the literal ones.

Fletcher, meanwhile, had taken the laptop from the officer and shooed him away. He joined them, speaking quietly.

"We need to move quickly. Word's out we have something, and Armstrong wants to know what it is."

"I thought he was on board with the subterfuge."

Fletcher shook his head. "Not yet," he said grimly.

"Oh, Fletcher. You are playing with fire."

"I know. Isn't it fun?"

"No, it's not. I want to see what's on the SD card. If you're avoiding your boss, where shall we go to look at it?"

"The only place in this town where there's any privacy, of course. Mine."

It was only a few minutes' drive to Fletcher's town house on Capitol Hill. Sam rode with Agent Daniels, who proved to be a pleasant companion for the short trip—he said not a word, leaving her to her thoughts. She couldn't get Amanda Souley-ret out of her mind. The helpless body, attacked from behind, the bloody spray on the ceiling and walls. The knife wound in the neck…

Now Sam had it, what had been bothering her all morning. Amanda hadn't fought back. When she was attacked, she'd run.

Running was counterintuitive. Souleyret was a trained pro-fessional. She would know how to defend herself, and how to defend Cattafi. Yet, when faced with an attack, she'd tried to get away instead of fighting her way out.

What in the world had spooked the girl so badly she'd turned tail instead of trying to fight?

The killer had gotten close to her, very close. There was no forced entry. Cattafi, or Souleyret, had let the killer in. Or the killer had a key and surprised them.

No, that long hallway from the door to the kitchen wouldn't dampen sound. They'd have heard him coming. So they must have let him in.

Was she trying to reason with him? Talk him down? Was she trying to surrender?

Worse, was she dealing with someone she knew? Someone trusted enough to get face-to-face?

That must be it, Sam decided. Whoever killed Amanda Souleyret was a known entity.

Which made this even harder. Betrayal resonated more deeply than any other motive, made it an ever deeper tragedy.

One last turn, and they were on Fletcher's street. His row house was charming white brick, situated on a street catty-corner to the Longworth Office Building on Capitol Hill, just down from the Capitol Hill Club and the RNC.

Sam had been to Fletcher's place before, and always wondered what the stone angel in his front yard symbolized to him. Darren Fletcher was as far from a religious man as she'd known, though he wasn't an atheist, not that she knew of. For a Catholic like herself, nominal as she may be, the idea of not having that mysterious support was anathema. She'd have to ask him about it sometime, like he had with her desire to be a medical examiner.

They parked on the street and followed Fletch up the stairs to the front door.

"Sorry for the mess," he said, and she knew he wasn't sorry for it at all. He was a man, a cop, and rarely if ever spent more than a few hours a day in his own home.

The house was surprisingly straight, though, and Sam detected a few homey touches she hadn't seen the last time—a potted plant in the corner, candleholders on the dining room table, black leather placemats. Surely that was Agent Jordan Blake's doing. The two were well-matched, Sam thought. She liked Jordan, respected her as a cop and thought, given a few drinks on consecutive relaxed Saturday afternoons, the two might even become friends. She was also wildly protective of Fletcher, another attribute. Fletch needed someone to care for him. He withered without a woman's touch.

"Does she have a drawer yet?" she asked him.

He looked at her sideways. "No. There's no point. Neither of us have time to settle in, you know? But I did buy her a toothbrush."

"Oh, Fletcher. The lengths you go to are mind-boggling. Even I'm overwhelmed."

"Hush, Owens." But he wasn't annoyed. He had the sort of suffused glow a man in the early throes of a love affair should have when imagining his woman spending the night.

Daniels was clearly unnerved by their banter. "Sir? Can I help with anything?"

"Can you cook?"

The kid shrugged. "I make a mean grilled cheese."

At the mention of food, Sam's stomach rumbled in a very unladylike manner. Fletcher gave a little laugh and pointed at the kitchen. "We'd be in your debt, Agent Daniels."

"Sure thing." The kid disappeared. Sam and Fletcher took seats across from each other at the dining room table. He put the secure laptop on the table, and Sam plunked down the black binder on Souleyret. He turned on the machine, plugged in the SD card.

"There's a lot of data here. It's going to take a while to upload."

"And off we go," she murmured, opened the stiff faux-leather cover and started to read.

★ ★ ★

Sam found the FBI file on Amanda Souleyret much more satisfying than the one the State Department had given her, and also more infuriating. Souleyret had definitely been operating under her own auspices for several years. She was an autonomous undercover agent, working around the edges of the pharmaceutical world, reporting to multiple people—including Girabaldi at State when necessary—sending reports back to the FBI. She made her own cases, did her own thing. She had few handlers, and even fewer people knew she was FBI. She seemed to take jobs from all sorts of agencies on an ad hoc basis. She was a freelancer, in many ways, with a variety of aliases to backstop her stories.

Clearly, Amanda Souleyret was a very accomplished spy.

As Girabaldi had told them, she specialized in getting information out of corporate databases. Which explained the SD card, Sam thought. She traveled the world on cases, settling into cities and jobs as needs be.

There was a photo in the file, too, one taken a few years earlier. Souleyret was smiling, lips closed, but there was a sparkle in her eyes. Sam was right; she'd been quite pretty. Not a bombshell by any means, but pretty. Sam imagined if you glammed her up with makeup and clothes she would stand out in a crowd, but dressed down, hair in a ponytail and no makeup on, she looked like a fresh-faced farm girl. Cute enough to use her looks if she needed them, but more than likely, she played it down in order to move around without notice.

And move around she did. Sam counted fifteen countries in the past two years. It seemed her specialty was getting close to a worker at whatever institution she needed to break into, steal their credentials, get the info and get out of Dodge. Simple, straightforward and effective. A friendly girl could wreak one hell of a lot of havoc if she knew what she was doing, and Souleyret obviously did.

There were specifics she hadn't seen in the other file, as well. Souleyret had gone to school at the University of Virginia, was recruited right out of the job fair, started at the academy three weeks after graduation. She'd scored top of her class in firearms and classwork, attracted the attention of the covert ops group, then went on to specialized training at the Farm, the CIA training center.

So Amanda had gotten the best of both worlds, and was sent out in the world to do her industrial espionage. And clearly more than that—the commendation had been for getting an FBI asset out of a firefight in Cairo. She got her hands dirty when it was needed.

Despite all the new information, Sam had the distinct impression she was being given a sanitized version of Amanda Souleyret's work life. The information was solid, but not detailed. Not redacted, to be sure, but Sam couldn't help but feel like something was still missing. And why would that be?

Either someone was trying to cover their tracks, or Amanda Souleyret was into something bigger than anyone knew, and someone was trying to keep her secrets.

TUESDAY: AFTERNOON

But evil is wrought by want of thought,

As well as want of heart.

—Thomas Hood

CHAPTER 26

BEAUTY WATCHED THE BROWN-HAIRED WREN WALK ACROSS THE STREET AND enter a town house with an angel out front. She moved like water, gliding gently, head up, shoulders back, a small spring in the last part of her step, like a little girl excited and bouncing on her toes.

He'd been watching her for days, months, years, it seemed. She was the ideal woman for him—just shy of being thin, pretty but not beautiful, brunette, good taste in clothes and restaurants, unmarried. He bet she'd know how to make conversation, be witty and clever, laugh at his jokes and fetch him cool drinks on hot days without asking.

He took his eyes off her long enough to look at himself in the rearview mirror. Narrowed his eyes, made himself look mean and started a vehement, virulent argument with himself.

I want her.

She doesn't fit the parameters.

I don't care. I want her. I want her now.

She has protections. She is not like the others.

And I'm supposed to do what, just sit back and content myself with looking? I want to feel her. That skin, so soft, so clean, so fresh.

The rules are there for your protection. You've spent twenty years making this work. You recognize the signs, it's happened before. It's simply an infatuation. Infatuation will be the end of you, of this. You won't be able to watch anymore. Do you want her more than you want your life?

An eyebrow raised.

No.

Good. You've been much too impetuous lately.

I'm bored.

Then we'll find something to make you unbored. But she isn't it. Now, drive away like a good little boy, and find another. Besides, your blood's still fizzing from the last one. Enjoy it. Relax. Go have a drink. You've taken two in the past two weeks. They are onto you. She will be onto you, as well, and soon. They are connecting the dots. Once they connect the kills, how long do you think you can stay ahead of this? Lie low for a bit, and see what happens.

I know she's onto me. That's what makes this so fun. I need something…more. A challenge. Yes, I think a challenge is in order. I can't stay cooped up anymore. I need to breathe the air and feel the breeze on my face. I need to touch her. I need to know what her hair smells like.

You need a challenge like a hole in the head. Are you an idiot? Do you want to get caught? Do you want to throw twenty years of work away? Because they will put this together sooner rather than later, mark my words. And then you'll be finished.

She will. She's the one who will see what I've done, and come after me.

And he licked his lips at the thought.

They fought for an hour, waiting for her to reemerge. When she did, with the cop and a younger guy who looked both scared and excited, he took a few discreet pictures for good measure, a little something for the road, so to speak. Thought about how nice it would be to touch that shiny hair, wind his fingers through it, bring it to his nose and sniff deeply of her essence. He knew she must use something expensive on it; her clothes were high-quality. She took care of herself.

Don't do it. Walk away. There are others, ones who fit the parameters, who are everything you're looking for and more. Rules exist for your protection, Beauty.

You're a fucking shit, you know that, right?

A smile in the mirror.

I'm the best friend you could ever have. Now, drive away.

And he did. Headed his car west, toward home. As much as he wanted her, Beauty knew it was better to let the anticipation build. It was too early. Too soon. There was so much more watching to be done.

He would leave the little wren alone.

For now.

CHAPTER 27

Capitol Hill

AS QUIETLY AS SHE'D COME, ROBIN LEFT HER SISTER'S TOWN HOUSE. SHE'D done a thorough search, looked in all the hiding spots Amanda had created throughout the place. Someone else had also done a thorough search of the house, especially of the renter's mail, but leaving practically no trace behind, which made the hair on the back of her neck stand up and her vision pulse with violet.

What did you get yourself into, little sister?

The dog next door was silent. Someone should ask the neighbor what time the dog had started barking yesterday. She hoped the police would be smart enough to think of it.

Back in her car, even more vigilant now. Down to Constitution, then up Indiana. Weaving around through the streets of the city, thinking furiously.

She called Lola, set her onto the email trail. If anyone could re-create a server bounce, it was her. The moment she hung up, the phone rang again. There was no caller ID. She had a special phone with its own operating system developed specifically for her team of miscreants, so they could operate in the shadows, unseen, unheard, untraceable.

When she hit Talk, there was a low tone. A signal.

She waited patiently, and a moment later, Atlantic came on the line.

"What's the matter?" he asked without preamble. Atlantic was a very busy man, the head of a number of secret task forces across all the agencies. Robin only knew the names and auspices of two—her own group, and Operation Angelmaker, Atlantic's attempt to keep a tight rein and eye on the world's government assassins. When one stepped out of line, he—or she—was brought back in or eliminated.

Robin had always been Atlantic's go-to girl in times of need.

"My sister was murdered last night."

She heard the soft intake of breath, was surprised. She'd only met him once in person, six years ago, when he recruited her. The rest of their communications had been by phone. But Atlantic was hard as nails, shrewd and unflappable. He was descended from the Ainu, the indigenous Japanese, and possessed one striking feature from this heritage—eyes that were an unholy, unnatural shade of pale ice blue, so light as to be nearly transparent.

"You'll never forget him if you meet him. He has a gaze colder than the depths of the Atlantic," she'd once been told by a colleague. It was true. Atlantic was an unnaturally gifted man, able to create great loyalty among his people, great respect among his peers and engender great fear among his enemies.

Compassion wasn't part of his lexicon.

"I heard," he said. "I am very sorry. Is there anything I can do?"

"Yes. Amanda got into something. I need to find out what. Since I can't exactly ask her employers..."

"You'd like me to do it in your stead. Fine."

And he was gone. Atlantic was never one to waste time.

She tapped her finger on the steering wheel. Wondered if she should make a call, ask for a welfare check on the men who rented her sister's house. No. If the D.C. cops were worth their salt, they'd eventually find the town house in Amanda's records and make their own gruesome discovery.

She wound down to Lafayette Square, found a spot on the street, paralleled expertly and walked into the park, staring across the way at the White House. She could never see the white marble without thinking of her swearing in, standing in the quiet Indian Treaty room, the flags whispering over the air-conditioning vents, the roughness of the pebbled leather of the Bible's cover beneath her palm.

I, Robin Souleyret, do solemnly swear that I will support and defend the Constitution of the United States against all enemies, foreign and domestic; that I will bear true faith and allegiance to the same; that I take this obligation freely, without any mental reservation or purpose of evasion; and that I will well and faithfully discharge the duties of the office on which I am about to enter. So help me God.

She had spoken the words of the oath with a deep sense of satisfaction, then took it to its most extreme meaning. She'd defended, all right. Fought and killed to protect the ideals and freedoms of her government. She'd done things no one should have to do, and had done them willingly, knowing she was serving the greater good. The sight of the building made her swell with pride. Regardless of occupant, regardless of political winds, she had played her role, and played it well.

Amanda had taken the same oath. She did her job well, too.

Amanda didn't know exactly what her older sister did, and Robin tried to keep it that way. The isolation from her only family was hard, but she wasn't sure Mandy would understand her vocation. Killing people under orders wasn't exactly meant for dinner conversation. As far as Amanda knew, Robin was a CIA field agent who went to multiple postings around the world. Her background was in physics, so it stood to reason she'd be keeping an eye out on the nation states with nuclear capabilities.

When, in actuality, Robin was a gun. That was all. A conscienceless gun. And Robin went to great lengths to make sure her little sister didn't know that.

Walking along the promenade in front of the White House, she took in the wandering black-clad spec ops detail on top of the building, the surface-to-air missile batteries, the cameras every few feet and other covert security measures. Had a moment of smugness—little did they know their greatest weapon was walking by at this very moment.

If they had known, if they had looked down and seen death walking past, they might not go so blithely about their day. Robin had a bit of a reputation in certain circles.

The smugness fled. Now Mandy would never know. Robin had fulfilled her greatest duty, to keep her sister ignorant of her sins.

Mandy had a law-and-order streak in her. Recruited into the FBI out of college, she wanted all the glamour and excitement that came with being a cop. She went through the academy, took all the tests, shot all the guns. And when her superiors started to see she had a knack for undercover work and was conversant in three languages, they'd seized the opportunity and started her onto a different tract.

Robin knew Mandy specialized in corporate espionage. Her normal MO was to falsify a résumé, get hired on by a company, find their weak spots, steal their secrets and get them back to whomever was paying. Or she was brought in to do the exact opposite—figure out who was stealing secrets, and where they were being sold. It all depended on where the company stood in line with the best interests of the US government.

Amanda answered to several different masters—whoever was directly affected, whoever had hired her, and her handlers, plus her FBI hierarchy. Robin had always admired her little sister's ability to juggle the sometimes vehemently opposing orders from several quarters. But like Robin, once on a case, she operated with autonomy, only reaching out when absolutely necessary.

A tidal wave of aquamarine the exact color of her sister's eyes clouded her vision, and Robin stifled a sob. Amanda had reached out. And Robin had been too busy to help.

She batted the cloud away. *Stop that. You're no use to her like this.*

Her phone rang, and she took a seat on an empty park bench and answered it.

Lola Jergens was on the line. "We have a trace. The email came from inside the State Department."

"Do we have a specific area, or a name?"

"The external address was fake, the whole thing was scrambled. No name, only the server section. It came from the Africa desk."

"Africa? She was supposed to be working out of France, or had been a month ago."

"There's no mistake."

Robin stood, started back toward her car. "Lola, I want you to pull every name in the section, figure out who would have been working with Amanda. I'm mobile. Call me when you have a target."

"What are you going to do?" Lola asked, wary. "You can't exactly walk in there. You're still persona non grata."

Robin smiled, and a homeless man on the edge of the park who was about to ask for money started and turned away, pretending he hadn't seen her.

"I just want to have a chat with whoever asked my sister to bring something into the country. Because whoever it is probably got her killed. Find out who it was, Lola, and let me know right away."

"And in the meantime?"

"I think it's time I go see Tommy Cattafi."

CHAPTER 28

Capitol Hill
Fletcher's house

IT DIDN'T TAKE AS LONG AS FLETCHER EXPECTED TO UPLOAD THE DATA FROM the SD card. The files were encrypted, not a huge surprise there. He opened the small package that came with the laptop, dumped out a thumb drive with a decryption software program on it, and a couple of other, more esoteric code-breaking tools should the thumb drive's program fail. Thankful for the forensic accounting seminar they'd been given last month, which covered how to run these programs in exactly this kind of scenario, he inserted the thumb drive and launched the program.

The more sophisticated the criminals became, the quicker the cops had to paddle to keep up. Jordan had introduced him to a number of fun toys the feds used to access information from both web accounts and hard drives, and he'd successfully lobbied for Metro to bring several of them on board.

The proletariat in him had qualms about the level of access the government now had, especially warrantless spying, which was happening more and more, but the cop in him appreciated the tools. They made his life easier, made an investigation of this nature go much, much faster than it normally would have.

The program finished running. The screen of the laptop went blank, then suddenly began filling with numbers. *Damn. Code. It was all in code. Son of a bitch.* Yes, he'd managed to crack the SD card, but he'd need a sophisticated cryptography program to decipher any of it.

Or a little help from his friends.

And he knew exactly who to call.

So much of the crime they saw now had links to the online world. When he'd become the homicide lieutenant, in addition to his appeal for more sophisticated technologies, he'd pushed for an outreach program into the technology community. They needed more confidential informants—CIs—who were on the hacker end of the spectrum. More deals done with boys and girls who were doing less-than-legal online work in exchange for information on their employers. His investigators agreed, and had done well rounding up some people they could use when the need arose.

One of the people who'd been fingered right away was a girl named Rosalind Lowe. In the hacker world, she went by the call sign Freedom Mouse.

Mousy she was not. A white hat hacker, she'd gotten herself involved with a small-time Mafia don in northeast D.C. who'd turned on her, and she'd come to them looking for help in extricating herself from the man's grip. She had information that was enough to take him down, but if he had any idea it had come from her, she'd be dead.

Fletcher liked Rosalind. She was smart and sassy, tattooed and pierced, and had a bullshit detector a mile wide. She could find work as a human lie detector, should the current technology ever fail. She'd also been specializing in cryptography at MIT before she'd gotten bored and dropped out.

She'd helped them take down the don, and in exchange they'd

forgiven her a small banking scam. Nothing that would hurt anyone. She was incredibly good at breaking into company's servers and then letting them know their firewalls were a joke, and had done just that.

He grabbed his phone, called Hart.

"Fletcher, where the hell are you?" he asked, sounding terribly annoyed.

"Home. With a wad of info I can't decipher. Can you get Mouse for me? I have a job for her."

Hart was quiet. "Armstrong is on the warpath looking for you."

"Which is why I called you. I need Mouse, Lonnie. Yesterday. And I can't call her, there's too much heat on this case as it is."

"Man," Hart said, dragging it out.

"Thou doth protest too much. Trust me, okay?"

"Okay. I'll make the call. I don't think we're going to be able to keep this thing quiet for much longer. Cattafi took a turn for the worse. His family won't be here for a few hours. They called from Chicago, asked if there was anything we could do. Which, of course, there isn't. And we're hitting a brick wall with Souleyret. I can't find out anything worthwhile. We're going through her financials right now. She owned a house on Capitol Hill for the past ten years, not too far from you. It's leased out. There's a BMW 3-series sitting in a long-term parking garage at Union Station registered to her name. That's it. She has no debt, no loans, no sketchy income, just a regular direct deposit from Uncle Sam. Girl was squeaky clean, with sugar on top."

"Why not park the car at the house?"

"Guess that's part of the lease agreement. Renters get the garage space."

"Credit cards?"

"Just one. An American Express she pays off automatically every month. We're going through the most recent charges now, but she must work on a cash basis, because it's barely being used.

There's nothing exciting here. Bank statements show ATM with-drawals, some with foreign activity fees, so we can build an idea of where she's been. But that's all we've got. There's nothing in her financials that screams, *Here's why someone wanted to off me.* We've got requests in for her phone and text records, but I gotta say, I'm getting the sense this chick is a bit careful. Contained. Or we're missing something huge. Now, when you gonna get here and start helping?"

"Not soon. I'm trying to find out what got Souleyret killed. She brought something else into the country—not the vac-cines—which is why I need Mouse."

"Oh. I see." His tone changed, from annoyance to interest. "And you think there may be some answers she can find?"

"I do. What about the sister? Have you found her yet?"

"Not yet. I was hoping Sam could dig into the official FBI files, see if she can't find her."

"I'll ask. Stay in touch. Text me the address on the Hill. When I finish here, I might as well go talk to the people who rented from her, find out if they know anything."

"You do that, boss. I'll just keep plugging away on nothing good."

Sam sat back in the chair. Fletcher was just hanging up his cell phone. "Anything?" she asked him.

"No. Hart's hitting a dead end with Souleyret. Nothing hinky in her financials, nothing unusual anywhere around her." He pointed at the computer. "My decryption program worked, but the files are all in code. I have a call in to a kid who might be able to crack it for me."

Sam's phone rang. "It's Baldwin. Finally. He might have a shortcut for us." She put the phone to her ear. "Where have you been?"

His deep voice always made her calm, but she heard a buzz

of excitement in it. "Confirming we definitely have another victim of the Hometown Killer."

"Why do you sound happy about this?"

"Because there's DNA at this crime scene. We have something to match him to now. He's starting to speed up, and he's starting to get sloppy. We're going to catch him, and soon. I hope."

"That is good news. I need to talk about our girl. Are you secure?"

"No. I won't be for an hour at least."

"All right. Let me say this, then. Are you aware of her code?"

He was quiet for a moment. "I was worried about that. Check the back pocket of the file. You'll find your help there. Listen, I'm sorry for being so cagey. I'll explain everything when I can get on a secure sat phone, or home."

"Okay. Be careful, Baldwin."

"You, too, Sam. See you."

She hung up and flipped to the back of the file Shultz had sent. Taped to the back of the last page was a small thumb drive.

She peeled it off and handed it to Fletcher, just as Daniels came back with a platter piled high with sandwiches.

"What's this?" Fletcher asked.

"I think it's a code breaker. Daniels, did Agent Shultz tell you this was in here?"

"Yes, ma'am."

Fletcher shrugged and slid it into the USB drive on the laptop. Nothing happened.

He disengaged the drive and handed it back to Sam. "Looks like it's a dud. Let's eat, I'm starved." Fletcher went to the kitchen and brought back some sodas, and they dug into the sandwiches.

Fletcher closed his eyes in bliss. "You weren't kidding, Marcos. Can I call you Marcos?"

"Yes, sir. Or Marc. Or Daniels. I get Agent a lot. I even answer to *Hey, you!*"

"Funny guy. I'm Fletcher. Or Fletch. Stick around, be my full-time chef? I'll make it worth your while."

"Not sure how Quantico could function without me, sir, but I'll ask."

Sam finished the first half of the sandwich, musing as she chewed. "We're missing something."

Fletcher tapped the top edge of the laptop, which had gone to sleep while they were eating. "Yeah, someone who can crack codes. Wish Lonnie would get back to me with Mouse already."

Daniels stopped eating. "I'm not bad at it, Fletcher. Code-breaking, I mean."

Sam eyed him, and he flushed a bit under her gaze, tucked his chin down and took a big bite of grilled cheese.

"Daniels, does Agent Shultz know that, too?"

He nodded. "I did a semester of cryptography at Yale."

Sam smiled. "I think I know why she asked you to stick around. Finish your sandwich, then you can have a go at the laptop."

Fifteen minutes later, Daniels said, "I'm in. This program is a little hard to get started—it doesn't launch by itself. You need to look at the codex and give it parameters before it can begin the process of identifying the initial code and rearranging the numbers into the codex." He turned the screen to face Sam.

Fletcher came to read over her shoulder.

At first, the words made no sense. Then Sam realized what she was seeing.

"Oh my God."

"What is it?" Fletcher asked. "This is all gibberish to me."

She pointed to the screen. "These are vaccination schedules, dated from last week all the way back to 2005. Throughout the pan-Africa region, but concentrating in Sierra Leone and Guinea. But that's not what's so interesting." She scrolled down. "Look at the findings. Wow. This isn't good."

"Are the vaccines killing people?"

She nodded. "Yes." She pointed at the screen. "See these two columns? These are inoculation dates and death dates. The death dates increase dramatically starting last March." She looked at Fletcher, troubled. "This wasn't a one-time test run. They've been at it for a year, injecting people with this new bug. God, Fletcher. Amanda's instincts were right. They've been perfecting it."

CHAPTER 29

FLETCHER WAS TRYING, AND FAILING, TO MAKE SENSE OF THE INFORMATION from the SD card. He stared at the screen, watched Sam scroll through the data. He had to take her word he was looking at vaccination schedules.

"Why would they do that?" he asked. "Why would they take the chance? This can't be quiet over there, people talk. Look at the massive Ebola outbreak last year—that was on every television station and in every paper around the world. How are they keeping this quiet?"

Sam was more pragmatic about things. She had a strange way of being able to separate herself from the case, to see it objectively. It was a skill that was turning her into an investigator, one he used to think he had, until his world blew up this morning.

"I think they're using the Ebola outbreak from last year as cover. The symptoms of Ebola hemorrhagic fever and this new bug are very similar. And as a result of the outbreak last year, the CDC and WHO fast-tracked human trials for an Ebola vaccine, too. They got desperate, and were given permission for compassionate use on the drugs they had that weren't fully tested. ZMapp, for example. It worked in several severe cases, boosting the immune systems, effectively curing them of the disease. So they sped things up, trying to find a way out of the epidemic."

"Could someone be trying to create their own vaccine? Using human trials?"

Sam shook her head. "There are always people who will offer up a cure. And there are always people who will be desperate enough to take them at their word. No, Fletcher, this is purposeful. I think Girabaldi is correct—this is the testing ground for a biological attack."

"Are you sure?"

She turned to face him and shrugged. "Until we find all of Amanda's notes, I don't think we'll know anything for sure. But we have to prepare as if an attack is coming."

Daniels was messing with the computer, scrolling through the pages. "There's something else that could be going on."

"What's that?" Sam asked.

"It could be one hell of a money-making scheme. If they have tainted vaccines, and they had engineered a cure, they could be slipping the illness into other inoculations or medicine, then selling their lifesaving medicine."

"True, it would be a boon to the bottom line of a company who was first to market with an all-encompassing vaccine. But this? All these deaths? It's catastrophic. If I were approaching this as a scientist, to me it looks like there is a completely new bug being given in the standard vaccines. I think Amanda was probably onto something. A mysterious man in the African bush, hundreds dead and the lead investigator and her pet doctor murdered? I think we're dealing with someone who's trying to cover their tracks."

They let that sink in.

"Fletcher, should we call Girabaldi? Tell her what we've found?" Sam said.

Fletcher shook his head. "Hell, no. This is the information she's after, I'm sure of it. This is why she sent us off to investigate the case, hoping we'd uncover something, then she'll swoop in and wrap it into her little cover-up."

Sam sat back in her chair and regarded him thoughtfully. "I don't know, Fletch. If what Amanda brought in does contain live viruses, we could have a major problem. Some infected with hemorrhagic fevers take up to twenty, twenty-five days to become symptomatic. People could be exposed and moving around the country, the world, and not know it. That could be the attack plan."

Daniels looked completely terrified. "You mean they could be bringing this new hemorrhagic fever into the country, and we wouldn't know?"

"Sure. It happens more than you'd think, sick people coming in from infected areas around the world, but we have such superior medical facilities and health standards that a full-blown outbreak here is extremely unlikely. But if someone's passing around a new disease without knowing it? That's a potential problem, sure." She turned to Fletcher. "Do you think Girabaldi's in on this? That she knows what's happening and condones it? And is trying to make sure the information doesn't leak?"

He shook his head. "I don't know what to think. She had the Africa desk at the meeting this morning—clearly he's in on it. What's the guy's name...Kronen?"

"Kruger," Sam said absently. "The on-site HAZMAT folks said the vials of viruses we found at Cattafi's place were simple vaccines, and so did State. What if... Let me see the computer again, Daniels."

He handed it over, and she looked through the pages of material, reading slowly this time, trying to make sense of the numbers and letters she was seeing. There was a medical shorthand here that she was thankfully familiar with. She looked for the pages that would have the behavioral risk factors, which could indicate how the disease might be spreading after the vaccine inoculations. She didn't see anything strange or out of place there. She went on to the reporting schedules. The files were far from perfect; self-reporting of this infection was practically nonexistent outside of the major population centers due to the ultraquick mortality, so the numbers were skewed to a representative sample of subjects vaccinated at a specific station in Uganda. But from what she could tell, ninety percent of those inoculated died within the first week. These entries were all labeled HR—high risk.

She scrolled faster, and at the very end of the file was rewarded with a small statement that made the blood leave her head.

Her voice was pitched higher than normal; she could hear the lingering fear in the question. "Fletcher, where are the vaccination vials we found at Cattafi's place?"

Fletcher raised an eyebrow at Sam. "What is it? What did you find?"

"Are you familiar with the concept of grafting?"

"Skin grafting?" Fletcher asked.

Daniels spoke up. "No, you mean the grafting done with wine, or roses. Creating new species by mixing two distinctly separate breeds." Sam and Fletcher both looked at him. He shrugged. "My mom is a gardener. She specializes in hybrids."

"Well, that's helpful knowledge, because that's exactly what I'm talking about. Diseases can act in the same way. You have a host disease, and you can graft a secondary disease onto it. It's a bit more complicated than wine or roses, but the disease can be made weaker, or create a hysteric response that allows it to be conquered. Or it could grow stronger, and become a superbug. Usually it happens by accident, but it looks to me like that's what they were doing. Trying to perfect a superbug that can be spread by casual contact, even making it airborne. It's one hell of a sophisticated weapon."

"And it could already be here on our shores," Fletcher said.

She took a deep breath and nodded.

"Sam, tell me there's a list of names and companies so we can start shutting them down."

"There isn't," Sam said, closing the laptop. "Amanda may have found out what they're up to, but she hadn't identified where the drugs are coming from. Fletch, we need those vaccines secured. If she's brought in samples of the actual superbug, we could all be in danger."

Agent Daniels pushed his plate away, appetite lost. "Sir, ma'am, there's no way we can keep this information quiet. There are too many lives at stake."

Sam nodded. "I agree with you, Agent Daniels. Amanda Souleyret was killed for this information, but I'm not inclined to hand it over to the very person who's asking for it. Not until we know she can be trusted. We need to keep this close hold for the time being, until we know who we can share it with. Are you okay with that?"

"If you say so, ma'am." He didn't look convinced.

Fletcher gave her a speculative look, then grabbed his phone and dialed. He put it on speaker.

"Hart here."

"Lonnie, where is the material taken from Cattafi's apartment?"

"Off the top of my head? I don't know, but I assume it's been taken into evidence by the crime scene unit."

"Get on the phone to Mel Robertson, have the bags pulled and waiting." He glanced at Sam. "We're going to, uh, get an outside, independent review of the material. Okay?"

"Okay. But what prompted this?"

"Too much to explain right now," Fletcher said darkly. "Just go do it, and I'll fill you in shortly."

"Will do," Hart said, and rang off. He called back within a minute.

Fletcher answered with a brusque, "You got 'em?"

"Fletcher, we have a problem. I've got Mel on the line."

"What's the problem?"

Robertson had a deep voice, and he sounded seriously pissed off. "HAZMAT took them. Claimed we were incapable of proper storage."

Sam felt her heart race. "Do you know who at HAZMAT took them?"

"I do, and I called them, but they've already handed them over to the CDC. Those vaccines are halfway to a field lab, or Atlanta."

"Son of a bitch." Fletcher slammed his hand on the table.

"Lieutenant, what aren't you telling me?"

"Those vials just became the most important piece of evidence we have. Mel, I don't want you to panic, but they may not have been safe, after all. I need you to find out exactly where they are, who has them and have them call me immediately. But no one outside, and I mean no one, can know about this. You read me?"

"Loud and clear. But when you say they aren't safe, what the hell do you mean?"

"Those vials might be carrying a live disease, Mel. One that could be used against us."

There was a sharp intake of breath from both men on the other side of the line. Robertson spoke first. "Jesus. Are we in danger? We were all exposed, even with the precautions we took. Everyone at the crime scene, you and Dr. Owens, too. And anyone who might come into contact with the courier. If this is airborne, we—"

Fletcher interrupted him. "I know. Find them, Mel. I don't care what you have to do. Just make sure this stays internal. We can't have the media up our asses about it. Not until we know for sure what we're dealing with." He hung up. "Great. That's just great."

Sam ran a hand along his shoulder. "Don't worry, Fletch. From what I'm seeing, they haven't managed to make this airborne. I'm pretty sure we'd need to be injected, or come into

contact with the blood or vomit or other bodily fluids of an infected body. Can they be engineered if they fall into the wrong
hands? Yes. But these hemorrhagic fevers aren't airborne. I do
think we're safe. If I didn't, I'd be jumping up and down right
now, insisting you pull out all the stops on a public health alert."

He was still white. "I hope you're right, Sam. We need to
go double-time into this investigation. We need to find Bromley and talk to him. Find out exactly what he and Cattafi had
stirred up."

"I'll call his office."

Sam used her phone to find the GW website and looked up
the number. A young woman's voice came through the line.
"The Office of International Medicine Programs, how may I
direct your call?"

"My name is Dr. Samantha Owens with the Federal Bureau of
Investigation. I need to speak with David Bromley immediately."

"Oh, I'm so sorry, but Dr. Bromley isn't in the country. Can
I take a message? He's been checking in, but I haven't heard
from him today."

"I know he's not. Where is he exactly?"

"Let me see…" There was tapping; she was looking it up on
the computer. "Cape Town, South Africa. He's doing something for the Infectious Diseases Research Training Program. I
don't know when he's expected back, but I do see he has office
hours next week. Should I put you down for an appointment?"

"Do you know a student of his named Thomas Cattafi?"

"Sorry, ma'am, no, I don't."

"All right. This is an extremely urgent matter. Can you reach
Dr. Bromley for me?"

"It's hit or miss with the time changes, but I can try."

"If you could reach out to him, that would be a huge help.
Please ask him to return my call immediately. Thank you." She
rattled off her name and information and hung up. Shook her
head at Fletcher.

"We're out of luck, for the time being, anyway. They're going to try and track him down."

Fletcher ran a hand along his chin. "Should we try on our own? Send someone to him?"

"Let's give her an hour, see if she can get through."

"We just can't win, can we?" She saw him thinking, deciding what they should do. After a minute he said, "We're going to have to share the information about the vaccines soon enough. They want us to investigate these murders—that's what we're going to do. Let's go to Souleyret's house, see if there's anything to be seen, then I'd like to check in on Cattafi. And where the hell is this mythical sister, huh?"

"We need to let Baldwin know what we've found. Him, I trust. He can help us decide what to do with this information, and maybe help us get a contact at the CDC to do an independent assessment of the vials from Cattafi's place. And he'll have an idea of whether Girabaldi is on our side, or her own."

"Call him, then, but from the road." He stood, put out a hand to Daniels. "Marcos, you can head back to Quantico now. Keep your mouth shut, you hear me? We'll take it from here. Thanks for all your help. I really appreciate it."

Sam saw the kid was disappointed to be dismissed. He was having fun, despite the horror of the information they'd just discovered. "Yes, sir. But I'm happy to hang around in case you need anything else."

"Fletcher, maybe Agent Daniels could start looking for Souleyret's sister for us. Save us some time? Since he's already here."

Daniels gave her a small smile. "I can find her."

Fletcher ran a hand through his dark hair. Sam saw the gray at his temples had spread, and felt a small shock. He'd aged in the time she'd known him, which wasn't very long, all things considered. A few months, really, cherry blossoms to autumn leaves.

And in that time, she'd never seen him as rattled as he was right now.

"Yeah. Yeah, okay. That's a good idea. Since you're already in this, Marcos, let's get you in all the way. You can work from here—you'll have everything you need, especially privacy. Do you need to call your boss? Tell her we need you?"

"She's already given me the day, sir. I'm yours. Do you have any information on the sister?"

Sam slid him the thin file State had given them, and the one from the FBI. "Here's everything we have on her. The sister's name is Robin. Robin Souleyret. Find her, and I'll buy you a drink."

He gave her a smile. He had a nice smile. It made him look even younger than he was.

"How old are you, Agent Daniels?"

"Twenty-eight yesterday, ma'am. Today's my first day working for NCAVC."

CHAPTER 30

Georgetown

XANDER SLAMMED THE PHONE DOWN AND UNPLUGGED IT FROM THE WALL.
How the media had found him so quickly was astonishing. No
one was parked outside yet, and he hoped that wouldn't happen,
but he wasn't at all convinced he could avoid it. Sam would be
upset with their life being played out on the news again. And
so would he.

He joined Chalk at the kitchen table, where they'd been sip-
ping water and booting up their respective computers. Xander
had eschewed the idea of them having an office, much prefer-
ring to work out of the town house in Georgetown, but now,
he was rethinking that decision.

"I don't know if we're secure here. That was CNN. This
isn't good."

"I'll fight them off for you, cupcake. Just point me at the
nearest news van with my grenades and they won't bother you
anymore."

Xander clutched his hands to his chest and batted his eye-
lashes. "Chalk, you're my hero."

Chalk flipped him the bird and started typing.

The smile left Xander's face. He wasn't kidding; he didn't feel secure here. Not with a professional contract hitter down by his hand, a client/target taking a nap on his living room couch and three possible suspects having Diet Cokes in the backyard under Thor's watchful eye.

Xander had come across a professional assassin once, been assigned to cover his ingress into a hot zone outside of Kandahar to take out a brutal Taliban leader, an executive order kept so quiet the press had no idea it was happening, back when the greater good was actually a point of sale in the war. The ride had been a long one—at night, overland in dangerous territory, scooting around known IED hotbeds, making sure they weren't seen. They talked. It was the natural thing to do to pass the time.

The assassin had his own code. He wasn't a believer, wasn't attached to any sort of dogma. If the job paid, he went, simple as that. But he'd felt it was his duty. There were too many lives being lost fighting unjust wars unnecessarily. He felt the best way to end a conflict was to take out the leadership, do it quickly and brutally, and watch the rebellion fall apart.

Xander had seen enough rebellions pop up after a leader's death to think this wasn't exactly accurate. He told the man—his code name had been Atlas—that he felt like they were fighting a hydra. The insurgents were true believers, and cutting off the head in this neck of the woods simply created five hundred more heads, all desperate for power, and the desire to crush the West.

Atlas had laughed and told him it didn't matter. There would always be another leader to eliminate. That was what made the world go around. One rebellion quashed, another rising from its ashes. More money for him. He was just the trigger. And in keeping with his pragmatic philosophy, he pointed out there were plenty more where he came from, too.

Xander supposed he was the same as the assassin, albeit with a slightly different code. He only killed under orders, too. He dragged himself back to the present, to his current crisis.

Beloved by many, Denon was still despised by a few, and they were clearly the ones behind the assassination attempt. The old axiom was true: powerful men and women drew powerful enemies. Xander had no illusions on that point. It was the thesis that would keep him and Chalk in business, long into their careers in close protection.

More importantly, if Xander could find who was funding the hit on Denon, they'd be able to stop the contract.

And he had no illusions on what that meant, either.

He was about to go hunting.

He knew he'd done the right thing protecting his principal. But now he'd brought down a world of hurt on himself and everyone around him. He couldn't stand the idea of putting Sam in danger. She managed to get herself in enough trouble without him adding to the mix.

Xander pulled up a file on his laptop. Maybe someone from Denon's past had a beef they'd missed, and was using his private staff to get close.

In the manner of all great—and rich—men, Denon had his fingers in a number of lucrative pies. The biggest entity by far was his interests in Britain's oil and gas. Twenty years earlier, as a young driller on an ocean platform, he'd seen a way to make their jobs more efficient, and his work resulted in a new method for getting the oil from the ocean's floor, one that had been adopted by every oil company in the world. Which made him a multibillionaire.

It was complicated stuff, and since he couldn't find any links from the past to support the current issues, it had no bearing to Xander's thoughts. He closed the backgrounder and moved into more recent information.

The specialized software Chalk had developed for their use was taking forever to run. Xander's internet connection was overloaded by the five laptops connected to the router.

It was taking quite a bit of effort not to rip the house apart in frustration.

"Anything yet?"

Chalk shook his head. "Patience, grasshopper."

Chalk was more tolerant than Xander, always had been, which was what made them a good team. He was quiet, tapping industriously into the program he'd designed, waiting for it to work. The software could search the netherworlds of contract hits, looking for any moves by the known hitters. Assassination was primarily a word-of-mouth business, but there were still people who used their computers and email to ask for "help," and Chalk was a genius when it came to programming. He'd written a software program that looked for the lingo special to the field. When it found a match to the usual buzzwords, it made a note, downloaded a piece of ingenious tracking software.

Some would call that hacking, but he didn't use the information he collected for his own personal gain, he simply fed it into his program to identify the threat. So white-hat hacking, definitely. The program followed everything from the computer of the person who'd initiated the contact, especially funds transfers. It was a handy tool to gauge where in the process certain plans were. Talk was one thing. When money started changing hands, it was clear matters had gotten more serious.

It was only one tool, and helpful or not, now they knew it was fallible. The program had picked up nothing of interest relating to James Denon before their detail began.

Chalk cracked his knuckles, drawing Xander's attention. "We're going to have to invest in a better wireless connection for you, my friend. I think I've got it finally." He clicked his mouse a few times. "Yeah, we're up." He read for a few seconds, shaking his head. "I see nothing here—no warnings, no threats. No contracts on Denon. No mutterings at all, in fact. I've been scoping conversations from the past two weeks—I did this before, too, and saw nothing, figured we must have missed something—but I'm coming up blank."

"So the program doesn't work perfectly. You can keep working on it, refine it."

"No, it works. Unlike some, *I* believe in my abilities." He grinned at Xander. "Seriously, maybe we're looking at this all wrong. Maybe Denon wasn't the target."

Xander came around to the back of Chalk's chair. "Let me have a go."

Chalk got up, fetched himself a Coke from the refrigerator. Xander took his spot, running through the program, searching for anything that might stand out. After ten minutes, he had to admit Chalk was right. There was nothing out of place, nothing that looked even remotely suspicious.

Xander leaned back in the chair and stretched. He needed fuel—caffeine, food, sleep. He grabbed himself a Coke and started making sandwiches for the crew. Chalk watched quietly, letting him think. After years together as Rangers, living in all corners of the world, there was no unnecessary chatter.

Finally, Xander turned, set a plate of sandwiches on the table, motioning for Chalk to dig in. He delivered a plate to the pool, left another on the table by Denon. Then he grabbed one for himself and in between bites ran through things with Chalk. "So if Denon wasn't the target of the hit, who was? Or did we just stop a madman from going all bell tower on that tarmac?"

"We need to run Denon's people through the system. None of them pulled a contract. Ergo, maybe one of them was the real target."

"Let's do that."

Chalk smiled. "Already am. Program's been running since you sat down. Should be about ready now. Of course, now that our target pool has expanded exponentially, we may find this has nothing to do with Denon at all."

Xander thought of the bloodstain spreading down the concrete wall. "Don't say that."

Chalk had green eyes with yellow centers that made him look like a raptor. He trained those hawklike eyes on Xander now. "Xander, man, you did right. Don't worry. You saved a life today, no matter what. Even if it wasn't our principal, you saved a life."

"We'll see about that. Where's this Senza guy from? Is there anything on him?"

Chalk sat back at the computer, pulled up a fresh screen. "He is Spanish, actually. Was. Worked under several names, so I don't know which one is real, but his history says he was a product of their spec ops. GOE—Grupos de Operaciones Especiales. Mean motherfuckers. Remember that guy, Pablo somebody, who came through Herat with those LAG 40 grenade launchers? He was GOE."

"I remember. He was posing as a translator. He was nuts. I didn't know if he was transporting those weapons or was setting up to shoot them at us." Another chunk of the sandwich disappeared. "So Senza had all the same training as we do."

"Yeah. His mandatory was up, they cut him loose in early 2000 and he went private."

"That's a nice long career for a private hitter. Any paper on who he'd been working for? Did he discriminate?"

"Not really. He'd taken ten jobs in four countries in the past two years. That's steady work, at a decent clip, too. You know how some of these guys are—they'll disappear for years, only come out if the target is huge, meaningful. And some of them will take the smaller jobs to keep in practice. Senza fell into that category."

"Someone like Denon is pretty meaningful."

"He is. But let's see who else might be of interest to the forces of evil."

He tapped on the keyboard, and a list popped up—the names

of Denon's small group that traveled with him to the US on his secret trip. "I've put in all the names of everyone in Denon's top echelons, from the staffers who traveled with him to the company's C-suite, and I've got nothing. Bebbington, Everson and Heedles are clean."

"Show me the files."

Xander ran through them. "Well, there's a ton more people in his company who could be a target."

"But it doesn't make sense, Mutant. We have to limit the target list to the people who knew about the trip. He kept it off the radar entirely. We should look at all the people he met with here in the States, too."

Xander agreed. "Get the itinerary, let's start marking off names, and see where we stand. I'm going to start at the beginning of the job and run through every contact made, from the pilots to the hotels, service and limos, everything external where there were strangers. You start running backgrounds on the people he was slated to see while he was here. Let's run them down, and see who Denon's doing business with who might be doing naughty things."

"Roger that. On it."

Twenty minutes later, Xander found what he was looking for. Or rather, an anomaly, which was enough to set his instincts on fire.

He was running the surveillance tapes from Teterboro, the first hour of the job, looking for anyone who might have been paying special attention to their principal's landing. Denon had specifically requested to meet them as he exited the terminal, not a moment before.

They'd been running the perimeter. He distinctly remembered casing the warehouse, looking for unseen threats, just as he'd done when Denon was leaving. Xander hadn't been looking at the plane. He'd had his back to it. Chalk had been inside the terminal scanning for problems there.

They'd missed it. Son of a bitch, they'd missed it.

On the tape, two females came down the steps of the private Gulfstream at Teterboro Friday night. Maureen Heedles, and a blonde he didn't recognize. She looked neither right, nor left, but marched directly into the terminal, and out of sight of the camera Xander had on his shoulder.

She wasn't listed on the manifest for the flight to London today. And she hadn't been on the flight that left this morning. That he was one hundred percent sure about.

Denon had brought a woman into the country, and left her behind.

CHAPTER
31

FLETCHER CALLED HART BACK AND GOT THE NAME OF THE RENTERS OF Souleyret's house on Capitol Hill—Michael Oread and Jared Lanter.

"They're both Congressional staffers," Hart said. "I called to talk to them, but neither man was at work today. I haven't had a chance to follow up. Also, Robertson is under sail to find and isolate the vaccines."

"Good. Good work, man. Where are we with the cameras around Cattafi's house?"

"Nothing yet. We still haven't been able to touch base with the neighbors. They must be out of town."

"The cameras will have a brand name on them. Get someone up on a ladder, find out who makes them, call the company and give them the address. They'll have an emergency contact for the owners."

"That's next on my extremely long list. Let me know if you find anything at Souleyret's house."

Fletch hung up with a bad feeling. Just something in his gut that told him things were all wrong, all off. How a simple case of domestic dispute had turned into an international intrigue and a possible bioterror attack in less than twelve hours was mind-boggling. There was no keeping this quiet; there were too many moving parts. He didn't feel the need to inform Girabaldi, though. He was going to handle this his way.

They got in his car and headed toward Souleyret's place. Sam was silent on the ride over, making notes in her round handwriting.

"Anything good coming?"

She shook her head "No. Nothing good. I'm having a hard time wrapping my head around the data we just saw. I keep hoping I'm wrong."

"Funny, I was just thinking the exact same thing. Moving that info, smuggling it in, is one thing—bringing live diseases and tissue samples? It's so risky. If Souleyret was working for us, for State, couldn't she just send an email or pick up the phone and blow it wide-open? For that matter, leak it to the press? Why run the risk of allowing an epidemic on our shores, too?"

"There must have been a very compelling reason. And you can't trust the press to work the information. Too much partisanship nowadays. It falls into the wrong hands, it gets swept under the rug, or blown into a different story, or starts an irretrievable panic. But yes, there are all sorts of ways to pass information, secure ways—interagency emails, diplomatic pouches, all that. She must have felt it was too important to chance, and I can understand why. There's a group out there killing people, and I imagine they'll do anything and everything in their power to keep it quiet."

She messed with her bangs for a moment, smoothing them down. "The problem is, we have no idea who Amanda was hiding the information from, Fletch. If she wasn't willing to risk coming in through her own service, or letting the people she was working with know where she was, that tells a lot about her situation. She clearly knew what was on the SD card. Why didn't she go to Girabaldi? Why did she sneak into the country, and how? And she went to a med student in Georgetown instead of her handlers? That's all kinds of messed up. We need to trace her last steps, find out when she came in and from where, in addition to figuring out why she was avoiding her own people. I don't see how we can do that without talking to someone who genuinely has her best interest at heart. Who might know what she was thinking."

"Like a sister."

"Exactly. I don't have one, but if I did, and I was in trouble, family is the first place I'd go. Who knows what sort of situation she had? They could be close, they could hate each other. But if they are close, the sister might be the key. She may have heard or seen something that she doesn't even realize is important. We have to find her. That data—if it's even remotely accurate—could be worth killing for. If Amanda shared, Robin is in danger, too."

"I agree. We're here." Fletcher made a right and pulled to the curb in front of Souleyret's place.

The tall shotgun house was quiet, undisturbed, situated on a street that was also quiet, undisturbed. Real estate agents would call it charming. The whole neighborhood was a small oasis, one of those tiny pockets of homeyness in the middle of the urban sprawl. D.C. was changing all around him. Places that used to be dangerous at all hours were suddenly filled with sidewalks and driveways and grass and flowers and baby strollers. It was disconcerting. He liked it, but didn't quite know what to make of it. He didn't trust anything that looked so good on the outside it made people yearn for it.

He imagined them all sick, dead and dying, the strollers rusting in the driveways, the flowers decaying in their pots. He couldn't let that happen.

He unbuckled his safety belt and climbed from the car. Sam followed him onto the small front porch, stood by his side as he slammed his fist into the door three times.

Nothing.

He rang the bell, and the dog next door, who apparently didn't mind knocking but hated the chimes of the tinny bell, went mad.

Still, nothing from the house.

He tried the knob, found it unlocked, and his heart gave a little thump. This might be a nice area of town, but no one in their right mind left their doors unlocked. It was still D.C., after all.

"Exigent circumstances," he said to Sam. "Back me up?" She nodded, eyes roving the neighborhood as if the answers were printed in the landscaping.

He called it in, told Hart they were entering the premises. Hart promised to have three patrols there momentarily. But Fletcher didn't want to wait. Something was pulling him into the house. His years of experience told him something wicked waited inside.

He stepped into the cool foyer, called out, "Hello? Mr. Oread? Mr. Lanter? Metro Police."

Nothing except the cool hiss of the air conditioner, which had been left on high. The whole place felt like the inside of a refrigerator. The floors were polished oak, the foyer empty of furniture aside from a small wooden bench, the walls painted a generic, builder-grade tan. A pair of muddy Wellies and dirt-covered work gloves stood in the corner—one of the renters had been gardening.

Fletcher cleared the rooms of the bottom floor out of habit; there was no one here, no one hiding, about to jump out. There was a table in the corner of the living room that had been disturbed. Searched, he thought, pointing toward it with his gun for Sam to see.

It was too quiet. Bad things awaited them above. He couldn't smell them, but he knew there was death here.

He saw Sam staring up the stairs. She'd sensed it, too.

He raised his weapon again and started up. Sam followed in his steps, careful and competent, hands in her pockets so she didn't accidentally touch anything. He appreciated not having to warn her to watch where she was going.

"Fletch," Sam said, low. He turned and saw where she was pointing. A long blond hair, tag attached, drifted from the banister. "We'll need to collect it. Amanda might have been here."

"Or we could have a suspect. You feel it, too, huh? It's all wrong in here."

"Definitely," she said. "Come on, let's see what's up there."

When they found the renters, facing each other, one tied up, the other reaching out, such a strange, dislocated scene, Fletcher started to curse. Sam could already hear the sirens approaching; their backup's arrival was imminent.

"How long have they been dead?" he demanded.

Sam touched the boy closest to the door on the arm. "You know I can't tell you that without a liver temp. And with the air-conditioning set this high, it might retard the decomposition process. A day, maybe. It wasn't recent, they're out of rigor, but they haven't begun to leak. The air-conditioning has helped preserve them a bit. I'd say within the past twenty-four hours."

"Goddamn it all. We've been fucking around with the damn SD card while these kids rotted."

She gently moved the boy's arm. "Fletcher, I can't tell you exactly, but they've been dead longer than you've been on the case. It wouldn't have made a difference. You couldn't have saved them."

But she understood his frustration.

She saw a small piece of paper under the unbound boy. Carefully eased it out. "Fletch. We have another note. Listen to this. *'I'm sorry, I had no choice. It's better this way.'* Do you think it's a coincidence? Could we have another murder-suicide?"

"I guaran-goddamn-tee you this isn't a coincidence."

There were voices outside. The police were here. Neighbors started to gather; Sam heard questions being shouted.

She ignored them, looked closer at the bodies, the positioning, the dried white strings of saliva around their mouths. Carefully eased a mouth open. Saw a brilliant red; the mucosa lining was irritated. "They ingested something. Something that worked fast. There are no signs of regurgitation, just froth. Whatever it was killed them very quickly."

"Any ideas?"

"Not until I get them on the table—or Amado does, I mean. OCME has the in-house tox screen. I'd advise you have a death investigator take a blood sample and hightail it through the system, so we can see what we might be dealing with. And we should check glasses, cups, anything that's been left out."

"We'll do that. I'm going to go let them in and get a crime scene unit here." He stopped in the door, looked back at her. "Who the hell are we dealing with?"

She shook her head. "I don't know, Fletch. But we're going to figure this out."

Hopefully, before too many more people die.

There was a big problem with being a professor, and not a medical examiner. Sam had to leave the room and let the D.C. people come in and do their work, without guidance or instruction from her. She could have pulled rank, thrown her FBI badge around, taken control, but honestly, she needed to keep herself separate and allow the investigation to continue.

She'd asked the death investigators to look carefully for injection sites, just in case her first instinct, that they drank some sort of poison, was incorrect. She had to assume whatever killed them had been administered against their wills, whether injected or ingested. She texted Nocek and asked him to rush the tox screen. But then she'd stepped away to let them do their jobs. There was nothing else she could do here.

Her fingers itched for a scalpel, to peel back the skin and see what sort of havoc the poison had wreaked. She checked her watch instead, counting silently. *One Mississippi. Two Mississippi. Three.*

She looked at her watch again. Baldwin should be calling soon; he'd promised her an explanation. She walked down the stairs and went through the kitchen into the tiny backyard. Sent Daniels a text: Anything yet?

He responded immediately: Yes, I'll have a full report shortly. Call you at this number?

Hurry. We have two more down.

She stowed the phone in her front pocket. She was good at waiting, but her agitation wouldn't allow her to sit still. She wondered about the long blond hair on the banister—both of the men had short, dark hair, and there was only one bedroom that seemed to be in use. There were three bedrooms upstairs, and the other two were set up as offices, with couches that looked like they could pull out into guest beds. She didn't like to make assumptions, but the setup screamed couple, not roommates. So probably no girlfriends staying the night. Which made exactly zero difference to the investigation. The hair could belong to anyone, friend or foe. But her first instinct when she saw it was to think it belonged to whomever had been here last. An automatic turn to the nefarious.

She started prowling the backyard, walked out into the alley and bumped into a small, portly woman with tightly marcelled white hair, wearing fluorescent yellow gardening clogs and holding a pair of dirty gloves. Her face was red, with both exertion and shock, Sam thought.

When Sam disentangled herself from the woman's grasp, she patted her down slightly under the guise of making sure she hadn't hurt her, but also looking for any surprises that might be coming. But the woman was clean, the gloves the only thing in her possession. She began asking questions immediately, voice high and breathless.

"I'm fine, I'm fine. Oh my. Whatever is happening? I saw all the police cars. I was coming over to make sure everything is okay. Do you know what's going on?"

"You're a neighbor?"

"I am. I live next door. Please tell me nothing's happened to Mike or Jared."

She seemed a kindly old soul, but Sam was well-marshaled in the ways of crime scene investigation. "What's your name?"

"Eloise Poe. I'm over there." She waved a hand absently toward her fence. The dog they'd heard earlier uttered a short, sharp bark. "Hush, Tervis." She turned to Sam, eyes full of concern. "Are the boys okay?"

Sam shook her head. "I'm sorry, ma'am."

"Oh my. Oh my." She had a hand on her chest, the red face going a duskier pink. Sam eyed her, making sure she didn't fall or faint, but the woman kept her feet, uttering small exclamations of distress until Sam touched her arm, which seemed to bring her back to the present moment.

"When I didn't see Jared on his run this morning I wondered if he was ill. I never imagined, oh my!"

"So they have a routine, a regular schedule?"

"They do...they did. Jared ran every morning at six. They both left for work at eight, together." She gave Sam an assessing look. "They were together, you should know that. It didn't matter to me. They were beautiful young men, very much in love. Jared said they might get married one day. And I thought that would be just grand. Well-suited to each other, did a nice job with the house, splitting the chores. And who am I to tell someone who they can love? I'm eighty-one and I've loved quite a few in my day who upset the people around me."

Sam smiled. God bless nosy neighbors.

"When was the last time you saw them, ma'am?"

"Eloise, please. Jared ran yesterday morning, but I don't re-member seeing them last night. They usually sit out on the porch at night, have a beer, talk about their day. Oh, how could this have happened? How did they die?"

"I'm sorry, ma'am, I can't discuss any details with you. I need you to come with me, though. You're going to have to talk to the detectives."

Eloise Poe stopped short. "You aren't a detective? Who are you?"

"My name is Dr. Owens, and I'm with the FBI."

"The FBI is here? Oh my."

Yes, Sam thought, *oh my indeed.*

CHAPTER 32

Capitol Hill

SAM PASSED OFF ELOISE POE TO THE UNIFORMS AT THE FRONT DOOR, AND went back inside to find Fletcher. Before she got very far, her cell phone rang.

Baldwin. *Finally.* She ducked off into the white-and-black kitchen, answered with, "I hope you have a whole lot of answers for me, because my list of questions is growing. I've got more dead."

"More dead? Where?"

She filled him in. He cursed once, very gently.

"Baldwin, I can't keep operating in the dark. We need to know what we're dealing with, because this case is getting weirder by the second."

"I know. I'm all yours."

"Then would you like to tell me why Souleyret was killed, and why someone seems to be knocking off people who have connections to her, too?"

"I've had some back-channel conversations since we talked last. You already know Souleyret was tasked with working on incidences of pharmaceutical espionage."

"That's what the file says. Girabaldi seems to feel otherwise. She thinks Amanda was working on a bioterror threat."

"Right. Well, Amanda had a specialized skill set. For lack of a better term, she was a honeypot. She'd get friendly with the people we needed to look at, get into their systems, load up the software that allowed us to take a look at these company's practices."

"I can imagine that would piss some people off. It sounds like she found the source of this threat, and someone realized they'd been taken. And now they're killing everyone around her."

"They're looking for something."

"I know what they're looking for." She told him about the SD card Souleyret had smuggled in and the vaccines they'd found. "We have the vaccination schedules for the whole region. Girabaldi thought the illness outbreak was an isolated incident. The files Amanda has here prove otherwise. They've been testing for a while now. It's scary stuff."

"Is that all you saw on the SD card?"

"All that we'd found as of an hour ago. We have an eager beaver from Quantico at Fletcher's place, looking for Robin Souleyret."

"Daniels, yes, Charlaine told me. He's very good."

"Yes, he is. The SD card was built on a sophisticated cipher, layers of encryptions. He cracked the initial code, but that doesn't mean there isn't more."

Baldwin was quiet.

"Come on, spill. We have no more time for secrets. We've got to find the sister, see if she knows anything and protect her."

"You won't have to protect her," he said.

"So you know where she is?"

"Where? No. Who? Yes. She's a CIA asset. Or was."

"Was CIA? Is she dead?"

"In a way. Listen, Robin works for a guy I know. She's unstable at best."

"Unstable, how?" Sam asked slowly.

"Robin got blown up a couple of years ago. Literally. She never recovered all the way. She was tough as nails, but the PTSD got her. CIA kept her on the payroll, but she hasn't been given real assignments in months. She works for my friend from time to time, on specialty jobs, but she's lost her edge."

"What did she do for them? What was her position? An analyst, a handler?"

"Um, her work was very specific. You know what Xander was used for often in his position with the Rangers? She was, too. That's all I'm willing to say. But she's messed up in the head. She's better left alone."

She knew exactly what Baldwin meant. Xander was an Army Ranger. He could do most anything well, without conscience or remorse, if he was given the order to do so. He'd been through every specialized school the Army had to offer, but he'd especially excelled at sniper school. Long-range hits.

Assassinations.

A cold finger paraded down her spine. Snipers scared her. Face-to-face assaults she could handle, but the idea of someone hundreds of yards away controlling your life genuinely freaked her out. Anytime, anywhere, Xander had told her. *Pow.*

"I see. What does Robin look like?"

"Like Amanda actually. They bear an uncanny resemblance to each other. She's smaller, though, and a natural blonde."

Sam thought of the long blond hair on the banister. About a woman who spent her life evading capture and arrest, who worked for the CIA.

Which led her straight to the meeting at the State Department, and Regina Girabaldi. That's why she was involved—Sam would bet this month's shoe budget the undersecretary knew Robin Souleyret, and had worked with her while she was still at the Agency. It explained the urgency of the meeting this morning. Sam had been right on the money; Girabaldi was closer to this than she let on.

"Did she work for our favorite undersecretary, perchance?"

"Wait," Baldwin said. "Go careful here, that's dangerous ground. Are you asking if I think she might be running this?"

"We know she is. She pulled us in this morning and gave us all sorts of crazy directions to cover all this up. Maybe the sister is more involved than we thought?"

"Involved how?"

"Working with the pharm company, moving information? Maybe she got on the wrong side of things? I don't know, it's silly to think she could kill her own sister. Isn't it? I mean, how messed up was she?"

She heard his breath hiss in. "From all accounts, she was pretty messed up, Sam. I'll get with my counterpart at the CIA, see if I can dig up something more on her. And look at the relationship between Regina and Robin. They were at the Agency at the same time. It stands to reason they know each other."

"I need to talk to her, Baldwin. I need to have a sit-down with Robin. At the very least, to inform her of her sister's death. And to ascertain if she's our suspect."

"I'll find her. Don't you dare go after her alone, you hear me? She's very, very good at her job, and those instincts die hard. If she's threatened, there's no telling what she might do."

"Why do I get the feeling there's a hell of a lot more you're not saying?"

A ghost of a laugh. "Because I only trust these phones so much. I'm done here. I'm catching a flight out this afternoon. I'll be back in D.C. late tonight. I'll come to your place. We can talk."

"All right. Hey, listen. In terms of diseases or vaccinations, have you ever heard of anything called Gransef?"

"Gransef? No. What is it?"

"It was the label on one of the vials we found at Tommy Cattafi's place. I've never heard of it before, and a basic search didn't bring it up. I'm worried it might be…the something new we're looking for. Which is no longer in our possession."

"Shit. I'll look it up, see if I can find anything on my end."

"Thank you. Which reminds me, speaking of Cattafi, do you have any idea how Amanda came to be working with him? Regina said they were friends from way back, but that goes against most everything I've seen about Amanda and the nature of her work."

"Now *that* I can help you with. I talked to Amanda's most recent handler. She recruited Thomas Cattafi a couple of years ago. He was on a rotation with Médecins Sans Frontières. He was perfect material for us. Smart, connected. Had an understanding of the basic nature of the industry. I don't know if he was doing actual work for her, but he was definitely a source, and a paid one—he's on the books. She may have thought he'd be a safer place to head to if she was on the run."

"It was a big mistake. Someone knew she was going to be there. I'm assuming they came here first, looking for her, and when they found the renters instead, they extracted what they could, killed them, either out of frustration or because they could provide an ID, left a note to try to make it look personal and headed straight for Cattafi's place. Which would mean someone's inside your system, Baldwin. I think Amanda's whole world had been hacked. If they knew where she could be found, and who she's recruited…"

"I hear you. It's either someone inside or someone close."

"Do you know when and where she came into the US?"

"No. There's nothing on her main passport, nor any of her provided identities. Though with the nature of her work, I'm sure she has a few legends we don't know about."

"Who knew the FBI was so secretive?"

"Every organization has its secrets, Samantha. Remember

that. And in the meantime? Be very careful. Something feels off about all of this, and I don't want you getting hurt."

She found Fletcher on the second floor, staring mournfully at the crime scene, watching his people collect evidence. He shrugged when he saw her.

"Anything new?" she asked.

"Nope. What about you?"

"I talked to Baldwin. He confirmed Cattafi worked for Souleyret. And we need to find the sister. Right now."

"Why the sudden urgency?"

"She's a CIA assassin. And she's a blonde."

He started. "You don't think she has something to do with this, do you?"

"Apparently, she had a bad go of it with an IED, and it scrambled her head. If she was approached by the wrong people...hey, while I'm cooking up theories, did anyone check exactly who these two work for?"

He checked his notebook. "One works for Marsha Harper, Republican out of Colorado. The other works for Joe Green, Democrat from New Mexico."

"That would make for some interesting dinner conversations. Those two are on the opposite sides of most everything. Where did these kids meet? Here in D.C.?"

"We're going to have to talk to their families and ask. They are both transplants. We're contacting the local authorities to make notifications. Once that's done, we can talk to them. Several hours at least."

"We might be able to take a shortcut. The next-door neighbor was friends with them. She's a sweet old thing—they clearly looked out for her. She's downstairs now."

"Yeah, all right. Nothing more I can do here, anyway. Let's go talk to the neighbor."

They went down the stairs to find Eloise Poe holding court

on the front porch. She was telling stories about her neighbors. Sam could hear her lilting, breathless voice, full of grief and memories.

She introduced Eloise to Fletcher, who pulled the woman from her adoring fans and started peppering her with questions. After he'd established she was close enough to them to know what was really going on in the house, he asked about the renters' backgrounds.

"They met in college. University of Colorado. Jared was the president of the Young Democrats, College Democrats, something like that. I understand it's quite a vocal force out there in Boulder. Michael was the head of the College Republicans. In the minority—he used to laugh about it. They fought like cats that first year, Jared told me once. And when there was some big hullabaloo on campus, they got hauled into the dean's office, and something clicked. They had coffee afterward and started dating. They knew it would be a contentious road with their backgrounds and their preferences, but they fell in love, and they fought for it all the time."

Sam thought about the two young men lying upstairs, their lives cut tragically short.

I'm sorry, I had no choice. It's better this way.

Anyone who knew their backgrounds would assume Michael had broken it off, and Jared couldn't handle it. A good ploy, and it made Sam nervous. Normally, it took time to find out personal information about people, what the push buttons would be. This wasn't hastily arranged.

She thought about Amanda Souleyret, and the note found at her crime scene.

You made me do this.

Something there.

She tuned back in to Mrs. Poe.

"And they moved to D.C., started renting this house. That was—what—four, no, five years ago now. Michael took a job with that pretty woman from his home district, Marsha Harper. She's a firecracker, that one, and he loved working for her. Jared bounced around a bit, but he was working for what's his name, Joe. Joe Green. He's been there for three months or so now. He was out of his probationary period, I do know that. They had us over for dinner to celebrate."

"Mrs. Poe, did you ever meet the owner of the house, Amanda Souleyret?" Fletcher asked.

Eloise waved at a gnat that was dive-bombing her head. "Of course I did. Amanda and I go way back. As a matter of fact, I'm a bit peeved with her. I saw her this morning, but she didn't even say hello. It's been a while since she's been by. She didn't need to babysit her renters, no, no. Those boys, bless their hearts, they were good kids. Quiet, respectful. Hardworking. No loud, crazy parties. They'd dog-sit for us when we went out of town. This is just so horrible, I don't understand how—"

Sam interrupted her. "Wait, Mrs. Poe, you saw Amanda this morning?"

"Well, yes. She's looking thin. She came to the fence and said hi to Tervis, then went in the back door. She wasn't in there long, no more than ten minutes. Came out, got into her car— she has a new car, too, a nice Lexus—then drove off. Didn't even bother to say hi, and it's been at least two years since I saw her last." Her eyes got wide, her mouth opened into a little O.

"You don't think she had anything to do with the boys, do you? Oh my!"

Sam spoke to Fletcher, sotto voce. "The sister. It had to be."

Eloise had sharp hearing. "Oh no, I'm sure it was Amanda. I was upset she didn't stick her head in to say hello."

"Have you ever met Amanda's sister, Robin, Mrs. Poe?"

"No, I haven't. Edgar has, though. Yes, my husband's name is Edgar Poe. Edgar Georgio Poe—his parents had a diabolical sense of humor."

Fletcher was already turning toward the Poes' house. "Ma'am, could we speak to Edgar? Mr. Poe? We need to speak with Amanda's sister right away, and we don't have any contact information for her."

She started trotting after him. "Well, Edgar's not all there, if you know what I mean. Alzheimer's. Bless his heart, he started to go two years ago, and now he only truly recognizes me and the boys, and that's not all the time. We can talk to him, but I can't guarantee you'll find out anything worthwhile. Why don't you just ask Amanda for her sister's information?"

Fletcher stopped and patted the old woman on the shoulder. "I'm sorry to tell you this, Mrs. Poe, but Amanda was killed last night. So you see, it's very important that we speak with your husband right now."

Eloise had done an admirable job of keeping it together, but with one last "Oh my," the tears began to fall down her wrinkled face.

CHAPTER 33

THE POES' HOUSE WAS CLEAN AND NEAT, SET UP ALMOST EXACTLY LIKE THEIR neighboring town house, but crammed cheek-to-jowl full of sixty-plus-odd years of a traveling life. Tchotchkes, antiques, tribal masks, French furniture, Italian paintings, bookshelves full of multicolored spines and squat Zen Buddhas competed for attention from what remained of the pristine ivory walls, which were covered in expertly taken black-and-white photographs. Everything was in its place; order reigned. But it seemed almost as if the whole house was holding its breath. If you moved one thing, the entire effect would be lost, crumbling down around their ears.

Eloise saw them looking, gave them a benevolent smile. "I took the photos. Edgar was in the Army, you know, and we moved all over the world. I needed something to keep me occupied. Even when he retired, we both still had the travel bug, and we weren't blessed with children, so it was always the two of us, off on our adventures."

They followed her into the surprisingly modern and uncluttered kitchen. Tervis the dog heard his master and came barreling in through the dog door. He turned out to be an adorable beagle who promptly sat on Sam's foot, begging for ear rubs.

Eloise poured out a small tot of brandy. "Sometimes Edgar likes a little drink in the afternoon. It seems to help him remember."

They paraded back into the living room and up the stairs. She stopped at the top.

"Let's not tell him about the boys just yet, or Amanda. I don't want him getting upset. I'll tell him later, when I think the time is right."

Fletcher nodded. "Of course."

Eloise led them to a spacious room overlooking the street out front, a den of sorts, a man's space, with flags from various sports teams on the walls, plus more of the unusual detritus from downstairs. The room was completed with two comfortable armchairs and a flat-screen television tuned to Fox News. It was turned down low, but Sam clearly heard the words *assassination attempt at Teterboro this morning.*

Xander should be home by now. She just wanted to see him, hear from his own mouth exactly what had happened. She pushed the thought away; she needed to stay focused.

Edgar Poe was trim and neat, bald as an egg, wearing comfortable slippers, jeans and a blue denim button-down. A set of binoculars sat on the table beside him, and a sweating glass of water. He smiled at Eloise when she came in, gaily singing, "We have visitors, Edgar, isn't that nice? This is Fletcher and this is Samantha. They want to talk about Robin and Amanda. I've brought you a drink to celebrate."

His voice was gravelly, but strong. He rolled his eyes and took the drink from her, setting it next to the binoculars. "Eloise, I may be losing my mind, but I'm not an idiot. I saw the police cars. Did something happen to the boys?"

She deflated immediately, all the air gone from her sails, and her resolve with it. "Oh, Edgar. They're gone. They're both gone."

He got up and folded his plump little wife into his arms,

patting her on the back while she cried. Tears formed in his own eyes, and he gave Fletcher and Sam an apologetic glance. "They're like sons to us. This is terrible. Just terrible. What happened?"

Fletcher sat on the small sofa. "We're not sure, sir." He gestured toward the binoculars, which Sam noticed sat on a book by the Audubon Society. "I notice you're a bird watcher. Did you happen to see anything or anyone out of place over the past few days?"

"I did. There was a car, parked down the street, night before last. Black sedan, like the kind you see in the motorcades. Government, without a doubt. Sat there for three hours, from dark until midnight, which is the reason it caught my eye. Those people come and go around here so often they're as common as a sneeze. But the cars don't linger. Drop-offs and pickups, that's all. No surveillance. And that's what this was."

"License plate?"

He shook his head. "It was facing us. I should have gone out to check on it or called the police. Were they staking out the joint?"

"I don't know, sir. Has anything else caught your attention in the past few days?"

Edgar urged Eloise toward the chair next to him. Sam saw they were just close enough for the occupants to hold hands while they sat, which they proceeded to do. It brought a lump to her throat. She knew how Alzheimer's worked. Forgetfulness was only one part of it. It was the isolation it caused in the mind of the sufferer that was the cruelest aspect.

He shook his head. "I was in Vietnam, you know. And Korea. Saw plenty I couldn't understand, plenty I'd like to forget. Sometimes I just turn it all off so I don't have to think about it. Other times, when my mind is still with me, I think I'd like to go back there. Talk to the families, see what happened to them. Know what I mean?" He grew silent. Tervis came to his daddy's side, whining gently, pushing his head under the gnarled old hand.

Sam glanced at Fletcher. The initial shock of their unfamiliar faces had been enough to startle Edgar Poe to the present, but Sam saw the sharp blue eyes were beginning to lose their focus. Eloise saw it, too, handed him the brandy glass.

"Drink, sweetheart." She gestured for Fletcher to talk quickly.

"Sir, your wife tells me you know Robin Souleyret, the sister of your next-door neighbor, the woman who owns the house, not the renters."

He took a sip of the brandy. "Yes. I remember her. Skinny blonde, good tits."

Eloise smacked him on the arm. "Edgar. Inappropriate."

"What? She did. I'm old, I'm allowed to look."

Fletcher was fighting back a laugh. Sam saw his lips twitch. "When did you meet her, sir?"

"She used to come around about eight, ten years ago. I don't do so well with time. But she'd stop by every once in a while, have a meal. She was government, just like Amanda. Spook, I think. We talked about the war."

"Have you seen her lately?"

"Naw. Haven't seen Amanda, either. You know, we killed a guy once, just plain scared the shit out of him. Hung him up by his thumbs in the forest. You could hear them crack when we yanked on the ropes."

And he drifted off, staring out the window.

Eloise stood, shaking her head. She motioned for them to step out.

Fletcher wasn't quite willing to let it go. "Sir? Mr. Poe?"

But Edgar said nothing, didn't even acknowledge them.

"I'm so sorry," Eloise said. "It's not a good day. He drifts like that, in and out of time. It must be so hard for him, so confusing."

Sam thought that was gracious. It had to be hard for Eloise, too.

They followed her down the stairs, out onto the porch.

Fletcher gave her his card, asked her to call if Edgar thought of anything else that might be of use, and they bid her farewell.

Tervis stayed behind to guard his daddy while he dreamed.

Out in the yard, Fletcher sighed deeply.

"That was a waste of time. Come on. Let's go see if anyone has found Dr. Bromley."

Sam fell into step with him. "I don't think it was a waste. We found out about the car. We can pull the cameras in the area, see if they captured it. Three hours is a long time to sit staring at a town house."

"Whoa, you don't think he was serious, do you?"

"I do. He was quite lucid when we came into the room. Sometimes a new pattern can shock the brain back to normalcy for a moment, almost like an electroshock. Seeing new faces in his own environment, the police cars—it was a change from his norm. It woke him up, so to speak."

"So we're going to rely on the eyewitness testimony of a guy with Alzheimer's who doesn't even know who he is? Sam, you know that's crazy."

"It's not as crazy as you think. He was very clear about what he saw before he drifted out. I think it's a good path to follow."

They got in the car, and he pulled away from the curb, thinking. "All right. Let's ask."

He called Hart, who answered quickly, sounding ragged.

"Boss, you gotta give me more than five minutes to do everything."

"I have something new for your list."

"God, now what?"

"Pull all the cameras from around Souleyret's Capitol Hill address, looking specifically at two nights ago between five and ten. We're looking for a black sedan, possibly government."

"Okay, I'll get Tech on it. By the way, I just got a call from the security company who handles the address in Georgetown, the house with the cameras on the gutters? They've gotten permission from the owners to release the footage to us. I asked them to send it over. You know Naomi Murray, right? Down in Tech? The brunette with legs to forever and gone?"

Fletcher cleared his throat and glanced over at Sam, who was smiling.

"I recall meeting Officer Murray once or twice, yes."

"Didn't you ask her out once?"

"Lonnie. Get on with it."

"Oh, sorry. Apparently, Naomi—Officer Murray—identified a gray Honda Accord on the camera. It circled the block four times, right before Emma and Cameron walked in on the scene. She's got the plates—they've traced to a guy named Toliver Pryce, out in Falls Church."

"Suspect?"

"Witness, I'd say. I thought I'd take a run out there and have a chat with him."

"Be careful, Lonnie. Don't you dare go out there alone. We've got all sorts of crazy shit going down here on the Hill."

"Roger that. I talked to Sophie Lewis—she's the head of the HAZMAT team from Homeland that was at the crime scene in Georgetown this morning. She's the one who handed off the samples to the CDC. She's got a call in to them to find out where the samples are now, and to warn them they may be unsafe."

"How many agencies are in on this now?"

"I don't know, the usual. Four or five at least. Plus the media. The story's all over the place—not that the samples are suspect, but that HAZMAT was on our scene this morning. Turn on WTOP in your car, you can listen in. It hasn't hit fever pitch, but they'll mention it at the top of the hour. If the wrong reporter gets a bee up their nose, we'll be fielding more than moderate interest."

"Great. Just great. So much for keeping things quiet. All right, my man. You keep chugging. Stay in touch."

He hung up, and Sam said, "Let's go back to your place and talk to young Daniels. He's got something for us. And I need a cup of coffee. I'm starting to drag."

Fletcher nodded. "That sounds like a damn good idea. I have a feeling it's going to be a long evening."

CHAPTER 34

GWUH

GEORGE WASHINGTON UNIVERSITY HOSPITAL WAS ON THE CORNER OF NEW Hampshire and I Street, and Robin had no problem walking right in the front doors and making her way through the corridors. Most visitors had to stop and present ID at the front desk, but Robin had pulled a few things out of the trunk of her car in order to make her ingress and potential interview go as smoothly as possible.

A wig made her hair a dirty salt-and-pepper gray; black reading glasses rested on a chain around her neck. She wore wrinkled blue scrubs and a white lab coat with the name M. Preston embroidered in blue over the pocket. She had a stethoscope sticking out of her pocket, carried a clipboard and moved with purpose.

It wasn't hard to gain access to hospitals. With so many people coming and going—friends and family, doctors and nurses, orderlies and techs—pretty much anyone could walk anywhere with impunity. In her doctor's outfit, she blended in seamlessly. GW had nearly nine hundred doctors on staff; she doubted anyone would bat an eye her way. It didn't hurt that she had an old ID from a shooting they'd worked, one she'd carefully lifted off a white coat lying on the back of a chair. Her people had done some work on it, and now it could be used pretty much anywhere with a quick holograph overlay.

Her phone flashed while she was in the elevator—Lola.

The email is from one of Girabaldi's people, message came through address labeled jkruger. There is a Jason Kruger on the rolls. Also checking on David Bromley, who was working with Cattafi. TC is in ICU, room 454.

Interesting. So it was one of Girabaldi's people trying to touch base with Mandy. With State this involved, Robin was going to have to move carefully and quickly before they decided to track her down and make her life miserable.

Get me everything you can on Kruger. STAT.

She sent the message, then destroyed the thread entirely. Damn it, what was Mandy up to? What was she trying to get "in"?

The elevator let her out on the fourth floor, and she found the ICU with no problem. A regular room would have been easier—there was less scrutiny—but she had enough of the lingo down from her own time in ICU that she was sure she could brazen it out.

She was lucky; they were in the midst of a shift change, and she strolled right past the nurses' station unnoticed. There was a guard outside Cattafi's door, and she nodded magnanimously at him, rattling her clipboard.

The cop, young, nervous, probably his first real assignment, smiled and held up a hand.

"ID?"

So predictable. She handed it over, reached for a pair of gloves.

He took great pains to write down the name and handed back the ID. "Dr. Margaret Preston. Got it."

"Thank you." She pushed past him into the room. She'd learned the less you said, the better. Act like you're supposed to be there, and you're bored with the procedures in place, and the world opened.

Robin avoided the window into the room, took in the boy on the bed. A dirty white haze struggled around his body, trying, and failing, to get in. Alone, broken, clinging to life. The last person to be with her sister.

They'd trached him, the air tube rising out of his throat like a triton from the sea. His face was waxy and pale, his eyes taped closed. Arterial ports ran plasma and medicines; the ventilator hissed with obscene regularity. A quiet but steady beeping came from the heart and pulse ox monitor; the volume had been turned down. Alarms would blare if there was a problem.

This was a waste of time. There'd be no talking to him; he was clearly not going to wake anytime soon. Whether he was in an induced coma or landed himself there naturally, she wasn't going to get anything from him in this state.

She crossed the room carefully, touched his hand. The flesh was slack, inert, cold. As the unhappy mist that clung stubbornly to him indicated, Tommy Cattafi was, for all practical purposes, dead.

A wave of grief passed through her. This man had a connection to her sister. He knew something, knew why she'd been killed. And who'd done it.

She gritted her teeth against the scream that rose in her throat, fury at the senseless deaths.

The young cop at the door looked at her searchingly as she came out. She shook her head, an indication that things hadn't changed and she didn't think they would. He nodded in return, a brief frown crossing his face, but workmanlike, understanding. Maybe not so young and inexperienced, after all, she thought. He'd seen enough death to know when it was staring him in the face.

To the elevator, ignoring a look from the charge nurse, though her heart sped up a little, just a teensy shot of adrenaline. As the doors began to close, she heard an alarm begin to go off, saw nurses start rushing down the hall. Someone called a code blue.

It couldn't be. Could it?

She needed to get out, now.

The elevator was fast, not stopping on its descent, and she was whisked back downstairs, made her way out the door and walked calmly back to her car. She'd been careful not to park near the hospital cameras, taking a spot on the street instead of in the garage across from the hospital. But she grabbed a cab, just in case, had him drop her three blocks away with a five-dollar tip for the short fare, walked a block and ducked into a Starbucks to change. In two minutes flat she was hoofing it back to her car as a flowing Victoria's Secret–haired brunette version of herself, in glamorous sunglasses, skinny jeans and knee-high boots.

She didn't think the precautions were absolutely necessary, but old habits died hard.

Now, she had to figure out what to do about Girabaldi.

Her instincts told her to keep gathering information. Going in with all chambers loaded was the only way to approach her old boss. She'd worked with the woman long enough to know she wouldn't admit a damn thing, so Robin needed proof, and lots of it, to force her to talk.

Because torturing her old boss for information felt wrong.

Bromley was the logical choice to talk to next, especially since she was so close to his office. But she itched to march into State and demand answers from Regina Girabaldi. They'd have words today, no matter what.

She texted Lola.

TC pointless, he's permanently out of commission. I'm going to Bromley next.

Lola hit her right back.

Be prepared for security.

OK.

Also, overheard Metro. They've been up on the Hill, found the bodies. IDK details. Running call through our system.

Well, hellfire. They were moving quicker than she expected. She needed to get a move on.

Exact coordinates for DB?

Lola sent her the address in latitude and longitude, which, on their personalized phone system, kept encryption codes better than street addresses. She was even closer than she'd realized; it would only take a couple of minutes walking. She set off, keeping an eye out for tails.

The rain was past, the city smelled fresh and clean. She hadn't been to this part of town in a while. It had changed, ever so slightly, in the way people age, a sudden shock at the sparse gray hair and expanded waist and wrinkles, then in a blink, the person you knew was back. Foggy Bottom would always be the same, regardless of the slight alterations to the veneer.

Her ears pricked. Something else that would never change in this city—the constant underlying wail of sirens.

She stretched her legs, hurrying. She wasn't doing anything wrong, but evading detection was ingrained in her DNA, so she wanted to get off the radar, off the streets, as quickly as humanly possible.

She was less than a block away now. A cop car came barreling down the street and she casually stopped and turned toward the building on her right, adjusted her sunglasses, reached into her bag like she was looking for something. The patrol kept moving, turning onto Twenty-third with a screech, and she resumed her walk.

Bromley's lab was on H Street, just around the corner from the hospital. She entered the building, noting the security cameras in the corners, and even though she'd been warned, stopped short when she saw the security desk and metal detector.

Damn it. You could have warned me what kind of security, Lola.

She wasn't going to be able to parade in here without some sort of story. She counted four guards behind the desk, a number of screens with clear shots of the building.

There was a building directory to her right. She glanced at it surreptitiously as she walked past, and breathed a sigh of relief. There was an OB/GYN office on the sixth floor. She noted one of the doctor's names—Thornburg—then marched to the visitor's log, wrote a fake name, inverting the names of the people before her, and Thornburg's suite number, then got in line for the metal detector, mentally running through her current state and the odds of making it through undetected—namely, the Glock under her left arm, the knife in her bag and the variety of weapons she always carried on her person. She and metal detectors were not friends.

Three people in front of her, two now. Only one thing to do.

In her purse, she had a mini-EMP—one of her own design, perfect for just these situations. Meant to work in a five-foot radius, the electromagnetic pulse was relatively simple technology, and had saved her ass more than once. As she dumped the bag on the conveyer, she discreetly hit the button, then smoothly withdrew her hand and, under the guise of undoing her belt, dropped the mini-EMP down the front of her pants.

Without so much as a squawk, the entire apparatus around her ground to a halt.

"What the hell?" the guard nearest her muttered. "This damn thing is going down again?"

"That's twice this week," the man next to him said. "Piece of crap."

There was luck. Of course, these devices were notorious for malfunctioning; she'd just played into that knowledge. They started to mess with the controls, turning the machine off, then on again, to no avail. The line of people coming into the building began to grow. After a few moments, a man behind her shouted, "Hey, I gotta get upstairs, I got an appointment."

More security guards poured out from behind the desk and a back room, messed with the mechanism of the metal detector, tried to get it working. After a few minutes, when it was clear they weren't in for an easy fix, they started waving people through, doing a brief visual scan in purses and gentle pat downs.

So, not that serious about their security, she thought as the man gave her buttocks a squeeze but neglected to reach under her arms. Good thing, too. She wanted to stay under the radar, and taking hostages and fighting her way in wasn't the way to go. She could have turned and left, but that would have drawn more attention than she'd like.

Another quick pat on the rear, and she was in.

And she was on her own. She needed a new phone. Hers had been wiped by the EMP, as had the ones around her, which meant her spare was shot, too. But that could wait until she had a look around Bromley's offices. She had to hurry, though. There was nothing she could do if someone figured out she'd been the source of the EMP, and the cops would show up here soon enough, especially if they'd already connected the two men from Mandy's town house to the murder.

She went to the sixth floor, walked past the OB/GYN offices and into the stairwell. Down two flights, fast, boots rattling on the stairs, to the fourth floor.

The door was plain, nothing inviting about it. And locked. Not a problem. She slipped a tensioner into the lock, wiggled the twist flex into place…and the lock popped. It took ten seconds. She was rusty.

The lights were off, so she didn't touch them, just pulled a small penlight from her bag and hurried into the gloom. The place was empty. She gave that a passing thought, wondering why. Lola said this was a private lab, but she'd expected at least one or two more people. Maybe he did his work completely alone? No, he'd worked with Cattafi. Surely there were other people around; the suite itself had several doors and the hallway angled off into another section of the floor. But it wasn't big enough to house much, which seemed odd to her. Maybe these were administrative offices, and the real lab work was done elsewhere. There simply weren't enough precautions in place here.

She prowled around, looking at the setup, confident she was right. This wasn't the real lab; this was for show-and-tell. Probably for investors and others Bromley would need to impress to fund his work.

Still, the silence was eerie, and she drew her weapon.

She found Bromley in the third room, off a small lab, slumped against a gray metal filing cabinet. Very dead. A neat job of it, too. Close range, shot through the right temple, the bullet spoiling what she assumed was his magnificent brain. She took another step closer. The gun, a .9 mm subcompact Smith & Wesson, was in his right hand, his arms sprawled out carelessly against the floor.

He'd killed himself.

She touched his neck briefly; his skin was pliant, his muscles loose and slack. He was completely out of rigor—and he was fully dressed. She couldn't check the lividity without disturbing the body, but the blood and matter on the cabinet and wall behind him told enough of the story. He'd been shot here. Not moved.

She was beginning to see a pattern. People around her sister were being systematically killed, and every one of them was supposed to look like a suicide. And more importantly, it looked like the kids on the Hill and the doctor had been taken out *before* Amanda was murdered.

She looked around, moving quickly, until she found the note.

Do I have your attention yet?

Jesus.

They'd been driving Amanda. She must have been on the run, and she must have holed up with Cattafi. A mistake that had cost her her life. But where else would she have gone?

To me. She could have come to me.

Robin pushed the thought away. It was too late for regrets.

Three different MOs—poison, shooting, stabbing—told Robin there was more than one killer out there. Multiple killers, with multiple targets, and all with a message. But who were the messages meant for? And what the hell had they been searching for? Had they found it when they found Amanda? Was she the end of the deaths?

With a sigh, Robin went into the small lab itself. It hadn't been ransacked, but there were clear signs someone had done a thorough search. She knew enough scientists to know they weren't all neat, but Bromley was. Everything had a place, and by the dust patterns, she could see what was missing. A computer for sure; there was a wireless mouse sitting alone on the right of the desk. The filing cabinet drawers were askew; on closer inspection, there was a large chunk of files missing from the well-organized G–I drawer.

So they were looking for something specific.

And now there were four dead that she knew of, one clinging to life. Who knew how many others?

The email came back to her: Did you get it in?

No response from Amanda. There wouldn't have been; she was already dead. And whoever killed her had called Robin's number.

Her sister had pissed someone off, and they were making sure there were no threads left behind. Which meant Robin needed to be a little more careful.

She searched the drawers, found nothing else of use. She wished she could use the phone, call Lola, but that would be an idiotic move. It would be traced, and then she'd be screwed.

She glanced out the window. The sun had finally broken out; there was a fine mist of condensation on the glass. It was time to start crunching data, see what they could come up with. Someone was following a rather clear path. Robin just needed to find out what path that was.

She turned to leave and walked into the barrel of a gun.

CHAPTER 35

Falls Church, Virginia

BEAUTY WAS WATCHING TELEVISION WHEN HE HEARD THE CAR. THERE HAD been little traffic since he moved in, one of the reasons he'd chosen this place. He went on alert, strode to the window. It was a cop. He wasn't in uniform—a detective, then—but there was no mistaking the demeanor. Cocky, arrogant, owned the world. He was a big meaty one, too, with arms the size of tree trunks and thick legs straining against his dark pants.

The cop took off his sunglasses and glanced toward the house. His hair was cut short and tight across his skull, his mouth was cruel. He held a red folder in his hands. Another patrol car slid up behind the unmarked, and two more cops got out. As they conferred among themselves, he felt the panic begin to rise.

Oh, God. They'd found him, already. He thought he'd have more time. He thought so many things.

The gun was in the cookie cabinet above the refrigerator. It was a nothing piece, one he'd picked up in Little Rock, a pearl-handled .22. It would do the job, though, if he positioned it in the right place. Just to the inside corner of his right eye, angled in twenty-five degrees. That should do it. He wasn't going to go back to jail yet. Not until he was damn good and ready, too old to lift a knife or get it up without pills.

He was breathing heavily; the very idea of this being *it* had frozen him in place. He had a plan. He wanted last meals and priests and television cameras and families surrounding him at the end. But it was too soon; he wasn't finished. He had so much more to do.

A deep breath shook him, and rational thought returned.

Would they send a lone detective to arrest him? One that would let himself be seen? No. If they had any idea, they'd have sent their SWAT team. Maybe this wasn't what he thought. Maybe they wanted something else.

There was a knock at the door. He propelled himself into motion, jumped across the room, grabbed the gun from its hiding place, stuck it in the waistband of his jeans, in the small of his back, where he could feel the metal growing hot and slick against his skin.

The knocking sounded again.

Breathe, cher. *Breathe.*

He turned up the burner under the potpourri on the stove, making sure the scent of cinnamon and apples was strong, then went to the door and opened it.

"Yes?"

The cop looked surprised. Most people did upon meeting him. The blessing and the curse that gave him his true name. He stifled a giggle. He did so love to see first reactions.

The cop's voice was deep, mellifluous. He'd have done well with voice-over work. "Good afternoon. I'm looking for Mr. Toliver Pryce."

"Yes, that's me. Is there a problem, Officer?"

The cop handed him a card. "I'm Detective Hart, with Metro D.C. homicide. You own a gray Honda Accord, is that correct?"

"Yes. But as far as I know, it hasn't killed anyone." Clever boy. Be amusing, disarming. Smile that perfect smile.

The cop had dropped eye contact now, was looking past Beauty's body, trying to see inside. "Ha-ha. That's pretty funny. Can I come in, Mr. Pryce?"

Beauty simply did not know what to do. If they wanted to search the house, he was screwed. The cop wasn't putting off any vibes, but that didn't mean he didn't know. No, he didn't. Beauty was safe. Of course he was. So careful, always so very careful.

He wanted to dance a little jig, but stopped himself. He must act accordingly.

"Goodness, forgive me. Of course. Please, come in." He opened the door farther, gestured for the cop to come in. "Can I get you a drink?" *And pour Drano in it so you'll turn into a choking mass of blue on my living room floor?*

Now, now. No need to get aggressive, cher.

"Thank you," Hart said.

He got the cop situated on the couch, handed him a glass of water. "So, how can I help you, Detective? My car was being naughty, I take it?"

"You were in Georgetown yesterday." It wasn't a question.

Go careful. Maybe they do know something. "Mmm-hmm?"

"Can I ask what you were doing?"

"In Georgetown? Nothing terribly exciting, I'm afraid. I was having dinner. A little place called the Tombs. Have you been there? I've always loved the food, the atmosphere—" he leaned forward, conspiratorially, winked "—the coeds."

Detective Hart didn't look surprised. "Girl watching? Aren't the college girls too young for you?"

"Not at all. What's the rule—half your age plus seven? They're well within the bounds. Well, the freshmen might be a little young. Now, tell me. What is this all about?"

"Did you go straight home after dinner, Mr. Pryce, or did you go elsewhere?"

Beauty gave him a frank look.

"Not…exactly. I met…a friend." He made an unmistakably lewd gesture with his hands, and the cop caught on.

"I see. I'm not here to make trouble for you, Mr. Pryce. What you did or didn't do was your own affair, though I'd advise you to be careful. We do run stings, and it can be very embarrassing for those men caught with the wrong sort of girl."

"I understand. Thank you for letting me know. I'd hate to get anyone in trouble."

"Noted. You drove past a crime scene at approximately twelve-thirty this morning. We were hoping you might have seen something."

"I did? How gruesome. Where was it?"

"On O Street. Almost to Wisconsin. If you were coming from the Tombs, heading out here to Falls Church, I'd expect you to go a different route."

"And yet, I've just made it clear I wasn't headed home after dinner. On the contrary, I drove down to the Mall, parked and took a moonlight stroll. I certainly don't recall seeing anything out of the ordinary on the drive. Can you be more specific— what might I have seen?"

Detective Hart smiled. He had cold eyes, Beauty thought, cold and shrewd. They belied his demeanor, and his physique.

"Can't tell you that, sir. I don't want to taint your testimony, should it come to a trial. Just take a moment, think about what you saw when you left the restaurant. People on the street, cars, sounds. Anything might help."

Beauty closed his eyes, envisioning the drive. He hadn't ex-actly been coming from the Tombs. Rather, he had, but he'd circled the block four times, watching until the light went off in the little wren's house.

His eyes popped open. "How did you know I was there?"

The cop smiled. "Cameras. All over the streets down there. Gotta keep the coeds safe."

So they knew he'd been around the block a few times, damn them. Lying wasn't an option.

"I'm sorry, Detective. I can't remember anything out of place. It was dark, I'd had a drink. I was…looking to hang out with someone. I didn't see anything of interest, if you will, in Georgetown. Which is why I headed farther into the city, in hopes of finding something a bit more to my liking."

"What about the ordinary? It was late, but were there people about? Any neighbors walking their dogs, any people at all?"

Give him something and get him the hell out of here.

He'd seen quite a bit that night, watching, but he didn't think the cop would appreciate those details. He turned inward, mentally replayed his loops around the neighborhood. It truly had been quiet, with few people around. "I saw a woman jogging, and two young girls—they looked like they were still in high school—standing on the corner of N and Wisconsin. Other than that, I'm afraid I can't help you."

"Which direction was the jogger going?"

"Toward M Street. She had reflective clothing on, she was easy to see. I didn't notice a face."

He gave his most charming smile and flexed the business card in his hand. He'd been gripping it so tightly his knuckle popped. "If I think of anything else that seemed out of place, I will absolutely give you a call."

Detective Hart nodded and stood. "Thank you, Mr. Pryce. I appreciate you being honest with me about what you were doing. It helps explain why you drove past the crime scene so many times that night."

Beauty gave him a thin smile. "Yes, well. World's oldest profession."

"Indeed." Hart didn't offer to shake hands, and Beauty was glad; his own was as wet as if he'd poured the glass of water over it. "Well, anything that comes to you, sir, please let me know. I'll see myself out."

Beauty watched him go, latched the door behind him. Moved quickly to the window, waited for the damn man to drive away and his minions to follow. Ran cold fingers along the gun at his back. So glad. So glad he hadn't overreacted.

But now he had to move, and move fast. The cop hadn't believed him. And he couldn't run the risk of anyone finding out what he was really doing.

It was time to move on.

The bedroom was small, the closet claustrophobic. He opened the door to see the real Toliver Pryce—a decent-looking man under normal circumstances, not quite as handsome as Beauty, but close enough to trick the cop—staring at him, his eyes wide, pleading, the gag in his mouth cutting into the soft flesh in the corners, his teeth comically bared.

"What shall we do with you, my friend?" Beauty murmured.

Pryce moaned against the gag, thrashed a bit. It didn't last long. He was tiring. He'd been in the closet for nearly two days now with no food or water. Beauty could just leave him there and he'd probably pass in another day or two, but he didn't think he could take the chance.

"No, I'm sorry. I can't let you go. I'm afraid it's time for you to meet your Maker." He flourished the gun, and pulled a knife out of a sheath that was secreted inside his pants. "Which shall it be? A bullet or the blade?"

Pryce became hysterical.

In the end, the blade was necessary. Beauty was careful not to splash blood on himself. When it was done, he stripped off his clothes and gloves while Pryce bled to death on his closet floor.

The adrenaline, the rush, the pure, unadulterated joy he derived from the fear on Pryce's face, would last him for weeks. He hoped. Freshly dressed, packed and ready to move on, Beauty picked up the phone with shaking hands. It took two tries to dial the number.

A thin voice answered. "US Marshal's office. How may I direct your call?"

"Extension 467 please."

A click, then a hearty, "Hello, Sauger here."

Beauty breathed a sigh of relief; he'd caught him in the office. Good. They could make things happen immediately. They'd done it before.

"Edward? Long time no talk."

"You son of a bitch. Where the fuck are you?"

"Now, now. There's no reason to resort to vulgarities. I had some business to attend to. Unfortunately, in the course of said business, I happened to come across the radar of a police detective in Washington, D.C."

"No reason? You dropped off the radar four months ago, you perverted little shit. After all I did to get you relocated to Arizona, fulfill all your bizarre requests, and you go AWOL on me? Damn right I'm going to call you names. You nearly cost me my job."

"Well, I am sorry, Edward dear. It was unavoidable."

"My ass it was. And now you're in trouble and you're asking me to get you back in the program?"

"I knew you'd be happy to hear from me," Beauty purred.

There was a heavy sigh from the other side of the call. "This is the last time. You understand? You disappear on me again and I'll let them have you."

CHAPTER 36

Georgetown

XANDER WOKE JAMES DENON WITH A NUDGE OF HIS BOOT TO THE MAN'S LEG.
He'd been sleeping like the dead on the couch, an arm thrown
over his face to block out the light. Only an innocent man could
sleep in the midst of such chaos. Or a guilty one, confident he
wasn't going to be caught.

Denon sat up and yawned. "What time is it?"

"Nearly five. You've been asleep for a couple of hours, and
the natives are getting restless." He pointed at Denon's people,
all sitting around the dining room table with laptops and cell
phones out, so absorbed in their work they didn't notice the
boss was awake.

"Didn't sleep last night." He spied the sandwich on the plate,
reached for it. "Thanks. I'm starving."

"Tell me about Juliet Bouchard."

Denon's hand paused, the sandwich halfway to his mouth.
He set it gently back onto the plate.

"Where did you get that name?"

Xander didn't budge. His face was hard, a look that would
make most men shake in their boots. His First Sergeant face.

Denon was susceptible. He looked at the floor and shifted uncomfortably. "She didn't have anything to do with this."

"How can you be so sure? She came to the States with you. She was on the plane's inbound manifest out of London. I have video of her getting off the jet at Teterboro. And then she just ups and disappears, and you nearly get shot? Too much of a coincidence for me."

Denon shook his head vehemently. Heedles noticed her boss was awake, started to rise from the table. Denon held up a hand, and she subsided back into the chair, looking worried. He spoke quietly, ducking his head. "Juliet's a friend. I gave her a ride. That's all."

"Where is she now?"

"I don't know."

"We need to find her." Xander nodded toward Denon's phone. "Why don't we give her a call, see where she is."

"I'm telling you, she's got nothing to do with this. I know her. You have to believe me." He was already speed-dialing a number.

He put the phone to his ear. Xander could hear the ringing, then voice mail pick up. "Call me," Denon said, then disconnected with a frown.

"That's odd. She usually answers whenever I call."

Xander changed tactics. "How well do you know this woman? What's her role in your organization?"

"I know her quite well, and she doesn't work for me." He crossed his arms and sat back against the white leather, clearly finished talking about the woman. But Xander wasn't deterred.

"Mr. Denon, let me tell you what I've found out about Juliet Bouchard. She's a French national. She came to the United States on your plane. She currently works for a company called BARE in Paris. She's got a degree in microbiology and worked at the Sorbonne and the Pasteur Institute."

"Yes?"

"And she died in 1942. So you can see why this raises my suspicions."

Denon squinted at him, tapped his fingers against his jaw.

"That's not possible. Juliet—"

"Sir. I can't protect you if you don't tell me everything that's going on. Chalk's in there ready to blow this woman up. If she's a friendly, you're going to have to prove it, and fast."

He put up his hands. "Don't. Don't. She *is* a friendly. We've been dating, okay? She's my girlfriend."

Xander glanced at Denon's thick gold wedding ring. "Your mistress, you mean. I take it Mrs. Denon doesn't know about it?"

"Mrs. Denon wouldn't care a whit, so long as her accounts are paid at the end of the month. We've had an *understanding* for a very long time. She does her thing, I do mine. We're discreet about it, very discreet. This is the sort of thing that brings down CEOs."

Xander crossed his arms on his chest. "Why don't you just get divorced?"

"Because I don't particularly want to be married to anyone else. This arrangement is beneficial to us both. My wife and I have been great friends for a very long time. We do things together. Events, parties, holidays. We have children, though they're grown now. We just don't have sex anymore. At least, not with each other. Divorce isn't necessary."

"And Juliet? The latest in a string of casual encounters, or someone special?"

"Very special. We've been exclusive for months now. She likes the arrangement, as well. It suits her needs. She's very busy, and doesn't have time to cater to a man any more than I do another wife."

"Where did you meet?"

Denon looked to his team, typing away, industriously keeping his company running through the air. He met Xander's eyes.

"Come now, my boy. Is this really necessary? This is my private life we're talking about."

Xander's smile was grim. "It is absolutely necessary. You've managed to keep something very personal under the radar, Mr. Denon. It makes me wonder what other secrets you're keeping."

"There are no other secrets. This is my great shame." He laughed, not pleasantly. "My wife's family is exceptionally rich. I need the funds to keep things running. It's as simple as that."

"Where did you meet Bouchard?"

Denon sighed heavily. "In Paris, June, last year. I was speaking at a conference, she was an attendee. She approached me after my speech, offered to buy me a drink. One thing led to another. I got a leg over, and she seemed not to mind too terribly much. We met up regularly after that."

"She's much younger."

The mischievous schoolboy was back. "Aren't they always?"

"Where is she now?"

"She had some sort of conference to attend in New York. I gave her a ride across the pond. She's finding her own way home."

"Does your staff know?"

"Only my secretary. And she's been with me longer than my wife."

"How did you explain her presence on the plane?"

"They all know Juliet is a colleague. It isn't unheard of for me to give colleagues rides."

Xander nearly groaned aloud. Why was it men never thought people knew about their affairs?

"Are we through?" Denon asked. "I need to check in with the office. I'm sure they're going mad by now."

Xander wanted to believe him. He liked the man, damn it. But his respect had dropped a few notches, and while the story rang true, Xander wasn't a fool. Something was up.

"One last thing. Why is she traveling under a fake name?"

Denon's eyes grew cold. "You're sure about this? Juliet Bouchard isn't her real name?"

"Absolutely. It wouldn't be readily apparent, but Chalk and I are very good at what we do. I'm certain it's an assumed identity. All the info she's using is attached to the woman who died in 1942." He paused for a moment. "I have to ask. Why didn't you have a background check run on her?"

Denon was troubled. Xander could see the far-off look in his eyes as he tried to rationalize what was happening. "I did, God help me. Apparently, my people missed it. Which is why, as I'm sure you can understand, I am bloody well going to fire everyone who worked on it." This anger was real, and the flare of it made Xander remember who, exactly, he was dealing with. James Denon was a very powerful man, and he could make or break Xander and Chalk at will. He needed to step carefully.

"We're looking into your staff right now, trying to see if anyone has a grudge or has been contacted by an outside group. And we're looking at everyone you met with while you were here in the States. But a mistress using a fake name is a good jumping-off point." He stood, shook Denon's hand. "I'm sorry to ruin your day. Hold off getting in touch with Juliet again for the moment. Let us see if we can find out more."

"I want to know everything you have the moment you have it."

"We're working from the kitchen. We won't be far."

He turned to leave, but Denon said, "Wait. What about the man who tried to kill me this morning?"

Xander shrugged. "We don't know much more than we did earlier—he's a Spanish national, a known assassin, very good at his job. We're trying to get into his private accounts and see where the money trail originated. That's the problem, Mr. Denon. We can't find any records of anyone putting a contract out on you personally. So we're operating under two theories. One, that someone inside your staff was the target, or two, someone inside your staff arranged for this so far off-book even we can't find a trace. But now we have another wrinkle."

"Juliet?"

"You've been dating a woman who's using a false identity. We need to find out who she really is, who she really works for and why she's targeted you."

Denon stood suddenly. There were more glances from the dining room table. "You can't think that. It's impossible. She loves me, and I love her," he whispered harshly.

Xander was several inches taller, and Denon had to look up when he spoke.

"Sir, I understand you have feelings for this woman. I will tread carefully. But everything is pointing in her direction. What kind of access has she had?"

"To what?"

"Your personal devices. Your laptop, your phone, your desktop at work."

He sank back onto the couch, head in his hands. "All of them. She's had access to all of them. I trusted her with everything. She was the one who suggested I work with you, for Chrissake."

"She did?"

"Said you were excellent, that you were trustworthy and capable. I was leery of hiring a new firm, untried, but she said you were the best. She was bloody well right, too. I'm still breathing."

"I wonder how she knew us."

"I've been wondering the same thing."

"Did she have contact with anyone else on your staff?"

He thought about it for a moment. "Only Lois, my secretary. No one else knows her personally that I'm aware of. Our world is a small one in London. Good Jesus in heaven, what have I done?"

"I may be off base, but I think we're onto something here.

What I need you to do is have the people you absolutely believe in look into your systems. See if they can find any anomalies."

Denon ran a hand across the schoolboy face. "What sort of anomalies are we looking for?"

"Money moving around to places it shouldn't, unauthorized accesses, anything that might tell us if someone's been inside your company's systems. Do you have a good IT person?"

"One of the best. And he's sitting at the table over there. Everson's been with me for several years. I trust him thoroughly."

"Good. When we're finished, I'll get him started looking for code anomalies, fake server proxies, anything that might indicate an outsider has built a back door into your system. What about the rest of your team? Any grievances, poor performance reports, firings? Who might be a problem for you?"

"I'll contact human resources, see if anyone's been fired recently. I can't think of another way to start looking at people outside of hire dates, and working backward." He glanced down at the coffee table. "I've been a fool."

"I wouldn't say that, sir. But we'll keep going at Bouchard from this end. Between the two of us, we may be able to find out what she's been up to. You should get Everson started on your files. I'm happy to help him."

"You really think Juliet, whatever her real name is, is up to something?"

"I do. And I'm afraid you may have been compromised along with your company."

"Bloody hell. Bloody fucking hell."

That about summed it up, Xander thought.

CHAPTER 37

Fletcher's house

MARCOS DANIELS MET THEM AT THE DOOR, SHIVERING IN EXCITEMENT. SAM was further reminded of an eager puppy, wanting to please, happy to see them home. She used to play a game with the twins, trying to match people to their canine counterparts. It was a teaching tool, giving them a way to learn different breeds. The moment Matthew and Madeline had figured out what *d-o-g* actually correlated to, they were obsessed, in the way only little ones could be. They'd both been wildly creative, precocious, able to pull breeds she'd never heard of from their tiny brains, enhanced with a book she'd bought them from the American Kennel Club.

What breed would Daniels be, if he were a dog? Loyal, smart, eager. Short-haired, clean, quiet unless agitated. Quick and lethal if necessary, she was sure of it; he wouldn't be assigned to Baldwin's unit if he wasn't very capable. A Doberman, then. Yes, looking closer, she could see it, a darkness inside him that would only be unleashed in the most dire of circumstances.

Her rumination was quickly interrupted by the Doberman himself. "I found Robin Souleyret. She has a carriage house out in McLean, lives on the estate of a couple of French diplomats. We have a BOLO out on the Lexus your witness saw this morning. It's registered to her, at this address in McLean. I've sent a car to start surveillance on the house, subtly, of course. From what I've been able to uncover, she'd pick up a tail a mile away. She's got a pretty impressive CV. Been all over the world, and most of it's redacted."

"Baldwin told me she was CIA black ops. How much did you actually find?" Sam asked.

Daniels grinned. "More than they'd want me to. Remember, I can work a little magic with the computer."

Sam grinned back at him, then shook her finger with mock sternness. "Agent Daniels, tell me you didn't hack the CIA databases."

"Oh no, ma'am. That would be illegal. I walked in through the front door and asked politely."

She clapped him on the shoulder. She was liking Daniels more and more. "Good job. What else did you find?"

"Souleyret was badly injured when the Humvee she was traveling in ran over an IED, north of Kirkuk. They were on a secret mission, traveling dark, with satellite guides, and someone screwed up royally, sent them off the road to hide from an oncoming patrol in exactly the wrong place. She pulled three men from the vehicle, saved their lives, got a big commendation for it, too. But she had to retire from field work. She had a pretty severe head injury which DQ'd her from active duty. Once she got out of the hospital, they sent her back to Langley, doing analyst work. She was bored, by all accounts, and difficult to work with. They blamed it on the head injury, but there were rumors—there always are—that she was aggressive and uncontrollable. They booted her, put her on administrative leave."

Sam looked at Fletcher. "We need to be looking at Robin closer."

"She could have been helping Amanda off book, for sure," he replied. "Good job, Daniels."

Fletcher started toward the kitchen, and Daniels grabbed his arm. "Um, before you go in there, a heads-up. Your friend is here."

"Jordan? She's back in town early." A smile lit his face, one that made Sam warm up inside. He really did dig the FBI agent he'd been dating.

"No, it's your other friend. The one you called to help. She said her name was Mouse."

"Ah, Rosie." Then he eyed Daniels. "What exactly is Freedom Mouse *doing* in my kitchen, Marcos?"

Daniels had the decency to look abashed. "If it won't piss you off, she's been dissecting the SD card. If it will piss you off, she's been cleaning up the lunch dishes."

Fletcher looked torn for a minute, and Sam knew he was thinking Mouse was yet another person to keep quiet. There was no way for them to manage a cover-up that had spread through so many people. At this point, she didn't give a whit what Regina Girabaldi wanted. This story was too big to contain, and doing so was hurting their chances of finding the killer.

"Don't worry, Daniels," Sam said. "I think Fletcher's level of aggravation will be in direct proportion to what, exactly, Mouse has found. Let's go see, shall we?"

The girl sitting at Fletcher's table was the furthest thing from a Mouse as Sam had ever seen, but she supposed that was the whole point of having an alias—you chose something to disguise yourself. Mouse's right arm was a sleeve of colorful tattoos that ended sharply at her wrist. Though she was clearly young, her dark honey-blond hair was streaked with silver. Whether it was natural or purposeful, its effect was stunning. She had a pierced septum, and she wasn't wearing a bra; her nipples were pierced, as well. Sam could see the outline of small barbells through the girl's thin shirt.

Mouse saw Fletcher, smiled widely and put up two fingers in a peace sign. "I come bearing good news."

"You better," Fletcher growled at her, but Sam could tell he was too interested to see what she'd found to be truly angry at Daniels's slipup.

"Good to see you, too, Lieutenant." She glanced at Sam, one eyebrow hiked.

Sam nodded in greeting. "Dr. Samantha Owens. FBI."

"Fletcher told me you were a professor at Georgetown."

"Normally I am. I'm an FBI consultant, too."

"Do you know anything about my world, Doc? What it is that I do?"

"A bit. Not enough to follow if you're going to talk hacker, though."

She smiled. The top teeth were perfect, gleaming white, but the bottom were crowded, the canines at an odd angle. More imperfections that looked utterly right on this mercurial girl.

"All right, then. When Marcos decoded the SD card, he only skimmed the top layer. There's a second level of encryption inside the card. Really advanced stuff, theoretical, even, if you want me to be honest. This card can take down the entire network of a company with a clean keystroke. It's a weapon, plain and simple. And if the wrong person gets their hands on it, someone's going to end up having a very bad day."

"In English, Mouse, for the old folks. Please," Fletcher said.

She nodded patiently. Genius she might be, but she was used to having to make herself clear. "You've heard of server proxies? It's what keeps a website secure, allows them to move and store people's private information. Some hackers sell proxies to the highest bidder. I'm talking millions of dollars changing hands. There's code on this card that will take down a website's secure proxy, and allow the hacker access to all the financial data stored in the servers."

"What would Amanda Souleyret be doing with this? Or what did she want it for? Is there any indication?" Fletcher asked.

Mouse took a gulp of her soda, her eyes never leaving Fletcher's. "To be honest, I'd assume she needed to get into a really secure database and steal something."

Sam nodded. "That makes sense. That's what her job was. Getting secrets out of databases. And the program worked, right? She was able to get the vaccination schedules, and the proof of the superbug..." She stopped. Mouse wasn't at all cleared to know anything more.

But the girl rolled her eyes. "I saw it all. Don't worry, I won't say anything. I assume your people will know what to do with this information more than me. It's wild, though, to think that they've managed to come up with a medication that might work. That's some cool shit, dude."

"What do you mean, *work*?" Sam asked. "The parts I read showed a ninety percent mortality rate."

"*Au contraire, mon frère*. Inside the second layer of information, there's a list of survivors, actual names and such. The data on the first layer was a year old—this is current, real time, like last week. There are a bunch more people who did survive. But here's the kicker. The ones who survived are being killed by the soldiers and families. They think they're zombies. There are a lot of superstitions in that part of the world. They know no one gets better once they contract the blood diseases. There's a patient in here who was in isolation for over a month, but got better, and when they released her and sent her home to her family, they stoned her to death, thinking she was a monster."

"Zombies?" Fletcher said. Skeptical had nothing on him.

Mouse shrugged. "That's what the files say."

"How many patients are we talking about who survived?" Sam asked.

"Of the people who were given the fake vaccine with the superbug in it, at least a hundred. The mortality rate is still tremendous, but some people are surviving. They're all identified by code letters. That's the important part of this, what was deeply encrypted. They are using antibodies in the blood of the ones who survived to create a real vaccine that will help fight the spread of the superbug. Which means there are samples somewhere—blood, tissue, all that icky stuff. I can't find where, but they exist. There's a log of them in the files."

Sam felt a spark of hope. "Who is *they*?"

"Some virologist here in D.C."

Bromley. It had to be. She exchanged a look with Fletcher. "So you're saying that they're using the samples from the survivors to work on a new vaccine that protects against the superbug?"

Mouse nodded. "They just have no idea how or why it works. And it still only works on about seventy percent. So the numbers are moving in the right direction, but it's still fatal for a lot of people."

"Tell me more," Sam said. "The physical samples taken from the survivors...what are they doing with them?"

"I'm not sure. The labeling system is a bit wonky, but it's consistent from area to area. That's the trick with codes—you find the similarities, and everything falls into place." She pointed to a line of code on the computer. "See, this one is from ground zero. It's a small village in Sierra Leone—Anchurra. AN. So all the samples from this area are labeled with a GR—for ground zero—and AN for Anchurra. The next letters are which strain they've been given, and lastly the patient number or letter. But I can't find where the samples got off to. Who knows where they are."

Sam felt a zing of recognition, looked at Fletcher. "I think I know where at least one is. God, I can't believe I didn't realize it before. I'm slipping."

"Where?"

"Remember the vials we pulled out of Cattafi's refrigerator?

The one no one could identify? *Gransef.* GR—ground zero. AN—Anchurra province. SE—the strain. F—the patient. We have one of the samples in evidence right now. It was rather elegantly hidden, wasn't it?"

Fletcher's smile grew wide, and he bumped Mouse on the shoulder. "Damn good work, kiddo." He nodded at Daniels. "You're forgiven."

"Wait. It's not all good news."

"What is it, Mouse?" Sam asked.

"It's the ultimate biological weapon, right? Even at its best, it still has a seventy to ninety percent mortality rate. You manage to slip this superbug into a shipment of flu vaccines heading to your local doctor's office or drugstore, and you can infect the populace. And even with our great sanitation and medical care, there would be a massive mortality rate, because the vaccine against the superbug still kills so many of the people who get it."

"What are you saying? That it's possible a terrorist organization might have their hands on some of this and is planning to put it into our vaccines?"

"Ma'am, I may be paranoid, but I think we can't rule it out. That would explain why the SD chip has the software proxies. So someone can load them into the firm's servers and download all their financial data. To condemn, or to prosecute or to cover all this up. If they're being funded by a terror group, or selling this superbug to them? We could have a much bigger problem on our hands."

The kitchen went silent. This was what Girabaldi had been worried about. Now they had proof, in one way.

Sam took a deep breath. "We need to get our hands on those vials from Cattafi's right now."

"And figure out who is actually behind this," Fletcher added. "What company has created this killer bug, and who was moving it in and out of Africa. All we know right now is there's a man with a British accent involved."

Mouse nodded, excitement shining in her eyes. "I've tracked the money to a shell company with French papers, but it's going to take some time to unravel exactly where this is coming from."

Fletcher's phone rang, jarring them all. He glanced at the screen. "This is the hospital. I asked for updates on Cattafi. Fingers crossed it's good news."

Sam watched him answer, and his face drained of color. "Are you sure?" he said. "Son of a bitch. Start running the name, right now. Find out who it is. You hear me? And send me the picture. Call me immediately when you know."

He hung up. "Cattafi threw a code blue. They've managed to bring him back. He's still in the coma, but he's breathing. Apparently, a doctor no one recognized came to see him just before he tried to croak. Put her name down as Margaret Preston. Problem is, there isn't a doctor named Margaret Preston at GW. I'm going to have heads over this."

"Wait, Fletch. An impostor doctor got in to see Cattafi? How?"

"Marched right in. They're sending a photo." His phone dinged. He opened the email.

There was a good shot of the impostor's face as she exited the room, taken from the nurses' station. It was grainy, but clear enough to work with. The doctor was small, gray-haired, stooped a bit.

He turned the phone around. "Look familiar?"

Sam had to strip away the hair, the demeanor, the attitude. Once she did, she saw someone she recognized. The hair was wrong, but the face was unmistakable. "That's Robin Souleyret."

"Yes, it is," Fletcher replied. "And she just tried to kill Tommy Cattafi."

CHAPTER 38

Foggy Bottom
Dr. David Bromley's lab

ROBIN SAW THE GLINT OF THE WEAPON, IMMEDIATELY WENT INTO A DEFENSIVE posture, crouched, ready to spring. She didn't hesitate; her fist struck out, nailing her assailant in the throat. With the other hand, she smashed her wrist against his forearm, knocking the gun loose. She whipped around and planted her left leg behind the gunman's right knee and shoved. He went over on his back— it was a he, she could smell the acrid scent of his sweat and feel the thick hair on his arms. He scrambled backward and landed heavily on his back with a curse—French, she thought dimly, did he just say *putain*?—then shot from flat on his back to his feet with breathtaking speed.

He came at her, both hands free now, confident in his skill, not even glancing for the gun she'd held. She took two punches, one to her cheek, one to her forehead, before she could turn to the side and kick him. He went for her leg and missed, but caught her sharply on the neck, right in the notch by her carotid, hard enough to make her see stars.

He had a momentary advantage, and he knew it. He grabbed

her by the wrist and flung her against the wall. She caught herself before she slammed headfirst, curled her body for the impact. Hit the wall with a dull thump, pain shooting from her shoulder.

He launched after her, teeth bared, his face so close she could see the small vertical lines that bisected his upper lip. Got his hands on her neck, but that was just where she wanted him. She went limp for a moment, surprising him, then turned in his arms and shoved hard against the wall with her legs, sent them toppling backward across the room. She beat him back to standing, but he was quick, right there. She didn't stop, turned and crashed an elbow into his throat and, without waiting to see the effect it had, threw her head back in a reverse Glasgow kiss.

She tagged him square in the nose, felt the crunch of the cartilage and a fine mist of blood warm down her back. He started to sag, and she jammed her right heel into his knee, which bent backward in an unholy way.

He screamed. The one–two head-knee combination was enough to stop him in his tracks. She felt him going down, sprang away so he didn't land on her, and calmly picked up his gun. A Beretta, with suppressor attached. Had it not, she wouldn't have had the luck she did to disarm him so quickly; the suppressor added just enough weight to make the gun off balance if you weren't gripping it tightly. She knew; she'd been disarmed once in the same way, not expecting the weight of the weapon to shift in her hand when her arm was hit.

She was breathing hard. It felt like the fight had taken years, not minutes.

The assassin was down, hands around his ruined knee. He wasn't crying, and she was impressed. She knew he must have been in an incredible amount of pain.

She stood near him, the gun trained on him, listening to a clever assortment of invectives in French. She'd been right; he had called her a *putain* and a *salope*, and suggested she do a few rather base things with her mother, father and grandmother.

She kicked him in the nuts and said, *"Baise-toi, connard.* Who sent you?"

"Nique ta mère."

She laughed, the adrenaline starting to fade a bit, leaving her light-headed. She spoke in French. "You're a nasty one, aren't you? I don't think I will. Tell me who sent you, or I'll pull the trigger. And if you know anything at all about me, you know I'm not kidding."

He shook his head. She debated for only a moment, then smoothly fired. The gun kicked gently in her hand, and the man's leg erupted in blood. He howled.

"Now both knees are shot. I'll give you one more chance. Tell me who sent you."

He was crying now, the pain and the shock of the gunshot too much on top of the fight. She took no pleasure in this conquest. He wasn't a worthy opponent. She'd taken him down too easily, too quickly.

"Quit crying like a little girl and tell me who you work for."

He shook his head and she started to move the gun. His eyes tracked it, moving slowly from his leg, to his groin, to right between his eyes.

"Who?"

"Denon," he said.

"James Denon?"

"Oui. Have mercy, sister." He was finished. He shut his eyes, ready. His throat convulsed once as he swallowed.

"Merci," she whispered, and with a small frown pulled the trigger twice more.

Riley showed up five minutes later. He found Robin sitting on the floor of Bromley's front office, the suppressed Beretta in her lap, a look of surprise on her face.

He dropped to his knees beside her, gently plucked the gun from her hand. She let him. She was tired. So tired.

Riley looked worried, but she hardly noticed it. She just wanted to close her eyes and sleep. The blood from the man she'd shot smelled of copper and iron, hot smoke, and when she finally relaxed against the wall, allowed herself to step away from warrior mode, she saw the whole lab was coated in a fine yellow smog, like bile.

Seeing the mess, Riley roughed her up, yanked her to her feet, whispering harshly in purple-veined words. "What are you still doing here? You need to leave. Now. You've been compromised. The police know you've been to see Cattafi. He coded right after you left. You're a suspect. What the hell were you thinking?"

Riley's fury brought her back to herself. "I didn't touch Cattafi. Rather, I touched his hand, but he was already gone. I didn't do anything else."

"The police don't think so. They think you went in disguised and shoved something into his IV. We need to get you safe, right now."

"It's fine, Riley. I'll just tell them what happened."

"And this?" He swung an arm out and she saw the detritus of the fight clearly for the first time—furniture toppled, paintings askew, the ruined husk of the French assassin on the floor opposite her.

She couldn't remember the last time she'd seen Riley so angry. It made her want to kiss away the frown lines between his brows. She settled for touching his jaw lightly.

"I didn't have a choice. But I found out something before he died. He told me James Denon had sent him after me. How is that possible? I thought Denon was on our side?"

"I don't give a rat's ass about Denon. Let's go. We need to get you out of the city."

"If I run, they'll think I'm guilty. There's another body here. The guy who ran the lab, Bromley. He was shot earlier, though it's been made to look like a suicide. Note and everything. He was already dead when I got here. Promise."

She gave him a wry smile.

Riley's green eyes glinted dangerously, then he threw his hands in the air. "So help me God, Robbie. Listen to me. If you don't run, *I'll* think you're mad. Get moving. Down the stairs. Now."

She resisted the urge to be flip and snap to in a salute. She cast a last glance at the body of the Frenchman, and holstered her Glock. Riley pocketed the Beretta, and they slipped out of the office toward the stairs.

This wasn't how her day was supposed to go. Then again, she assumed Amanda had felt exactly the same way when faced with the silver power of the knife.

They got out of the building without notice. Riley marched her down the street and into his truck. Reached over and fastened her seat belt. She felt hollow and strange, the way she always did after a massive adrenaline rush, and a few choice bruises were beginning to throb. She pulled down the visor, looked in the mirror. She had the beginnings of a nice black eye; she didn't remember receiving that particular punch.

"Where's your car?" Riley asked.

"Back on I Street. At a meter."

"Lola will get it. I'm taking you to my place. You're too damn hot to go home now."

He yanked the gearshift into Drive, and she put a hand on his leg. "I'm sorry. I didn't have a choice."

He looked at her strangely. "You always have a choice, Robin. He could have been of use to us."

She retracted the hand, watched the cloud of red follow. Sat up straighter. "He wasn't. He killed my sister, and there wasn't any reason to keep him alive."

"Except he didn't kill your sister."

The world around her pulsed *red, red, red.*

CHAPTER 39

Fletcher's house

SAM'S PHONE RANG. IT WAS A 202 EXCHANGE, BUT SHE DIDN'T RECOGNIZE the number. She answered, anyway.

"Dr. Owens? Agent Owens? Uh… This is Peggy at GW. We talked earlier about Dr. Bromley?"

"Doctor is fine. Thanks for getting back to me. Were you able to find him?"

"No, ma'am, because my info was wrong. He got back into the country yesterday, and he should be at his office. I tried calling over there, but no one answered. He might have gone home because of the jet lag, but I know he likes to do some work right away when he gets back, just trying to catch up, and sometimes he turns off the phones. I left a message on his cell for him to call you, but if you really need to talk to him now, you might just head on over there and try to see him in person. If I talk to him, I'll tell him to expect you."

"Peggy, you deserve a raise. Thank you for following up."

She told Fletcher.

"Good. We're heading there now," he said.

They sent Daniels to join the surveillance team looking for

Robin Souleyret, and sent Mouse on her merry path to follow the money trail, with extreme injunctions to keep her mouth shut. She'd assured them she wouldn't say anything to anyone— she knew which side her bread was buttered on—and had given Sam the key to the encryption codes so they could access the SD card's multilevels of security in Fletcher's office.

Sam was sorry to see the girl go. She was smart and funny, and had added a bit of needed levity to the day, despite the horrifying information she'd uncovered. She made a good teammate.

In the car, Fletcher got on the phone with Hart, who'd tracked down the gray Honda that had been lurking around the Cattafi crime scene, so Sam took five minutes to write up her notes, trying to prioritize. The information they were uncovering was coming fast and furious, and she wanted to be sure they had all the threads together. They needed to find Amanda's laptop, which Sam was certain had more information on it. They needed to know who the SD card was meant for. Sam assumed it was Girabaldi, but perhaps it was for Robin Souleyret.

Why kill the renters? Why kill Amanda? Why try to take out Cattafi? And who the hell was manufacturing the superbug?

There were too many *whys* floating around. So much information, so many threads. They needed Bromley, needed to understand what, exactly, he and Tommy Cattafi were up to, whether they had indeed developed a vaccine against the superbug. They needed the samples Amanda had smuggled into the country themselves. They needed to find out where the hell Robin Souleyret was hiding in plain sight; Daniels's tail had reported in that she was not at her residence. The afternoon was slipping away, and Sam was starting to get tired.

She made Fletcher stop at Starbucks so she could grab a large coffee. She offered to get him one, but he demurred, running into the market across the street for a Diet Coke. While she was in line, she called Xander.

"Where are you?" He sounded stressed, and she felt bad. He

needed her. She knew just how hard this morning must have been for him, and here she was, completely caught up in this case.

"We're at the Starbucks in Foggy Bottom. There is so much going on with this case I can barely keep it straight. Are you okay?"

"I am, but, Sam, I need you here. As soon as possible."

He wasn't kidding, and he wasn't asking. She recognized his tone; he was in operational mode. Something bad was happening. "I'll come right now. I'll have Fletcher drop me off. He can survive without me for a while."

Xander got quiet for a minute, then said, "No, actually, stick with Fletcher. Stick to him like glue. He can keep you safe. I trust him."

His tone made her anxious. She stepped closer to the window, edging herself between the glass and the wall, looked outside. Living with Xander, who was a Ranger through and through despite the fact he no longer worked for the government, had instilled a sense of danger in her. She was more wary, had a different level of focus as she moved around the city, was more attuned to her surroundings. She immediately began watching to see if anyone was paying attention to her. From what she could see, no one was. She pitched her voice low. "What's wrong, Xander? What's going on?"

"Remember the code I gave you for your phone?"

"Yes."

"Turn it on and call me back."

The "code" was an encryption key that allowed her to make secure calls. He really was into something. She did as he asked, inputting the code, waiting for the dial tone to beep at her three times to indicate it was encrypted and active, then called him back.

"Okay, I'm secure. Xander, what in the world is wrong?"

"The man I killed this morning was a pro. We thought he was hired to kill my principal, James Denon."

"You thought?"

"It's looking like he wasn't the target, that someone on his staff was. The problem is, we're missing one of his people. We're looking for her now. French national using the name Juliet Bouchard. She came in with his team three days ago, but she wasn't with them when they were flying home, and she's not listed on any manifests leaving the country. Nor does she have a visa on file. I'm pretty sure she's behind the assassination attempt."

Sam felt a punch of recognition when she heard the name. "Bouchard. Bouchard. Why does that name sound familiar?"

"You've heard of this woman?"

The barista at the counter called Sam's name. "Hang on a sec, my drink's ready." She grabbed the coffee, dumped in cream and sugar, enough to give her a real boost, then headed back out onto the street, coffee in one hand, phone in the other. She used her bottom to push open the door.

"Sam? Talk to me."

"I'm here, babe. I'm just thinking." She set her coffee on top of Fletcher's vehicle, opened the door. And then it hit her, where she'd seen the name, and her blood went cold. The list of Amanda's aliases. Juliet Bouchard was one of them.

"Xander. I know who she is. And I know where she is."

"Tell me, right now. I need to lock her down."

"You're too late. The woman's real name is Amanda Souley-ret. And she's in the morgue."

Sam put Xander on the speaker and filled him in on everything she knew as Fletcher drove them to Bromley's office. He absorbed the story, asking only one question.

"Do you have any idea who might have killed Souleyret?"

"There's only one suspect right now. Her sister, Robin," Fletcher answered.

"The spook? Great. Where exactly is Robin Souleyret?"

Sam glanced at Fletcher. "That's what we want to know."

"Listen, can you do some background on Denon, see if he has any official ties to Souleyret or the State Department? Might save us some time, if we can find the name of the company Amanda was investigating in Denon's files," Fletcher said. "Look at Regina Girabaldi, too."

Xander whistled. "That Girabaldi?"

"Yes. She's into this, we just don't know in what capacity."

"I'll add her to the mix. Listen, though the threat level might have gone down if Souleyret is dead, someone killed her, and until you find the sister, I won't be sitting easy. I'm not kidding when I say keep Sam close, Fletcher."

"You know I will," he replied. "We're at Bromley's office right now. We'll touch base when we get out."

"One more thing. Bouchard—Amanda Souleyret—she suggested Denon hire me and Chalk to do his protection detail here in the States. Souleyret may have involved us for some reason, and if she did, I intend to find out exactly why. We're looking into everything he's done since he set foot on our soil. She may have involved you on purpose, too, Sam. Made sure you'd be called in to work this case. Please be careful."

"I hear you, though I think I'm simply a coincidence. Baldwin put me on the case because he was tied up on another."

"This woman was murdered a block from our house. That's one hell of a coincidence."

"Not everything is a conspiracy, Xander. Cattafi happened to live near the school I teach at, one he attended himself. This isn't Timothy Savage all over again."

"Just be aware, hon. I killed a guy this morning. The media's already tracked me here. How long do you think it will take them to start putting the parts together?"

"Then we'll work faster. You mind your six, soldier."

She heard a snort of amusement. "Since it's such a pretty six, I will do my best."

She hung up and looked at Fletcher. "Some good news there."

"What? That the media is hounding your boyfriend?" he said, pulling up to the curb.

"No, goof. If Amanda brought the vials in on Denon's plane, they mustn't be dangerous in and of themselves. If we'd found out she'd brought them stowed in a specialized container, or taken clear precautions to negate the danger, I'd be much more worried. She must have had them in her bags, perhaps in a small cooler. I think Denon and his people would have noticed if she were trying to hide something lethal."

"We'll want to ask, but I hope you're right, Sam. I've got a headache just thinking about those diseases."

She looked him over, concerned, but he smiled. "Don't worry. It's nothing some Advil won't fix. Do you have any?"

She fished a bottle from her bag, dumped two in his hand. He downed them, then tossed a POLICE card on the dash of his car. "Let's do this."

Sam glanced around before she got out of the car, just in case. She saw nothing out of place. The street was crawling with coeds and businesspeople and runners, all wrapping up their afternoons, beginning the slow march into night. The normalcy hid a multitude of sinners, and she didn't feel entirely safe until they'd gone through the revolving doors and entered the cool lobby of Bromley's building.

There was a metal detector, two guards standing near it and a workman in a leather tool belt perched on a small ladder, the mechanism panel pulled off to show dangling wires. More guards were at the desk; they were all on alert.

Fletcher badged them, jerked a head toward the repairs. "Problems?"

"As always. Who're you here to see?"

"Dr. David Bromley."

"Fourth floor. Mind signing in?"

Sam reached for the pen. She scanned the list of names as she wrote hers down. Something was odd. The list had a Fred Horace, a Jennifer Wilde, then a Jorace Filde.

"Fletcher. Look at this."

She pointed at the name. His brows pulled together. "Weird."

"Purposeful? Or am I just being totally paranoid?"

"You're being appropriately paranoid." He signaled to the guard. "Do you remember these people? Do you have any identification on them?"

"Just the cameras." He pointed to the camera over the desk. "Don't know if it's working, though. Pretty much everything electronic on the first floor got all kinds of wonky this afternoon."

Fletcher tapped his fingers on the counter. "We're going up to Bromley's office. You pull the camera feed for this time slot. I need to see who this person is."

The guard looked exceedingly uncomfortable. "Uh, sir, do you have a warrant? 'Cause the building management won't like that a bit."

"Get on the phone with them, tell them we're looking for a murder suspect who may have been in the building. And if they give you any crap, come up and get me. I'll talk to them directly. Can you do that?"

He nodded. "Why not? Everything else around here is screwy today."

Fletcher motioned for Sam to follow him, and they went to the elevators. Once the doors were closed, he said, "Good catch. Think Robin has been here already?"

"It stands to reason. First she visits her sister's town house, then Cattafi, then stops here? I'd say she's looking for something."

They were whisked up to the fourth floor, out into the tan carpeted fluorescently lit hallway. Bromley's office was halfway down the hall. The door was locked. Fletcher banged on it a few times, but no one answered.

"Damn it. Not answering the phone, not answering the door. Where the hell is this guy?"

"Fletcher. We'd better get security to let us in."

He turned to her. "Why?"

Sam pointed at the floor. There was a small smudge of red on the carpet.

"Aww...shit."

CHAPTER 40

Bromley's office

THE INTERIOR OF BROMLEY'S OFFICE WAS SPLASHED WITH A VIVID RED. THEY could see a body from the doorway. The scent of blood was rich and fresh in the air—whoever this was, he hadn't been dead for very long. He was young with black hair, and Sam knew from the photos on the wall he wasn't David Bromley.

While Fletcher called it in, Sam edged carefully into the room, taking gloves from her pocket. She used her phone to take a few pictures, wanting to preserve the integrity of the room as much as possible before they stepped inside.

Fletcher grabbed her arm, making her jump. He whispered in her ear. "You, stop. Stay right here. I need to make sure we don't have any company."

She nodded, let him lead the way. He had his gun out. When the guard from downstairs arrived, they cleared the office. She stood watching the dead body in the outer office, saw his twisted leg, the gunshot to his knee, his crushed face, the disarray. There'd been a huge fight here, and he'd lost. The question was, who the hell was he, and who had he encountered?

And if this was Robin Souleyret's work, they needed more gun power. Maybe a couple of Abrams battle tanks.

A few moments later, Fletcher called out to Sam, "Come back here, carefully."

She followed his voice down the hall, and found him standing over another body.

"Bromley?" she asked.

The guard nodded. He was pale, but holding it together. "God, oh, God. Yes, it's Dr. Bromley. He came in this morning real early, right at the beginning of my shift. How could he do this? I don't understand. He didn't seem the suicidal type, you know?"

"The man in the anteroom, does he work here, too? He wasn't wearing lab clothes," Fletcher said.

"Him, I've never seen. I don't know who that is. Someone really did a number on him. I don't recall him coming through security today, but I had a break at lunchtime."

Fletcher stepped back, motioned for them both to do the same, so they were at least less likely to contaminate the crime scene further. "Now you want to get that camera footage rolling for me, buddy?"

"I was checking it out when you called me up here, Lieutenant. There's a problem with it, like I told you. Everything from this afternoon is erased. It's almost like we had a power surge. Something weird happened. The metal detector goes down all the time, but this was everything—cameras, the machines, even some of the guys' phones."

"That sounds like more than a power surge."

Sam shoved her hands into the pockets of her pants. "It sounds like a deliberate attack. Like someone needed to get in here and didn't want to be seen. I wonder who that might be?"

Fletcher nodded at her from across Bromley's body. "Look." He pointed at the small piece of paper left carelessly near the body. He took a picture of its placement, then picked it up with a gloved hand and read it aloud.

"*'Do I have your attention yet?'* Yes, by God, you do."

Sam's phone rang. She glanced at the screen. "It's Nocek. Maybe we'll get some answers." She stepped into the hall and answered the phone.

Nocek was excited. "Samantha, I have most gratifying news. We know what sort of poison was used on the young men. You were very quick to think of having the samples sent ahead."

"We're in a time crunch, Amado, and I have more bad news. Two more bodies related to this case. So thank you for taking me seriously and running the blood. What did you find?"

"Scopolamine and morphine."

"That's an odd pairing. An anticholinergic mixed with an opioid? I'd be more inclined to expect that in a 1940s delivery room than now."

"You are correct. It is not a commonly used concoction now."

"It would be a painless way to go. Easy to administer, too— no taste, no scent, no color. Just mix it in water and feed it to your victim. It would explain why their mucosa was red."

"Painless, yes. And simple to acquire. More importantly, if one were an expert in its use, if administered properly, it would also induce a state of well-being, bordering on hypnotic."

She sucked in her breath. She knew exactly where he was going. "The CIA used to use scopolamine for interrogations. It was one of the first effective truth serums. The renters were questioned before they were killed. Is that what you're telling me?"

"As always, Dr. Owens, your astuteness astounds even me. Yes, I believe this to be the case. And the sample from Michael Oread registered nearly twice the dosage given to Jared Lanter. I will be paying special attention to each man's time of death to see if there is a differential that would prove this theory."

"Do you think Oread was killed first? It would make sense.

If you're trying to get information out of someone, killing the second person would give them incentive to cooperate."

"I think that may be the case, yes."

"Thank you, Amado. Call me if you find anything else interesting. And I'm sure you're going to be getting a call to come here, so I'll give you the information." She rattled off the address and suite number. "I won't be here. I have another stop to make. But be careful, and have your people paying attention. We have someone on a spree, and I don't want anything to happen to you."

"I would extend the same warning to you, my dear. Be very careful."

Sam told Fletcher Nocek's theory. He was already bouncing on the balls of his feet, ready to get out of there and track down Robin Souleyret. When she told him the possible reasoning behind the specific drugs given to the renters, he started shaking his head.

"Should have known we were dealing with Agency crap when Girabaldi dragged us in this morning. This all leads back to her. She's trying to pull us in to clean up her mess. She's going to dump this whole case at our feet and blame us for not stopping these deaths. I can already see the press conference."

The security guard stationed by the door to wait for the crime scene techs gawked at Fletcher. Sam grabbed Fletcher's arm and pulled him deeper into the lab.

"Whoa there, cowboy. Don't let anyone else hear you say that. She's a very powerful woman with a lot of friends."

"And a rogue agent from her past tying up loose ends."

"Do you really think Robin Souleyret killed her own sister?"

"I don't know, Sam, but at this point? We're five bodies down in a twenty-four-hour stretch, with another clinging to life. We have notes from the scenes that are giving us some sort of message. Talk of cell regeneration, zombies in Africa, tainted vaccines. Pressure from the State Department. Some big muckety-muck out of England helping Amanda Souleyret get into the country. Despite all this information, we don't know anything more than we did this morning, and I've got another four murders to deal with. I am not at all happy."

"I know. We need someone good to take apart Bromley's records, see if we can find anything that might help explain what he and Cattafi were doing."

"I'm thinking it's time we push Girabaldi a bit. See what we can shake loose. If she'd been clearer with us this morning, we might have gotten ahead of this."

Sam thought about it for a minute. "I understand the urge, but Fletcher, again, Bromley's been dead since this morning at least, well before we got pulled into State. I think finding Robin Souleyret is the primary goal right now. Whether she's our suspect, or she's working the case of her sister's death on her own, a face-to-face is imperative. What did Hart tell you about the Honda Accord that was circling the crime scene? Could that have been her?"

"It wasn't a woman, it was a guy. Hart said he claimed to be looking for 'companionship,' trolling the late-night Georgetown scene before heading downtown for some action. He wasn't sure about him. Said the dude was weird. He's going to do a background check on him, see if anything pops."

"All right. Let's go down and see what the tapes say, see if Robin Souleyret was even here. Then I think it would be smart to hook up with Xander. See what he and his partner, Chalk, have come up with. They have a tie into this case now, too. And Baldwin is flying back as we speak. He has more information for us that he couldn't share over the phone about Robin's background. We have a lot of balls in the air, and to be honest, I think it's time to regroup before we go marching into the State Department and start making accusations. You good with that?"

He blew out a breath. "I'm good with that."

★ ★ ★

Sam hung back while Fletcher and the guards went over the footage from the day. Thought about everything—about the senseless murders, the secrets and lies. Wondered about James Denon. She knew the name, of course; he was in the news often. What was his tie to the tainted vaccines?

She wasn't an idiot—the pattern was clear. Everywhere they went, they seemed to be just missing the elder Souleyret sister. And in her wake was a deluge of dead bodies, killed in a variety of manners and methods. There was no way they couldn't consider Robin Souleyret as a suspect, at least until she was caught and questioned.

Something else was niggling at her, and she knew exactly what it was. She simply couldn't imagine Robin killing her little sister. Yes, the woman was black ops, which meant she followed orders and knew how to keep to the shadows. Yes, she had a record of assassinations longer than Sam's arm. But it would have to be one hell of a head injury to allow her to stab her own sister in the back.

Thought some more, about life. About what it must be like to be out on your own, making life and death decisions on a daily basis, the subterfuge that went into that kind of existence, the ability to go for extended periods without touching base with anyone. Xander had been in the business himself, in a way. She knew how hard it had been on him. Surely it was hard on Robin Souleyret, as well. And maybe, just maybe, she wasn't totally alone in this world.

Fletcher was arguing with the head of security now. She left him to it, dialed her Doberman, Marcos Daniels. He answered on the first ring.

"Dr. Owens? Can I help you?"

"I hope you can, Agent Daniels. Anything show up from the surveillance on Robin Souleyret's place?"

"No, ma'am. Nothing. She's not there, and we haven't seen her go boo yet. The girl's in the wind."

"Maybe not entirely. She's almost certainly in D.C. I think someone's helping her, and it's time to put some pressure on."

"What do you want me to do?"

"First, find out who Robin might be working with. Even though she's a sole operator and used to being on her own, she needs resources—money, weapons, everything. Find out who might be offering her succor. See if she has a man, or any record of boyfriends or girlfriends, all that jazz. These people can't operate without a little help from their friends. I don't think she's on a sanctioned job, but just in case, you might want to take a look at our friends from Langley, too."

"Got it."

"And then, I need you to do a massive triage on Amanda Souleyret. Find me anyone and everyone she's been in contact with in the past few weeks. Crash her systems, get into her email, rumble her life, everything you know how to do, and do it fast. Can you do that?"

"I can. Sure wish Mouse was around. That girl…" He drifted off.

"Call her in. Tell her we'll pay her as a consultant. Make her sign every nondisclosure agreement we have, and make it very clear to her what the parameters are." She went silent for a second, then said, "You did get her number, didn't you, Daniels?"

"Um, yes, ma'am, I did."

She couldn't help it; she smiled. She thought she'd caught a flicker of interest between them. "Good. If you hit a brick wall with Amanda's real accounts, try tying in the name Juliet Bouchard. It's an alias she was using. I'm assuming, if she's any good at her job, that the legend is backstopped well. Find the legend, and we'll start finding some answers. Get moving. Report to me only, do you understand? And, Daniels? Watch your tracks. Robin Souleyret is a suspect now, and she's dangerous. All right?"

"On it, ma'am. I'll be back to you soon."

He hung up, and she pocketed her phone. Maybe working for the FBI wouldn't be all bad. And this protected Fletcher completely. If he didn't know what she was up to, it wouldn't rain down on his head. She was pretty damn sure Baldwin would have done exactly the same thing. Which meant he'd have her back.

Or she was becoming power-hungry.

Fletcher huffed over to her. "Who were you talking to?"

"Daniels. Checking on our surveillance. So far, we've got nada."

"The security guard was right. The tapes were wiped. Not only from the afternoon, either. Whatever happened cleaned the whole day."

"And what do you think happened?"

"Some sort of electronic surge, that's my best guess."

"Robin Souleyret has a great deal of electronic experience, yes?"

"Yes, she does."

"I'm not up on all the latest spy technology, but I assume it's very possible to have a micro-EMP made that would only work in a small area?"

"Entirely possible. Hell, you can get directions to make one of those on the internet—it's not hard."

"Then let's throw that in as the possible cause of the problem and move along."

The doors opened and the crime scene techs started rolling through, and Hart arrived right behind them.

When he saw Fletcher, he narrowed his eyes and marched over. "What in the name of hell is going on? We got bodies and crime scenes coming out our ears."

"We're trying to find out." Fletcher filled him in as best he could. "We're going to Sam's place and regroup." Hart smelled like pizza—he'd grabbed a slice on his way over—and Sam heard Fletcher's stomach growl. "And eat, hopefully. Been a long time since lunch."

"Ah," Hart said. "You've got Xander the wunderkind working on this, don't you?"

Sam smiled. "He found a link between his principal and Amanda Souleyret. I can only imagine what he'll have for us when we get there."

"Before you go, I have some bad news," Hart said, and Fletcher groaned.

"More bad news? This day keeps getting better, doesn't it?"

"The vaccines from Cattafi's place never made it to the CDC lab they were supposedly heading to. It's taken a while to sort through everything, but the gist is this—the CDC claims they were never contacted, and never picked up the vaccines."

"What? Who the hell signed out the vaccines?" Fletcher asked tightly.

"The signature is scribbled, so we don't have a name. He said he was from the CDC, picked up the vaccines from HAZMAT, signed all the paperwork, got in his car and left. Got him on camera—a big guy, wearing a ball cap with the name of a courier company that doesn't exist on it. He's gone, and the evidence is gone with him."

Fletcher turned white with anger. "Holy shit. Holy shit, people. We are well and truly fucked."

"Fletcher, now it's time to call Girabaldi," Sam said. "Everyone who's tangled up in this case or discovers a facet of it is being tracked down and eliminated. We can't contain the story if we can't stop the people involved from being killed. Not to mention whoever is behind this has their hands on the vaccines. This is not good, and we need to move quickly."

He breathed deeply a few times, thinking, then nodded. "I'm

afraid you're right. Girabaldi is the key. I just don't know which side she's on."

Sam shook her head. "I don't, either."

"We'll head over there right now, explain what's been happening, and that we're going public. We can't let those vaccines be used against us. I will not have a terror attack in this city on my watch."

"That's a good plan, boss. I'm with you. You be careful," Hart said.

"Yeah. You, too."

Fletcher gave Hart some directions on what to recover from upstairs, and they set off, knowing the crime scene was well in hand.

They stepped out into the cooling fall evening. Sam had the oddest sense of dislocation. The gloaming was hovering around them, everything so clear, so perfect, and for that fraction of a moment as the sun began to set, light bouncing off the windshields of the cars lined up at the meters on the street, she saw the world around her with an unearthly clarity. It made her uneasy; things were too far out of control.

They started toward Fletcher's car, and out of the corner of her eye, she saw a car turn onto the street. A black sedan, very similar to the one Edgar Poe had described. The window started down.

Sam turned abruptly, grabbed Fletcher's arm and pulled him toward her just as the bullet crashed into the building behind her.

CHAPTER 41

THERE WAS A SECOND OF CALM BEFORE PANDEMONIUM BROKE OUT AROUND them, and the gunman managed to get off another few shots.

Fletcher reacted quickly. He shoved Sam to the ground, stepped forward to the curb and returned fire. It wasn't SOP, and the sedan was already pulling away, the tires screeching smoke. Suddenly Hart was there, too, the two men shoulder to shoulder, firing in unison, both in perfect triangle stances, mimicking each other, and the rear window of the sedan shattered.

The car lurched hard to the right, up onto the sidewalk, scattering pedestrians like a flock of birds hit with shrapnel, and slammed into the building one block down.

Fletcher and Hart took off. Sam was right behind them, up and running hard. The smell of gas reached her nostrils as she skidded to a stop next to the car. She saw someone bolt from the passenger seat. Hart saw him, too, took off running after him.

Fletcher shouted at her to get back and yanked the driver from the car. The man flopped from the driver's seat onto the pavement. She heard the shouts and screams of the people around, blocked it all out.

The driver's head was ruined. He'd taken one of their bullets to the back of his skull, but he wasn't dead yet. She pushed

Fletcher to the side, pressed her fingers into the man's neck, felt the feeble pulse starting to skip. There was nothing to be done, nothing at least that she could do. The bullet had decimated his brain; his heart was just waiting for its last signal to stop pumping.

Fletcher was rolling the body, slapping the man's pockets, looking for ID and other weapons, getting blood on the pavement and his pants. There was brass all over the car, and thick red blood, and Sam sighed heavily as the man died with her hand on his neck.

She sat down on the curb. Her knees and her palms were skinned from landing hard on the concrete sidewalk. Fletcher saw her, his face filled with concern, and more—anger, frustration, an almost feral gleam from the adrenaline she knew was punching through his system. Killing was hard, but the first rush was impossible to avoid. It was the power of taking a life, of being the stronger creature, that drove the limbic system into overdrive. It didn't care about morality, it simply was.

He shook himself a little, trying to get back to normal. "Are you okay? You're not hit?"

She shook her head. "He's gone," she said unnecessarily, gesturing to the man at her feet.

The adrenaline was fleeting, and now Fletcher was starting to freak out. Sam didn't blame him a bit. She was feeling quite rattled herself.

"Holy shit, holy shit. Do you know who it is?" He wasn't asking, he wasn't looking at the body. He was walking in circles, letting his body and mind get back onto the same plane.

Hart came back, panting, shaking his head, talking a mile a minute. "He got away. Bastard got away. I lost him in the crowd on M Street. What the hell was that about? Who'd we shoot?"

He grabbed the wallet Fletcher had stripped from the pants pocket, opened it. "Jesus, he's one of ours."

Sam nodded. She'd recognized the man from their meeting

earlier in the day. As she'd stood over him, a finger on his er-ratic pulse, her mind tried to reconcile the situation—an ally turned enemy. And there was going to be hell to pay.

The man who'd tried to kill them was Jason Kruger, head of the Africa desk, from the State Department.

And now they had to figure out who had been in the car with him.

Sam watched Kruger's body being loaded into the blue morgue van. The sun was setting in earnest, night coming on fast. The lights of Foggy Bottom were ringed in haze, leftover precipitation from the afternoon rains. Small wisps of fog drifted up from the Potomac, and Sam listened to the conversation tak-ing place beside her with half an ear.

She'd just received a text from Daniels. He was in Robin Sou-leyret's world; they were crashing her email. He hadn't found anything yet, but he'd only gotten started five minutes earlier. She texted him back an OK, then tuned in to Fletcher and Hart's hushed tête-à-tête.

"It was a man who fled the scene, right, Lonnie? I wasn't imaging that?"

"Looked like a dude to me. Moved like one, too. Big, wear-ing a baseball cap. Yes, I'm pretty sure it was a guy. Why?"

"Just wanted to be sure we weren't dealing with Robin Sou-leyret face-to-face. We keep finding evidence that points in her direction."

"Media's here. You want to make a statement?" Hart asked.

Fletcher shook his head. "Hell, no. What I want is to get in Regina Girabaldi's face, find out what the fuck her acolyte was doing shooting at us."

Sam saw a large black man making his way toward them, and pointed him out to Fletcher. "Isn't that your big boss?"

Fletcher groaned slightly, stood to meet the man. "Chief, I can explain—"

Fred Roosevelt, the D.C. chief of police, held up a hand. "I don't want to hear it. There are cameras and reporters thick as lice on the street behind me, and who knows who's managed to point a boom mike in our direction."

Fletcher nodded. "I'll save it, then. You're up to speed?"

"I am. You're all okay?"

"We are."

Roosevelt glanced over his shoulder. Sam saw a reporter staring their way. He didn't mince words. "Captain Armstrong's here. He's going to have to take your guns. Let's do that quietly, inside, with a crime scene tech. Then you and Hart need to go home."

"Sir, I can't—"

Roosevelt shook his head. "Not now, and not here. Go surrender your weapon, then go home. You're off the case, effective immediately. We'll hand it over to Woolrich—he'll do it right."

Fletcher nodded, red-faced, swallowing down his anger, and turned, signaling to Hart. There was no fighting this; it was how things had to be. There were some protocols even Fletcher couldn't outmaneuver.

Roosevelt turned his attention to Sam. He gave her a long, lingering, thoughtful look. She knew he had never liked her, not since he was the captain running Homicide and Fletcher and Hart got involved in a shooting trying to protect her. She'd just moved to D.C.; she barely knew any of them. Hart hadn't even held it against her, and he was the one who'd been shot. Roosevelt always had it in for her after that. The higher he rose on the food chain, the more difficult it became. She knew Fletcher had been shielding her from Roosevelt's animosity, but there were no barriers to entry now.

His eyes were appraising and unfriendly. "Trouble follows you, doesn't it, lady?"

She squared her shoulders. "We—"

He bent closer, voice low. "Get off my scene. You may have

Lieutenant Fletcher wound around your little finger, but you're going to end his career one of these days, whether you mean to or not. I'd prefer you not end it with a bullet. Now, go play with your FBI friends and leave my boys alone. You hear me?"

She opened her mouth to retort, then closed it. He was right. Any time she got involved, things went from bad to worse. Instead, she decided to play it cool. She nodded, turned and started to walk away. There were muffled words, then she clearly heard him mutter, "Bitch," under his breath.

She turned around and stepped to his side.

"That is entirely uncalled for. Fletcher originally brought me into this case, yes, but I was assigned to work it by the Federal Bureau of Investigation, and I don't care if you have a problem with me. I intend to help Lieutenant Fletcher and Detective Hart solve this case, and finish it, whether you want me involved or not. As a matter of fact, Chief Roosevelt, the FBI should probably take over the investigation from here. I'll send a liaison with official instructions."

His mouth dropped open. "You can't do that. This is my case, my jurisdiction."

"I can't take you over, no, but I am already conducting an investigation, and I am going to make an official request for jurisdiction. I'm a federal officer, and I've been shot at. The suspect in question is a government official. This should be our case, and I'm going to make sure it is. You're welcome to continue working it—your team is a great asset. But the FBI is officially in the mix." She gave him a smile. "Now you can call me a bitch to my face, because I've earned it."

His eyes bugged out and a vein popped up in his forehead. He started to sputter, but before he had a chance to form words, she went up the stairs toward Fletcher, who was staring at her narrow-eyed. She didn't bother to look back.

"What was that all about?" he asked.

"Not now," she replied.

They went inside the building. There was a crime scene tech waiting near the broken metal detector. He was quiet, did his job quickly and efficiently, taking swabs of both Hart's and Fletcher's hands, bagging their guns. Sam realized her hands were covered in blood. The crime scene tech handed her a wipe. It stung obscenely against her abraded flesh.

They were done in five minutes, and Fletcher's immediate boss, Captain Armstrong, was waiting for them. If he'd seen Sam's exchange with Roosevelt, he chose not to mention it. He leaned in, spoke quietly in Fletcher's ear, close enough that she saw him twitch when Armstrong's mustache tickled the lobe. "Go home, Fletcher. Let me deal with Roosevelt. You hear me?"

"Yes, sir."

Armstrong shot her a strange glance, and she could have sworn he smiled, albeit briefly. So he had heard their tiff, damn it. She was beginning to feel foolish for losing her temper, then decided to hell with it. Part of working with the FBI, as Baldwin had explained, was putting up with the occasional skirmish with the locals. Of course, she hadn't expected to get into one so soon, but Roosevelt had it coming.

Sam spared a glance toward the front doors, saw a bevy of microphones and camera flashes, the black stalks of camera tripods being hurried into place. Roosevelt was going to do a presser right here at the scene, and distract the media long enough to get his men away.

"Good of him," Fletcher said to Hart. "He could have thrown us to the wolves." And to Sam, "Now are you ready to tell me what all that was about? You seemed a bit heated talking to the big dog."

"You don't want to know. Suffice it to say, I just jacked your case."

"You did what?"

She grabbed his arm as the flashbulbs started behind them.

"Come on. We need to get out of here."

"I'm off the case. I'm supposed to go home and sit on my hands like a good little boy."

She chewed on her lip for a moment. "Well, you can do that. Or you can come with me and solve this case."

Fletcher shrugged back into his jacket. "I don't know what you're up to, Samantha, but I'm with you." He turned to Hart. "Go home. Watch your back. I'll stay in touch."

"Hey, dude, we're off the case. What do you think you're doing?"

Fletcher glanced at Sam, gave his old partner a shrug and a grin. "We'll see."

Sam called Quantico as she walked out the back door of Bromley's building, avoiding the press corps and that puffed-up rooster Roosevelt. Fletcher followed Sam. He looked troubled, not that she blamed him. What she'd just done was impulsive, but necessary. She couldn't let someone like Roosevelt get in and muck things up. He used to be a cop, but now he was a politician, and everything was going to turn his way if they weren't careful. And this way, she could protect Fletcher, too.

Charlaine answered on the first ring. "You've got my kid Daniels working hard, don't you?"

"I do. Listen, I may have just mouthed off to D.C.'s chief of police that I'm requesting jurisdiction of this case."

Charlaine started to laugh, and Sam told her the whole story with relief, fighting down her own laughter as Charlaine hooted. "You don't waste any time, do you, Dr. Owens?"

"Apparently not. I felt it was justified. We were just shot at, and the shooter was an employee of the State Department. And the chief was being a jerk. He's a politician. He'll screw everything up."

Charlaine laughed again. "Then you did exactly the right thing. Set up at the Hoover Building. I'll brief them on what's happening. You'll have to go in and give them the rundown. Do you want to run this yourself, or do you need more help?"

"I think we need all the help we can get right now, Charlaine. Night has fallen, and we're chasing our tails. We've got a manhunt ongoing, a spree killer shooting his way through D.C., five dead and two suspects missing, plus a load of possibly hot vaccines in the wind. We have a dead State Department official in the street outside. This is bigger than even my capable hands, and we need to work with the D.C. police, too. And someone needs to get Regina Girabaldi in a private room."

Charlaine whistled. "She's involved?"

"To her perfectly waxed eyebrows. I'm not sure exactly how, but she pulled us in this morning and asked us to cover the whole thing up. It's beyond that now."

"I hear you. You're smart, Sam. We do our best work when we work together. I'll handle things from this end. And I'll let Baldwin know. He just checked in from the plane. I think he's headed your way when he lands in a couple of hours, so you can coordinate together."

"Roger that. I have to go home. There's a whole separate branch of this case brewing in my living room. You saw the assassination attempt of James Denon this morning, right?"

"I did."

"That was my guy who shot the would-be assassin. He's got Denon holed up at our place while he tracks down who was involved. Turns out, I think we're working the same case. There's a common player between the two. Our girl."

"Seriously? Sam, be careful. Go take a breath, let me get things moving."

"I will. And, Charlaine? Thanks."

"You got it, kid. Nice to have you on board."

Fletcher listened to Sam's call and decided he needed to make one of his own. It might get him fired; he knew continuing to work the case was dangerous to his career, but he had a feeling in the long run, it would be better to keep pushing than step back and wait like he'd been told. Armstrong would agree, he was sure of it.

When Armstrong had replaced Fred Roosevelt as captain, Fletcher had been worried. Armstrong was tough, no-nonsense, a careerist who liked to see his numbers move in the right direction. He'd spotted Fletcher as a troublemaker from the beginning, and Fletcher naturally assumed the two would clash constantly.

His concerns had been unwarranted. Roosevelt had been a hard-ass, kept himself separate from the troops. Armstrong, on the other hand, was one of them, had risen up through the ranks. He and Lonnie worked out together. He'd given Fletcher the chance to work on the Joint Terrorism Task Force and promoted him to lieutenant, allowed him the autonomy to continue investigating in the field as he wished, instead of letting him ride out his twenty at a desk.

Fletcher knew he had an ally in Armstrong, but he was still reluctant to tell him all of his suppositions at this point. If he was wrong, it *would* cost him his job, and no amount of bonhomie from his boss would save it.

It was time to talk to Girabaldi, but Fletcher wanted to do it in his house, not in hers. Rattle her up, make her uncomfortable, find out why Kruger had tried to kill him, and who had been riding in the car with the would-be assassin.

But that wasn't meant to be. He had to watch his back, make sure he didn't get fired. As they drove back to Sam's house, Fletcher called the number he'd been given earlier. The phone was answered almost immediately by Ashleigh Cavort.

"Is it true? Did Jason shoot at you?"

"Yes."

"Oh my God. The shooting was on the news, but I didn't believe it. His car was gone, his desk was empty. They said it was a State Department official. We knew it had to be him. How could he do this?"

"Ms. Cavort, I know this is a difficult time. But I need everything you have on Jason Kruger, and I need it now. And put Girabaldi on the line. She and I need to have a chat."

Cavort gulped back her tears, adopted a more professional tone. "The undersecretary has been placed under protection, Lieutenant. With the events unfolding as they are, we can't help you. We have to protect her—she's our number-one priority. Even I can't get in touch with the undersecretary right now."

"Then screw Girabaldi, you have to get me Kruger's file. Ashleigh, please. We're under attack, and we don't know why, or from whom. You gotta let me see who this guy really was. I don't have time to go through the proper channels."

She was quiet for a moment. "Do you have a secure email?"

"Sure."

"Give me the address."

He rattled off the combination of letters and numbers.

"I'll do my best," she said, and hung up.

CHAPTER 42

George Washington Parkway

RILEY DIDN'T SPEAK AFTER HE DROPPED THE BOMB THAT ROBIN HAD JUST killed the wrong man. He wouldn't answer any questions about who might have killed Amanda, and she finally grew frustrated and stared out the window at the darkening sky.

She watched the dimly lit scenery pass as Riley drove them into Virginia, getting her far away from D.C., to someplace safe. That place being his house. He was giving off clouds of black and gray shadows; she was trying very hard to control the synesthesia and ignore his anger. But it was becoming more and more difficult the crazier the day became. Riley was the first person who'd understood her gifts, accepted her despite them.

No. That wasn't true. Amanda had, as well. Grief made her stomach seize, and she reached out to Riley, put her hand on his arm, seeking some sort of connection. She had to fix things, fast.

"Riley. I'm sorry. I reacted without thinking. He attacked me, and I, well, honestly, I don't remember much."

He shrugged off her hand. She set the offending palm in her lap and stared at it. It still had bits of his blackness swirling from the tips of her fingers.

He didn't look at her, kept his eyes on the road. The sun had set; the lights of oncoming traffic were blinding her.

"You shot the man three times. Tortured him, and didn't manage to gain any usable information. Is it that easy to forget, Robin? Can you turn yourself off so well now that you don't even feel?"

She shook her head. "That's not fair. I feel. I feel *too* much. That's the problem. It sounds like a convenient excuse, but I've never lied to you, Riley. I've lost the edge that allowed me to stay neutral all these years. I can't find it. And until I do…"

He ignored that. "Atlantic called. Amanda got herself into some serious shit. She smuggled out an SD card with encrypted data she'd stolen from a pharmaceutical company in France. And she brought a group of vaccines into the country. I can only assume someone followed her, tried to retrieve the info and killed her in the process."

She thought about Cattafi, lying gray and unmoving in the hospital bed. "If Amanda was the target, why kill all the people around her, too? Because everyone she's been in contact with is dead, or near to it."

"We don't know."

She looked at his big, sure hands on the wheel. Was it possible that those hands had caressed her body in the night? They were lethal, deadly hands, worse even than her own. It was what drew them together, the understanding they had about why and how they needed to do their jobs. No wasted energy. No wasted death. Their code. How their lives operated.

She'd broken that unspoken pledge. She'd killed out of anger. Shame flooded through her, waves and waves of pulsing red.

She tried to pull it together. Weakness wasn't allowed. Even admitting she'd lost her edge was a betrayal of their code. They weren't allowed human emotions. And she knew she had them, and that was going to cost her everything.

"Does Atlantic know what was on the SD card?"

"No," Riley said. "And the D.C. police have it in their evidence locker."

"I wouldn't worry about that. There's no way they'd be able to get through the encryptions. They'd need a major cryptographer, all the right programs, everything. I know my sister. She is—was—the best at what she did. The information is safe for now at least."

"If only that were true, Robin, but I think you're wrong. Metro has a chick from the FBI working with them. I'm sure the stiffs from Quantico have already gotten their grubby little paws on it and decrypted the information."

She let that sink in. If the FBI was involved, things would be more difficult, but not unsalvageable. Not yet.

"Damn it, Riley, what the hell did Amanda stumble across? And why did the State Department want it? The email she received came directly from the Africa desk. She was bringing it in for this Kruger guy."

"I don't have an answer for you, Robbie."

She took the nickname as a good sign. Maybe he had forgiven her. She straightened, forced his darkness away, filled her space with a light blue fog that felt calming, took a breath. "So what is our mission?"

He looked over to her, his green eyes muddy with anger. He was volatile, that was part of the attraction. He was so very much alive. Her calm vanished; the car went black again.

"*My* mission is to get you to safety and recover the SD card and the vaccines so we know what the hell is going on. Your mission is to lay low. You'll stay here until I return."

"Come on. That's not fair. I need to do something. I can't just sit around, knowing my sister's killer is prowling the streets." *And that I did nothing to help her when she asked*, she thought, but kept it to herself.

"Atlantic's orders," he growled. "Nonnegotiable. So don't even try lobbying me."

Damn it all. Atlantic had given her a life when hers was collapsing in on itself. If he was pissed at her, it was like going to jail, or worse. Siberia, without a coat.

"I want to talk to him."

"He's out of touch. We're here."

Riley turned down a dirt track toward the water. He lived on a houseboat south of Old Town Alexandria. He liked that he could pull up anchor at any time and sail away, though he never really did. He wasn't ever home long enough to enjoy more than a glass of wine on the deck, watching the sun slip into the horizon, or the occasional sunrise, billowing pinks leading into soft yellow days, or, more often, sleepless nights, the water around him glowing silver in the moonlight.

At least, that's what he told her. He could be poetic when he wanted to, when the night made anything possible. Now was definitely not one of those times.

She had never been here. He always came to her. It was how they worked. Compartmentalized from each other. She couldn't help herself; she was dead curious about where he lived.

He pulled into the parking lot and practically dragged her to the boat. Inside the sliding glass doors, he gestured toward a round wooden table, built into the floor. He opened a cabinet, pulled out a scrambler and a laptop, set things up and called in on his satellite phone.

"I have Nightingale. She's A-OK."

They heard three clicks, affirmation of the transmission, then he shut it all down and stowed the gear. "There's food in the fridge. Help yourself."

He started toward the doors.

"Hey. Where are you going?"

He turned and gave her a sharp green glance. "To clean up your mess."

"That's uncalled for. Why are you so mad at me?"

He ignored her, kept moving toward the door, a big man with

broad shoulders and strong arms, the swirling black accompanying him like a matador's dirty cape.

"Riley. Don't walk away."

That stopped him.

Back still to her, he spoke carefully and evenly. "I can't do this anymore. I'm sorry."

He turned, and she was overcome by the colors of the emotions swirling around him. Greens and blues and pinks and yellows. Colors at odds with his harsh words. Before she could process things properly, he had her in his arms, his mouth hard on hers.

The kiss lasted forever, or only a moment, she wasn't sure. Then he pushed her away savagely and walked out the doors and up the dock, away from her, without looking back, and when the engine of his car turned over, she felt the small interior walls she'd built over the past months with him crumble to dust.

He'd just said goodbye, and she hadn't stopped him.

She didn't cry. There was no point. They'd always been prickly together, and it was a thing of convenience, of mutual admiration, not love. Never love. She didn't do love. And God knows, neither did Riley.

She tried to get the computer out of its cabinet, but it was locked. And not just any lock—it was biometric, the bastard. She'd need a thumbprint to open it.

She checked her phone, saw there was no service.

The pity party was over, replaced by a fine sheen of rage. He'd left her here on his boat, in total isolation. Not the most chivalrous act he'd ever committed.

If he was done with her, perhaps she should be done with him, as well.

The darkness of the Potomac was all-encompassing. But she didn't mind the dark. It gave her more room to move, held the synesthesia at bay. She turned off the lights of the houseboat so she wouldn't be backlit in case anyone was watching, stepped out the doors, slid them closed behind her and jumped quietly off the boat onto dry land.

Robin knew how to disappear. She didn't even have to go back to her house if she didn't want to. She had a stash out in Woodbridge at the bus station, a go-bag she could access, with money and passports and weapons, one of the many she had all over the world just for these kinds of situations.

These kinds of situations.

She almost laughed. She didn't know what the exact protocol was when your sister was murdered, your boss dissed you, your lover broke it off, you crossed your own moral lines and you had nothing left to live for. She checked her bag—yes, the small locker key she'd clipped to her key chain months ago was there. She might have been a bit crazy, but she was meticulous.

She started off into the night. She'd need a car. It was a few miles back into Old Town; she was sure she'd find one that met her needs along the way. She laid out a mental map in her head as she walked. She could be at the station by nine and gone from the world five minutes later.

The bright lights of a car's high beams swung into the gravel lane that led to Riley's dock. Robin froze, then ducked into the brush, crouching against a small sapling, feeling the sticky wetness of its leaves covering her legs. The car drove in slowly, as if the driver was looking for something. Or someone.

She pulled her gun from its holster, screwed on the suppressor. Felt something inside her—the last shreds of hope—break. Riley had left her here to be eliminated. She'd faced a hell of a lot of betrayals in her day, but this, her own team turning on her? This was beyond the pale.

She felt the anger and hurt leave; icy certainty flooded her. She was calm, breathing slowly, heart rate dropping, eyes laser focused. Not a girl with synesthesia who felt too much, but a stone-cold killer who wasn't about to be taken alive.

The car passed her. It was a black Lincoln Town Car with

diplomatic plates. French, if she wasn't mistaken. The glass was dark; she couldn't see who was inside.

Curiosity kept her in place, watching dispassionately as the car pulled up carefully to the small dock. The engine idled. No doors opened.

Who had they sent to kill her? She knew most of the top assassins in the world, if not by name, at least by face. She'd spent years building dossiers on her competition. In her job, she needed to be aware at all times of who might be coming, and whether they were friend or foe.

Of course, the two roles could be reversed at a moment's notice.

They'd need a top contractor to take her out, someone simply outstanding. She ran through a list of the few people she thought might be able to take her, preparing scenarios for each. Realized these could be her last thoughts ever, and forced that away. No. She wouldn't go down without a serious fight.

At last, the door opened. The driver emerged, male Caucasian, five-ten, buzz cut, eyes roving, a hand on his waist. An operator. When he was satisfied no shots were coming, he walked around to the passenger's side. She laughed to herself. She could knock him off in a heartbeat, and his passenger, too. She leveled the gun against her arm, sighted as the car door finally opened.

They *had* sent their best. Out stepped her old boss. Regina Girabaldi.

Robin lowered the weapon, took a deep breath to dispel the surge of adrenaline that tried to punch through her system.

There were few things in this world she was certain about. That Regina Girabaldi would want her dead, or even try to have her killed, wasn't on the list.

She stood up, made her way carefully back to the boat. Regina was already on board, tapping gently at the glass. Her bodyguard—Secret Service, most likely, and nervous to be out alone, away from his flock—was watching intensely. While Regina wouldn't hurt her, this loon might.

Silent as a doe in a thicket, she stepped to his side, pulled the earwig from his ear and pressed the suppressor gently against his temple. She felt his muscles bunch; he was going to attack.

"You're looking for me," she said softly. "I won't hurt her."

He didn't relax, but he didn't move, either. She took his weapons, just in case, and with a small jab to his ribs, started him onto the path down the dock to the boat.

CHAPTER 43

Georgetown

XANDER WAS DEEP INTO JAMES DENON'S COMPUTER FILES WHEN SAM CAME through the door with Darren Fletcher fast on her heels. Thor jumped up with a bark and ran to Sam, tail wagging, tongue lolling. Xander watched her greet the animal with a loving caress across the ears, but she had her eyes locked on his, and he felt that jump in his stomach he always had when she looked at him. She was clearly exhausted and running on caffeine; her hands were shaking a little as they stroked Thor's coat. She was beautiful, though. Beautiful, and his.

He stood, shook Fletcher's hand, then pulled Sam to him. The hug was brief, but the connection between them was all he needed. He could feel her shivering, though it wasn't at all cold in the room. Fear, then, adrenaline from the close call.

"I'm so glad you're okay," he said in her ear. She nodded, held on tighter, until Fletcher cleared his throat.

"Hey, don't I get a hug? He nearly shot me, too."

Xander let her loose and reached for Fletcher, who ducked away, laughing. It felt good to goof off for a minute, but Xander got serious again almost immediately. He jerked his head toward the living room.

"I have Denon here. He's ready to talk when you are. I haven't told him yet. About Amanda's death."

Sam sighed. She hated this part of the job. "Let's get to it, then. Living room?"

"That seems to be the best place."

"Xander, you need to be watching our backs until we find Robin Souleyret. I'm supposed to be getting the background on Jason Kruger any minute," Fletcher said.

"You really think he was working with Souleyret?"

"I don't know. But Souleyret's the closest thing we have to a suspect until she presents herself and proves us wrong."

Sam glanced through the house, saw the crowd of people gathered. "We need some extra security here. I don't want to be paranoid, but until we do locate Souleyret, I won't feel safe. Almost the entire working knowledge of this case is in a three-thousand-square-foot area, and from what I hear, she's one hell of a shot. I don't want to get picked off before we finish this."

Fletcher nodded. "I agree. I can call in a few people."

Xander shook his head. "Additional protection isn't a bad idea, but let Chalk handle it. He can be discreet."

"Screw discreet," Sam said. "I want a show of force. Make her rethink any ideas of attacking us here."

"Chalk *is* a show of force. Let me get him going." He went to the kitchen, conferred with his partner for a minute. Sam saw Chalk smile and nod, then he slipped out the back door with Thor at his side.

Xander came back to her. "I wish we were at the cabin. I could protect all of you better there."

She gave him a smile, ran a hand along his jaw. "Me, too. But we're stuck here. So let's make it work, soldier."

Her cell phone rang. Daniels was calling. She put up a finger and answered, put it on speaker. "What's up, Daniels?"

"Dr. Owens, I've got something. I'm still staking out Souleyret's place. We've gotten into her files through her wireless connection—sloppy of her. She's barely got any encryption on it at all. She was looking into her sister's email. She downloaded a draft email that looks like it came from the State Department, though I don't know if she knows that."

"Who sent it? Girabaldi?"

"Nope. Jason Kruger. It came from his email. It says, *'Did you get it in?'*"

"When was it sent?"

She heard him typing. She could imagine him, sitting there in the car, his laptops spread out, Mouse working by his side. They were going to make a great team—Sam had to find a way to get the girl on board at the FBI full-time.

"It was drafted at eight-thirty this morning."

"Before State called us in. That's really interesting. You heard about Kruger, right?"

"That he tried to kill you and Detective Fletcher? Yes. I'm very glad he didn't succeed."

"Me, too. Unfortunately, he's dead, and we can't ask him what he was looking for, though I think we can guess. I can only assume he was talking about one of two things. The SD card or the vaccines. Which are in the wind, by the way. Someone posing as a CDC courier took them from D.C.'s HAZMAT team."

"Jeez. Sounds to me like we have multiple people working the angles of this case, Dr. Owens. There's no way only one person could be in so many places at once. It has to be a full assault team."

"I agree. Two of them are down that we know of. One had been killed at Bromley's office. We're still waiting for an ID on him. And now Kruger's dead. Assuming the attack on James Denon was a part of this, that's three assassins down. One got away when Kruger was shot. We can only hope that's the last player. And Robin Souleyret is still out there somewhere."

"So you think she's managing this? Someone has to be calling the shots."

"I don't know."

"If there's a team, ma'am, you need to be really careful. Even if you think three of the four are down."

"You're right, we do. It almost feels like there were multiple assassinations planned to be carried out simultaneously. This is incredibly well-coordinated. If Kruger was behind it, we might be in luck, but since he was out doing the shooting, I'm afraid someone else is running the show. I feel like everything is leading back to Girabaldi. Is she clean? Can you find out?"

"I can. I'll have to pull out of Souleyret's files, though."

Sam thought for a minute. "Okay. Just dump them all, and let Mouse start going through them. You shift to Girabaldi. Be careful, Daniels. This is a very powerful woman were talking about."

"I will. Hey, hold on a second."

She could hear Mouse talking in the background.

"What is it?"

"A courier. DHL. He just pulled into the driveway."

"Where's he headed?"

"Hang on. He's driven past the circular drive entrance for the main house. He's heading down the track to Souleyret's."

"Is he for real? Or is this someone coming to eliminate Souleyret?"

"I'm watching. I've got night-vision goggles on. We're well hidden in the woods."

"What the hell is he doing out delivering so late?"

"I don't know. That's pretty sketchy. Want us to intercept? I've got another couple of cops here."

Fletcher was standing to her left. Both he and Xander nodded. "Yes. Intercept him. Right now."

She heard the squelch from the radio. Daniels was calling to the cops, telling them to get the guy. "I'll be back to you in a minute. Talk to Mouse."

And he was gone. Mouse came on the line. "Hi, Doc."

"Hi yourself. Give me the play-by-play."

"They've boxed him in. The cops are driving right up to him, guns drawn. He just dropped a package on the ground and put up his hands. No one went boom. That's a good sign."

Sam laughed. "Yes, that's a very good sign."

"Marc's got the package, he's opening it now. Looks like a CD of some kind. He just gave me a thumbs-up. It's nothing dangerous. The guy has ID, looks like he really is just a courier. They're checking the truck, too, just in case, but we look good here."

Sam let out the breath she hadn't realized she was holding. "All right. You and Daniels finish up there and bring that package to me. Right now." She gave the girl her address.

"I've got a copy of Souleyret's hard drive, too. We'll be there in ten."

She hung up. Fletcher raised an eyebrow. "I kind of like it when you take over the show."

"Hush. What do you think is in that package?"

"I don't know."

"Do we know where Girabaldi is now?" she asked.

"Cavort said they have her under protection, so she's probably reading a magazine in some bunker somewhere. I can push things, bump it up to her bosses, have them release her into my custody."

"You're off the case, Fletcher. You better stay put. You can't lose your job over this."

She could see the frustration on his face. "Honestly, Sam, right now, I'm more concerned about the idea of a gang of assassins on the loose in my city. I know this Chalk character is good, but I'm going to get some people watching the house, just in case. Armstrong will help with that." He peeled off into the den near the back door. It was the only unoccupied room on the lower floor.

Xander watched him go, put a hand on Sam's shoulder, dug his thumb deep into the tissue. She sighed as the muscle relaxed and released.

"That's better. Thank you."

He nodded. "No worries. Listen, I do have some news for you. I think Denon's company is the one Amanda Souleyret infiltrated. I think he's the money behind the vaccines."

She reared back, nearly toppling a crystal vase from the small hall table. She managed to get a hand on it before it hit the floor. "What did you say?"

"His IT guy, Everson, just told me he found a back door that's been in place for several months. He doesn't know how bad the damage is yet, so we haven't told Denon."

"Do we know who's responsible?"

He shook his head. "Not yet, but think about it. Amanda was sleeping with Denon. The affair had been going on for almost a year. You said she was trained as a honeypot, technologically and otherwise. What better way to bilk a company than bedding down with its CEO and putting a spike in his systems?"

Sam brushed her hair back from her face. It made an awful kind of sense.

"We've been assuming all along that she was working the right side of this. Are you saying you think she was behind it instead? And crossed the wrong person, who had her killed?"

"Her, and everyone who had anything to do with this case. They're eliminating the knowledge base. Systematically."

"Did you find a money trail for the man from this morning? The Spaniard?"

His face darkened. "The assassin I killed, you mean? Not yet, but we're working on it." He rubbed a big hand over his face, smoothing out his eyebrows. She could see he was tired, bone-deep. They all were. "This is a clusterfuck, you know that."

"I do. And we have a bunch of possibly deadly drugs out there, most likely in the wrong hands. Who knows what they're planning."

"Let's talk to Denon."

"First, Xander, hon, are you okay? Tell me the truth."

He glanced over her head, then put a hand under her chin, lifted her face so she was staring deep into his coffee eyes. He gave her a quick but thorough kiss, then a grin. "Are you?"

"I am now."

He hitched his arm over her shoulders. "Then let's do this."

CHAPTER 44

THEY SAT WITH DENON IN THE LIVING ROOM—SAM, FLETCHER AND XANDER, a triumvirate of frustration and exhaustion and hands shaky from too much caffeine, facing their last hope for an explanation of the day's events. Sam sipped on a cup of tea, wishing for a stiff shot of Scotch, knowing it would just put her to sleep. Still, a girl could dream.

She set the cup down. Denon watched her motions. He knew something was up; she could see it in his face. He looked from her to Xander to Fletcher, then cleared his throat.

"You might as well tell me. I can see you have bad news."

Sam nodded. "Then I'll be blunt, Mr. Denon, and please forgive me. We know where Juliet Bouchard is. And who she is. Her real name is Amanda Souleyret. She's a deep undercover agent run out of the FBI, and I'm sorry to have to tell you this, but she's dead. She was murdered last night, quite near here. There was a man with her, a young researcher named Thomas Cattafi. He's alive, but barely."

The color drained from Denon's face as she spoke. "We don't know who killed her, but it stands to reason, considering she came in on your plane, it was the same people who tried to murder you this morning. So anything you can tell us about her would be a huge help in ending this mess."

He was silent for a moment. Closed his eyes. Breathed out once through his nose, heavily. When he opened his eyes again, his emotions were mastered, but still raw and on the surface, like the tension of a bubble's edge. A breath in the wrong place and he would burst.

His voice was shaky. "I know the name. Tommy Cattafi, I mean."

That got her attention. "From where?"

He stood, walked to the edge of the room, called into the dining room. "Mo? Maureen? Hang up, right now."

She did, stood, brushing her hair back from her face. Sam hadn't really noticed her before now, but she was a pretty girl, with one bright blue eye and one brown, that took her from interesting to exotic. "Sir?"

"Remember that kid Tommy Cattafi? Juliet sent him your way. You brought him on as an intern to work on the offshore pipeline we were planning into Sierra Leone. He was working with the Doctors Without Borders organization there. You said he knew the area and could help us liaise with the locals."

Heedles shook her head. "I don't remember that name. But, sir, we have so many interns. And not all of us have your eidetic memory."

"I'm sure that was it. I'm not losing it all quite yet."

She bit her lip. "I'll have to check the personnel files."

"Do that."

"I'm on it, but it will take me a minute." She sat down and started typing furiously. Everson gave her a long glance, then followed suit. Bebbington, though, came over to his boss. He turned him away from the table, and they walked back into the living room to where Sam was standing, watching the exchanges with interest. So Amanda had sent Tommy into the fray. It made sense, he was her recruit. He would have been a great candidate for anyone to hire on.

Bebbington shot Xander a knowing glance. He had a quiet voice, befitting a mathematical genius.

"Sir, I've found an anomaly you need to know about."

"Speak up, Louis, I can barely hear you."

The man swallowed hard. His voice was shaking. Sam saw him swipe his palms against his too-tight pants leg, leaving a small dark smear on the fine worsted wool. "Someone has siphoned off an exceptionally large amount of money from the accounts."

She didn't think it was possible for Denon to get any whiter, but he did.

"What in the bloody hell are you talking about, Louis? Who?"

"I don't know yet, sir."

"How much?"

"In the range of forty to fifty million pounds. Out of the African pipeline project."

"How is that possible? We closed that down last year. We don't have an African pipeline project anymore."

"Sir, I can't believe I'm telling you this, but someone kept a line open on it. They've been funneling money out of the program budgets for all the Venezuela accounts. A little here, and a little there. Nothing that would cause us to notice. Until it was too late."

Denon's fists clenched. He looked like he was about to knock the younger man to the ground. "Louis, you're my CFO. How is it, exactly, someone has managed to embezzle fifty million pounds out from under your nose?"

Bebbington swallowed hard, his Adam's apple bobbing in his thin throat. "It's an incredibly sophisticated siphon program. I wouldn't have seen it if we weren't looking at the back door. Everson found tracks in the system. Sir, we have been compromised. Badly. And, sir, I must tender my resignation. This happened on my watch—"

"Shut it, Louis. Now's not the time. Where did the funds go?"

The man looked only slightly relieved. "Everson followed the trail to the Banque de France. The money moved through circuitous routes, from numbered accounts in the Caymans to a Swiss bank to the current resting place, a branch in the Côte d'Azur."

"Can we access it?"

"We can try. There have been regular disbursements, also through coded accounts. It's going to take a full forensic examination to unspool the thread, though. Weeks, if not months."

Xander's cell rang. He stepped away, put it to his ear, listened for a moment. Sam heard him say, "Roger that. Friendlies at the door. Cover us."

The doorbell rang, and all the Brits started.

Sam smiled. "Relax, gentlemen. That will be Agent Daniels and Rosalind Lowe, who have been working on the SD card Amanda Souleyret brought into the country. They've seized a package that was being sent to her sister. We might get some answers from it."

She started toward the door, but Xander put a hand on her arm. "You let me get it."

Sam stopped, nodded. Xander already had his SIG out, was moving quickly down the hall into the foyer. Thor appeared in the hallway, followed his master. With a few guttural German commands from Xander, Thor went on alert. Chalk came in from the back door, guns drawn, loaded for bear. With a look toward Xander, who sent him some sort of telepathic shorthand, he melted into the hallway by the dining room where he could see out the front windows.

The doorbell rang again. Chalk called out, "All clear."

Xander carefully inched open the door, leading with the nose of the gun.

Sam heard Daniels. "Whoa! FBI, man, I'm FBI."

"Xander, let them in already," she said.

He opened the door wider, and Daniels and Mouse trooped in, looking exceedingly excited. He slammed the door shut, and the dog relaxed. They were secure again. For now. Sam saw Chalk detach himself from the window and quickly move to the rear of the house, where he disappeared out the back door to secure their perimeter again. She had to admit, she felt safer with him and Xander on such high alert.

There were brief introductions, then Daniels held up a laptop. "We have something major to show you."

Sam gestured to the mixed company. "Is it appropriate for all, or do we need to find someplace quiet?"

He flipped open the screen, hit Play. "Just watch."

The video was black, then Amanda Souleyret's face filled the screen. Her voice was strong, but quiet, as if she didn't want to be overheard. The room behind her was dark; it was hard to see where she was. Sam thought it looked like a hotel room, but it could have been a private flat. Even subdued, she was so very alive. It was all Sam could do not to remind herself of this same body on the stainless-steel slab, cuts in her neck and back, the heart no longer beating, but still and inert. And Fletcher's voice: *"You've never told me why you do it."*

Quit it, Owens. This isn't the first time you've seen someone from the grave.

But when Amanda began to speak, Sam felt goose bumps parade up and down her arms.

"Robin, I hope I've had a chance to talk to you in person before you receive this message. If not...well, I'm most likely dead. I'm so sorry. I didn't want to put you in any danger. You've had too much to deal with since the accident. No matter what, I want you to know that I love you, and everything that happens from here on out, well, if I didn't stop them, I know you'll find the means to do so.

"Gina is in danger. You need to protect her, no matter what. I have done all I can to keep her safe, but I fear it's too late, and she will get

sucked into this maelstrom. *She's too important to us both to let that happen. I also need you to watch Thomas Cattafi's and David Bromley's backs. They are the key to all I'm about to tell you, and they must be protected at all costs.*

"*I was working on a case with a small pharm company in Paris when I accidentally downloaded information about a possible bioterror attack using our own flu vaccines. I briefed Gina, then set about trying to gather information about the attack. From what I found, a small group was testing out a new 'drug' in Sierra Leone, claiming it was a vaccine for measles. Instead, it contained a new, undocumented viral hemorrhagic fever that is especially virulent. They were testing a weapon, perfecting it and planning to use it to attack the United States and Israel.*"

There was a brief pause, and Amanda shook her head.

"*It gets worse. This new hemorrhagic fever kills in forty-eight hours, and it could be airborne. Right now, it is unstoppable, especially in an unsecured environment like Africa. The data points were absolutely terrifying, and just as I was making progress on discovering who, exactly, is behind this, they shut things down, wiped the files clean, destroyed every bit of evidence, and everything I had went up in smoke. And I knew my word wasn't going to be enough. You know how this administration works. You have to have a knife to their throat for them to pay any attention to these threats.*

"*I'd only gotten the name of a single company that was involved— Denon Industries, out of London. The money trail led directly to them. They have a charitable arm that has been funding the development of this horrible weapon.*"

Denon jumped up from his seat. "That's preposterous. I had nothing to do with this!"

Sam hit Stop on the video. "Mr. Denon, please, sit back down. We will hear everything Amanda has to say before making any assumptions or judgments."

"Sir?" It was Bebbington, excited now, standing in the doorway to the living room. "Ms. Bouchard, she's right. I've tracked some of the funds. Whoever embezzled them from us set up a trust under the guise of being a charitable organization. It traces back to the pipeline project, but it's in your name, under your private accounts. According to the records, you've been pumping money into this experimental medical treatment for two years."

"Jesus H. Christ on a piece of toast, Bebbington. How the hell did this happen?"

"I haven't been able to trace the information all the way back to the perpetrators yet, sir. Whoever did it has managed to obfuscate their trail masterfully. It's going to take us a while to figure out who's behind it. But I'll keep working on it. I'll find them, I swear it."

"You do that." Denon drew himself up to full height, faced Sam and Fletcher. "Denon Industries will cooperate fully with the FBI and any other international law enforcement organization you see fit to involve here. These actions are clearly of a single person who set out to deceive me and the company. I would never sign off on such a thing. It goes against everything I believe in."

Sam put her hand on his arm. "Sir, I appreciate that, but please sit down. Let's hear the rest of Amanda's story."

Fletcher moved a step closer, and Denon glanced at him, then sat, looking miserable. Sam pressed Play on the video, and Amanda Souleyret continued her confession from the grave.

"Something seemed odd about the trail suddenly leading me to a single organization, but I had to move quickly. I set up an infiltration strategy and implemented it. It didn't take long to get inside the company. What I found showed my earlier suspicions were right. I believe Denon Industries is being set up as the fall guy behind this massive genocide. And genocide it is, I'm sure of it. First in Africa, and, soon enough, in Europe and America. It is a perfect weapon.

"You know what I do, Robin. I've been intimate with James Denon for nearly a year now. I do not believe he is aware that his company's finances are being used to fund the operation, nor do I believe him personally capable of knowingly authorizing such devastation. My software

found a back door that was bleeding funds, but quietly. He has a mole, but I haven't been able to figure out who it is."

Sam saw Denon's face collapse at this news. He loved this woman, and she'd just exonerated him. Sam felt infinitesimally better. At least she wasn't sitting in her living room with a mass murderer.

"I sent Thomas Cattafi into the company to see if he could work this from another angle. He hired on to their African pipeline project as an intern, a liaison between the company and the locals, and in that guise was able to get into the areas affected in Sierra Leone. What he saw there was frightening. David Bromley is Thomas's mentor. He's a virologist at George Washington University and a preeminent scholar in hemorrhagic fevers. Tommy explained what was happening, and took Bromley's guidance on testing the blood of the people affected and reporting back with his findings. Tommy told me that there are reports of a British man who comes to the area once a month. We think this is how the bug is being delivered, in the medications that are supposed to be relieving the suffering of those afflicted.

"Tommy brought out the samples, and he and Dr. Bromley have been working for the past few months on a real vaccine. It's complicated to explain, but Tommy figured out that stem cells from cadavers showed the most promise in combating this disease."

Sam looked at Fletcher. That explained what Thomas Cattafi was doing at the anatomy lab. He'd been taking samples to use in his fight against the bug.

"Cattafi and Bromley have been working hard to reengineer the stem cells to create a workable therapeutic vaccine against this superbug, which means they can give it to people who've been exposed and halt the spread of the disease. I know they're very close to success. They've had to test in the field, with Bromley going directly to Africa to inoculate the infected people, and I understand it's been rough going, but they are starting to see a positive response. Their work will save the people affected, if they can get to them in time. And if we are attacked, we need to have the means to stop an epidemic.

"Meanwhile, I followed the money. I believe I have identified at least eighty percent of the people involved, from the terrorist organization in Africa to the company manufacturing the bug. I infiltrated their systems and stole the material I hope contains the answers to stopping the spread of the disease. It's time to turn this information over to State and let them sort it out. I've included a list in this package. You'll see some familiar names. Jason Kruger, for one, who works for Gina, which is why she's in so much danger. I believe he is the 'British' man they talk about—you can look at his official travel to prove where he's been, and though he grew up in South Africa, he has a British accent, probably from early schooling there."

Amanda shook her head.

"Greed, sister. Greed drives terrorism, and the people who are trying to do good are being overwhelmed by the ones trying to make a buck on the backs and lives of the people. It sickens me, and I'm sorry I couldn't be the one to end their attack.

"Please, Robin, act quickly. I have a lot of evidence, but not a lot of answers. It's time for me to let Gina shut down the funneled funds from Denon's company. With any luck, they will be able to discover who, exactly, is behind all of this. They're going to need James's cooperation, and I promise you, he will cooperate. He'd never want anything like this to happen. He's a good man, and I care for him deeply. If you get a chance, please tell him so. And while you're at it, will you tell him my real name? He only knows me as Juliet Bouchard, and it's important that he understand why I deceived him. I wanted to tell him myself, when all this was over, but I don't think I'm going to get a chance."

A small sob leaked from Denon's mouth. The screen went black, and everyone froze, then began speaking at once.

"Hold on a minute, there's more," Daniels shouted.

A few seconds later, Amanda came back onto the screen. She was in a different place, a hotel room, from the looks of it, and it was full daylight out. She looked disheveled and scared.

"Robin, I screwed up. I'm pretty sure Kruger discovered what I've been up to, and has warned his people I'm coming to the States. Kru-

ger opened a dialogue with me out of the blue, asking for my help on a case they were working in Sierra Leone. He began emailing me, asking for information, said they had word there was a terrorist attack in motion. I know he works for Gina, but this has been close hold—she hasn't told anyone what I'm doing.

"I played along, but I've found a money trail that leads directly to his accounts. Right after that, my house was tossed, my passports stolen, my phones were tapped. I knew I was being followed, despite my precautions, so I cleared out of France immediately, but it's probably too late. I'm in London right now, and will be taking a flight tonight to New York with James. We leave in a few hours, and I pray I make the flight. I'll have the samples with me. I have to get them to Cattafi. That's the only thing that can save us now.

"My enemies are in the shadows. I've taken precautions to make sure the information I have is making it to the people who need it. I've mailed this to my house in D.C., and to you. Gina will also receive this, and I'm bringing in more information on my person, in the way you told me about a couple of years ago.

"I know you can pick up where I left off. But, Robin, I have to warn you, I think everyone who knows about this is in great danger. Something I saw before the trail disappeared scared the hell out of me. I believe the bad medications have been sold to the highest bidder. The terrorist organizations in Africa have been in the market for anything and everything they can use to attack the United States, and this is the perfect weapon. If they've already gotten their hands on the medicine, it may be too late for us to stop their infiltration into our health system. It's as easy as infecting several of their people and putting them on a plane to the US. We won't even see it coming.

"I've already warned Gina of the possibility we're going to be attacked, and that her life is in danger. She needs eyes on Kruger immediately. He will lead us to the rest of the people involved.

"Please, for the sake of all the people we serve, catch the person behind this, and do it now. I've failed our country, our people, James, Gina *and you. Worse, I've failed myself. I should have come forward with this information sooner, but I had no idea how far things had progressed."*

Amanda was openly crying now. Through the tears, she put her fingers to her lips, then blew a kiss toward the screen.

"I love you, sis. I have faith in you. I'll see you again someday."

And the video ended.

TUESDAY: EVENING

Death is a delightful hiding place for weary men.
—Herodotus

CHAPTER 45

Riley's houseboat
Tuesday evening

REGINA GIRABALDI HAD BEEN IN THE CATBIRD SEAT AND OUT OF THE FIELD for too long. Robin almost laughed at the look on her face as she marched the woman's bodyguard toward her, the gun still nestled against his temple.

Girabaldi's hand went to her side for a moment, in search of the cool weight of a gun holster on her hip she'd become accustomed to after years in the field, but, finding no weapon, raised both hands slightly in a defensive gesture.

"Robin. Don't hurt him. We're just here to talk."

"Gina, do you really think I'd be stupid enough to shoot a Secret Service agent?"

"No. But you might shoot *me*. I'd rather we talk like civilized adults."

Robin bared her teeth at her mentor in an approximation of a smile. "Then you'll understand why I don't put my weapon away. The door's unlocked, just pull the latch."

Girabaldi stared at the barrel of the gun for a few moments, took a deep breath, swallowed and turned around with her shoulder blades tensed as if expecting the firing to commence immediately. When Robin didn't shoot her in the back, the proud shoulders dropped an inch, and she slid open the doors and entered. The Secret Service agent followed her, looking like a dog that had just been kicked.

Robin walked after them, pulled the sliding glass door shut behind her. She knocked the guard in the shoulder good-naturedly.

"Don't worry about it. I'm pretty good at sneaking up on people. I was taught by the best, remember." She used the gun to gesture toward a chair. "Sit."

He stiffened.

"Please," she added, and he acquiesced, taking a seat at the table and muttering the words "I'm sorry" to Girabaldi. Regina shook her head as if to say, *Don't worry, it was my fault,* and he looked even more unhappy.

Robin sat down, as well, leaned back in the chair. Girabaldi's eyes were wide, but she, too, sat, running her hands along her arms as if she were cold.

"Do you want to do this in front of him?" Robin asked.

"Do we have a choice?"

Robin shrugged. "I'm not comfortable letting him loose into the wild just yet. I can tie him up and gag him, stash him in the trunk of your car, but I have nothing to hide. I've done nothing wrong, and I want you to tell me what in the hell is going on. So if you need him to disappear, just say the word."

"Witnesses can be handy. He stays." Girabaldi smiled then, and set her hands on the table. Robin was shocked by how aged they'd become. Seeing those capable hands, ones she'd emulated so many times, wrinkled and spotted and heavily veined, hit her hard. She dropped the nose of the weapon, let it dangle casually toward the floor.

"What the hell, Gina? Who killed Mandy?"

"I don't know. And I'm being honest with you. She'd been

working on a case deep undercover. I'm talking off the grid entirely. A long game, which put her in an unbelievable amount of danger."

"Were you running her?"

"Yes."

"So no matter who wielded the knife, you're responsible for her death." Her fingers caressed the gun gently, raising it slightly. Girabaldi's chin rose to match it. "How could you let it get this far?"

"Amanda went offline two weeks ago. All she had to do was call me and I would have moved heaven and earth to save her. Instead, she got too cute by half, and someone caught on."

"What was the job, Gina? Quit beating around the bush and tell me. I know it has something to do with James Denon, but that's as far as I've gotten."

"First, I need to ask you a question. Did Amanda say anything to you about what she was working on?"

Robin caught the anxious tone in Girabaldi's voice, the lavender words spilling out of her mouth. It put her even more on alert.

"She sent me a note a month ago. Asked for a spot. I couldn't break away." *Couldn't, because you'd just fucked up your own world and you were too busy trying to bail yourself out, and where did that get you? Sidelined. Well done, you.*

She told the voices to shut the fuck up, and felt better.

"I heard about that. I'm sorry. If I were still your boss, I wouldn't have shuffled you off. You're too good for that."

"Quit trying to make this all okay. It won't be. Ever. Tell me about Amanda. Now."

"We have the beginnings of another pandemic in Africa. Worse than the terrible Ebola outbreak of 2014. We have a generalized viral hemorrhagic fever that mimics Ebola, but the time from exposure to death is less than forty-eight hours. It developed by accident, and we still aren't one hundred percent sure how it was spread. A pseudovaccine was engineered and used. Unfortunately, the new vaccine kills half the people who contract the illness, and heals the other half. There's no way to know which will happen. But if they aren't treated, the mortality rate is one hundred percent. We think this outbreak is simply a testing ground. Some very undesirable people want to use the sickness as a weapon, since its efficacy in killing people is so high."

"Great. Wonderful. So you unleashed a bug you can't stop. That's terrible, but this involved my sister how?"

"We didn't unleash the bug. Amanda found proof of an attack plan in the works, and she got in bed with the money trail for us."

Robin raised an eyebrow. She hadn't particularly liked the methods her sister used to get to the information she needed, but that was her choice. Amanda was a grown-up. She could bed whoever she wanted, for whatever reason she wanted.

"And the money had her killed when she exposed him?"

"No. He hasn't been exposed. We think someone in his company had her killed, and then killed everyone who was working the project along with her. We're still trying to find out who that person might be. In the meantime, Mandy had found a couple of doctors who thought they could reengineer the vaccine. Apparently, they'd been working on it privately, and were close to having a cure."

"So why would someone want to kill her for it? It sounds like a great thing. She may have found a way to fix a very bad situation."

"I believe the truth of the matter is they don't want it fixed. The people behind this are selling the illness to a terrorist organization. Amanda thought we might be attacked in the near future. She got one of her own recruits into the mix, genius kid, to see if he could help."

"Cattafi?"

"Yes."

"His buddy Bromley is dead. In case you hadn't heard."

Girabaldi collapsed then, from proud face and shoulders to the bottom of her spine. She hunched over the table, put her head in her hands. "Everyone who worked on this is dead. Someone's trying to clean up their mess."

"And you're next?"

Regina nodded.

"Why didn't you save her, Gina? Why did you let my sister die?"

"I didn't. I would have done anything within my power to protect her, you know that. She wasn't like you. She needed me. She's always needed me."

Robin felt the familiar flame of jealousy rise up in her, pushed it away. "I needed you, too, *Mom*. It would have been nice if you'd realized that."

"Your sister—"

"Your daughter."

Regina closed her eyes. "You're my daughter, too. Don't think this hurts me any less than it hurts you. I've already lost one of you. I can't lose you, too. I've done all I could for you. But now I need your help. Please, Robin. Don't make me beg."

"Done all you could except be a mother when I needed one. A boss, a mentor, yes. You taught me how to kill, how to hide in the shadows, how to be the woman I am today. But you never could talk yourself into loving me. You reserved all of that for Amanda. And now you want me to be your shield. To protect you. That's rich, Gina. Really, really rich."

Girabaldi gritted her teeth, trying to gain control, the upper hand, as she always had. Robin watched the familiar strangeness of her mother's face as she struggled for composure.

She'd given them up when they were so young, when Robin was only four and Amanda two. Left their father, left their life, to globe-trot for the CIA. Her dad, bless his heart, was crushed, but remarried, giving them a mother figure, a sweet lady who they both called Mom. Regina returned to her maiden name and was referred to—if she ever needed to be—as their distant aunt.

Amanda was too young. She never really knew what had happened. But Robin remembered. She remembered it all. When she was eighteen, she showed up on Regina's doorstep, wanting answers. Regina turned her into a weapon instead, then came for Amanda when she, too, came of age.

Clouds of purple were billowing around Robin, and she fought through the darkness. Regina had made sure they were both taken care of, put to work in the family business. She took one look at an adult Amanda and nestled her sweetness into her bosom, under her arm, where she could be protected. And one look at Robin—the coldness, the emptiness, the lack of empathy and the potential for destruction—and put a long-range rifle in her hands.

Robin had seen her private CIA induction file once. It read like a clinical wasteland. *Emotionless sociopathy. Lack of empathy. Penchant for violence. Ability to compartmentalize. Comfortable with extreme isolation.* And then the ultimate stamp of approval. *Recommended for field work.*

Amanda's file was different. It had always been different. Warmer. Nicer. Plays well with others and shares with her friends. Shares herself with her friends, it should have read. In more ways than one.

Robin didn't know what was worse, being completely closed off and frigid, or finding love in the arms of strangers. She knew both their lives were in direct reaction to the abandonment of their mother. The anger boiled up again, threatening to overflow.

"You made us both, Gina. And now you've killed one of us. I don't think I'll let you kill me, too." She stood and started toward the sliding glass door, to the darkness, the anonymity that was her world.

Regina spoke softly. "Robin. Please don't leave. You need to see this." She nodded at the Secret Service agent. He reached into his jacket and pulled out a small tablet.

"This will explain everything."

She hit Play, and Robin stopped at the door, halted her escape and nearly cracked into pieces.

Amanda.

She listened to her sister's honey-colored words, wondering what it all meant. Why she had to die for this case. Why she hadn't pushed for help when she got in too deep.

She wanted to prove herself, Robin. To you, to Gina. You know that. She always did. And she had asked. You abandoned her when she needed you the most. You are no better than your mother.

When the video was finished, she sat down, trying not to lose it. Trying to compartmentalize, as was her forte. Pushing away the horror and loss of her baby sister to a cause that would kill them all, and going into a more operational state. It was too late to save Amanda. It wasn't yet too late to save the world.

If what Amanda said was true, about the coming attack, this was bigger than all of them and their petty family squabbles. An attack on their soil with a biological weapon delivered in a most innocuous manner would derail the world.

The now-familiar doubt crept in. It had come recently, borne on a piece of shrapnel, sanded with desert muck, into her side, and whispered to her of all her failings.

She couldn't stop this. They were screwed. Absolutely, one hundred percent screwed.

Robin walked to the small kitchenette and fixed herself a stiff shot of bourbon. Forced all the emotions that had been swirling around her since the accident back into the black hole inside her, found her focus, her bitter cold center, the one place she felt truly herself. She shot the bourbon, then turned and leaned against the hard counter.

"Why me, Regina? You have two agencies at your beck and call."

Girabaldi's face creased in relief. Her daughter had acquiesced once again, and she was back on top, calling the shots.

"I don't trust anyone but you right now, Robin. I need your protection. I need you to find out who killed Amanda, and who is after me. I've already had one team member involved in this killed today. I wish I could convince myself he's the only one involved, but I can't. Only a handful of people knew about the medicine and vaccine."

"Who was it?"

"Jason Kruger. I would have never expected him to betray me like this. I'm not sure how deep his betrayal goes, though. And the D.C. police killed him an hour ago."

"He was onto Amanda. Chasing her."

"She brought the samples in, and he managed to take them from her. I have no doubt they were—at some point today—in his possession."

"Did he kill her? Was it Kruger?"

"I don't know. I don't know who else it could be, but there could be any number of people working this, Robin. You know how terrorists work." Girabaldi grew cold then, back into her role. "I want you to hunt them down and eliminate them. You heard your sister. She knew she was in danger and that I am in danger. We will all be affected if there's an attack."

Robin laughed, the sound harsh against the night air. "So you want to wind up your little sociopath and watch her go?"

Those hands, those old-woman hands, clutching at the wooden tabletop, leaving filmy prints on the shellacked finish. The voice had always been stronger than the flesh, and it held a familiar hint of annoyance.

"Now is not the time, Robin. When we've secured the tainted medicine and arrested all those involved, you and I will talk. You can berate me, you can beat me up, hell, you can kill me. But our duty lies with this country, and we must stop this attack."

"Is this sanctioned? Or are we off book?"

"This is sanctioned. I have cleared it with your superiors. I spent the day having you reinstated. Do this, and I will make sure you're given your old position. Or a new one, should you desire. You can have anything you want. Robin, we're talking about an unknown terrorist attack that could come at any time. I need you. Your country needs you."

Your country needs you. The very words that had driven all three Souleyret women into a life of public service, into the morass of death and destruction, the carnage of their beliefs and duty laid to waste behind them.

Family was always second to country.

Robin shook herself, and the cloud cleared away. "Riley says I'm a suspect in Amanda's murder. How exactly do you propose I do this job? I can't have people hunting me. I need my back clear."

"I will work everything. Consider yourself cleared. I've already got the FBI on board."

"I want to talk to the investigators. I want to hear firsthand what they have to say."

"I can arrange a meeting for you."

"No, Gina. I want to do this myself. I want to talk to the woman, the FBI agent, the medical examiner who did Amanda's autopsy. I want her. And no one else. If I get a hint that there's someone else involved, I pull out and disappear, and you can go fuck yourself."

"That's fine, Robin. I don't blame you a bit. But you need to be careful. I don't know who to trust anymore. I've been compromised, and so was Amanda. You should operate under the assumption that you have, as well."

CHAPTER 46

Georgetown

THERE WAS SILENCE WHEN THE SCREEN WENT BLACK. XANDER HAD GRABBED Sam's hand a few moments before Amanda finished the recitation of what led to her death. She was glad of the familiar pressure; she felt like she might fall down otherwise. This was as bad as it got. How in the hell were they going to stop an attack they couldn't see coming? They still had no idea who was behind the plot. Not to mention, if Amanda was right, and the superbug was airborne, spreading it through the populace *was* as easy as importing sick people on planes. Sam shuddered at the thought.

No one moved as Daniels closed the laptop. Mouse was by his side, eyes wide, unconsciously seeking what succor she could find during Souleyret's recitation. She met Sam's eyes and shrugged.

"Jesus," Fletcher said, visibly shaken. "This is bad. This is really bad. She did get the medications in, and we've lost them, and Bromley, and probably Cattafi, too."

Daniels looked pleadingly at Sam. "We have to raise the alarm now, ma'am. If what she says is true, we can't take the chance. If this is already in our inoculation system, we're too late. We have to stop all the vaccines being given nationwide immediately."

Sam didn't hesitate. "I agree. We can't take the chance. Call Charlaine, tell her what we've learned. This will take a massive coordination—let her get things started. We'll have to talk to the CDC and Homeland immediately. Get them to pull all the vaccines that have shipped this season. And we need to warn them we could have an attack coming, or even under way. But, Daniels, this has to be done very carefully. We can't take the chance of starting a panic."

Daniels raised a brow. "I'm panicked already. I got a flu shot last week."

"Then you needn't worry. She specifically said the virus kills within forty-eight hours. If she's right, and terrorists have gotten hold of this, they haven't managed to get it into our systems yet, or we'd have bodies stacked like cordwood in the street. It would be hard to do now. The vaccines for this season were produced months ago. We'd already know. But going forward, anything new coming in—yes, we need to get everyone on alert. And we need Regina Girabaldi in real protective custody, right now. Go, Daniels, now!"

Sam turned to Denon. "Sir, we have to find out who in your company might be behind this, and we need to get that name immediately. There's no more time to waste. Are you willing to allow us access? Xander and Chalk, plus Mouse—if you let them into your servers, they'll be able to find the link."

He nodded. "What do you need? Passwords? Everson can get you everything you—"

There was a commotion in the kitchen. The shatter of breaking glass, guttural shouts, a strange gurgling choke. Sam sprinted into the hall just in time to see the front door swing closed, a smear of reddest blood in bas relief against the white paint. She started toward the door as a babble of voices filled the house. She heard Xander shout, "Fletcher, call 9-1-1, we've got two down."

A heartbeat later Xander was in the hallway, blood on his chest, moving fast, the SIG Sauer in his hand. "Watch it, watch it. They need you in the kitchen. Stay inside." Then he was out the door, Thor a blur of tan-and-black fur beside him. She saw Chalk sprinting down the street. Daniels pushed past her, going after them. The door slammed behind him.

Sam ran toward the kitchen and into utter chaos.

Everson was on the floor, clutching at his throat, gouts of red spouting from a slit in his carotid. Bebbington was already dead, his head nearly severed, tipped to the side as if he were listening to his shoulder tell a story.

Sam caught the spray of Everson's blood in her face as she knelt beside him. She yanked a tea towel off the cabinet below the sink and held it hard to his throat. "Hang on, damn it. Hang on," she yelled at him, but she could see it was too late. His eyes were unfocused, staring at a world only the dying could see, and the warm stickiness pulsing over her hands was slowing.

Denon was standing, horrified, in the entrance to the kitchen. Fletcher was on the phone calling for help. And Sam knelt in blood again, holding the useless towel to Everson's neck as he left this world. He gave one last burbling gasp, and then he was gone.

Damn it.

She forced her focus back to the surroundings and counted. There was someone missing.

She let the soaked fabric drop to the tile floor and grabbed Fletcher, dragged him toward the front door. She caught Denon's sleeve as she went, towed them both into the shockingly clean hall with its eerie handprint on the door. "Where is Heedles? Where is Maureen Heedles?"

Fletcher shook his head, shoved the phone in his pocket. "I don't know. We have to search the house. You stay here, cover Denon."

Sam pointed at the bloody handprint. "She must have run out the front, but wait." Sam pulled open the closet door and quickly punched in the code to the gun safe. She pulled out two automatics and two handguns. She pressed a Glock .40

into Fletcher's hand, and two magazines. She tucked the second into her pants at the small of her back, filled her pockets with two more magazines. "Now go," she said, nodding toward the kitchen. "I've got this."

Fletcher bent down and pulled his throw-down gun from his ankle, then, double-fisted, started moving toward the kitchen, walking soft. The sudden silence bled around them. Sam arranged the M4 strap around her shoulder and handed the other to Denon. "Do you know how to shoot?"

He nodded. "A shotgun. We hunt. Fox hunt. In the country. Not allowed to shoot the buggers now, but I have done in the past."

He was in shock. She stepped right up to his face, shook his shoulders a little to get his attention.

"Maureen Heedles. I need to know her background. You said she's your head of R and D. What does she research for you?"

"The best places to put in pipelines, terminals, offshore drilling. She's a geologist. She's a fucking geologist. Not a killer."

"James," Sam said, softer now. "There are two men dead in the kitchen to refute your claim. She's on the run. She lit out of here with a knife, and God knows what other weapons she has. Xander and Chalk and Daniels are after her. She's betrayed you. She's killed your people. She must be the leak. She must be the one who is funneling the money into the development of this medicine. Think, man. When did she come to you? How did she get hired?"

And thought to herself, Xander, where are you? Please tell me that was Mo Heedles we saw tearing out of here, and not Robin Souleyret.

She saw Denon starting to come back to himself, just as Fletcher came back into the hall. "We're clear. She must have gone out the front door after she killed the two men. I—"

Denon raised the rifle, and suddenly Sam was standing between two well-armed men on alert and pointing guns at each other.

Denon's voice cracked. "He wasn't in the room. The lieutenant had stepped away. He could have done this."

Fletcher didn't move an inch. "You're imagining things, Denon. I was behind you the whole time. It was your woman who did this. Now, put the weapon down, slowly, and no one will get hurt."

Sam faced Denon, her own gun casual in her hands. "James? We're all friends here. We're all just trying to help you. Please lower the weapon. Lieutenant Fletcher is on our side. I swear to you."

Denon took a ragged breath and the nose of the gun began drifting down. Sam gently relieved the man of the weapon. "I think I'll hold on to this, if you don't mind."

Denon nodded, slumping back against the wall, pale and sweating. "Forgive me. I was hasty."

Fletcher nodded. "Sam, my people are converging on the neighborhood."

"Warn them that Xander and Chalk and Daniels are out there with Thor."

"Already did. Why don't we go into the living room, and we can talk some more."

Fletcher jerked his head, and Denon started moving. He stuck his head into the guest bath, pulled out a towel and tossed it to Sam. "You're covered in blood."

"Seems to be a pattern," she said, wiping her face. Sam saw Mouse crouched on the floor in the corner of the living room, fingers going wild over her laptop.

"Sorry, Mouse. We're clear, you can come out."

"It's okay. I've tapped into the CCTV cameras. They have her cornered near the university entrance."

Sam hurried over and stared at the screen. It was black-and-white, but she could see clearly enough to make out what was happening. Thor had Heedles backed against the steps. Xander and Chalk had drawn down on her. Daniels had both a hand-

gun and a phone. The only light came from the soda vapors lining the street. It appeared Heedles was taunting them, shouting
something, and Sam saw Xander's hand flex on the gun.

"This is it. They're going to take her."

Heedles dropped to the pavement.

CHAPTER 47

XANDER WAS BREATHING HARD, MORE FROM ANGER THAN ANYTHING ELSE. His night vision was messed up; he'd run in front of an SUV and the driver had flashed the brights at him in annoyance. He was following Thor's barks—the dog was at least fifty yards ahead of them. He went frantic, and Xander knew he'd cornered the woman.

He called to Chalk. "Thor's got her. Turn around forty-five degrees, come down from the north. We'll take her from the street. Daniels, to me."

Daniels was right behind him.

"Where do you want me?"

"Loose box, coming up the southern perimeter, your back to Key Bridge. Make sure she doesn't dart down there. We might lose her if she manages to hit the bridge. Clear the civilians as you can, and be quiet about it."

"Yeah, we might lose her over the edge, when I toss her off," he muttered, jogging into the darkness.

Xander moved carefully toward Heedles. He wanted to take her alive, that's why he'd set Thor on her. He regulated his breathing, shut his eyes to help them readjust, then jogged the last half block to her location.

Heedles was stuck at the base of the main entrance steps to Georgetown University. Thor was dancing near her, snapping and growling. She caught Xander's gaze, watched him come into view. He saw fright on her face, but defiance, and that certain sense of inevitability he'd seen on the face of every terrorist he'd cut down. She knew she was going to die, and she wasn't afraid. It was a foregone conclusion.

There was a siren behind him, but he didn't break eye contact.

"Thor, *achtung!*"

Thor stopped barking immediately, but still had his teeth bared, a rumbling growl emanating from his belly. Xander had seen huge men cower in front of a dog, but Heedles decided to stand her ground. She was trapped, and she knew it, but she wasn't going to be backed down.

"Call him off. Call him off now," she yelled at Xander.

Daniels appeared to Xander's left. Chalk was inching in from the right. They had her, and she knew it.

"I'm not kidding. Call him off or I'll shoot him dead." From the folds of her jacket, she produced a Glock with a lightning draw. She was practiced with the weapon; she didn't hesitate or allow it to waver in her hand.

"Don't even think about it, Heedles." All three men had their guns trained on her in a flash. She hadn't stopped staring at Xander. She began moving the weapon toward Thor, and Xander called, *"Fuss."* Thor whined once, then came to his master's side and sat heavily, still on alert, his hair bristling along his back. Xander touched the dog once on the back in reassurance. *"Braver hund,"* he whispered, low. *"Bleib."*

Heedles relaxed when the dog stopped growling at her. Considering she had three highly trained men with guns on her, she became almost conversational. Still defiant, she tossed her hair and gave Xander a manic grin. "It's too late, you know. We've already launched. There's no way to stop things now. We've won."

"What are you talking about?"

"The Pyramid was activated last week. We've eliminated everyone who could stop us. You're the only ones left who know about us, and trust me, you won't see another dawn before your throats are slit and you're left mewling in the gutters."

Her bitter words, delivered in a polite, upper-crust British accent, were completely incongruous.

"Who, or what, is the Pyramid, Maureen? Tell me. If I'm going to die, anyway, what's to stop you?"

"I'm not stupid. I'm not falling for that. I won't tell you anything more. You can torture me, you can rape me, you can tear me limb from limb. I know that's what you do, that's what you enjoy. But I've done my job, and done it well, and I will not give up my people."

Daniels called out to her. "We don't torture and rape, Ms. Heedles. But we will put you in a four-by-six room for the rest of your natural life if you don't cooperate."

She laughed, a high-pitched shriek. Xander was reminded of a woman he'd seen in Afghanistan, keening and wailing over the body of her dead child, killed while playing after he ran over a neglected roadside bomb. An unfortunate mistake with everlasting consequences.

Xander knew there was no reasoning with Heedles. She was mad, and she'd done enough damage.

"What was your job in this plot? At least you can tell us that. We know you're the one who was stealing the money. Was that all you were asked to do?"

Heedles shook her head, her strangely asymmetrical eyes flashing in the streetlamps. "I killed the girl and the doctor. Juliet. She's had Denon by the cock from the first. He'd do anything she said, anything she wanted. She was his perfect little toy, and he had no idea she had double-crossed him. She had to be eliminated. She was going to expose us all."

"So you, what, dropped by Cattafi's place last night with a knife, like you just did in my kitchen?"

"I was the only one who could get close. I was the one she trusted. She told me a month ago she and Denon were fuck buddies. We were having drinks, and she had too much, and I got her back to my place. I asked her if she was usually into women, and she let it slip that she was into Denon, big-time, but she wanted me, too. So we screwed, and I realized then she must be a decoy. She'd been sent in to destabilize us."

"Who is *us*, Maureen? Who are you talking about?"

That hysterical laugh again. "Don't you wish I'd tell you? The Pyramid is sacred. We only know the person above us and below us. We are safe. We are impenetrable. But I will say this. Feeling the knife go into her flesh was one of the best moments of my life."

"Stand down," Xander said, nodding at Daniels, and at Chalk, who both looked shocked, but listened. They lowered their weapons, and Heedles reacted like a mirror, and did the same.

In that fraction of a moment, inside the breath they had all just taken, he shot her.

Xander felt the familiar rush he always did when a gun went off in his hands, and watched the woman drop to the ground, screaming in pain.

He'd hit her in the right knee, and the second she began falling, Chalk hurtled forward and knocked the weapon from her hands. Where she'd gotten the gun, Xander didn't know, but he was cursing himself for letting his guard down. He should have known it was someone with Denon, someone who'd want to stay close. They were damn lucky she hadn't managed to murder them all. She'd tried to get out of the house silently by cutting the throats of the men she worked with day in and day out. Couldn't risk the gun, there were too many people in the house who knew how to disarm her and wouldn't hesitate to do so.

Chalk stood by him, weapon pointed at the crying woman.

Daniels converged from the south, and while they covered him, he rolled her and slapped a pair of cuffs on her. It was over.

She was crying and yelling, making no sense. Daniels was on his phone, calling for help.

Xander heard applause. Some students had gathered behind him. They were taking pictures and one was filming with his iPhone. His first thought was one of fear and relief. *Son of a bitch. They'd been right in the line of fire. They were lucky not to have been shot or worse.* His second was more disturbing. *They had it all documented. Great.*

Chalk realized the issue, went to talk to them, and a bright light flooded from behind them with a snap. Xander heard footsteps approaching. He turned to see the reporter from CNN who'd called him earlier in the day, with a cameraman in tow, a smile crossing her face, the wail of sirens a distant howl to accompany her.

"Sergeant Whitfield, Rebecca Gorman, CNN. You've done it again—you've shot your second person today. How does that feel, sir?"

Chalk was back, a few cell phones bulging out of his pockets. Xander gave him a dark look, and moments later, the cameraman was lifted off his feet, arms twisted behind his back, the expensive camera clattering to the ground.

"You can't do that! You're interfering with our first amendment right to—"

One of the students, the one who'd been filming with his phone, joined in. "Yeah, you can't steal our stuff, man."

"I respect your right to report on this story, and I'd lay down my life to make sure you can, but we're not going to do this right now," Xander said.

Gorman was losing control. "I have it all, *we* have it all, on tape. It doesn't matter. We can approach one of those kids over there. They have it all, too. We can be live in five minutes. Our viewers need to see what's happening here. I can get an uplink to New York in a few minutes."

Xander sighed. "Ma'am, when the FBI clears these videos for public consumption, then I'll be happy to sit down with you and give a comment. Until then, you're going to have to shut this down. We're in the middle of a case. There's a killer on the loose."

Chalk stepped in, taking up much of the space between the woman and her cameraman. "Seriously, if you put our faces out there now, we lose our tactical advantage. We can't have you broadcasting this footage, not until we find him. Do you understand?"

She nodded, wide-eyed, let the mike drop to her side. The student's eyes grew big. "Are we safe, dude?"

Chalk shook his head. "No."

The reporter turned white. "Why didn't you say so?"

"I just did. Please get back in your van, and lock the doors. Metro will be here momentarily. Take this one with you." He pulled the kid's sleeve, and he happily cozied up to the pretty reporter. "Don't worry, we'll be in touch. You guys are witnesses, after all. The police will want to talk to you."

"I need my equipment," the cameraman said.

Chalk obliged, but not before removing the cassette that held their footage of the shooting and handing it to Daniels.

"Dude, totally uncool."

Daniels had Heedles by the arm. She was sitting up, back against the stairs, blood leaking onto the sidewalk. She kept up a steady string of curses at them.

"Ma'am, I'm Agent Daniels, FBI," he called to the reporter. "He's not kidding. We will return your footage as soon as we're cleared, but you want to get off the street right now." The cameraman backed off, nursing his bruised hand.

"Xander, Chalk," Daniels said. "I'll stay here, deal with Metro. You should head back to the house." The sirens were coming closer; Fletcher's call had been answered. A patrol car whipped onto the street. Daniels turned his head toward it, then yelled, "Go. Now!"

Xander didn't hesitate. The last thing he needed was to be detained like he had this morning. He took off at a jog, Thor and Chalk right with him. They had no more time; he knew Gorman was already on the phone to her producer. There was no help for it. Even without the footage they'd just shot, word would be out in moments. Too many people had seen him shoot Heedles. It was how things moved now. They had to act quickly, before they became bigger targets than they already were.

"She's just the money," Chalk said as they cut across to N Street. "We still need to find the brain."

Xander nodded. "This is a seriously fucked-up day, man. Let's get back to the house, go from there. But keep an eye out for anything Heedles might have discarded on the way."

CHAPTER 48

WHEN THE DOOR OPENED AND SAM SAW XANDER AND CHALK COME THROUGH, she felt overwhelming relief. She hurried to them. "Xander, are you okay?"

"I am. Daniels sent us back here. We cornered Maureen Heedles, and I shot her in the leg. Where's Fletcher? I need to make sure he knows what's happening."

Fletcher came into the hall, clapped him on the shoulder. "I know. We saw the whole thing. Mouse tapped into the CCTV cameras. You did good."

"I should have killed her," he said grimly.

"Probably. But it's good that you didn't. She might be able to give us information. I should head down to the scene. I'll make sure they understand what happened."

"It's all on video," Chalk said. "A fucking reporter was there, plus a bunch of kids." He dropped the phones and film cassette onto the hall table. "Lucky they weren't killed."

They went into the den. Mouse was on the floor, stretched out like a teenager on her stomach, typing faster than anyone Sam had ever seen.

"Mouse," Xander said. "Heedles said there was a pyramid, or the group is called the Pyramid. We need to see if we can find what she's referring to. Here's her phone. We found it in the bushes at the end of the street. She didn't have time to destroy it when she was on the run. Can you see who she's been talking to?"

"I'm on it," Mouse said. "While you two were off being heroes, I found a seek-and-destroy program on Heedles's computer. She launched it when we asked her to look at the personnel files. She's managed to destroy half the servers in Denon's company. They're totally wiped clean."

"Can you restore them?" Xander asked.

"Maybe. We have the SD card Amanda smuggled out, and it has a pretty sophisticated program on it that could be used to restore what's been wiped. It's almost as if she knew this would happen, and put her own fail-safe into play. I can't promise it will work, and it's going to take a while. She's very good. She's had the attack built into the system for a while. This kind of recovery, it's hit or miss. It all depends on what I can reconstruct. It's like a puzzle—without the corners, you can't make the insides work."

"Did she kill the information about Africa, and the medicine?" Sam asked.

Mouse nodded. "I'm sorry, but she did. She's destroyed this so thoroughly even I am going to have trouble recovering it. She had at least thirty minutes' head start, and it was enough time to wipe most everything clean. I'll do my best, but without another backup to run and fill in the blanks, I can't promise anything."

"Another backup? You mean, like another computer where the information could be stored?"

"Yes. I've reconstructed a bit. I can see threads to other computers. But she's severed them, and sent the attack program into their systems to wipe them clean, too. There are at least two other machines that hold the answers she was trying to get rid of. One is here in D.C., and one is in France. Probably the home of the terrorist who organized this in the first place."

"If there's one in D.C.... Can you trace an address, Mouse?" Fletcher asked.

"It's on Connecticut Avenue."

"Where does Jason Kruger live? What's his address?"

Mouse typed some more, her tongue caught between her teeth. "There's a Kruger on...hey, you're good. Here it is—3700 Connecticut Avenue, apartment 303." She flipped the screen, and Sam saw a satellite shot of D.C. The image zoomed in to a small spot. "It's a match," Mouse announced.

Fletcher had his phone in his hand, was squinting at the small screen. "My vote is someone gets over to Kruger's house ASAP. He was up to his eyeballs in this. He must have a backup for safekeeping in case he needed to use it to try and play the hero instead of the villain." He hit Refresh for the hundredth time in the past fifteen minutes. "Where the hell is Cavort with that file?"

On cue, Fletcher's phone rang. He glanced at the screen, then answered with a frown. "Woolrich? What's wrong?"

"Hey, boss. I've got a major problem."

"Don't we all," he said. "Hit me."

"I know you're off on admin, but I thought you might want to hear this. That guy Hart interviewed earlier today, the one driving the gray Honda in circles around the crime scene? Hart told me something felt off about him, asked me to do a background check. The guy he described who opened the door and said he was Toliver Pryce doesn't match the driver's license photo Virginia has on file. It's not even close."

"Son of a bitch. Get back over there. Right now."

"I'm already here. No one's answering the door."

"Shit, shit, shit, shit. Does this Pryce guy have family?"

"Not that I can find. I called his work—he's an actuary out in Ballston. Boss said he's a loner, keeps to himself. He was genuinely worried about the guy. Apparently, missing work is completely out of character. Without a family, if he were hurt or missing, no one would come forward to ask for a welfare check, right? We'd need to take the boss's word on things?"

"That's right. If you're asking permission, I absolutely think you have enough to go in."

"Armstrong's getting paper right now. He wanted to be sure we were all taken care of. I just wanted you to know."

"Break down the fucking door, Woolrich. I don't give a shit if we have paper or not. This might be the key to stopping our killer."

"Goddamn it. This is on you, Fletch."

Fletcher heard a crash, then a muffled groan.

"Ah, man. Smells awful in here. We've got a body." More shuffling, a murmur of voices in the background, then Woolrich came back on the line. "Fletch, we found him. Pryce has been stabbed. He's in the closet. We've got another fucking crime scene."

"Turn it over. You need to grab Tony and hightail it out to Hart's place. We need a composite sketch of the guy he saw, and we need it yesterday. Have crime scene run the entire place for DNA, trace, anything they can find. We're missing one last assassin. This might be him."

"I'll hand the scene over and get on my way. You think he's in cahoots with the woman?"

"Maybe. What did Hart say he looked like?"

"Pretty boy. Really handsome guy, could have been a model. Blue eyes, midthirties. I'll get with Tony and get a sketch together."

"Is the Honda still there?"

"Yes. It's in the driveway."

"So we don't know for sure whether this guy was really driving it last night or not."

"Nope. Which puts everything he said into question. His whole statement is worthless."

"Go get me a composite drawing, Woolrich. We'll worry about the rest later."

"Roger that."

He hung up, and Fletcher's phone dinged. It was the email from Cavort. "Finally," he said, opening the file.

Kruger was thirty-four, born in Cape Town to an American mother and South African father. His mother was a diplomat, and they moved around a lot—he spent most of his time in England and South Africa. He went to the embassy schools, and followed in their footsteps into the Foreign Service. He requested the Africa desk, wanting to work closely with the various countries he'd fallen in love with as a boy.

He scanned the rest. This wasn't going to do it. They needed more. Financials. Private emails. Phones. All the things that took time. He saw Sam, face pale but composed, moving from the kitchen to the living room, and intercepted her in the hall.

"We gotta go to Kruger's place, ASAP. This file doesn't give us diddly-squat."

"You can't show up there, Fletch. You'll get into all kinds of trouble."

"Then you go. Take Xander as backup. Someone needs to get into his place immediately. I'll stay here and see that Bebbington and Everson are taken care of properly."

Their raw scent had permeated the house. She didn't want to go anywhere near the kitchen. Fletcher was giving her an out, and she was more than tempted to take it. She knew how to handle a crime scene, but this was her home. Her refuge. And it had been defiled in the most horrible way possible. She would never be able to stand in her kitchen again without seeing the vast emptiness of Everson's face, and Bebbington's head falling off his shoulders.

A wave of panic washed through her. *One Mississippi. Two Mississippi. Three Mississippi. Four.*

Get it together, Owens.

She wanted out of this house. Right now.

She ducked into the guest bath, turned the water on hot, scrubbed her hands until they felt clean, counting, counting, counting. Fletcher said nothing, waited outside the door for her.

When she finally twisted off the tap and dried her hands, they were bloodred, but she had herself somewhat under control. She reached for the Glock at the small of her back, then deliberately inserted it into a small leather holster she'd taken from the closet and clipped it to her belt. She stashed a few extra magazines in her back pockets, grabbed her Birkin bag and said, "Ready."

"You good?" Fletcher asked, giving her a veiled look.

She nodded. "I'm good. I trust your gut. We'll go. Denon's in shock. He bears watching. You don't know that he won't freak out and try to shoot you again."

"Yeah, that wouldn't be good. Honestly, I'd rather get him out of here, too, but he needs to stay somewhere that we can keep an eye on him. Leave Chalk with me. We'll watch over him, make sure everything gets handled here. Sam, you have to hurry. I have a feeling about this."

She'd known him long enough not to discount his instincts.

"Won't there already be homicide people there?"

"Maybe. But if you get going, you could get ahead of them. We're stretched pretty fucking thin right now, with all these crime scenes. Besides, you're working this case. You have every right to be there. Come on. We don't have time to lose."

She stared him in the eye for a moment, and he saw the gold flecks in the honey brown that seemed to dance in the light from the hall lamp. She nodded once. "Feels like the roof is about to be on fire."

Fletcher grinned wide. He'd told her how much he loved singing that song when he and his band were together. "Too right it is. I vote we let the motherfucker burn."

"Baldwin will be here shortly."

"I'll fill him in. He'll be good for the coordination of everything, since Daniels is stuck down there with Heedles. I'll make sure the CDC is notified, take care of beginning the co-ordination of shutting down the vaccines. You go. Please, Sam."

She nodded. "Xander," she called. "Where are you?"

He came around the corner, Thor padding at his feet, the M4 resting easily in his arms, like a father cradling a baby.

"Gear up, babe. We have to go to Jason Kruger's house, right now."

CHAPTER 49

Potomac River

ROBIN HADN'T BEEN COMPROMISED, THAT SHE KNEW FOR SURE. SHE WAS VUL-
nerable, yes, she had the last vestiges of a head injury lingering about, was shattered by the death of her little sister and her
mother's constant betrayals, but she wasn't compromised. She
was going to end this before it spread any further.

First, she needed weapons. She wasn't about to go into the
breach unarmed.

The gun the Secret Service agent carried was already in her
pocket. She started combing through Riley's place, looking for
guns and ammo, anything that might help. She found his gun
safe in the small, tailored closet in his tiny bedroom. A combination lock and a key, double fail-safes. *Shit.* If she could only get
back to her own place, she had an arsenal there. But she knew
the cops had to be crawling all over it by now. Home was no
longer an option.

She was surprised to feel the loss of her sanctuary keenly, wondered if she'd ever be able to go home again, but pushed away
the emotional intrusion and kept searching. She found the safe's

key taped to the back of a painting of a sunset in the bathroom. She inserted it into the gun safe lock, turned it. One part down.

Think, Robin. Riley wasn't trying to keep people out of his safe. Not really. It was for defense, but he was more likely to stay constantly on offense. He'd want to be able to get into it, and quickly. So if Riley was in a hurry, what would the simplest code be?

000.

She lined up the numbers, and the safe opened. She laughed to herself. Riley hadn't expected her to toss his place looking for weapons. He hadn't taken enough precautions. Regardless of what he'd been expecting, it was sloppy. Which surprised her. Riley wasn't normally the sloppy type.

She pulled out a 5.56 Tracking Point 500 series AR, admired the state-of-the-art long-range weapon for a moment, followed it with a 9mm Smith & Wesson M&P. The TP AR would be good for a long-range shot, and it fit well against her back if she needed to run. She slapped on a leg holster with a K-Bar knife in the sheath, filled a pouch with multiple magazines for the handgun, and an extra clip for the AR, strapped it to her waist. She slammed the door to the safe and returned the key to its hiding place. If she couldn't take them down with this arsenal, it was time for her to quietly retire.

She needed to call Lola, get her brain moving on things.

She picked up Riley's phone, started dialing the number, then stopped and set the phone gently back in the cradle.

Don't trust anyone, Robin.

Maybe Gina was right. Maybe she was better off handling things herself. The only problem was, she didn't know where to start.

She needed some help. Riley's unsecured desktop computer was sitting on his desk. She booted it up, hijacked the system, bypassed the passcode, encrypted the hell out of the system and was in.

It took her fifteen precious minutes to get all the addresses, phone numbers and maps she needed. She turned the computer off, picked up the phone and made a single call. She had to talk to Atlantic. She had to find out what was going on.

She was shocked when he answered.

"Riley?"

"No, sir, it's Souleyret. I'm at Riley's place."

"Where is he?" There was a note of urgency in his voice she'd never heard before.

"I don't know, sir. He told me you sent him to clean up my mess." There was an edge to her own words, but she'd long ago stopped being frightened of powerful men. Atlantic could have her murdered in her sleep if he wanted, but why would he? She was an asset to him, until the moment she stopped being one. When he'd brought her on board, he'd pledged that he would let her know when she stopped being of use to him. It was nice to know she would be informed of her own expiration date.

Atlantic was quiet for a moment, then she heard a sigh. "I was afraid of this."

She was shocked at her anger, but there was no stopping it now. "I'm sorry I'm such a disappointment. I'll just go off quietly and eat a bullet. Will that do for you? *Sir?*"

"Robin. Riley is unsanctioned."

The words hit her like a speeding train. "What did you say?"

"I have been searching for answers to your sister's death since you called me this morning. I unearthed some tremendously frightening information. Riley has been working with Jason Kruger at the State Department. He is a part of an organization known as Pyramid. They come from Tripoli, an offshoot of al Qaeda. They went to Africa to raise an army. Their scientists, who have been funded handsomely over the past few years, were tasked with finding a way to attack the United States and Israel. These cowards are behind the terrorist attack planned on American soil tomorrow. I understand Mr. Kruger is dead, and the samples Amanda brought into the US are missing. They have stolen them. *Riley* has stolen them. There has been increasing chatter about an attack coming shortly. They're planning to release a genetically modified superbug into the United States. They've been working on several different delivery methods. Water. Vaccines. Grenades. Putting sick people into airplanes. Their theory is, if they spread it widely enough, chances are good they can sicken thousands of people. This superbug kills in forty-eight hours, and it's airborne. We will have a pandemic on our hands almost immediately."

She felt the world breaking into fragments around her. Riley. Riley was behind this. All his anger today, his comfort, his words.

I can't do this anymore.

He didn't kill your sister.

She thought her heart might burst from her chest, the blood pumping so hard she could feel the individual beats against her ribs. "Did you know this threat was under way?"

"Yes. But we didn't know who the players were. Now we know some of them. Maureen Heedles, who worked R and D for James Denon. Jason Kruger from State. We have the name of an organization. It will take time to track down all those involved, but we have a beginning."

"And Riley is a part of this. Are you absolutely certain?"

"I am. I'm sorry. I know you have been friends for some time." The word *friends* floated from the phone, spinning lazily in the air, tinged in green.

You could call it that, she thought, then her stomach seized and she fought down a sickening bout of nausea. Riley, who'd been helping her recover, who'd slid into her bed and into her body with ease. The head injury had forced down her walls. She'd been vulnerable for the first time in her adult life.

And he'd taken advantage of her temporary lull.

Gina was right, after all. She *had* been compromised.

Riley had been using her this whole time. He'd been wait-

ing, biding his time, knowing exactly what Amanda was working on. That was why he'd always inquired after her. Not every
day, just sprinkled into conversation here and there.

Where's Amanda these days? What is she up to?

I'd love to meet her sometime. Does she ever come back to the States?

*She must be pretty important if you can't touch base with her. Where
did you say she worked again?*

Innocuous chatter. Getting-to-know-you conversations.
Fucking pillow talk.

She'd walked into the oldest trick in the book. Seduction.

Robin stared out into the dark water, listened to its hypnotic
lapping, the maddeningly regular splashes against the hull of the
boat as the tide forced its way into the marshes. *He who controls
the tides...* She had no choice. Riley had killed her sister. She
had to take him down. There was no decision to be made here.
It was Riley and his terrorists or her.

"Atlantic, where would he be? Where did he go? Do you
have eyes on him?"

"He's shielding himself from us. Or they're doing it for him.
Our satellites over D.C. have been deactivated. That was my
first clue Riley had turncoated. We're awaiting help from the
NSA. But until we're back online, our usual tools are useless."

"Jesus. And he knows exactly how to make a satellite go dark.
Please tell me you have a fix on his tracker."

"It's gone. He cut it out of his arm, or he's lying dead at the
bottom of the Potomac, right under your feet."

"He's not here. I saw him leave. He must have tossed the
tracker as he left."

Right after he kissed me goodbye.

"I'm sorry, Robin. You're going to have to use old-
fashioned methods to find him. Because he's managed to blind
us. We've flagged his passports, all the identities we know of,
but you know he has friends. He could be in the air right now,
and we'd never know it."

"Where would he go? Back to Africa? No, sir. He's here. If they're planning an attack, he's going to be in the midst of things. That's his way."

"Lola has the names of the other members involved in the day's events. Kruger is dead. Maureen Heedles has been neutralized, is being taken to the hospital with a gunshot wound. A Spaniard, Senza, was killed this morning trying to eliminate James Denon."

"I've crossed paths with him before. Not sorry he's gone."

"And the man you found at Dr. Bromley's office? He was a French national named Alain Montague. Very nasty business, how we lost him."

She caught the rebuke. "Yes, I should have left him alive. But why? He was a hired gun. He knew nothing. He'd been sent to kill, and he nearly succeeded." *Riley sent the man to kill you, Robin. Remember that. There could be more.*

"Bygones."

"I'll find Riley, sir. And I will end him."

"I trust you know where to start?"

"I do. I'll report back when I have news."

She hung up the phone, stared at the arsenal she'd just accumulated. Did a press check on the Glock, and headed into the living room. Girabaldi and her pet Secret Service agent were still dutifully sitting at the table where she'd left them.

"We have a problem," she said.

"Another?" Girabaldi responded.

"Yes. We need to get you out of here."

Robin grabbed the shoulder of her mother's perpetually elegant Chanel jacket and pulled her from her seat. She tossed the agent his gun and backup. "Car. Now."

He listened, ran to the car, and by the time Robin hurried Girabaldi out of the houseboat, he had the car started. Robin shoved Gina into the backseat and climbed in behind her.

As they drove up the deserted lane, Robin asked, "Do you

have a safe house? Someplace you can go that no one knows about?"

"I have a place on the Chesapeake. It's sheltered. No one can trace it to me."

"Go there, now. Use your most secure protocols. No phones, nothing that can be used to track you." She took Girabaldi's cell and tossed it in the bushes.

"I'm safer with you."

"No, you're absolutely not. Our host here is involved in the plot."

"Riley Dixon? Working against our interests? That's not possible."

"It is possible, because it's true. He's gone dark. I just talked to our...to a friend, who's warned me what Riley is really up to. I have to find him and eliminate him. You won't be safe with me. Head to your beach. Have Fumbles here watch your back."

The agent gave her an exceptionally dirty look in the rearview. Robin smiled at him. "Let me off on the corner of Prince and South Pitt, then get her the hell out of here. Think you can do that?"

"Yes," he grumbled.

"Good."

Gina actually looked frightened, something Robin couldn't remember ever seeing. "What are you planning, Robin? You can't go up against Riley alone. He'll see you coming a mile away."

"No, he won't." Robin stared out the window for a moment. "You don't know me very well, Gina. I will do whatever I must. That's how I was raised, and that's how I was trained."

They were moving quickly now. There was very little traffic. They'd be at her drop-off point in a few minutes.

"Listen to me. You need to disappear. Riley is going to be hard to stop, yes, and I don't need to be worrying that you're safe, as well. When you see this splashed on the news, and that we have a resolution, you'll know it's time to come home. Can you do that for me? Just trust me for once and disappear?"

Gina nodded. "I've always trusted you," she said quietly. "Be careful, Robin."

She gave her mother a cocky smile. "I always am."

CHAPTER 50

Kruger's condo

JASON KRUGER LIVED ON CONNECTICUT AVENUE, A FEW BLOCKS NORTHWEST of the National Zoo. This was an area for professionals; there was a Metro stop almost across the street from his tan brick building, and multiple bars and restaurants spilling late-night light onto the sidewalks. Despite it being nearly two in the morning, there were plenty of people wandering around. It was last call, and the bars were beginning to empty.

Kruger's building was guarded by a glass door requiring a keycard. There were no cops around. Fletcher's instincts were right; they'd beaten them to the scene. Sam was about to pick up the phone and ask the condo company to buzz them in when Xander knocked the butt of his SIG hard against the plastic reader, and they heard a familiar buzz. The door was briefly unlocked.

"Where'd you learn that trick?" she asked, scooting inside.

"Denver, actually. Guy out there showed me. It doesn't work all the time, but there's a certain frequency that gets interrupted in some of them, and we just got lucky."

"My little juvenile delinquent."

He huffed out a laugh. The lobby was dark. They made

their way toward the back, found the elevators. Inside, Xander brushed his lips across her forehead. "You hanging in there? It's been a crazy day."

Sam nodded. "Yeah. But I'm telling you, Xander, the second this case is over, we are moving. I'm sick of my house being used as a halfway station for crime scenes."

"Sounds like a plan."

She reached for the Glock at her hip, so aware of its strange weight. Hefted the cold, hard metal in her hand. Xander was watching her. "You don't have to do this," he whispered, clearly concerned.

Sam didn't like guns. She didn't like shooting them, cleaning them, having them around day in and day out. And right now, she abhorred the fact that she held one in her hand. But she wasn't about to step into Kruger's apartment without it.

She gave him a half smile. "Yes, I do."

The elevator dinged, and the doors opened to the third floor. They crept down the hall, Xander leading the way, the M4 ready in his hands. The lighting was eerie, on some sort of dimmer, so the walls shone orange. The carpet cushioned their steps, and they made it to apartment 303 without a problem.

Xander shouldered his M4 and pulled a small brown suede case out of his back pocket. His lock picks. Sam the FBI consultant looked the other way. Moments later, the lock disengaged, and Xander slipped inside. She followed, the gun warming in her hand.

Kruger's home was dark, the milky glow of the streetlamps on Connecticut their only source of light. The furniture was minimalist, modern, black leather with white accents. The walls were covered in tribal masks and wooden sticks. A large black-and-white painting of the Buddha took up nearly the entire living room wall.

It did not look like the home of a terrorist.

Sam put on a pair of purple nitrile gloves. Xander had already pulled on his thin supple leather shooting gloves. At least they wouldn't contaminate anything.

Xander made a motion with his right hand, which Sam knew meant spread out. He started toward the bedroom. She went directly to the refrigerator. If they were going to get lucky, it might start here.

She swung open the stainless doors. A gust of cool air enveloped her. Aside from a knocked-over bottle of ketchup, some hard cheese and bologna, a four-pack of Innis & Gunn, the fridge was empty.

A hardworking man like Jason Kruger would certainly spend little time at home cooking. Worse, there was no sign of the vaccines.

She felt her earlier hope dissipate. Fletcher had been so sure there was something here. She'd bought into it, feeling the same way. She thought there would be some sort of resolution, something to put a period on this awful day. But there was nothing visible. Their only hope was the computer.

She did a perfunctory search of the rest of the kitchen and dining room, pushing on panels and hoping for the same kind of surprises they'd found in Cattafi's apartment. Nothing.

The unit was small, only a single bedroom and bath off the living room. Xander rounded back into the living room, shaking his head. His voice was low.

"You need to come see this."

She followed him into the bedroom. The closet door was ajar. The left half was filled with two rows of hanging clothes, pants and suit coats and shirts, with a double rack for shoes below. Very neat, very organized. The right side held a small, stackable washer and dryer. Xander played his light over the edge. "What's that?"

Sam got closer. "Blood." She opened the washer. The contents were wet. Inside was a pair of running shoes, pink-and-orange running shorts, a dark shirt and a dark jacket.

The girls who'd been headed to Cattafi's apartment said they'd seen a jogger, a woman. The witness Hart had spoken to, the weirdo in the gray Honda, also said he'd seen a woman jogging.

These clothes had to belong to Maureen Heedles. She was the jogger.

"Xander, we have three witnesses from this morning who saw a woman jogging in our neighborhood around the same time as the murder. I think Heedles was telling the truth. She's our killer. Let's tear this place apart. Where's the computer?"

"Over in the corner. I've already copied the hard drive." He dangled a flash drive in front of her.

They started a thorough search of the bedroom. Sam hit pay dirt five minutes in.

"Xander, I've got something." Kruger had a European-style bed with drawers underneath for storage. "There's a false panel in here. Look what I've found." She held up a cell phone, a thin MacBook Air and a black leather bag. "Wanna bet these are Amanda's?"

"All the proof we need to tie Heedles directly to Kruger. It's a thread we need to unravel, though. They were supposed to be in New York. How did she get to D.C. and back without Denon noticing?"

"It was night. Unless they were sharing a bed, I assume she had her own room. It's a little over three hours by train, and Amtrak has overnight runs between the two cities. Train down, kill Amanda, dump her clothes and the laptop here with Kruger, back on the train up to New York. Boom. You could do the whole shebang in less than eight hours, and it's faster than driving. Rather elegant, actually."

"Smart. So what's Kruger's role in this?"

"I don't know. Other than he works for Girabaldi, who used to be Robin's boss. I think Heedles was meant to appear to be Robin Souleyret. It's all a big setup, with her as the scapegoat. We need to let Fletcher's people process the entire place. But we have to take this with us. Let's go call him, let him know what we've got."

"Sounds good."

They started back toward the door. Sam noticed light bouncing in the hallway and froze. She grabbed Xander's hand, pulled him to a stop. Leaned close. "Someone's out there."

The light went off, and they heard the distinct sound of a key being inserted into the lock.

Xander moved quickly, blended into the shadows by the door, pulling Sam behind him. He raised the M4 toward the breach.

The door opened gently, silent on its hinges. Someone else was breaking in, trying to be quiet about things. But this person had a key, and it wasn't Fletcher's people from Metro.

Xander waited for the bulk of the body to be in the apartment, then reached out with a hand and grabbed whoever was coming in the door.

The world exploded into action.

No longer worried about making noise, Xander yanked the person into the apartment and slammed the door behind them. The battle raged on for a few minutes, the two thumping and pulling and scrabbling, trying to gain purchase on the slick hardwood floor. Sam saw the intruder was small, dressed in black, fists moving at a rapid pace. Fighting, fighting hard. One punch caught Xander on the nose, another in the jaw. Sam felt a warm spray of blood across her hand. She stepped forward into the scrum, caught a kick in the shin.

But Xander was on top now, wrestling the person to the ground. After a breathless curse, Sam realized it was a woman. She saw a flash of blond hair, realized who this must be. Before she could intervene, the woman was pinned on her back, breathing hard. Xander was sitting on her chest, a large K-Bar knife to her throat.

"You broke my nose, you bitch."

"You shouldn't have attacked me, then, you stupid oaf. Get off me."

Sam flashed the light across the woman's face, which gave her the last bit of confirmation she needed. She sighed heavily.

"Xander. You can let her up. But watch yourself. It's Robin Souleyret."

Seeing the sister gave Sam chills. It was always hard talking to family members of the dead, but when they bore such a striking resemblance to the corpse she'd just worked on, it made things much more difficult.

All her imaginings about Amanda Souleyret went out the window when her sister Robin stood up. It was almost as if Sam could suddenly see the corpse animate, and it gave her the creeps. Eyes that sparkled with life, even in their grief, a dancer's stride, blond hair in a long bob past her shoulders. Robin was taller than her sister, and a few years older, but the resemblance was uncanny.

Robin had also been through the ringer. She had a well-formed black eye, and new injuries from her altercation with Xander. Her right eye was swelling, her knuckles were abraded. A bruise peeked out of the top of her shirt.

"Had a rough day, I take it?" Sam asked.

Xander was still holding the knife on her, ready to use it if she bolted. She eyed him with distaste. "You could say that."

"Why don't you start at the beginning. Explain to me why I shouldn't call Metro and have them come arrest you for murder."

"I didn't kill anyone who wasn't trying to kill me. And I don't owe you an explanation. I have my own reasons for being here, and now that I see what I'm looking for isn't available, I'll be going."

"You aren't going anywhere," Sam replied coolly. "I can link you to three crime scenes today. Not to mention your sister's murder. There's a stack of women's clothes in the washer, which has blood on it. I don't doubt that it's your sister's. You want to tell me what your connection is to Kruger?"

"Please," Robin said, rolling her eyes. "Are you accusing me of murdering my sister?"

"Did you?"

"Hardly," she spat.

Sam knew she couldn't trust the woman, but a knot released in her chest. She held out the bag with Amanda's things, and Robin flinched.

"Want to tell me how these got here?"

Souleyret was getting upset now. "I have no idea. I have no connection to this man. I'm investigating these crimes, just like you. Besides, do you think I'm dumb enough to leave evidence behind? I've been doing this for a very, very long time, Dr. Owens. I wouldn't be alive today if I was as sloppy as these fools."

"And yet, you've been a part of every crime scene I've been to today, and we have DNA to prove it."

This clearly surprised her. "Bullshit."

"You left a hair behind this morning at your sister's place. And the neighbor saw your vehicle. It's circumstantial, but it will stand up in court."

Robin was shaking her head. "I didn't kill those men. And I didn't kill Bromley, or my sister, or Cattafi. I've been searching for her killer, just like you." She couldn't resist adding a gibe. "Though it seems I was a few steps ahead, until this moment."

Sam narrowed her eyes at the woman. "So you're just exceptionally clever, and someone's setting you up? That's what you're trying to tell me?"

"Yes." Robin seemed to be on the edge of losing control. Sam wanted to push her there. It would be the most expedient way to get information from her.

"Any idea who might have it in for you?"

Instead of answering, Robin said, "Think about it. Why

would I kill my sister? Why would I kill any of these people? Now, the man who attacked me in Dr. Bromley's office, him I had to stop. He was trying to kill me, and I wasn't about to let that happen. But I had nothing to do with Amanda's world, on purpose. It was the best way for me to keep her safe. I love my sister. I'm heartbroken that she's gone. And I didn't kill her."

She must have seen something on Sam's face. She backed against the sofa and sat down, arms at her sides. Defenseless. Shocked. "But you know who did. And you've been playing me. You know I'm innocent."

Sam nodded. "You're hardly innocent. But yes, we know who killed Amanda. We have her killer in custody, and a confession."

Robin took a deep, long breath, her shoulders relaxing. "I'll show you mine if you show me yours. But first, I need some ice." She gave Xander a rueful glance and touched her eye. "Didn't your mommy teach you it's not nice to hit girls?"

"My mommy makes exceptions when the girl in question leads with a Smith & Wesson."

They assembled in the kitchen. Xander plopped some ice from Kruger's freezer in a dishcloth, handed it to Robin. He made another ice pack, cautiously held it up to his nose. When it was numbed a bit, he signaled to Sam, who ran her fingers along the edge, squeezed the sides. He grimaced, pulled back from her touch, eyes watering.

"It's not broken. Just banged up. You'll be pretty again when the swelling goes down."

Robin, whose face was hidden behind her own ice pack, laughed a little. Sam turned on her.

"You've been our number-one suspect in several murders today. You're damn lucky he didn't shoot you. I hardly think this is the time to laugh. Explain what you're doing here. Now."

"You're feisty. I like that. I'm just looking for a guy I know," Robin said lightly.

Sam wasn't in the mood. "Quit fucking around and tell me how you know Jason Kruger."

A shadow passed across Robin's eyes. "That's not who I'm looking for."

"Who, then?"

"A ghost."

Sam got in the smaller woman's face. "Robin. Listen to me. We have a very bad situation brewing right now. So if you know anything about it, now is the time to talk."

She did. And the more she told them, the more frightened Sam became.

CHAPTER
51

Georgetown

CRIME SCENE TECHS WERE CAUTIOUSLY ASSESSING SAMANTHA'S KITCHEN, AND Fletcher watched the clock, drumming his fingers on the table. They should have called by now. He'd managed to stall the team heading to Kruger's place, but they would get there soon, and there was nothing he could do.

Heedles had been taken to GW, and the media had their videocassette back. There would be no holding the story down. He was just thankful it was the middle of the night, or they would have already been paraded onto the morning news shows like chickens to the slaughter. It was going to be bad enough when the sun came up.

Armstrong had shown up on scene furious to find Fletcher giving directions, but when he explained what had happened, Armstrong calmed down. He sent Fletcher back to babysit the crime scene at Sam's place with extreme injunctions to stay put and not move an inch and to get Xander Whitfield back to the scene, then started working with Marcos Daniels to keep the media firestorm under control.

Fletch was tired as hell. The adrenaline spikes throughout

the day, the lack of sleep, not enough food and not enough caffeine—it was all catching up to him. He'd hiked across N Street,
gotten back to Sam's, avoided the mess in the kitchen and found
Denon grieving alone in the darkened living room. Mouse had
stayed nearby, lending quiet comfort, her face glowing in the
screen of her computer—didn't that girl ever get tired?

It was almost quiet when his cell rang. Finally.

"Sam. What did you find?"

"Robin Souleyret, for starters. We know what's going on.
We're looking for a man named Riley Dixon. Fletcher, we need
to drop everything and get everyone in town looking for him.
I'm pretty sure he has the vaccines from Cattafi's place, and he
is armed and exceptionally dangerous."

"Do we have a file on him?"

"He's CIA black ops. I doubt they'll let you see it. But I'm
sending a picture your way."

"Where the hell might this guy be, Sam? What's he up to?"

"He's going for the aquifer, Fletch. They're going to release
this pathogen into the water supply. It works like cholera, and
apparently they've developed a strain that is resistant to the treatment they do at the plants. It could already be in the water supply. We're heading there right now."

"I'm right behind you."

"Fletcher. You have to stay there. Send Chalk. Send everyone you have."

"Samantha, I appreciate you being concerned for my well-
being, but there's no way I'm staying here. MacArthur Road is
residential. You're going to have a lot of scared people if we go
in there with lights and sirens. Word gets out, and we'll have
more than a panic on our hands. We could scare him off, and
he'll just find another place to empty his poison into the water."

"We can't take this guy ourselves, Fletch. He's a trained assassin. We need SWAT. And HRT. And every other acronym
with a bunch of guns we can find."

"We have Xander and Chalk. They're probably more capable than half a dozen SWAT officers. By the time I make the call, rally these guys, this could be over. We have to stop them ourselves. I'll make the call from the car, get everyone rolling, but we're going, now."

"I'm glad you have so much faith in their abilities."

"Sam, you're wasting time. To hell with protocol. We're trying to stop a terror attack. I'm back in the game. Meet me at the aquifer. I'm on my way."

He heard her curse once before he turned off the phone.

He had no desire to be a hero, but now was the time for them to strap it on and stop this Riley Dixon character before it was too late.

The D.C. aquifer was quiet, the humming of the engines the only noise. Those who lived in the area were asleep in their beds, completely unaware that a potential terrorist attack was under way.

Fletcher and Chalk headed northwest on the divided highway, driving slowly, watching for anything that might be out of place.

Fletcher had always worried about the aquifer. Though it was well-guarded and the water treated so thoroughly and deeply that pathogens couldn't possibly pass through, it was open and exposed. If there was a weaponized pathogen that *could* be distributed in water, where it would grow into something bigger, maintain its effectiveness and manage not to be killed by the treatment itself—this was the perfect place to attack.

Sam had emailed a photo of Riley Dixon, so at least they knew who they were looking for.

Fletcher pulled to the side of the road, parked. He and Chalk got out and started toward the plant. A few moments later, Sam, Xander and Robin Souleyret drove up. They converged a block away from the aquifer.

Sam had Robin fill them in on her information—that her

source assured her there were at least three methods being tested to get the superbug into the general population, and they were going for the water tonight.

Chalk handed Xander another clip for his M4. "Why do you think he's here? He could be anywhere."

"It's just a feeling," Robin said. "Something Riley said to me this morning. He asked me if I'd seen today's bulletin. It's the daily threat risk assessment we get. There was a story about a white paper done several years ago on terrorism and water supplies. A reminder of the threats we face, asking them to tighten security at all the water treatment plants across the country. We have threats like this all the time, but he's never once mentioned the bulletin to me, and my boss mentioned the possibility of a water attack. It was clearly on everyone's minds today, but I think it was more. I think he was trying to tell me something."

"You never saw this coming?" Fletcher asked.

Robin shook her head. "I haven't seen much past the end of my nose for a long time, Lieutenant. And if you'd asked me two hours ago if Riley Dixon could be involved in a terrorist attack on this country, I would have shot you just for being stupid. But I'm seeing clearly now. He removed his GPS tracker, he shut down our company's satellites and he's off the grid entirely. And that thought frightens me more than anything else. Now. Shall we?"

"One last thing," Chalk said. "Do you think he's alone?"

Robin paused a second, then shook her head. "Probably not. We normally operate alone, yes, but with a job this big? If it were me, I'd bring backup. At least a few people to cover me. But I like our odds."

Xander gave Sam a smile. It was a compliment, one operator to another. He liked Robin, she could tell. She was tough and ballsy and ruthless. All things he respected.

With a glance at Chalk, Xander spun his finger in the air. He took the lead and they bled into the darkness, weapons drawn, a silent black wedge moving toward the treatment plant.

CHAPTER
52

The D.C. aquifer

THE TEAM RILEY HAD ASSEMBLED WAS SMALL, BUT LETHAL. THEY'D LOST TIME getting the superbug out of the vials and into the weaponized containers that would leak the poison into the water supply. There were so many ways to do this, but Riley had done a risk analysis on every aquifer in the area, and determined this one was the best chance they had to make a devastating statement.

For the thousandth time since he'd been forced into this mess, he shrugged off the voices in his head that screamed, *Don't do this—if you do this, you're lost forever.*

He had no choice. He'd fucked up. The Pyramid owned him, and he wasn't willing to give up his own life when it could be lived out in relative comfort and happiness half a world away. He'd spent his entire adult life being pulled through the machine that was his government, watching it disintegrate into a mocking portrait of itself.

An attack of this scale, when they weren't looking, weren't expecting it, would wake them up, if nothing else.

The attack had been exceptionally well coordinated from the first. The team had spread out, eliminated everyone who might be a problem. James Denon had gotten lucky, having a sharp-shooter protecting him. Riley himself was one of the few people who could have made that shot this morning, across the roofs of two buildings with a SIG. He was duly impressed.

His guards watched him, balaclavas dropped over their dark-skinned faces, with something akin to wonder and mistrust in their sloe eyes. They'd killed the plant manager on duty, and all the security guards they'd come across, quickly and silently, but he could tell they hungered for more. Death was never enough to a jihadist. They wouldn't be satisfied with blood, not until it ran in the rivers across the US. They'd been on him for three weeks now, as everything was being put into place. He knew they were ruthless. He knew they wouldn't give a second thought to putting bullet in his head. If he tried to back out, or even hesitated, they would simply shoot him and finish the job themselves.

He was better than them. He only killed for his own purpose, not to answer the call of another.

As he loaded the canisters, each bearing waves of death, he told himself that, over and over and over.

CHAPTER 53

SAM PACED HER STEPS WITH XANDER, THE GLOCK TIGHT IN HER HAND. HER shoulders were already starting to ache from holding up the weapon, a knot forming between her scapulae. Fletcher was behind her. Robin and Chalk brought up the eastern edge of their triangle.

They were moving fast, low and tight, and it only took a minute to get past the perimeter and into the plant itself. Someone had cut the chain on the fence. They were definitely in the right place. Sam wondered for a brief moment how Robin had known it would be this particular plant, or if it was a lucky guess, then all thoughts were pushed away when she smelled the blood.

She touched Xander's back, made him stop. They all halted. "Over there," she whispered, and he broke off silently, returning a minute later, his lips drawn tight together.

"Five down. Executed. Stripped of weapons. Must have been the night shift." He turned to Chalk and murmured in his ear.

"What did you tell him?" Sam whispered.

"That we might have more than one bad guy in here. Come on."

Great, she thought. *Just what I need, more bad guys*. Started off after him again.

The whir and hum of the machinery covered their tracks, but it wasn't until Xander suddenly fired into the darkness that Sam heard anything unnatural. The *foopt* of the silenced bullet seemed overly loud and out of place. Chalk was right there, catching the body before it hit the ground, and Robin stepped into the breach and took another silenced shot. Fletcher worked with her, and Sam felt so oddly out of place, watching them eliminate threat after threat, the terrorists falling like chess pieces.

The men who guarded Riley were lazy and undisciplined. They assumed they were safe because they'd killed the people on duty. They hadn't expected a threat from outside. It was their only advantage.

Sam kept moving, pushing forward in the darkness. There were small lights on the ceiling that gave her the direction she needed to go. Xander stepped to her side, their flying V complete again. They wound in, farther and farther, and the hall opened into a great room, with three large water tanks draining into pools, and huge metal arms swirling through the water so it didn't stagnate.

Riley Dixon was standing over the middle pool, dropping steel canisters into the water. Sam tripped over something metallic, sent it skittering into the darkness. It was their first stroke of bad luck. Dixon froze, then dove away.

Sam thought Robin was the one who yelled first. "Riley! Riley, stop!"

And then it was a cacophony, voices and bullets echoing off the steel containers. Xander pushed her down onto the ground, practically kneeled on her back as he emptied his magazine into the darkness, calling directions in a bizarre military shorthand that everyone but her seemed to understand.

There was a brief pause in the gunfire. He hauled her to her feet and pushed her behind a huge steel vat. She could smell the chemicals, something akin to chlorine, almost like the pool she used to swim in as a child. He whispered harshly, "Stay put," and disappeared into the darkness.

She had every intention of listening to him. The firefight was moving away from her, deeper into the plant. She grasped her Glock hard. Her fingers started to sweat on the trigger.

She heard a shuffling sound. Someone was running toward her. The footsteps coming closer. *Friend or foe?*

She didn't have a choice. She had to stop whoever it was. She swallowed hard, then whipped out to her left, into Riley Dixon's path.

He was huge, taller than Xander, bulkier and desperate. The lights above showed his face, eyes wild, mouth grim. An enraged bull on the run.

She didn't think. She didn't move. She held her ground and squeezed the trigger, three times, in quick succession, just as she'd been taught.

Riley's momentum carried him right into Sam, and they both went down hard on the cement floor. He was on top of her. He must have weighed two hundred twenty-five pounds. He was big. Really big. So big he was starting to crush her.

She could hear him wheezing, and felt wetness begin to seep onto her chest. She'd definitely hit him at least once.

Center mass. She'd gone for center mass, and Riley hadn't been wearing body armor.

He must have been stunned, or bordering on unconscious. He was laid out flat on top of her, breathing stentoriously, arms dangling to the side. She was trapped, and she started to panic.

She tried pushing him off her, but two-hundred-plus pounds of dead weight was too much to shove from the angle she had without help. Finally, she was able to wiggle out, scraping her fingers and back on the hard floor.

She wanted to call out to Xander, listened hard for the rest of the team. She couldn't hear anything but Riley's heavy wheezing. Out of habit, she put her hand on his neck, feeling for a pulse. It was fast, but steady. He wasn't about to die on her.

She couldn't see the gunshot wound, though she knew vaguely where it must be. She tugged at his shoulder, braced her feet and rolled him onto his back. He flopped over, and his head smacked the floor. It sounded like a knock against a ripe canta-loupe. *Serves you right*, she thought. *I hope that hurt.*

She skimmed her hands along his chest until she found the wettest spot. Ripped his shirt open. Without good light, she had to feel her way through the wounds. She was surprised; she'd hit him all three times. Two bullets had passed through his side. She could feel the exit wounds in the back, but one had landed more centrally, breaking a rib, which must have punctured his lung when he fell.

"Leave him be." Robin Souleyret was standing over her, gun pointed at Riley's head. She kicked away his weapon, and Sam heard it skitter away into the darkness.

"Did you get the canisters?" she asked.

"We did. We stopped him. The stupid, arrogant fucking bas-tard. Don't you dare try to help him. Let him bleed out like the animal he is."

"I'm half tempted to listen to you, but I'm afraid I have to help him."

Then Xander was there. "No, you don't. Leave him. Fletch-er's called for backup—they'll send an ambulance."

She wanted to argue, but acquiesced. She stood, feeling slightly dizzy. She'd just shot a man. She, who was honor bound to save lives, had very nearly taken one. From scalpel to gun, she thought dimly.

Robin was staring at her strangely. "Dr. Owens? Dr. Owens?"

Sam heard the words, saw Robin's mouth working. But she suddenly sounded so far away, almost as if she were in a tunnel. She could hear Xander shouting, and saw his face, a kaleido-scope of horror. There was pain then, sharp and awful. It took her breath away. From far away, she heard other voices raised in alarm, but then she was floating, and felt nothing but warmth, and peace…

CHAPTER 54

SAM WOKE TO SUNLIGHT STREAMING AGGRESSIVELY THROUGH AN UNFAMIL-
iar window. She was on her side, facing this explosion of light,
and it hurt her eyes. Groaning at the intrusion, she tried to roll
away, and a fire started in her ribs and spread into her left arm,
leaving her breathless.

"Sam? Samantha? Honey, are you awake?"

Her eyes began to focus again. Xander was standing over her
like an avenging angel, his hair sticking out at all angles, face
bruised and blackened, deep shadows of worry under his eyes.

"You look like hell," she croaked. He started to laugh, and
she slipped away.

When she woke again, she felt much more lucid. It was dark
outside the window, but there was a humming white light over
her head, long and strangely artificial. A fluorescent bulb. Lord,
she was in the hospital. She recognized the smells and the noises,
the faint beeping of her heart monitor. Her hand went to her
face. She felt the soft *whish* of oxygen shooting up her nose,
burning as it went.

Xander was asleep in the chair to her right, his head at an awkward angle. She hated to wake him, but her side ached, and inside, too, a pain she'd never felt before, and she wanted to know what was happening.

"Xander," she said, voice like gravel. He didn't move. She cleared her throat, and the ripping noise woke him. He smiled at her and scooted over to the bed. His voice was gentle, soft, completely at odds with the wild man he looked.

"Hi, babe. You're back."

"What happened?"

"Who told you it would be a good idea to step in the path of a bullet?"

"I was shot?"

"Yeah. Nicked a few organs, but you're okay. They got all of it, though it took them a while. It fragmented against a rib when it ricocheted out. You're gonna have a couple of kick-ass scars."

He sat on the edge of the bed gingerly, wiped her hair back from her face.

"Did we stop him? I shot Riley, but that's all I remember."

He nodded. "He'd managed to get three canisters into position in the water, but Fletcher—that man's smart, and quick—called for Metro to kill the power grid. The emergency generators kicked on, but not before we pulled the canisters out of the water. Then we shut down the whole plant. They are monitoring the water closely. They've advised no one to drink it for a while."

"Dixon? Is he alive?"

Xander's face hardened. "Yes. I really need to teach you to shoot better. You hit him three times, but none of them counted."

"I wasn't trying to kill him, just stop him."

"Like I said, I really need to teach you better." But the tenderness of his touch belied the gruffness of his words. "The shithead managed to get a shot off as he was going down. We think it ricocheted, came up at an angle, nicked your spleen and liver, hit your rib, then came out your side and buried in your bicep. You're kind of a wuss, you totally fainted on me. So we got you here to GW lickety-split, and they fixed you up."

"I'm a wuss, huh? Where's Fletcher?"

"He went to grab us some coffee. You should taste it. I swear, I think they make it vile on purpose."

"Chalk? And Robin? Is everyone okay?"

"We're all fine, baby. We saved the world. It's you we're worried about."

She shifted, felt the knife-hot pain in her side, decided she'd stay right where she was. "Ouch."

"Let me get the nurse. She wanted to know when you woke up."

Fletcher came in the door then, saw her awake. A huge grin split his face. He handed Xander his coffee, kissed Sam on the forehead, then stood over her with a mock frown on his face, shaking a finger. "You are not allowed to do that to us ever again."

"Yes, sir."

"Does it hurt?"

"Yes."

He softened. "I'm sorry. We shouldn't have left you there alone. I thought you'd be safe."

"Then next time, don't chase a big scary man into my path."

"No next time. Deal?"

"Deal," she said, smiling. She didn't dare laugh; she had the feeling it would hurt like hell. "When do I get to go home?"

"Doc says a day or two. They want to make sure you don't leak anywhere by surprise," Xander said, grimacing as he tasted the coffee.

"What an elegant concept." Her head went back onto the pillow, the crackling barrenness of it hard under her neck. "So we saved the day. That's good."

Her nurse came in, clucked over her a bit, then shot something wonderful into her IV, and admonished her to hit the red button if she needed anything.

Sam recognized the strange softening of the edges that came from the pain medication. She started to float and didn't fight it.

Fletcher's phone rang. "Jesus, it's like Grand Central around here. I'm going to throw this thing in the trash." But he put his ear to the phone, and a moment later, a grin erupted on his face. The effect of the medicine made it seem like the edges of his lips were exceptionally wide, and Sam stifled a giggle.

He thanked whoever it was and hung up. He patted her on the knee.

"Our luck's changing, Doc. Not only did we save the world, that was Dr. Bayer up in ICU. He has good news. Thomas Cattafi just woke up."

CHAPTER 55

FLETCHER LEFT TO TALK TO CATTAFI'S FAMILY, AND SAM DRIFTED FOR A BIT until Xander told her he was going to grab some food, and left her to sleep it off. Sam was comfortably numb from the drugs, but dreamed for what seemed like hours, of dark caves and monsters with huge, gnashing teeth that pinned her down and shoved sharp sticks in her side.

She awakened to full daylight. She squinted at the sun coming in from the blinds, then realized a familiar face was sitting in the chair previously occupied by Xander. It took her a minute to make sure she wasn't dreaming. The chair's occupant was tall, blonde, with one gray eye darker than the other.

"Taylor!" she shouted, jerking her best friend's attention from the novel in her lap.

Taylor Jackson jumped up from her chair and started to throw her arms around Sam, but stopped when Sam hissed in a breath.

"Oh, honey, I'm so sorry. I hit your bullet wound."

"Words I never thought to hear coming out of *your* mouth. Getting shot is your job."

Taylor grinned, and Sam felt immediately better. "No kidding. Hurts, doesn't it?"

Sam nodded. "Like hell."

Taylor contented herself with sitting on the side of the bed, holding Sam's good hand tight in hers, a huge grin on her lovely face.

"I came as soon as I heard. Baldwin called me when he landed. He showed up to your house, found two dead men in the kitchen and was just in time to hear the radio call that you'd been hit." The smile faded, and she touched Sam's cheek. "You scared me, Sammy. Don't do that again."

Sam laughed, shakily. "Scared myself, too. I'm so glad you're here. I've missed you."

"I've missed you, too, sugar." Sam could see Taylor was wrestling with her emotions. Never one to cry over spilled milk, her best friend, but she wasn't good when it came to her people getting hurt.

But there was something else there, too, and Sam knew Taylor well enough to know when she was holding something back.

"What is it? What's wrong?"

The gray eyes crinkled in amusement. "Never could put one past you, could I?"

Sam shook her head. "No, you can't. Spill."

Taylor took a small breath. "Okay. It's about the Hometown Killer."

It took Sam's muzzy head a moment to place the name. "Right. The serial killer who isn't a serial killer, except Baldwin and I think he is. Baldwin told me there was DNA at the crime scene in Denver. That's great news, right?"

"Absolutely. There's only one problem. Remember the man Lieutenant Fletcher was investigating, the one who drove the gray Honda near the Cattafi crime scene?"

Sam felt her stomach start to sink, a pit forming that made her breath come faster. "Yes. It all happened really quickly, but if I remember correctly, one of Fletcher's guys found the real owner dead, and we thought he was a part of the plot to contaminate the water system. When we went into the aquifer, they were doing a sketch of him to release to the public, find out who he was."

"That's right. Metro's crime scene collected foreign DNA from Toliver Pryce's house. There was a match in CODIS to the DNA at the crime scene in Denver."

Sam felt the alarm begin to build in her system. "Wait. What are you saying? The Hometown Killer was a part of this?"

Taylor shook her head, her blond hair *shurring* past her shoulders and getting in her face. She tucked a strand behind her ear. "He wasn't involved in the terror plot."

"Then why…" She broke off. It was a stupid question. Why else would a serial killer be circling her block? "He knows who I am," she said flatly.

Taylor nodded. "We're afraid he might, honey. Don't worry, though. Nothing is going to happen to you. We're going to find this son of a bitch and put him behind bars where he can't hurt anyone ever again."

Taylor brushed a hand across Sam's cheek, and she realized her best friend had just lied to her.

CHAPTER 56

BEFORE SHE WAS DISCHARGED FROM THE HOSPITAL, SAM WENT TO VISIT
Thomas Cattafi.

He was on the third floor, in a private room, still hooked into the ventilator, but improving daily. She'd visited before, slowly wheeling herself down to the elevator and onto his ward, but he'd been asleep, and she hadn't the heart to wake him.

But today, his mother was in the room with him, and spied Sam out in the hall. She was small and blonde and compact, and incredibly cheerful. She came out and shook Sam's hand. "We've seen you on the news, Dr. Owens. Thank you for finding the horrible woman who did this to our Tommy."

Maureen Heedles had been paraded all over the local and national news, and it was up for debate who was actually going to prosecute, the US government or the British. Sam bet they'd both get a turn—the woman wouldn't see freedom again. The same for Riley Dixon, though his story was more difficult to discern. He was in federal custody at an undisclosed location, and Sam had a feeling he'd be disappeared from his world completely soon enough.

"I didn't do much, ma'am, but thank you. Is Tommy up for a visitor? I'd like to talk to him."

Mrs. Cattafi nodded. "He's been writing down everything he can to help the police. Did you know, he's discovered a real vaccine for this terrible virus he and Dr. Bromley were working on, one that will work on other hemorrhagic fevers? I always thought he'd cure cancer, and here he goes and saves a continent."

Sam smiled at the woman. "He's a brilliant boy. I'm just so glad we were able to save him."

And I wish to hell we could have saved Amanda.

Cattafi's face lit up when he saw her. So he recognized her from the news, too. She didn't know what they'd been saying. She was avoiding the television like the plague, instead catching up with Taylor and Xander and getting reports from Fletcher, who, along with Lonnie Hart, had been put back on active duty with no stain on their records.

Fletcher had filled her in on Cattafi's research. In trying to find a cure for the engineered superbug, he and Bromley had found the key to a comprehensive broad-spectrum vaccine that could inoculate people against the disease. Cattafi had found that decaying stem cells, from people already deceased, mixed with the blood of those who'd survived, could be manipulated to kill the mutated superbug. He was able to use this to engineer a therapeutic, killing the bug from within.

It was groundbreaking work. It was too early to know if they could use the therapeutic vaccine to create a prophylactic to vaccinate against all hemorrhagic fevers, but their vaccine could halt the spread of the superbug if it were released into the world, removing the dire threat from the terrorist organization known as the Pyramid.

Sam wouldn't be surprised to see the kid nominated for a Nobel Prize, alongside his deceased mentor.

Cattafi was pale, but wrote, *Hi,* on his whiteboard.

"Hi to you, too, Tommy. I just wanted to thank you for pulling through. You're going to save a lot of lives, kiddo."

He smiled sadly, wrote, *Couldn't have done it without Bromley. He was a genius.*

"He was. His death is a great loss, as is Amanda's. You did all you could, I know that. She'd want you to move on, to follow this dream you've created."

He nodded, tears in his eyes.

"I talked to the dean, Tommy. He is happy to reinstate you immediately. As soon as you're up and around, would you like to come back to school?"

He grinned and wrote, *Yes!* She smiled, smoothed down his hair. "Good. I want to be there the day you take your oath. Remember to invite me, okay?"

Always, Dr. Owens.

He was tiring, so she gave him a smile, squeezed his hand. "You're a rock star, kiddo. Get better."

Back in her room, she eased herself onto the bed and stretched, happy to feel the stitches pulling. They were knitting, her wounds were healing; she'd be out of here shortly. And then she'd have to deal with the Hometown Killer, and finding a new home, and getting back to her classes and a million other things.

But for now, she rested. She was safe here, with Xander and Fletcher and Taylor and Baldwin. Nothing would touch her.

They discharged Sam on Tuesday, exactly a week after the craziness began, when Amanda Souleyret was killed and Cattafi stabbed. It had been a bloody day with too many lives lost, and Sam prayed nothing like that would ever find her again.

She and Xander drove Taylor and Baldwin to the airport. They were heading back to Nashville, and Baldwin was going to throw all his resources into the Hometown Killer. Not only did they now have DNA, they had a visual on the man, and a description provided by a very smart, very observant cop. Baldwin was certain they would nail the bastard quickly, but Sam wasn't so sure. Someone who'd managed to kill for years unnoticed wasn't going to just walk into their arms.

But she didn't tell Baldwin that. She knew he wanted her to feel reassured. And she did, in a way. Because she knew now what she was capable of. That she could stand in the face of death and danger, and fire a gun into the darkness to save herself.

It was a new kind of strength, one she hadn't wanted, but was grateful for.

The short drive home from the airport was a revelation—autumn had seized D.C. overnight, it seemed. The trees were a riot of colors, their street charming and quaint, leaves accumulating on the sidewalks. The scent of fires and the sharp crisp air made her long for the mountains.

The house had been professionally cleaned. She still didn't want to stay there. She wasn't ready. She was only renting the place, and she'd already decided to break the lease and move on. For the meantime, Xander had arranged for a quick trip for them, to go see his parents in Colorado. She could heal and enjoy the crisp fall air and turning leaves.

Her boss, Hilary, had put her on a medical leave with indeterminate dates. She encouraged her to take as much time as she needed to recover. Sam secretly thought Hilary was so enjoying being out of the administrative world and being a part of the teaching world once again that she'd like Sam to stay away longer.

Sam wasn't in the house for five minutes before the phone began to ring. She wasn't surprised. Between the cops, the media and their own people trying to check in, everyone wanted a piece of her. So she answered each call without bothering to look at the caller ID. This time, a familiar female voice greeted her.

"Dr. Owens? It's Robin Souleyret."

"How are you, Robin?"

"I'm fine. Did you see the press conference State did?"

She had—Ashleigh Cavort, facing the camera, an American

flag over her right shoulder, the State Department's to her left. Face pale and voice tumbling. She knew she was about to get slaughtered by the press, and Sam had felt bad for her. She wasn't the one who'd done wrong here, and she was going to have to fall on her sword in public. State was desperately trying to track the members of the group called Pyramid, but they'd rabbited, just as everyone feared. Hopefully, Heedles and Dixon would be forced to share something, and the forensic examinations of the money trail would lead them to the right people. The threat still existed. Would always exist, from this group or another.

"I turned it off. I didn't want to see the fallout."

Robin laughed. "Smart of you. I live for the fallout."

"So I gathered."

"James Denon came on after. He congratulated you personally."

"That's lovely. He sent flowers, too. What can I do for you, Robin?"

"I wanted to thank you. You were the only one who believed in me, and it's because of that I'm not in prison right now. You helped save Gina, you helped save us all. I wanted to let you know if you ever need me for anything, I'm a call away."

"That's kind."

"I'm serious. Shit gets strange in the world today. You never know when you might need a helping hand. Don't ever hesitate."

"What are you going to do?"

"Didn't you hear? I've been reinstated. I'm going back in the field. I'm going to find these bastards if it kills me."

"Dare I say congratulations?" Sam asked.

Robin laughed. "You're a brave chick, Dr. Owens. It's been nice knowing you. Thanks for the assist." And then she was gone, and Sam hung up the phone with a goofy smile on her face, not quite certain why.

CHAPTER 57

POOR, DELICATE LITTLE WREN.

Shot in the side, face splashed on the news, on leave from her job.

They were onto him now. He needed to be very careful. He'd made the long drive just to watch her come home. Wondered what she felt knowing the ghosts of the men who'd died in her house were still watching.

He wished she spent more time on the computer; he would be able to see into her head, see her thoughts. But she was one of the old-school ones. She didn't like to text, didn't have social media accounts, rarely used her email. She was self-reliant and strong and didn't need the approval of others to function.

It made her more intoxicating than the rest.

Her phone was the only way in. He knew she used it; old-fashioned girl that she was, she actually called her friends when she wanted to speak with them. One had come to visit, and she was intriguing in her own right—tall and rangy and blonde as a sunbeam. She carried a gun like she'd been born with it, and he wondered what she smelled like.

Focus, cher. You have work to do.

He'd have to spoof the phone, which meant breaking into the house. The man wasn't the problem, it was the dog. The glossy, healthy German shepherd clearly worshipped the woman and wouldn't hesitate for a moment to sink his teeth into the first threat that came along.

He'd have to wait for the man to take the dog on a run, and her to take a shower.

It would happen, if he were patient.

Just be patient.

Oh, I will.

Said the spider to the fly.

EPILOGUE

Two weeks later
Washington, D.C.

SAM WALKED INTO THE SMALL LIVING ROOM AND COLLAPSED GENTLY ONTO the dusty couch. The flight back from Colorado had been delayed, and it was past midnight. She was tired and ready for bed. She wanted to sleep for a week. Preferably with Xander by her side.

Thor clambered onto the couch with her, put his head on her knee. He was tired, too.

Xander followed her into the living room, dropped their bags on the floor. Fletcher had rented the apartment for them while they were in Colorado. They were staying here until they found a new place.

"Come on, sleepyhead. Let's go to bed," Xander said.

She smiled at him, patted the seat next to her. "Come here."

He grinned and joined her, plopping down with a groan. "Oh, that does feel good, doesn't it?"

She swung her legs up into his lap. "It does. It's good to be back. I didn't think I'd miss D.C., but I did."

"Well, we have the whole weekend in front of us. With nothing planned, either. We can wander the streets, take in the sights. Or spend the weekend in bed, if you prefer."

It was her turn to grin. "I think that sounds like a fine idea. I don't think I can keep my eyes open for another minute. But I have no intention of sleeping, just in case you were wondering."

She batted her lashes, and he laughed. She leaned up and touched his cheek, and his lips found hers, hungry and warm. She let the tide of relief flood through her, thought back to the moment three weeks earlier when she'd seen him on television, in cuffs and being hauled off to parts unknown. She'd had a wild dose of terror course through her then, a sudden fear that she'd never see him again. *Thank God*, she whispered mentally, adjusting her body to fit his better, deepening the kiss. *Thank God he's all right, and here.*

He released her too soon, stood her up, wrapped his arms around her. She melted into him, feeling his strength, enjoying the sense of protection being in his arms always afforded her.

Then he stiffened and pulled away. She felt bereft; the loss of him was so intense as to be painful. Opened her eyes to see concern etched on his face.

"What is it? What's wrong?"

He bent down to the coffee table. It was an ugly faux wood, but she didn't care. They wouldn't be here long.

"What is this?"

He didn't touch it, just pointed. Sam saw what she'd missed before—a small red rose lying on top of a folded piece of paper, her name written in spiky black letters on the paper.

Worry flooded her. "I don't know."

"Son of a bitch." Xander used a knuckle to knock the rose away and open the paper. He read the words, then let the note close.

"Come away," he said, his voice hard as glass. "Right now. We're leaving."

"What does it say, Xander?" She heard the fear in her voice, the quavering tone. *Be strong, damn you. Don't be afraid.*

But she was. She was so afraid.

Xander steered her into the kitchen, picked up the phone. She heard him vaguely, through a fog, the pounding of her heart too loud to allow rational thought.

"Baldwin. It's Xander. He was here. He was in the apartment Fletcher rented for us. We're fine, but the bastard was here. He left a note."

Xander gave her a concerned look, listening to Baldwin. She took a deep breath and started back toward the living room.

"Sam, wait. Don't—"

But she was already there. She grabbed the note and opened it, vaguely recognized the handwriting from somewhere. Reminded herself to breathe, that she was safe. For now.

It was from him. There was no mistaking the message. Or its intent.

Come find me, Samantha. I'm waiting.

★ ★ ★ ★ ★

ACKNOWLEDGMENTS

I owe a debt of gratitude to so many people for their kind help, expertise, good humor and support during the writing of this book:

Acclaimed virologist Eric Mossel, Ph.D., who was instrumental in helping me develop the story, lent authenticity to a variety of situations, and helped me find the right path between fiction and reality. He's a mean copy editor, to boot.

Lee Mossel, for hooking me up with his son, and laughs on the golf course.

Sherrie Saint, who did a load of legwork tracking down just the right way to kill a bunch of people.

David Achord, for clarifying the finer legal points for Xander's little situation.

Randy Ellison, for all the on-point articles, talking points and napkin sessions over margaritas. And calming the hysterics...

Catherine Coulter, for helping me see the original story wasn't personal enough.

Anton Pogany, for even more medical expertise.

Karen Evans, for *all* the things.

Laura Benedict, for countless phone calls and machinations and treats in the mail.

As always, all mistakes, exaggerations or pure literary license are mine, and mine alone.

Several wonderful people bid on character names for charity (the Brenda Novak Diabetes Auction) and on my Facebook fan page. Robin Souleyret, Thomas Cattafi and Maureen Heedles, you are all fabulous. So are you, fellow Langley-ite Emma Cattafi, for getting this for your BIL. It was my honor to capture your names for this work. Thank you!

Thanks to the usual suspects, without whom I'd never get anything accomplished: my lovely agent, Scott Miller; my wonderful editor, Nicole Brebner (thank you twice); everyone at Trident Media Group and MIRA Books who work tirelessly behind the scenes to get these books into readers' hands; my hoodoo guru Paige Crutcher; my soul sister Ariel Lawhon; my sister from another mister Jennifer Brooks; my wine and chat for five (uh—fifty) Erica Spindler; the indomitable Alex Kava; Deb Carlin, for so much; my dear productivity buddy Jeff Abbott; the ever-fabulous and funny Andy Levy; the one and only Joan Huston, grammar goddess extraordinaire; Blake Leyers, for edits and manis and pedis and lunches and being a fellow tall chick! The Wild Women—River Jordan, Susan Gregg Gilmore, Kerry Madden, Lisa Patton—for a weekend to remember forever; Sheldon, my UPS guy, and Chris, my postman, who are bloody patient with all the packages; Anna Benjamin, for the best care package evah!; my incredible friends on Facebook and Twitter, who laugh at my jokes even when they aren't funny; the indie booksellers and librarians who've been working so hard to get me into readers' hands—couldn't do it without you!; and Writerspace.com—Cissy, Susan, Celeste and Dee—ladies, you're the bees knees!

Special thanks as always to my awesome parents, for whom there are never enough adjectives, and my bros.

No book is ever truly finished without thanking (yes, again!)

my Randy. *Je t'aime, je t'adore, et je vous aime aussi.* Thanks for Paris, bunny.

Finally, this book is dedicated to the memory of a dear friend who passed away this year. John Seigenthaler was an extraordinary man who gave so much to this world, to the Nashville literary community and, of course, to me personally. He is dreadfully missed.